Cal recalled, yet again, the incident which had occurred only hours before the Japanese attack on Pearl Harbor, although he hadn't known that then. There'd been a full moon that night and the seas were friendly, flat and glistening like the smoothest of silk. He was on the night watch and several ships in the convoy were clearly visible, including one of their naval escorts . . . Suddenly, without warning, the *Magnolia* erupted in front of them. It exploded like a firework, showering sparks and flames. Cal quickly went outside. He could hear the crackle of burning and the sizzle of red–hot metal as parts fell back in the water. He could hear men shouting and screaming for help . . .

'What are you thinking about, luv?' asked Sheila.

'Nothing,' smiled Cal. How could he tell her, when he knew she was already worried sick? But it dismayed him when she said there was 'nothing happening'. It had been the same in the pub, where all the talk was of the football match that afternoon, as if they'd grown so used to their country being at war, it was so much part of their everyday existence, they no longer took any notice of what was going on elsewhere unless tragedy hit their own particular family . . .

Maureen Lee was born in Bootle and now lives in Colchester, Essex. She has had numerous short stories published and a play staged. *Stepping Stones, Liverpool Annie, Dancing in the Dark, The Girl from Barefoot House, Laceys of Liverpool* and *The House by Princes Park*, and the three novels in the Pearl Street series, *Lights Out Liverpool, Put Out the Fires* and *Through the Storm* are all available in Orion paperback. Her novel *Dancing in the Dark* won the Parker Romantic Novel of the Year Award. Her latest novel in Orion paperback is *Lime Street Blues*. Her latest novel in hardback, *Queen of the Mersey*, is also available from Orion. Visit her website at www.maureenlee.co.uk.

BY MAUREEN LEE

The Pearl Street Series
Lights Out Liverpool
Put Out the Fires
Through the Storm

Stepping Stones
Liverpool Annie
Dancing in the Dark
The Girl from Barefoot House
Laceys of Liverpool
The House by Princes Park
Lime Street Blues
Queen of the Mersey

Through the Storm

Maureen Lee

ORION

An Orion paperback

First published in Great Britain in 1997
by Orion
This paperback edition published in 1998
by Orion Books Ltd,
Orion House, 5 Upper St Martin's Lane,
London WC2H 9EA

A CIP catalogue record for this book
is available from the British Library.

ISBN-13 978-1-4072-0706-3

Printed and bound in the EU

The Orion Publishing Group's policy is to use papers that
are natural, renewable and recyclable products and
made from wood grown in sustainable forests. The logging
and manufacturing processes are expected to conform to
the environmental regulations of the country of origin.

www.orionbooks.co.uk

The third for Patrick

Chapter 1

A slice of hazy yellow sun had begun to peep over the grey slate roofs of the small cul-de-sac. The blue sky was cloudless, heralding a fine late September day. There was a slight breeze, and a salty smell hung in the air, fresh and bracing. In the distance, a ship's hooter sounded on the River Mersey, a deep, sonorous sound, and two seagulls came swooping down, squawking raucously. They perched side by side on the gutter of the King's Arms, their eyes raking the ground below for scraps. Seeing nothing, they took off again, even more noisily.

Pearl Street was gradually waking up. Blackout curtains, upstairs and down, were drawn back and smoke began to curl lazily out of the chimneys as fires were lit to boil water for the first cup of tea of the day. The tea would be only half as strong as people would have liked – two ounces a week, which was all the ration allowed, didn't last long if you drank it strong. Even if you drank it weak, you were quite likely to run out before next week's ration was due. Few people complained. They knew too many merchant seamen from Bootle who had lost their lives in the struggle to keep the nation fed.

Dishes rattled, a welcome sound to those awake and still in bed. They snuggled further under the clothes in order to savour the last few peaceful minutes before getting up for work or school.

Every house shook briefly as an electric train left

Marsh Lane station and clattered along behind the roof-high railway wall at the far end of the street. The trains ran to Liverpool one way and Southport the other.

It was a peaceful scene, tranquil, despite the disparate noises; the boats, the trains, the gulls, and the people inside the houses much appreciated waking up to the sounds they knew so well after the carnage and destruction of the past year, culminating in the May Blitz, when Liverpool had been subjected to an entire week of saturation bombing. The centre of the city had been left a veritable wasteland of dust and debris. In Bootle alone, nearly a thousand people had been killed or injured, and many thousands more had lost their homes along with everything they possessed. Scarcely a house had been left undamaged in some way.

Until that fateful May, there'd been thirty houses in Pearl Street, a terrace of fifteen each side, the front doors opening directly onto the pavement. Now there were only twenty-seven, and an ugly gap on one side where numbers 19 to 23 used to be. They were gone as smoothly as if they'd been cut away from their neighbours with a giant knife, leaving only a crater surrounded by a jumble of broken bricks, smashed slates and jutting beams as a sign that houses had ever stood there. A bedroom fireplace remained, looking pathetic and incongruous, halfway up the wall of number 17, which was miraculously intact. The broken windows, the lost slates, the smashed front doors in the rest of the street, had long since been repaired or replaced in the mammoth and united effort to get the town back on its feet.

The air-raid siren still went occasionally. Everyone felt the same awful hair-raising sensation when they heard its unearthly wail, and waited anxiously for the soothing drone of the All Clear. Planes rarely got through nowadays, much to their relief. No-one, even if they lived to be a hundred, could have got used to the

2

almost nightly raids which had terrorised Liverpool for so long.

It was incredible, people said to themselves and each other, that all this was due to one power-crazed man, Adolf Hitler, who had turned the entire world inside out and upside down and now had virtually the whole of Europe in his evil, vice-like grip. Great Britain had been left to stand alone, with the alarming threat of invasion ever present until June, when Germany invaded Russia, which diverted Hitler's attention away from the British Isles.

The sun was becoming less hazy as it rose higher in the sky. It shone directly through the upstairs windows, and those in bed felt the welcome warmth on their faces.

In the coalyard next to the railway wall, Nelson the horse munched his oats contentedly as Bill Harrison began to load the cart with sacks of nutty slack and coke, which was sometimes all he could get in wartime. Fuel was in short supply and the Government had recently urged people to share their firesides with their neighbours.

A stout uniformed figure came marching round the corner, whistling cheerfully, and began to deliver letters. The figure was no longer a cause for astonishment or mirth or both; people had got used to seeing a woman doing the job of postman by now. In fact, the population had got used to women doing all sorts of strange things since the war began.

Two girls virtually fell out of the front door of their house, giggling hysterically. They linked arms and ran down the street and around the corner, already late for the bus to work.

Another door slammed and a small man in overalls emerged who tipped his soiled tweed cap, winked at the postwoman and said, 'Good morning, Vera.'

'Morning, Dai.'

Dai Evans always tried to time his exit so he would

3

come face to face with Vera Dodds. There was something about a buxom woman in uniform, particularly when she wore trousers . . .

'Lovely day,' he ventured.

Vera nodded. 'Going to be hot, I reckon.' She flipped through the letters in her hand. 'Nothing for you.'

'I weren't expecting anything.'

'Though there's something for your neighbours, from America.'

'America! I wonder what that can be?' mused Dai.

'And a letter for the Harrisons from their daughter in Newcastle.'

'I hope it's not bad news.' The Harrisons had already lost two of their grandsons in the fighting in North Africa.

'This looks official. It's from the Ministry of Labour for Miss Kathleen Quigley.' Vera showed Dai a brown envelope on which the name and address were typed.

'Jimmy'll have a fit if Kitty has to get a job,' Dai grinned. Like most of the street, Dai had sized up Jimmy Quigley's incapacity as being wholly put on, a fake. They didn't blame him – any man able to get a pension out of those mean buggers who ran the docks was a man to be admired – but it wasn't right, the way he took advantage of his daughter, Kitty. He'd had the poor girl running round after him like a blue-arsed fly for nearly ten years. 'That'll cause ructions in number twenty.'

'We've all got to do our bit,' Vera said primly.

'I'd best be off,' Dai said, adding casually, 'Perhaps I'll see you in the pub tonight, like?'

'Perhaps you will,' Vera replied, equally casually. A spinster in her late forties, she wasn't sure why, but since she'd started delivering letters there were men in their dozens panting after her. She rather liked Dai Evans with his lovely Welsh sing-song voice. It was rumoured his wife, Ellis, gave him a terrible time at home.

An elderly woman opened an upstairs window, sat

her small wiry frame backwards on the sill, and began to clean the glass with a chamois leather. 'Morning, Vera,' she shouted. 'Anything interesting today?'

'No,' Vera said shortly. There was no way she would discuss the post with Aggie Donovan, the nosy ould bugger. She finished the street and continued with her round, just as the milkman arrived. He left the cart in Opal Street – it was impossible to turn a horse and cart round in the narrow cul-de-sac – and brought the bottles in metal containers, two in each hand.

A couple of young boys ran out of a house in front of him and began to kick a football to each other. 'Mind the milk,' he warned. 'I don't have none to spare, not with the rationing. If you break one, your mam'll have to give up one of hers and she'll murder you.'

One of the boys stuck out his tongue. 'No she won't.'

'Oh yes she will.'

'She won't.'

The milkman gave up. The stable door opened and Nelson came trotting out with Bill Harrison, his face already black with coal dust, sitting behind holding the reins loosely in his even blacker hands. His eyes lit up when he saw the milkman and he pulled the cart to a halt.

'Just in time. Our Nelson can have a word with your Daisy.'

The milkman chuckled. 'We should let him get stuck across her one of these days. It must be lousy being a horse and the only oats you get come from a bag.'

'We might come up with a racehorse between us.'

Nelson had already noticed Daisy waiting on the corner and whinnied impatiently for his owner to get a move on. Mr Harrison slapped his broad brown rump. 'Giddeup, boy.'

The wooden wheels of the coal-cart rattled noisily over the cobbles and a few seconds later the two horses were nuzzling each other gently.

5

More people left for work, the men mainly in the direction of the docks. One or two who'd been on night shift arrived home, worn out and eager for something to eat and a good kip.

Aggie Donovan had finished cleaning the bedroom window, but stayed where she was. It was a good vantage point from where she could see everything that was going on. Her beady eyes swept this way and that as eagerly as the seagulls. She could even see into some of the bedrooms opposite if she tried.

A van drove into the street and stopped outside number 10, Miss Brazier's old house. Two workmen got out and carried in a ladder and several tins of paint. Although Aggie had approached them yesterday, the workmen professed to have no knowledge of who the new tenants were.

'Funny colours,' she remarked, staring down the hall which was painted pink. As far as she could see, the living room was white, but perhaps that was just an undercoat.

'Everyone to their own taste,' the workman said and slammed the door when it looked as if Aggie were about to elbow her way in for an inspection.

The two boys had been joined by several others, and Aggie nearly jumped out of her skin when a football hit her bony behind with considerable force.

'Who did that?' she screeched. 'I could have fell.' She struggled into the bedroom and ran downstairs, but when she opened the door the street was empty apart from Nan Wright already sitting on the doorstep of number 1, soaking up the early morning sun in a pink hairnet and bedroom slippers, looking like a great fat wrinkled whale. The boys had vanished as if by magic.

Soon afterwards, the children started to call for each other for school. They began to leave in small groups, gasmasks over their shoulders. They went more cheerfully than they used to. Since the bombs had started falling, their school, St Joan of Arc's, situated dangerously near to the docks, had closed, and now they went for just half a day to St Monica's. It was a long walk, but better than spending an entire day being bossed around by teachers.

Aggie waited on her doorstep, hopping impatiently from one foot to the other. 'Who kicked that ball?' she demanded when several young lads appeared looking as if butter wouldn't melt in their mouths.

'What ball?' they asked innocently.

Like the milkman, Aggie gave up. Kids today, she thought disgustedly, they had no respect for their elders. They got away with murder, unlike when she was a girl. Many's the time she'd received a clip around the ear for merely looking at a grown-up the wrong way round.

She crossed over to the end house and began to air her grievances to Nan Wright, but Nan appeared irritated at having her sunbathing interrupted and stubbornly refused to agree with a word Aggie said.

'We weren't bombed when we were kids, were we, Mrs Donovan? We didn't have rationing, either, and our dads weren't away fighting in a terrible war.'

'No,' Aggie conceded grudgingly. Her behind still hurt where the football had hit it. 'Even so . . .'

'Seems to me,' said Nan, 'that kids bear up remarkably well, all things considering. They brighten up the street no end. I couldn't stand it when most of 'em were evacuated and everywhere was dead quiet.' Her only child, Ruby, then twelve, had died of scarlet fever in the last month of the last century, and Nan, already a widow, had lived on her own ever since.

Aggie, annoyed, decided to change tack. She put her hands on her hips and glared down at the woman. 'I'm surprised at you, Nan Wright, sitting out so early in the morning,' she said spitefully. 'I'd've thought you'd have work to do inside.' She hadn't even got her teeth in, Aggie noticed, and there were gravy stains all down the front of her cotton pinny which hadn't been near a drop of starch when it had last been washed. Her nearly bald head shone through the pink hairnet, and Aggie wondered why she bothered to put one on.

Nan Wright rubbed the bright purple knotted veins on her bare sagging legs and seemed unperturbed by the attack. 'I have, but that sun's too good to miss. I can always do me work later. When you get to seventy-two, some things don't seem to matter as much as they used to.'

'Huh!' Aggie was seventy-four and as thin and small as Nan was big and fat. An eternally agitated woman, never still, she had the energy of someone half her age and an unquenchable interest in everybody else's affairs. Almost universally loathed throughout the street, nevertheless she was listened to avidly as she relayed juicy bits of gossip she'd managed to pick up. Every now and then, she surprised the neighbours with acts of unexpected kindness and generosity.

Aggie returned home and decided to clean the back bedroom window, which would give her an entirely different aspect to view.

The street was silent for a while as the women made the beds, washed the breakfast dishes and carried out their other indoor tasks. Then, as if an alarm had been set, at least a dozen emerged to attend to the outside of their houses; to brush the pavement, clean the brass on the front door, wipe the window sills. Several came armed with buckets of warm suds and proceeded to scrub their steps, whitening the centre and neatly finishing off the edges with a border of red raddle. Ellis Evans, a big woman with a florid, unhealthy face, attacked the walls of her house with a yardbrush, rubbing them so hard that clouds of brick dust gently floated down.

Everyone waved to Nan, who sat watching this hive of activity with amusement. Ellis would brush her house

8

away altogether one of these days. There'd been a time, not all that long ago, when she'd been just as house-proud herself, but nowadays she felt thankful just to be alive and able to enjoy God's warm sunshine when so many people had died over the past two years, including several of her dear neighbours.

Most of the women went indoors, though a few remained, leaning on their mops or brooms talking to each other. Nan watched the steam rising gently from the washed steps as they quickly dried in the heat. Her own doorstep was a disgrace, but she didn't care. If it got too bad, someone would offer to scrub it for her.

In the house next door, Mrs Singerman began to play a gentle tune on her piano, and Nan felt a wave of blissful happiness pass over her old body. What a beautiful world it was! What a pity folks couldn't be left to get on with their own affairs without interference from monsters like Adolf Hitler! She closed her eyes and promptly fell asleep.

She was woken by Kitty Quigley shaking her by the shoulder. 'Would you like me to get your shopping, luv?'

'Well, I wouldn't mind . . .' Nan said the same thing every day when someone offered to do her shopping. She made to get up, but getting up was such a struggle nowadays.

'Of course I don't mind. Don't budge,' Kitty said kindly. 'I'll fetch your ration book off the mantelpiece.'

Nan leaned sideways to allow the girl to get past into the house. Kitty came back seconds later, tucking the ration book in her shopping bag. 'Is there anything you particularly need?'

'A pound of 'taters, and any sort of meat that's going, as long as it's not that whalemeat. It's dead horrible, tastes like cod liver oil. Even Paddy O'Hara's dog wouldn't eat it when I offered him a bit.'

Kitty sighed. 'Me dad doesn't like it, either.'

9

'Are you all right, Kitty? You don't look at all yourself this morning.' She was a pretty girl, Kitty Quigley – well, not so much a girl, she must be all of twenty-six or seven – with a mass of unruly brown curls and wide-apart hazel eyes that looked at you with an almost startling clarity. Although she never used a scrap of that make-up stuff, her cheeks and lips were a pale rosy pink. She was always dressed nice, even if it was only to go to the Marsh Lane shops: but then, thought Nan, the shops were as far as Kitty ever got, what with her dad being virtually housebound and needing constant attention since his accident on the docks. She was wearing her lemon-coloured cotton frock with white piping on the collar and the belt. A timid girl, though with a sunny personality, today she looked unusually wan and down-cast.

'I'm okay,' she said in a tone of voice that told Nan she wasn't okay at all. 'I'll be as quick as I can with the shopping. You can give me the money when I get back.'

'All right, luv. There's no hurry. I'll see you later.'

Kitty left, and Aggie Donovan came sidling over and nodded at her retreating figure. 'They got a letter this morning at number twenty. It came in a brown envelope.'

'Did it now!' said Nan, adding sarcastically, 'What did it say?'

But the sarcasm was wasted on Aggie. 'How should I know?' she asked indignantly.

As she made her way towards the shops in Marsh Lane, Kitty thought about the letter that had arrived for her that morning. Apparently, the Ministry of Labour classified her as a single woman without dependants and demanded that she present herself at the local Labour Exchange next Monday morning at half past ten to register for war work.

There was nothing in the world Kitty wanted more

than to get a job and do her bit towards the war effort. There were times when she felt as if the conflict was passing her by; that one morning she would wake up and it would all be over and Kitty Quigley wouldn't have done a single thing to help her country win, not even in a voluntary capacity. In 1939, when it first started, Dad had nearly been in tears when she suggested she become an Air-Raid Warden or an Auxiliary Fire Fighter or join the Women's Voluntary Service.

'But what happens if those air raids they're all talking about get going?' he asked piteously. 'Your poor ould dad'll be left all on his own.'

'You can always go to the shelter,' Kitty said reasonably. 'They've built one only just round the corner. One of the neighbours'll come in and help you get there,' she added quickly before he could raise that particular objection.

But Dad immediately thought of another. 'Say if the worst happens and you're killed! Who'll look after me then? I'd have to go in a home.' His eyes became moist. 'I couldn't stand that, Kitty, luv. I'd sooner be dead meself than go in a home. No, I think we should stick together. That's what families are supposed to do during wartime, stick together if they can.'

Kitty loved her dad dearly. She couldn't stand it when he cried. She knew he missed his mates and the camaraderie of the docks. He hated being an invalid and dependent on his daughter for virtually every little thing. For his sake, she immediately gave up all thought of joining a voluntary organisation and later on, during the raids, she and Dad sat under the stairs when the bombs fell on Bootle. Sometimes, during a lull, she could hear singing coming from the shelter around the corner, where everyone seemed to be having a dead good time despite the horrendous things happening outside.

There was a queue outside Costigans when Kitty

arrived. There was always a queue outside any sort of shop that sold food – some women came well before they were due to open in order to be first – but this queue seemed unusually long, which meant there must be something special on sale.

'What have they got?' Kitty asked the woman at the back.

'I dunno, luv. Look, keep me place a mo, and I'll pop up to the front and see.'

Kitty willingly agreed. 'Okay.'

'I hope it's biscuits,' another woman said. 'I haven't had a biscuit in ages.'

'I wouldn't mind biscuits either, custard creams.' Kitty's mouth watered at the idea of dipping a custard cream in a cup of tea. It hadn't exactly seemed a delicacy before the war, but now . . . 'On the other hand, me dad was only saying the other night he really fancied sardines on toast.'

'Aye, sardines'd be a nice treat.'

The first woman returned to reclaim her place. 'It's baked beans,' she announced excitedly. 'One for each ration book.'

Two more women had come up behind Kitty. 'What's the queue for, luv?' one asked.

'Baked beans.'

Kitty waited for nearly an hour, praying all the time the beans wouldn't be sold out before her turn came. She emerged, triumphant, with three tins, one for Nan Wright, together with some other rations; tea, sugar and half a pound of nice lean bacon. They could have bacon and beans for dinner today.

She then queued for bread, queued for potatoes, and decided not to bother with the butcher's when she discovered there was only the hated whalemeat on offer. Perhaps Nan would like a few slices of the bacon? Several women were waiting outside the shop as there was a rumour sausages might be available soon. The butcher didn't dare announce the sausages were definite, else word would flash round like wildfire, and he'd end up with a queue a mile long and a possible riot on his hands if there wasn't enough to go round.

On the way home, Kitty called in the newsagent's shop to collect the *Daily Herald*. 'I don't suppose you've got any ciggies?' she asked hopefully.

Ernie Johnson, a middle-aged man with a severe squint, gave her a suggestive wink from behind the counter with his best eye. 'Give us a kiss, and I'll let you have ten Woodbines.'

'I'll do no such thing,' said Kitty indignantly. 'Have you really got Woodbines, Ernie? Me dad hasn't had a smoke in weeks.'

'Can I pinch your bum, then?'

'No you can't!'

'In that case, what'll you give me for ten Woodbines?'

'The money!'

Ernie sighed as he produced the ciggies from underneath the counter. 'There's some women'd dance round me shop stark naked for them.'

'I'm not sure if I'll come in here again once the war's over,' Kitty said threateningly.

'Can you imagine it being over, Kitty?' Ernie's face grew serious.

Kitty thought, then shook her head. 'No. It's funny, but it feels as if we've always been at war and it'll never stop. I've even got used to the bomb sites. I can hardly remember Marsh Lane all built up like it used to be.'

'I feel the same.' Ernie seemed to be looking at Kitty with one eye and the door with the other. She remembered he had two sons, both in the army, though he was always good-humoured in a crude sort of way. 'I wonder if things'll ever be normal again?'

The door opened and a man poked his head in. 'Any ciggies?'

'No, mate,' Ernie shook his head.

'Ernie!' Kitty said reproachfully when the door had closed.

'Well, I've never seen him before. I keep the ciggies for me favourite customers — and there's none more favourite than you, Kitty.'

He smacked his lips and made to come round the counter, and Kitty quickly escaped. She was never quite sure if Ernie was joking or not.

'Kitty!'

A pretty, harassed-looking woman pushing a black pram containing two rather large children came panting up when Kitty emerged from the newsagent's. 'They've got baked beans in Costigans.'

Sheila Reilly had been in the same class as Kitty at school. She'd been Sheila Doyle from Garnet Street in those days, but had moved to Pearl Street when she married Calum Reilly, a merchant seaman who was away most of the time.

'I know, I got some. I got one for Nan Wright, too. Did you know Ernie Johnson's got ciggies?'

'I've already bought a packet for me dad. He's a dirty bugger, that Ernie. The things he asked me to do!' She stopped the pram and fanned her face with her hand. 'Phew! I'm sweating like a cob. Here, put your bags in the pram, Kit. That's why I bring it. Our Mary's two and Ryan's three and they're far too big to be pushed round, but it saves having to carry all me shopping. There's no way I could cart home seven tins of beans, along with everything else.'

'Mam!' the children complained in unison as Kitty gratefully planted her two bags on their feet.

'Shurrup, youse two, else I'll make you walk,' Sheila told them severely. She smiled at Kitty. 'Kids!'

Sheila had six children; the older four were at school. The two women had been good friends once, though nowadays Kitty avoided her whenever she could as long as it didn't involve being rude. Sheila Reilly with her

14

vast family made her feel uncomfortable, like a dried-up old maid. Sometimes, Kitty felt it wasn't just the war which was passing her by, but life itself.

'How are you doing?' Sheila asked as they walked back home. 'I haven't seen you for a natter in ages. Why don't you pop in for a cup of tea now'n again? We could talk about old times.'

Because they're the last thing I want to talk about, thought Kitty. It would only remind her of the hopes and dreams she'd once had, that the three of them had had; Brenda Mahon, Sheila and Kitty. They'd stayed friends after they left school at thirteen and went out to work. They'd done the First Fridays together, made the Stations of the Cross each Easter, gone to the pictures, giggled breathlessly over boys. She muttered something about how she'd love to pop in for a cup of tea, but her father always kept her busy.

'Remember us hanging round North Park when it was dusk waiting for the Parkie to lock up? We used to have a fine ould time with the lads. We even had a bet once on which of us would be kissed first.'

'I remember,' Kitty said shortly.

'You won. You were the best looking and drove the lads wild. Me and Brenda always thought you'd beat us getting married by a mile . . .' Sheila paused as she turned the pram into Pearl Street, as if aware of how tactless she was being. Kitty Quigley had been stuck at home with her dad for ten whole years and denied the opportunity even of meeting a man, let alone marrying one. 'Still,' she finished lamely, 'marriage isn't the be-all and end-all of a woman's existence, is it?'

'I didn't particularly want to get married, did I?' Kitty did her best to sound cool and unperturbed. 'I wanted to be a florist. I intended having me own shop eventually.' She'd been working in Garlands in Stanley Road for nearly a year learning the trade, and distinctly remembered the day someone came running in to say her dad had been taken to Bootle hospital. Kitty left immediately to go and see him, never dreaming at the time she was leaving for good.

Sheila began to manoeuvre the pram down the back entry. 'That's right, so you did. You were always the artistic one at school.'

Though Kitty had assumed other things would be on the cards eventually; a husband, children, a home of her own. When they reached the Quigleys' back door, she put her hand on the latch to go in.

'Y'know,' Sheila said, looking at Kitty thoughtfully, 'I've often wondered what would have happened when your dad was hurt if you'd been a boy? Would you still have been expected to give up your job to look after him?'

It was something Kitty had wondered herself, lately; not at first, but when she saw the young men being called up to fight regardless of their family circumstances. If she was a man, if she was called up, Dad would have no alternative but to manage on his own.

'I dunno,' she muttered. 'I had a letter this morning from the Ministry of Labour.' She had to tell someone. 'They want me to register next Monday for war work.'

'That's good – isn't it?'

'I suppose so.'

'Our Eileen had ever such a good time when she worked in the munitions factory. The women there were an absolute scream.'

'I know. She told me about them.' Sheila's sister, Eileen, had lost her husband and little boy in the raids last Christmas. She'd recently remarried and left Pearl Street to live in Melling, a small village outside Liverpool. 'It's just that . . .' Kitty paused.

'What, luv?'

A voice piped from the pram, 'Mam, I'm thirsty.'

'And I'm dying for a wee wee, Mam.'

The children were becoming impatient waiting in the entry. Sheila plucked them out and shooed them into the house next door but one. She turned back to Kitty, aware something was wrong, her good-natured face full of concern. 'What is it, luv?' she asked again.

'It's just that . . . that me dad's started writing down all the things I've got to say on Monday to persuade them not to take me,' Kitty said in a rush. She felt cross with herself when halfway through her voice actually broke and she felt as if she could very easily cry.

'C'mon, luv.' Sheila put her hand on Kitty's arm. 'Let's have that cup of tea and you can tell me all about it.'

'But I'm already late,' Kitty said tearfully. 'I was ages in that queue waiting for the beans.'

'So what? It won't hurt your dad to wait a while longer.' Sheila took Kitty's hand and began to pull her along the entry as if she were a recalcitrant child. 'I refuse to take no for an answer,' she said firmly.

The inside of Sheila's house was more modern than most others in the street, one of the few to have electricity. It had once belonged to her sister and Sheila had lived opposite, but number 21 had been blown to smithereens in May, leaving the Reillys with nothing except the clothes they stood up in.

'Still, we're alive, that's all that really matters,' Sheila said staunchly at the time.

Everywhere was cheerfully untidy when Kitty went in. There were toys on the floor, and in front of the green-tiled fireplace stood a clothes maiden heaped with children's underwear in a variety of sizes; vests, underpants and an assortment of petticoats, liberty vests and knickers, all of which had been provided by the WVS. The wireless had been left on, loudly, and Vera Lynn was singing 'Yours till the stars lose their glory . . .' a song Kitty particularly liked. There was a large picture of the Sacred Heart over the mantelpiece, which Sheila had retrieved from their old house. The glass hadn't even been scratched.

Sheila immediately put the kettle on and Mary and Ryan went out to play. Soon, the two women were ensconced in front of the fire drinking the most insipid cup of tea Kitty had ever tasted.

Sheila apologised for its paleness. 'That's this morning's, with another few leaves added. Now,' she said sternly, 'what's all this about your dad writing down what you've got to say on Monday?'

'He doesn't want me to go to work,' Kitty said in a small voice. 'He's terrified of being left alone.'

'As if he'd be alone in Pearl Street!' Sheila snorted. 'Why, the neighbours'd pop in and do everything that's needed. Look at the way they all looked after Tony when our Eileen went to work in that factory!'

'Yes, but it's me he wants, Sheil, his own flesh and blood,' Kitty explained. 'I understand how he feels. He was such a strong man before the accident. He doesn't want everyone to see the way he is now.'

'He can't be all that bad, luv, if he can get as far as the King's Arms most nights for a pint.'

'But it's only on the corner, Sheil,' Kitty protested. 'And he has to use his sticks.'

Sheila said casually, 'According to me dad, once he's there, he's the life and soul of the party.' Like most people, she was convinced Jimmy Quigley was taking his poor daughter for a ride. He wasn't nearly as ill as he cracked up to be, not now. Of course, he'd been badly injured when the crate had fallen on his legs, breaking them in several places, but, as Kitty said, he was a strong man with strong bones, and strong bones mended easily. No-one minded the long drawn-out skive, but Sheila, in particular, minded the way he took advantage of her old friend's affection and let her waste her life tending to his every need.

Kitty's already pink cheeks flushed even pinker with

18

irritation. People were forever hinting Dad wasn't as ill as he made out, but they weren't there when she helped him up to bed at night, they didn't hear him groan in agony with each step. He was only putting on a brave show in the King's Arms, trying to make out he was better than he was.

Noticing the flush, Sheila said gently, 'I suppose you feel in a terrible pickle, wondering what to do?'

'That's right,' Kitty nodded. 'I feel torn in two sometimes. I'd love to go to work, I really would, but I feel dead selfish just thinking about it. Even when I suggest a part-time job, he gets upset. It's not as if we need the money, though sometimes it's hard scraping along on his pension. On the other hand . . .' It would be nice to wear clothes that weren't secondhand from Paddy's Market. Although clothes rationing had begun earlier in the year, Kitty had never used a single coupon so far.

'Everyone's entitled to a life of their own, luv.'

'Are they?'

'Of course they are!' Sheila affirmed heartily. 'I mean, your dad's only fifty, three years younger than mine. He could live another thirty years – and you'll be nearing sixty yourself by then!'

Kitty shuddered. 'Oh, Sheil!'

'Of course, it's none of my business, but even so, Kit, I hate to see you sacrifice yourself like this. I mean, you've never even had a proper boyfriend, have you? Those lads we used to knock around with were never serious.' Despite the fact that Kitty's face froze, Sheila pressed on, determined to make her friend see sense if at all possible. 'You don't get out to the pictures or go dancing like other girls.'

'Well, y'see, me dad . . .'

Sheila interrupted with, 'I remember when it first happened and I used to try and persuade you to come out in a foursome with our Calum and his mate, Kevin

Woods. Your dad always seemed to take a turn for the worse when the time came to go.'

'I wonder what happened to Kevin Woods?' Kitty said brightly.

'That's a nifty way of changing the subject. If you must know, he married a girl from Browning Street and they had two kids. He went down two years ago on the *City of Benares* when it was torpedoed on the way to America.'

'Oh, God!' Kitty made a face. 'I didn't know.' He'd seemed a nice lad, Kevin Woods, very thin, with sharp elbows and an Adam's apple that wobbled noticeably when he spoke.

Sheila supposed she'd better take the hint and talk about something other than Jimmy Quigley and his relationship with his daughter. She began to discuss that morning's shopping. She'd considered joining the queue for sausages, but the whole thing was too up in the air. 'I would have done if it had been definite, but I wasn't prepared to wait when it might have been a waste of time. Anyroad, the kids'll be thrilled to bits when they find there's baked beans on toast for their tea. We were dead lucky, weren't we, eh?'

What Sheila didn't realise was that this sort of discussion only made Kitty feel worse. People, particularly in queues, often spoke to her as if she were a housewife. They grumbled over prices, complained about the fact onions and lemons had virtually disappeared from the shops, wondered what had happened to offal – 'Have you tried to get a bit of liver or kidney lately, luv?' – asked her how many coupons you needed for sheets and pillowcases. No-one ever talked about hairstyles or the latest fashions. They assumed she was a married woman, as they all were.

I suppose I *am* a housewife, in a sort of way, Kitty thought miserably. I do the shopping, the cleaning, the washing, make the meals, I darn socks, mend clothes, and do everything housewives usually do, except I don't have any of the advantages, such as a husband and children to make it all seem worthwhile. She began to feel guilty again, because Dad needed her every bit as much as the other women's families did. He wouldn't be so desperate for her to stay with him if he didn't.

When Sheila asked if she'd washed her blackout curtains lately, Kitty decided it was time to go.

'Well, I'd better be off. Nan Wright's probably waiting for her 'taters. Thanks for the tea.'

'She eats too many 'taters, that woman,' Sheila said darkly. 'She's growing to look like one in her ould age.'

'Where on earth have you been? I was getting worried about you.'

Jimmy Quigley was sitting in his chair underneath the window, listening to the wireless and reading yesterday's *Daily Herald* for the second time. The room was neatly dull compared to the Reillys', reflecting Jimmy's personality rather than his daughter's. He abhorred fuss or ornaments and distracting colours which he claimed made him feel restless and on edge, so only a small chiming clock on a plain white runner stood on the otherwise bare sideboard, and the wooden mantelpiece held merely a solitary wedding photograph. The marble-patterned oilcloth was worn right through in places, but Kitty couldn't imagine the time ever coming when there would be enough money to replace it.

Her dad reached out eagerly for the newspaper, which he usually read from cover to cover. He wasn't a tall man, Jimmy, but his shoulders were broad, his well-muscled arms brown from sitting outside in the yard. He looked younger than his years, with wild brown curly hair and a fresh complexion similar to his daughter's, and appeared remarkably athletic, despite his crippled state. Jimmy had played for Everton Football Club Reserves when he was a teenager and had hoped to become a professional player, but although he was good, he wasn't quite good enough.

'There was a long queue at the grocer's,' Kitty explained as she handed the paper over. 'I managed to get some baked beans.'

'I could've sworn I heard your voice in the entry a while ago.'

'That's right, you did. I met Sheila Reilly on the way home and I went in hers for a cup of tea.'

'And here's me, been dying for a cuppa meself,' he said peevishly.

'In that case, I'll fetch some water and put the kettle on.'

Kitty went into the back kitchen and plonked her shopping on the wooden draining board with slightly more force than was necessary. She couldn't even do what other *housewives* did, let alone a young single woman: in other words, pop into a neighbour's for a jangle and a cup of tea, without feeling she was neglecting him.

She filled the kettle, took it into the living room and put it on the hob over the fire to boil. Her dad had laid the paper down on his knee and was looking at her rather bemusedly. It was rare his Kitty appeared out of sorts.

'What's the matter, kiddo? Have you got the hump over something?'

'No, Dad.'

'Yes you have. Come on, spit it out. What's up?'

'I don't see anything wrong with having a cup of tea with Sheila,' Kitty burst out.

'Of course there's nothing wrong,' he said, astonished. 'Who said there was?'

Kitty felt confused. 'The way you spoke just now, as if you were annoyed.'

'Me, annoyed? Never! I was worried, that's all. You can see Sheila Reilly whenever y'like, y'don't have to

22

mind me.' He winced and rubbed his knee. 'It's just that me legs have been playing up a bit this morning, particularly the right one . . .'

'Oh, Dad, you should have said!' It was just like him to suffer in silence. 'Would you like me to make a hot water bottle to put on them?'

'It doesn't matter, luv,' he said stoutly. 'It'll pass eventually, it usually does.'

'Are you sure now?' Kitty began to fuss around, taking the cushion from behind his head and plumping it up before putting it back carefully.

'I'm sure.'

'Oh, I nearly forgot. I got you ten Woodies.' She fished in her handbag for the cigarettes.

'What would I do without you, kiddo! Where's the matches? I'm dying for a smoke.'

Kitty brought a box of Swan Vestas and sat watching him indulgently while he lit a ciggie, took a deep breath and blew the smoke out with a long contented sigh. Their eyes met and they grinned at each other. All her previous resentment was forgotten. She knew that after he'd finished the *Daily Herald* they would have their dinner, bacon and beans, and he would suggest they play draughts or cards before he took his afternoon nap in the chair. Then they would listen to the six o'clock news on the wireless while they ate their tea. It being Thursday, *ITMA* with the Liverpool comedian, Tommy Handley, was on at half past eight, his favourite programme. Often Paddy O'Hara, his best mate, would come in and listen with them. Afterwards, they would go to the King's Arms, Dad somewhat painfully on his sticks, and she would tidy up, fetch in the coke and kindling ready for morning, set the table for their breakfast, put the washing in to soak. Finally, she would make a butty for his supper and start preparing the cocoa.

She told herself she was very lucky. All over the country, people had lost their homes or, even worse, their families. Kitty Quigley had a warm house to live in and a dad who loved her, and although there were more exciting ways of spending her days, she was better off than many young women of her age.

Even when Dad produced a piece of paper on which he'd written down what to say when she went to the Labour Exchange on Monday, urging her to learn it off by heart so it would sound natural, Kitty merely nodded her head obediently and didn't say a word.

Chapter 2

The Labour Exchange in Breeze Hill was busy and an air of mild chaos reigned. The original office in Oriel Road had been bombed in May, and it appeared as if the staff had not yet settled properly into their new home. Although Kitty arrived early for her appointment, feeling somewhat nervous, it was almost half past eleven by the time she was told to go to the counter where an official, a beautifully made-up girl much younger than herself, was waiting impatiently as if Kitty were late. There was a little cardboard sign in front of her which told the world she was called Miss G. Ellis.

'Where's your form?' she asked crisply.

'I haven't got a form.'

'You're supposed to have filled in a form while you were waiting.'

'No-one asked me to,' Kitty said humbly, feeling it was entirely her own fault she hadn't filled in a form. She found Miss Ellis, in her navy-blue tailored suit with a crisp white blouse underneath, and with perfectly waved hair, rather intimidating, despite her tender years. She spoke dead posh in a forceful, staccato way, as if she was in a hurry to get the proceedings over with as quickly as possible.

She tut-tutted and produced a form from behind the counter, snapping, 'In that case, I'll fill it in for you to save time. Name?'

'Kathleen Patricia Quigley, but everyone calls me Kitty.'

'Is that Miss or Mrs?'

'Miss,' Kitty said meekly.

'Address?'

'Twenty Pearl Street, Bootle.'

'Age?'

'Twenty-seven.'

'And what sort of work are you experienced to do?'

Kitty cleared her throat. 'Well, I worked in Williams Toffee Factory when I first left school. When I was sixteen, I started training to be a florist. But the thing is . . .'

'A florist!' Miss Ellis wrinkled her nose. 'There's not much call for florists in wartime.'

Kitty ignored the interruption and pressed on, '. . . the thing is, there's something I want to explain first.'

The girl looked irritated. 'And what's that?'

'I know I'm single and I don't appear to have any dependants, but the fact is, I do. Me dad's an invalid and he needs me to look after him.'

'It's amazing how many women turn out to have invalid fathers, invalid mothers and even invalid cousins and grandparents, when they're called up for war work,' Miss Ellis said sarcastically.

'But it's true,' Kitty protested, hurt. 'He had this terrible accident on the docks and he's never recovered. He needs his sticks to go everywhere. I have to get him up of a morning and put him to bed at night.'

'Can he make his own meals?'

'No.'

'Wash himself?'

'Yes.' He'd never wanted her to do intimate things, like wash him. When he took his weekly bath in front of the fire, he would only allow her to fill, then empty the tin tub. Whilst he bathed, she had to go upstairs or shut herself in the back kitchen till he finished.

'Is he under a doctor?'

26

'No.'

Miss Ellis paused and looked at Kitty, her perfectly plucked eyebrows raised enquiringly. 'No? How can he be an invalid, yet not be under a doctor?'

'We can't afford it, can we? Anyroad, he doesn't need a doctor. He's not *ill*, he just can't get around as well as he should. If his legs ache, he takes a couple of aspirin for the pain.'

'Is he incontinent?'

Kitty looked at her blankly. 'What?'

The girl said impatiently, 'Does he wet the bed?'

'Good gracious me, no! He goes to the lavatory at the bottom of the yard like everybody else.'

'Alone?'

'Of course.' Kitty tried vainly to remember the things Dad had written down which she'd learnt by heart. Something about him needing twenty-four-hour care and it being dangerous for him to be left alone in case he fell during one of his dizzy spells, though she couldn't recall him having had a dizzy spell in years. She racked her brains, but nothing else would come.

'He has dizzy spells,' she said desperately.

'So do I,' Miss Ellis said bluntly. 'I'm epileptic. No-one would employ me before the war. It's wonderful feeling useful for the first time in my life. I can't understand women,' she went on coldly, 'who perform contortions in order to avoid doing their bit.'

Epileptic! Kitty stared at the girl, who stared back in a slightly aggressive way as if she expected the remark she looked quite normal, which she did.

'I'm sorry, I didn't know,' Kitty stammered.

'There's no reason for you to be sorry, and even less reason why you should have known. I don't usually tell anyone, it's just that people like you give me a pain. Working for one's country during a war is a privilege, not a chore. I'd far sooner be in a factory, but office work is all they'd let me do.'

27

'I'm sorry,' Kitty said again, feeling as if she would like the floor to open up and swallow her. She hated being regarded as a shirker when she'd been dying to work for years. The women on either side of her seemed to be having quite animated and friendly conversations with their interviewers, which only made her feel worse.

Miss Ellis shrugged. 'As to your father, it appears he can do everything for himself except cook, but if he can get as far as the lavatory in the yard, he must pass through the kitchen where you keep the food. Surely he could prepare a small meal for himself, even if he does it sitting down?'

'I suppose he could,' Kitty sighed. If she left everything ready, put it in the oven if necessary, and did the washing, the shopping and most of the housework at the weekend, Dad should be able to manage on his own, though she wished she didn't feel quite so glad she hadn't managed to convince Miss Ellis of the need to stay at home. 'It's me company he'll miss more than anything else,' she muttered half to herself.

'If he complains,' Miss Ellis said unsympathetically, 'tell him you could be sent anywhere in the country. He'd miss your company even more if he didn't see you at all.'

'Oh, you wouldn't do that, surely?' cried Kitty, alarmed.

'I could, but I won't. There's enough vacancies in Liverpool to avoid such extreme measures.' She pulled open the drawer of a little wooden box which appeared to be full of white cards and began to leaf through them. For the very first time, she smiled and said sweetly, 'Now, let's see what those vacancies are.'

Half an hour later, Kitty emerged from the Labour Exchange, dazed.

'I've got a job!'

She said the words aloud in order to convince herself,

28

then repeated them, because even she found it hard to believe the words were true.

'I've got a job!'

Next Monday morning at six o'clock sharp, she was to report to Staff Nurse Bellamy at Seafield House in Seaforth which was now a Royal Naval Hospital, where she would be employed as an auxiliary nurse, working morning or afternoon shifts for alternate months. She could have started before, tomorrow if she'd wanted, but thought it wise to leave it till Monday so Dad would have time to get used to the idea of being left by himself.

A nurse! She visualised herself in a white uniform tending to sick and injured sailors. She really would be doing her bit towards the war effort from now on.

'Apparently, you can catch a bus to the hospital from the tram terminal in Rimrose Road,' Miss Ellis said when she came off the telephone after fixing everything up. 'It leaves at twenty to six. A uniform is supplied, but don't forget to wear a pair of flat shoes.' There was no need for an interview, the hospital was desperate, though she'd described Kitty in quite glowing terms over the phone.

'Oh, she looks terribly capable to me – and she's cared for her invalid father for many years,' Kitty heard her say.

Miss Ellis had turned out to be reasonably pleasant in the end, and shook Kitty's hand when she left. 'Good luck with the job, Kitty,' she said a touch patronisingly.

'Good luck to you,' said Kitty.

She didn't go straight home, but wandered around the shops in Stanley Road, partly to put off telling her dad he was about to be abandoned, partly because she would soon be earning two pounds seventeen and sixpence a week, which meant she'd have money to spend on herself for the first time since she left Garlands.

According to Miss Ellis, it was rather more than an

auxiliary nurse would normally expect to receive; the rate was higher because Kitty was being employed by the Admiralty. 'You'll be the equivalent of what they call a Sick Bay Attendant in the Navy, though you won't have quite so much responsibility.' On the other hand, the hours were horrendous. Qualified nurses were in short supply and three shifts had been merged into two; six till four on mornings, two till ten on afternoons, six days a week. 'That two hours' overlap is the only time the hospital has its full quota of staff,' Miss Ellis said.

There seemed to be plenty of clothes available in the shops. By the time she'd seen a coat she'd like to buy, two frocks, a nice blue cable-knit jumper, a pair of shoes and a broderie anglaise petticoat and knicker set, Kitty had spent an imaginary six months' wages, though she'd ask Brenda Mahon to run up a few things for her. Brenda was a dressmaker and only charged her friends a pittance for making clothes.

She went into the Co-op to look at their material, and an entire year's pay had gone by the time she came out again.

Kitty wasn't sure what reaction to expect when she told her father the news; anger, perhaps, dismay, indignation? She was confounded when, after a short interrogation, he appeared stoically resigned to the fact he was about to be left to his own devices as from Monday.

'Did you tell them about me dizzy spells?' he asked querulously.

'Of course I did, Dad,' Kitty assured him, 'but the woman didn't seem much interested.' She decided to put the entire blame on the shoulders of Miss Ellis.

'And me palpitations?'

'Yes,' lied Kitty. She'd forgotten all about his palpitations. 'She wasn't interested in them, either.'

'I'm sure there's something wrong with me heart, the

way it beats all crooked like. I was thinking of calling in the doctor one of these days.'

'Would you like me to fetch him in while I'm still home, like?'

He shook his head. 'No, luv, it doesn't matter. It's just something I'll have to put up with. You don't have to worry about me,' he said bravely. 'I'll manage on me own. I'll have to, won't I?'

'The neighbours'll come in and see to you,' Kitty promised. 'I'll have a word with Aggie Donovan, she's always keen to lend a hand. And Sheila Reilly'll pop in from time to time and make you a cup of tea. You won't be on your own, Dad, don't worry.'

'I'd sooner you didn't have a word with anyone, luv. I don't want people poking around, least of all that Aggie woman. It's not good for a man's dignity, having folks see him, particularly women, when his body's all broke up, like.' His mouth pursed in pain and he rubbed his knee.

'You look perfectly fine, Dad.' If the truth be known, he looked the picture of health. 'You just have trouble getting round, that's all.'

'That's all!' He regarded her with moist eyes. 'Your mam, God rest her soul, wouldn't think "that's all" if she could see me. It'd break her heart if she knew the way I was.'

Kitty's mam had died when she was four. She had only vague memories of a quiet, brown-haired woman who smiled a lot and smelt of lavender when they went to church.

'That's why I didn't put you in an orphanage when your mam passed away, like a lot of folk suggested,' Dad said, his voice quivering with emotion. ''Cos I knew it'd break her heart.'

'Oh, Dad!' Kitty felt so full of guilt, she could easily have burst into tears. Perhaps she should go back to the Labour Exchange and tell them there was no way she could go to work. She would ask to see a different official, someone who might be a bit more sympathetic than Miss Ellis. It was her dad who, perhaps unintentionally, made her see that this wasn't the right thing to do.

'Still,' he said, 'all those injured sailors need you more than your ould dad does, eh, kiddo?'

'I suppose they do,' she agreed.

'Just leave a butty and a glass of water on the table before you go to work, and that'll see me through the day till you come home and make something proper to eat.'

Kitty remembered what Miss Ellis had said; that if he could get as far as the lavatory, it meant he passed through the kitchen and could make a meal for himself, but felt it wasn't quite the right time to point this out.

That night, he didn't feel well enough for the King's Arms and decided to go to bed early. He groaned, clearly in terrible agony, as she helped him upstairs. After he'd changed into his pyjamas and she went to tuck him in, he panted, 'Don't know what I'm going to do about getting downstairs next week, luv. I'm not keen on getting up at half past five. Perhaps it might be best if I stayed in bed till you came home.'

'But, Dad,' she cried. 'You'd be bored silly stuck in bed all day.'

'Not if you brought the wireless up. You might even find time to buy the paper before you went to work.'

'I'll do me best,' vowed Kitty, though she was already worried she wouldn't be out in time to catch the bus. 'Goodnight, Dad.' She kissed his forehead. 'Don't worry. It's going to be all right.'

'Of course it is, luv. After all, there's a war on. Everyone's got to make sacrifices, haven't they?'

Jessica Fleming stood in the window staring out at the undulating Westmorland countryside, her baby daugh-

32

ter in her arms. From here, on the second floor, you could see for miles and miles. There was not a building in sight, just smooth green hills dotted here and there with smudges of purple heather and vivid yellow gorse. Hedges of a darker green ran haphazardly across the flat ground where the grass was longer and wilder. Some of the trees had already turned gold and were surrounded by a scattering of fallen leaves. The trunks of a row of silver birches glinted as brightly as if they had been painted.

Directly below the window, in their private garden, the lawn was strewn with conkers and cones. The cones were supposed to indicate the weather; closed it would rain, and the sun would shine if they were open, though Jessica had never found them very accurate.

She jumped as two grey squirrels suddenly appeared only yards from where she stood, chasing each other in and out the branches of a massive oak tree. The baby chuckled and reached for the squirrels, slightly surprised when her chubby hands came up against the glass. The animals disappeared. A few seconds later, they were scampering across the conkers and cones on the lawn.

It was a magnificent view, spectacular. This was England as it had been a thousand years ago, unspoilt and natural.

But Jessica hated it. She appreciated the beauty, yet it made her feel exposed, unsafe, unshielded. She wasn't quite sure how to describe what she felt when she looked out of the window – and it was impossible not to look out a hundred times a day, for it stretched the entire wall – and saw such a vast expanse of the earth, yet never another human being in sight. She preferred the winter, when she would draw the curtains and turn on the lamps far sooner than was necessary. It was only then she felt safe.

The little girl began to struggle, and Jessica shifted her

weight onto her other arm. 'It won't be long, Penny love, then we'll go,' she whispered.

Had anyone been outside the window looking in, they would have considered Jessica Fleming herself to be as spectacular as the view, with milk-white skin and a gleaming cascade of russet hair which she secretly hennaed nowadays to keep the grey streaks at bay. As if her glorious head of hair wasn't enough to attract attention, her eyes were an unusual sea-green. Tall, and perhaps slightly overweight, her figure had a Rubensesque voluptuousness accentuated by her clinging blue jersey dress. Penny was equally outstanding, even though she was only twelve months old; a Christmas card baby, with plump rosy cheeks, firm rounded limbs and hair not quite so thick and red as her mother's, more a tawny gold. Penny's eyes were a bright clear blue.

Outside, the sun began to slip behind a cloud, and a shadow crept swiftly across the hills and fields as if someone was laying a dark blanket over it all. Jessica shuddered and turned away. She sat Penny on the floor, where she immediately got to her feet and began to lurch unsteadily from the chair to the sideboard to the sofa, until she fell full length on the rug in front of the fire. She didn't cry, but a look of gritty determination came over her little face and she crawled as far as a chair, pulled herself to her feet and began another precarious journey around the room. Penny had only started walking two weeks ago.

Her mother laughed and cooed. 'What a clever girl you are!' She sat on the velvet sofa, her back to the window, and said aloud, 'I wish Arthur would hurry up.' He'd promised faithfully to see her off by half past twelve. Glancing at the clock, she saw it was quarter to one.

A few seconds later, there were footsteps on the stairs, slow and rather weary, as if the person coming was either very old or didn't relish whatever was waiting for him in the room upstairs. A man entered, handsome in a gentle, subdued way. He muttered, 'I'm sorry I'm late, but we had a visitor.' He regarded the woman wretchedly. 'Are you sure about this, Jess?'

'I'm positive, Arthur. I want to go home.'

'But . . .'

The woman raised a white hand on which the nails had been painted a delicate pink. 'Please don't start again, dear. We've gone over this a hundred times over the last few days. I want to be in Pearl Street, and that's all there is to it.'

'But you hated Pearl Street, Jess,' he said wildly. 'You couldn't stand it when you were forced to go back two years ago.'

She nodded in agreement. 'I know. I'm being awkward. I'm not even sure myself why I feel the way I do.' She'd been born in the street forty-five years ago; Jessie Hennessy, whose dad was a rag-and-bone man, operating from the end house which was now a coalyard. Bert Hennessy, a widower, turned to removing furniture on his cart, eventually bought a lorry and was soon running ten. By the time Jessie was sixteen, they'd moved to a better house in Walton Vale. When she met Arthur, who'd taken a part-time job with the company to help himself through university, the Hennessys were living in a detached mock Tudor residence in Calderstones, the best part of Liverpool.

'It's all my fault,' moaned Arthur. 'If we hadn't gone bankrupt, we'd still be in Calderstones. There'd have been no need to move to Pearl Street. Everything would have been fine.'

'Oh, Arthur! How many times have you said that over the last few days? It wasn't your fault. You're an intellectual, not a businessman. If it was anyone's fault, it was mine. I should have paid more attention to what was going on.' She was the one with the head for commerce, but she'd been too busy climbing up the social ladder to take an interest in the business after her father died. It had all been left to Arthur and he couldn't cope. When the crash came, she'd been taken totally by surprise. They'd returned to Pearl Street, where Bert Hennessy had invested in several properties, to live in one of the houses she owned. The shock to her system had seemed unbearable at the time. She'd never dreamt that nearly a quarter of a century later she'd return to live in the mean little street where she'd grown up. It was almost as great a shock to discover she didn't want to leave when Arthur got this job, curator of the museum downstairs.

'Anyroad, Arthur,' she said gently. 'Everything wasn't fine, was it? Our marriage wasn't exactly what you'd call perfect.'

'It wasn't so bad,' he said sulkily. Penny was trying to climb up his legs. He reached down, picked her up and pressed his face against her round cheek. Jess could tell he was close to tears. 'I suppose you're going back to her father!'

'I wish you wouldn't take that attitude, dear. My going back's nothing to do with him. He knows nothing about Penny.'

'Not that I blame you,' he went on, his face still muffled against the little girl's. 'He gave you a child, which was something I never managed to do.'

'I told you never to think like that. Penny's your daughter, every bit as much as she's mine.' She felt irritated at having to repeat, virtually word for word, the things she'd already said so many times, but supposed it was only fair to let him have one final try at changing her mind, despite the fact she knew it was useless. She was leaving, no matter what Arthur said.

'That doesn't stop you taking her away from me.'

'I'm not taking her away, I'm going home.'

36

Arthur sighed and carried the little girl over to the window. 'I can't understand how you can bring yourself to leave all this.' He gestured towards the view. 'It's glorious.'

'I know,' said Jess, 'but I loathe it. It's dead. I feel as if I'm living in a graveyard, particularly being on top of a museum.' *The Higginbotham Museum of Prehistoric Egyptian and Greek Art*, it said on the engraved brass plate outside.

'I should never have brought you here,' Arthur said miserably. 'I wasn't exactly unhappy myself during the time we spent in Bootle.'

Jess went over and stood beside him. Their shoulders touched. 'You love it here, Arthur. It's an archaeologist's heaven.' He spent hours downstairs long after the doors closed, poring over the artefacts, studying papers, writing letters to people all over the world who were as infatuated as he was with Greek and Roman remains. It was the first time since leaving university he'd had the opportunity to indulge in the subject which interested him to the point of obsession. Perhaps if they had more time together, she wouldn't have felt so cut off from life, Jess thought without rancour.

'I don't think I can go on living if you're not here.' He buried his head in Penny's hair and began to cry.

'Then why don't you come with me?' challenged Jess. She loved him, though he was weak and made her feel more like a mother than a wife. She wasn't quite sure why, but she prayed he would duck the challenge. He did.

'No,' he said. 'I'd sooner wait and hope you'll come back.'

Jess knew that she and Penny wouldn't be gone for long before he'd be downstairs immersed in his treasures and they'd both be forgotten, at least for a while.

'Would you mind carrying the suitcase out to the van?'

He nodded numbly and put the little girl in her arms. 'You'll write?'

'Of course. We'll still see each other.'

They went wordlessly down the two flights of stairs. Penny seemed to have grasped something serious was happening. She stared solemnly at her mother and held grimly to her ear.

Outside, the picturesque High Street was deserted. It was Wednesday, half day closing, and the only sign of life was a cat washing itself on a windowsill opposite.

Arthur put the suitcase in the back of the van and Jess tied Penny into the passenger seat with her reins. Her pushchair was already there, along with her white painted cot and mattress and her toys, bundles of bedding and several other household items.

'This is stupid!' Arthur cried. In a frantic gesture, he put both hands to his forehead. 'Why are you doing this to me, Jess?'

Jess kissed his cheek. 'I'm sorry, dear. It's just that I was beginning to feel as dead as the scenery. I'm a city person, Arthur, a Liverpudlian through and through. I need bricks and mortar around me, people, shops. I've never felt so alive as that year we spent in Bootle.' She seemed to experience all sorts of emotions she'd never thought existed.

Arthur glanced at Penny through the van window. 'I can understand that,' he said bitterly. It was the other man who'd made her feel alive.

'It's nothing to do with Penny,' Jess protested, though it was. 'It was all sorts of things, like the troop concerts I used to give with Jacob Singerman . . .'

'Jacob Singerman's dead.'

'I know,' Jess said sadly. 'Lots of people are dead, like Eileen Costello's husband and Tony, her little boy, all gone in the Blitz. That's something else. It hardly feels as if there's a war on, living here. Liverpool's at the very hub, what with the docks being so important.' One of the first things she'd do when she got back was take Penny for a walk along the Dock Road. 'I feel as if I'm missing out on all the excitement.'

'Excitement!' Arthur said derisively. 'The air raids weren't exciting.'

'How would we know, Arthur, we weren't there.' If it hadn't been for Penny, she would have left months ago, raids or no raids. She felt the need to be in the thick of things. She opened the door of the van and slid into the driving seat. 'Goodbye, love.'

He bent down and kissed her on the lips, his face stricken with grief. 'Goodbye, my darling Jess.'

'You're sure you don't mind my taking the van?' Jess had plans for the van once she was ensconced in Bootle.

'I'll get something else.' He needed transport occasionally to collect items which had been donated to the museum.

'Is there enough petrol?'

'I've put in the entire month's ration. The rest of the coupons are in your handbag.'

'Thanks,' she said briefly, and for the very first time since she'd told him she was leaving three days ago, Arthur felt a surge of resentment. She was selfish, always putting herself first, never him. Nevertheless, he said, 'I'll send you a cheque each month.'

Jess had been about to slam the door, but paused. 'I told you, Arthur, I don't expect you to keep us, not under the circumstances.'

'I'll send a cheque all the same. You can tear it up if you like.'

'As you wish, dear.' She closed the door, switched the engine on and shoved the gear lever into first. 'Goodbye,' she shouted.

The van was moving when she heard banging on the side. She braked impatiently and Arthur opened the door. 'Who was it, Jess?' he said pleadingly. 'Just tell me his name?'

But Jess merely shook her head, and once again the van started to move and Arthur was left with no alternative but to release the door. He watched as a white hand reached out and slammed it shut. He still watched until the van reached the end of the High Street, turned the corner, and Jess was gone.

Miss Helen Brazier was getting married and vacating number 10, one of Jess's properties, though no-one in Pearl Street knew she was the landlord of a dozen houses in the area. They'd been purchased by Bert Hennessy many years ago as an investment. An agent collected the rent, took his commission and deposited the remainder of the money in her and Arthur's joint bank account, where it went towards paying off debts that were still outstanding to the bank from when the firm went bankrupt.

According to the agent, with his approval Miss Brazier had been subletting number 10 ever since she'd joined the ATS fifteen months ago. Now stationed in Suffolk, she was about to wed a sergeant in the Royal Air Force who already *owned* his own house in Potters Bar – Jess read the letter to the agent, and Helen Brazier had actually underlined 'owned' twice. Normally, the tenancy would automatically be transferred to the people subletting, but the Grahams were bad payers, never in when the agent called for the rent, and several weeks in arrears for the umpteenth time. He suggested they be given Notice to Quit.

Go ahead, Jess wrote back when she received his letter. She couldn't stand people who didn't pay their bills. *Though it's not me who should suffer the shortfall in rent, but Miss Brazier. She's the person ultimately responsible.* Jessica had a heart of stone when it came to business matters.

Helen Brazier saw the justice in this when it was put to her, and offered her furniture to make up the shortfall. *It's good stuff*, she wrote. *It belonged to my mother. I'm sure*

40

it's worth much more than what is owed. My hubby-to-be already has his own furniture. Anyroad, it would cost the earth to have it sent to Potters Bar.

The agent asked what he should do? *The Grahams have moved out and left the place a proper midden. It needs cleaning and redecorating throughout before it can be re-let, though the wallpaper's the sort that'll take a coat of distemper. The furniture's good quality, like she said.* He wanted to know if he should sell it, or let the house furnished. *Lots of people lost their stuff in the raids. You could get as much as half a crown a week more by letting it fully furnished.* If Jess wanted it sold, he would charge a fee of ten shillings for his trouble.

All this correspondence had been going on without Arthur's knowledge. Jess liked to keep her own affairs private, not that he would have been interested if she'd told him – if she'd had an opportunity to tell him, that is, whilst he was so engrossed in bits and pieces several thousand years old.

It was when she got this last letter that Jess had her great idea. *She* would live in Helen Brazier's house. She would move back to Pearl Street with Penny, which was what she'd been yearning to do ever since she'd left for the second time.

She told the agent to have the house cleaned and decorated; *pastel colours; pale pinks, blues, white.* She'd recently read in a magazine that pale colours were all the rage in Mayfair. *Leave the furniture where it is,* she wrote. *I've some business to sort out in Liverpool which might take quite a while. I'll live there myself.*

It was almost dark by the time Jessica neared Liverpool. Although Arthur had drawn a map of the route she should take, the road signs had been taken down some time ago when there'd been the threat of invasion, and she got lost several times. Penny was in the back by now, fast asleep on the cot mattress.

41

Jessica threw back her head and sang at full throttle: 'In Dublin's fair city where the girls are so pretty . . .'

The enclosed space seemed to enhance and give even greater depth to her already glorious soprano voice. She'd joined a choir whilst she was away, but choirs seemed dull in the extreme compared to the troop concerts she used to give, at which she'd sung all the latest hits. The audience, men perhaps on the point of going off to fight within a matter of hours, had joined in the chorus if they knew the words, cheering to the echo when the concert finished. The atmosphere had been charged with emotion. Sometimes dear old Jacob Singerman, who accompanied Jess on the piano, had been close to tears at the end.

When Jessica drove into the dusk of the great city where she was born she felt her heart lift. She found the headlights worse than useless to see by with their metal caps which left merely a narrow slit of illumination. But she didn't need lights to witness the damage that had been wrought. Parts had been reduced to little more than brickyards and elsewhere bare skeletons of buildings remained, silhouetted black against the grey sky. She drove around, almost aimlessly, for a while, forgetting she was wasting petrol, her horror increasing with each corner she turned. Eileen Costello had told her what had happened in her letters, but nothing could have prepared her for actually seeing the terrible destruction for herself. It was as if the city had been hit by an earthquake.

Jessica sighed, thought about the petrol, and turned the van in the direction of Bootle.

Yet more destruction and broken buildings. Some streets seemed to have disappeared completely, wiped with ruthless finality off the face of the earth. She felt a strange sort of resentment that she'd missed all this, though she knew she was being ridiculous and silly. It didn't seem right that she, a Liverpudlian, had avoided the suffering that everyone else in the city had endured.

She pressed her foot on the accelerator, anxious to get to Bootle, to Pearl Street, to be home.

The first thing she did when she entered the house was draw the curtains everywhere and turn the gaslights on. She was pleased to find the place looked quite respectable, and as the agent had said, the furniture was good, if rather ornate and over-large, and had thoughtfully been polished. The heavy embossed wallpaper had taken the distemper well and the rooms were bright and cheerful, and would look even brighter once she got some pretty chintz to cover the ugly blackout material. She'd just have to go without carpets until she earned money of her own, though the quaintly old-fashioned oilcloth looked the sort that was quite likely to come back in vogue.

'What do you think, Penny?' Jessica asked as she carried her daughter upstairs to show her around. Penny had woken up the very second the van stopped. She seemed enchanted with everything, particularly the gas mantles which she'd never seen before, but then the most insignificant little thing could enchant Penny.

The mattress on the double bed in the front bedroom had seen better days, but Jessica supposed it would have to do. The rear room contained only a single bed. She'd brought her own bedding and a few other things – dishes, cutlery, a few cooking utensils – though when she went downstairs again, she found the back kitchen fully equipped and supposed it had all belonged to Miss Brazier.

There was a brass coal scuttle half full of coal on the hearth in the living room, and the fire was partially laid with rolled-up paper topped with kindling. The agent was obviously keen to make a good impression on his employer. Jess lit the paper and gradually began to add

43

the coal, lump by lump. She was dying for a cup of tea. She thought wistfully of the house across the road, number 5, where they'd returned to live. It had been snapped up by the people next door, the Evanses, when Jess and Arthur left. She'd had it modernised throughout in the short time they'd been there; a proper fireplace instead of the ugly black range, a bath fitted in the washhouse, a stove in the back kitchen. And she'd had electricity installed throughout . . .

Jessica felt herself grow hot. If it hadn't been for the electricity, she would never have had Penny!

'Oh, God!' She felt her stomach turn over at the memory of that night.

The fire had begun to take hold. Jessica fetched a kettle of water and put it on to boil. It was only then she realised there was no fireguard. 'I'll buy one tomorrow,' she resolved. There was a second-hand shop in Marsh Lane, who'd be sure to have one in stock.

She gave Penny a bottle of concentrated orange juice and warm water and hooked her reins to the leg of the table. Then she began to unload the van. Everyone in Pearl Street would be dying to know where it came from when they saw it there tomorrow, Aggie Donovan in particular. She'd have to find a garage. That van was going to be a source of income, and she couldn't risk it being damaged. Her father had started with a horse and cart; Jessica was starting with a van. She was determined not to sponge off Arthur.

The kettle boiled and the tea was made, when Jessica discovered she'd forgotten to bring milk.

'Damn!' she muttered. She couldn't possibly wait until tomorrow for a cuppa, she'd just have to borrow some. Eileen Costello, who she would automatically have gone to, was now living in Melling, and Jacob Singerman, the dear old soul, was dead. Still, Eileen's sister, Sheila, wouldn't mind lending her some.

Jessica undid Penny's reins, picked her up and tripped

along in her high-heeled suede sandals to number 16 to borrow a cup of milk. She would have sooner died of thirst than borrow milk when she lived in Calderstones, but something seemed to have happened to her when the business went bust and she'd returned to her roots in Bootle. Things that had mattered then didn't seem important any more. She no longer cared if she made a good impression. In fact, she didn't give a toss what people thought. She knocked on Sheila's door and waited.

Sheila Reilly stared in disbelief at the glamorous figure in the clinging blue dress and fluffy white mohair cardigan who was standing on her doorstep, a cherubic baby in her arms.

'Strewth, if it isn't Jess Fleming! What on earth are you doing here?'

'I'm here to borrow a cup of milk. I've moved into number ten.'

'Come in,' Sheila cried, delighted. 'The kids are in bed and I was just listening to the wireless on me own. Does our Eileen know you're back? I bet she's thrilled to bits if she does.'

'No. No-one knows – except you.'

'Is Arthur with you? Surely he hasn't given up that nice job in the museum?'

'Arthur might come later,' Jessica said briefly.

Sheila turned her gaze on the baby. 'Is this Penelope? Oh, let me hold her. Isn't she beautiful? Come to your Auntie Sheila, there's a good girl. Sit down, Jess. Make yourself at home.'

This is what I've missed, Jessica thought warmly; the feeling that people care, the togetherness, as if everyone in the street belonged to the same family. It was something she'd never been aware of when she'd lived there as a child.

'It seems dead funny, seeing women with children

45

younger than me own,' Sheila said, chucking Penny under her fat chin. 'I had six in seven years, which meant I always had a baby, but our Cal refuses to have any more till the war's over. He says six kids and a wife are already enough to worry about whilst he's away at sea.'

'Well, you can't blame him,' Jess said reasonably. 'How is Calum?'

'He was fine when I last saw him in July. He's on the Atlantic convoys. I never know when to expect him home.' She looked at Jessica with scared eyes. 'It's terrible dangerous, Jess. Most nights I can't sleep for thinking about Cal, stuck on a little boat somewhere in the middle of the ocean and all those U-boats about. I've lost track of the number of his mates who've been killed.'

Jessica was unsure how to reply. What on earth were you supposed to say to someone in Sheila's position? The loss of life at sea, the tonnage of ships sunk, was horrendous, and had been so since the very first day war started and the *Athenia* had been torpedoed on its way to Canada.

'Never mind,' Sheila sighed. 'If I say enough prayers, God won't dare let anything happen to Cal.' She stared at Penny curiously. 'Y'know, it's awful funny, Jess, but she's got a definite look of our Siobhan – y'know, me oldest girl. Isn't that peculiar?'

'Very peculiar,' Jess agreed.

'Anyroad, now's you're here, you may as well have a cup of tea with us. I was just about to make one, me dad'll be along in a minute on his way home from the pub, though you can put the kettle on yourself.' She hugged Penny, who looked quite content in a strange woman's arms. 'There's no way I'm going to give up this lovely little bundle.'

'I've already made tea,' Jessica said. 'I'll go and fetch it. It would be a shame to waste a whole pot.'

She fetched a dozen eggs at the same time – she'd

brought a whole tray with her which she'd intended keeping for herself, but Sheila's open-hearted welcome had touched her. She remembered the way people usually shared things, particularly good fortune if it came their way.

Sheila was overwhelmed when Jess returned. 'Eggs! A whole dozen! I'll give some of them to Brenda.'

'You can buy eggs from the farms,' Jess explained. She went into the back kitchen and poured the tea.

'Our Eileen's started keeping hens out in Melling, though none of them have laid yet, they're only little.'

'I must go and see her.'

'Perhaps we could all go together one weekend?'

'That'd be nice.' Jess could hear laughter in the street, men's voices. The King's Arms was letting out. She held her breath, feeling on edge as she waited for the key to be drawn through the letterbox, for the door to open. She wondered if she'd purposely forgotten the milk, so she would have an excuse to call on Sheila Reilly the minute she arrived.

A few minutes later came the sound which she'd been so anxiously expecting. The front door was opened. 'It's only me, luv,' a man's voice called.

'Come on in, Dad,' Sheila called back.

And the giant figure of Jack Doyle appeared, almost entirely filling the doorway of the living room.

Chapter 3

Jack Doyle stood immobile in the doorway, his face totally expressionless. He was better dressed than usual, in a cheap navy-blue suit and a collar and tie.

'Jess's home,' sang Sheila. 'She's moved into number ten, Miss Brazier's old house. And this is Penelope. Isn't she lovely? And it's ever so strange, Dad, but from certain angles, she's the image of our Siobhan.'

Jack blinked and came shuffling awkwardly into the room. 'Where's Arthur?' he growled, directing his question at Sheila, as if the red-headed figure in the blue dress were invisible.

'Arthur might come later,' Sheila explained.

'What happened to the Grahams?'

'Dai Evans said the rent collector told him they were bad payers – they both had the same landlord. They were chucked out. I already told you that, Dad.'

'That's not fair,' Jack exploded. 'There were five kids in that family and Alfie Graham hasn't worked in years.'

'Only because he didn't want to,' Sheila argued. 'There's plenty of work for everyone since the war began.' She regarded him with a certain amount of disapproval. 'You're dead rude, Dad. You haven't said hello to Jess.'

'Hello,' he said grudgingly.

'Hello, Jack,' said Jessica. Her face was as expressionless as his, disguising entirely the thrill of excitement that coursed through her.

She'd loved Jack Doyle since she was twelve, when he

had come to the yard to complain bitterly because her father had given only coppers to some old lady for a family treasure which was worth far more. He was eight years older than she was, already courting, and barely aware of Jessie Hennessy's existence. Anyroad, he wouldn't be interested in someone like her, the daughter of a capitalist, a man who made his living like a leech on the backs of the poor – or so she'd heard him yell at her father on more than one occasion.

After they left Pearl Street, she still had hankerings after the young firebrand who'd been the bane of her father's life for so many years, though gradually, as time passed, the memory faded and if she thought about him at all, she regarded him as part of a working-class past long out-grown. She married Arthur. She was happy living in Calderstones, surrounded by every luxury money could buy. Her wardrobe was stuffed with the latest fashions, they owned the latest car, the kitchen was fitted with the most modern appliances. Jessica Fleming wanted for nothing.

At least she told herself she was happy. There was always a sense of sadness that she'd never had children. At times, she felt she would have given everything, the clothes, the car, all the equipment in the kitchen, if only she could conceive a child of her own. Of course, it was her own fault. There was something wrong with her. Jessica Fleming might well be the epitome of woman-hood, with her broad hips just made for childbirth, and full breasts waiting to be filled with milk, but inside she was barren . . .

'Jess!'

Jessica came to. Sheila was standing over her, a cup and saucer in her hand.

'You were miles away,' she laughed. 'I've poured you another cup of tea.'

'Thanks. You're right, I was miles away.'

'With Arthur?'

'I'm not quite sure where I was.'

Penny had been transferred to Jack Doyle's knee while Jess was in her daydream. She was standing, exploring his face with her hands, whilst he stared at her, a curious, almost mystified expression on his craggy features. When Penny pulled his ears, he couldn't resist it, he smiled.

The smile transformed his rather sombre face. He was still a good-looking man, Jack Doyle, thought Jessica, perhaps better looking now than when he was young, with a rugged, almost exaggerated handsomeness and eyes that were a vivid blue. Both his daughters had inherited the same colour eyes. He wore the cheap suit with a sort of rough elegance that better-dressed men might have envied. He was so very different from Arthur, who was delicately boned, much thinner, with small, almost feminine, hands. Jack's hands were like spades, workman's hands, rough and worn at the knuckles from the hard manual work he did every day on the docks.

Jessica shivered, remembering the way those hands had touched every part of her the night she conceived Penny. She wondered if he was having the same sort of thoughts. There'd only been the once, and neither of them had referred to it again. They'd acted as if the night had never happened, as if he'd never come into the house to get on with the electricity, thinking the place was empty. Instead, he found Jessica, naked in the bath in front of the fire.

He lifted Penny high above his head, his hands almost meeting around her small body, and she squealed in delight. 'She's lovely,' he said, for the first time addressing Jessica directly. 'But Penelope's a daft name to give her. What made you think of that?'

'We call her Penny.'

'That's better.'

'What was the lecture like, Dad?' Sheila turned to

Jessica. 'He went to a lecture earlier on with his girlfriend.'

Jack flushed a ruddy red. 'She's not me girlfriend, don't be so bloody stupid.'

'Your womanfriend, then,' Sheila giggled. 'Did you ever meet Kate Thomas, Jess? She was the overseer in our Eileen's factory.'

When Jessica shook her head, Sheila continued, 'Her and Dad get on like a house on fire – don't you, Dad? Me and our Eileen really fancy having Kate Thomas for a stepmother.'

'For Christ's sake, girl, shut up your nonsense. There's nothing like that between me and Kate.' He grew even redder and Penny patted his cheeks curiously.

'More's the pity.' Sheila sighed and winked at Jessica. 'You've been a widower for a long time, Dad. It seems a shame, a man like you going to waste. I bet there's loads of women dying to get their hands on you – and Kate Thomas is probably first in line.'

'What was the lecture about?' asked Jessica, who was finding the conversation irritating.

Jack looked relieved that the subject had been changed. 'Anglo–Soviet Co-operation,' he replied. Then his big face twisted contemptuously. 'It makes you sick, the way the official line on our Russian comrades has changed out of all proportion since June. No-one had a good word to say about them until then. Now, Communism's respectable, Russia's our "Great Ally", and Stalin can't do a thing wrong. It's "Uncle Joe" this, and "Uncle Joe" that, and everyone's falling over themselves to send help, from "Tanks for Russia" week to knitting blankets. They even sent an entire wing of the RAF over there. In fact,' he said proudly, 'that's where Nick is, our Eileen's husband, Russia.'

'I know,' said Jessica.

'Brenda Mahon's making gloves and socks for the Russians,' Sheila put in.

Jack nodded approvingly. 'They'll need them, what with the winter coming on.'

The Germans had thought the conquest would be easy – Hitler himself had said Russia would fall like a leaf – but the Russians, although they were retreating, were fighting like demons for every single inch of soil. Not only that, they adopted a scorched-earth policy which meant the enemy might capture a town, but there was nothing left to capture; the people had left, the buildings had been razed to the ground.

'Did you listen to the news tonight, luv?' Jack asked his daughter.

'Yes, Dad,' Sheila said obediently, 'but there's not much happening anywhere, at least not much worth reporting. Everything's in the doldrums at the moment, except for Russia.'

'I'd better be getting home,' said Jessica. 'Penny must be tired.' Penny didn't look the least bit tired. She appeared to be trying to walk up Jack's chest. 'Oh, I mustn't forget the teapot, Sheila, and I'd still like to borrow a bit of milk if you've got some to spare, so's I can have a cup of tea first thing in the morning. I'll register with the milkman tomorrow.' She got to her feet. 'I'll take them first and come back for Penny.'

'That's all right, luv. Me dad'll take Penny. You take the other things.'

Jessica had left the gas light on low in the living room, and the fire was burning cheerfully in the grate.

'Don't put her on the floor,' she said to Jack when he came in carrying Penny. 'There's no fireguard. I'll take her upstairs with me and assemble the cot.'

'I'll do the cot for you, it's no job for a woman,' he mumbled. 'Where is it?'

Jessica felt amused. Her father had taught her how to strip a lorry's engine and put it back together. She'd been his chief mechanic when there'd only been the two of them trying to get the haulage business off the ground. She could have assembled the cot in a jiffy. Nevertheless, she replied, 'It's in the front bedroom. I thought I'd have her in with me till she gets used to things. It might all seem a bit strange at first.' Penny was used to her own white painted nursery with teddy bear transfers on the walls.

Jack put the little girl in Jessica's arms without a word and tramped upstairs. Jessica took her into the back kitchen, sat her on the draining board, and washed her face and hands and cleaned her teeth. 'You can have a bath in the morning, a different bath than usual, in front of the fire.'

Penny waved her arms in delight, as if she understood every word and looked forward to the treat. 'And Mummy will give you a nice drink of milk in a minute.'

She breastfed her daughter at least once a day, unwilling to give up the last real physical link between mother and child. There was still a sense of wonderment when she saw Penny's rosy lips sucking greedily at her white breast that she'd actually become a mother after all those barren years – and it hadn't been her fault, after all.

There was a shout from upstairs. 'It's done.'

'Is this where you want it?' Jack asked when Jessica entered the bedroom carrying Penny. He'd erected it on the far side of the bed, against the wall. 'It'd have stopped you opening the wardrobe if I'd put it on the other side.'

'That's fine.'

The big double bed, with its tumble of blankets and sheets and the green satin eiderdown thrown carelessly on waiting to be made, seemed to loom significantly between them. Jessica wondered if it reminded him, as it reminded her, of that night, *the* night, when both of them had seemed to reach a higher plane, a sort of seventh heaven, full of delights and delicious feelings she wasn't aware existed. It had been good with Arthur, but she'd never thought it possible it could be as good as it was with Jack. And to think all that tenderness and passion was hidden behind his gruff, taciturn exterior, and she, Jessica Fleming, was the only one who knew it was there!

'When did you say Arthur was coming?' he asked suddenly.

He'd been good friends with her husband, and he was an honourable man, Jack Doyle, as straight as a die, a man who under normal circumstances would regard sleeping with another man's wife, let alone the wife of a friend, as little short of traitorous. But the minute he'd walked into the room across the road, events had gone completely out of control. Neither could help themselves.

'I didn't say he was coming. I just said he might.'

'That was a good job he got. It'd be a shame if he gave it up.'

'Wild horses wouldn't drag Arthur away from the museum.'

Jack looked puzzled. 'But . . .' he began.

'I've left him,' said Jessica. There! She'd put it into words. She and Arthur had been fencing around each other rather cautiously for days. There'd been no mention of Jessica leaving permanently, not even of a proper separation; they'd behaved as if she were merely going away for a while, though both had known in their hearts she was going for good.

'I hated it there,' she said spiritedly. 'I missed Liverpool. I couldn't wait to get back.'

'A woman's place is beside her husband,' Jack growled. 'Y'should have stayed whether you liked it or not.'

Jessica stared at him angrily, and at the same time tried to discern from his expression if he was pleased she was back within his reach, but he looked sternly censorious.

'You could say a man's place is beside his wife,' she said. She wasn't going to take lectures on where her place should be from anyone. 'I asked Arthur to come with me, but he preferred to stay.' She tossed her head. 'Anyway, it's none of your business.'

'You're right, it's not.' He came towards the door where she was standing. 'I'd better be going. I'm on firewatching duty at midnight.'

He touched Penny's cheek briefly as he pushed past. 'She's a bonny little girl,' he said, smiling briefly.

Jessica was conscious of his muscular arm brushing against hers. She almost wished Penny wasn't there so she could grab Jack and pull him back towards the bed. But Penny *was* there, waving bye-byes as Jack made his departure.

There was no moon and it was pitch dark, blacker than she'd ever known it.

Kitty Quigley felt her way along the walls of the houses in Opal Street and nearly fell over when the wall ended and she realised she'd reached Garnet Street. She began to panic. It was like walking through thick black soup. She'd never get to and from the newsagent's in time to catch the twenty to six bus at this rate, and if she was late on her first day, she'd die. She imagined the hospital telephoning Miss Ellis to complain.

'Oh, God!' she moaned as she kicked over a milk bottle and spent several precious minutes searching for it, without success.

Brisk footsteps sounded in the otherwise totally silent world, but Kitty had no way of knowing whether the steps were coming or going or which side of the street they were on. She screamed when she bumped into a figure so solidly built that she almost bounced off.

'Who's that?' the figure demanded.

'It's Kitty Quigley from Pearl Street. Who's that?'

'Vera Dodds, the postwoman. I'm just on me way to

55

the sorting office. What on earth are you doing, Kitty, wandering round at this time of the morning?'

'I'm going to Ernie Robinson's for the *Daily Herald* for me dad. He wants to read it while I'm at work,' Kitty explained to the dark, as Vera was invisible, adding proudly, 'I'm starting at the Royal Navy Hospital, Seaforth, this morning as an auxiliary nurse.'

'Aye, so I heard. Well, you're on a fruitless journey at the moment, girl. Ernie doesn't open till six o'clock.'

'Damn!' muttered Kitty, cursing her stupidity for not finding out before, though she felt slightly relieved. It meant she could return home and have a bite of breakfast. 'Me dad'll be dead disappointed when he finds he hasn't got a paper.'

'I'll get your dad his *Daily Herald* if you like,' Vera offered. 'I'll pop it through the letterbox when I'm doing me round.'

'Thanks all the same, Vera, but he'll be in bed and he can't manage the stairs on his own.'

'In that case, I'll take it up. Don't worry about your dad, luv. I'll see to him.'

Kitty had a feeling her dad mightn't be too pleased if Vera Dodds suddenly appeared in the bedroom, but she found it awfully hard to turn down people's kind offers of help and risk hurting their feelings.

She didn't mention Vera when she got home, just as she hadn't mentioned all the other people who had promised to see to him whilst she was at work. She merely apologised for the lack of a paper, made herself a piece of toast and left him propped up against the pillow looking hard done by.

'I hope I don't get one of me dizzy spells while you're gone.' The dizzy spells had returned in full force over the last few days.

'Well, at least you're safe lying down, Dad,' Kitty said comfortably.

It was slightly lighter by the time she left for the bus;

not much, but enough to see by as she made her way towards Rimrose Road. It was lighter still when she got off at the hospital.

Seafield House was a lonely place, fronting Seaforth Sands and reached from the road through an iron gate and along a tree-lined path. A massive five-storey grey brick building with narrow windows, some with iron bars, it had square solid turrets at either end and rows of unnaturally tall chimneys protruding like fingers into the lightening sky. Before only recently becoming a naval hospital, it had belonged to the Lancashire Asylums Board, and had a sinister, forbidding air. No-one had ever been seen going in or coming out, and people were unsure whether the place was occupied or not. Kitty felt very small as she trailed behind a handful of people who'd got off the bus at the same time towards the arched double doors, one of which was wide open.

The others had disappeared by the time Kitty entered the door herself, and she found herself in a dismal reception area two floors high with a black and grey tiled floor and walls painted a colour she couldn't put a name to, a mixture of putty and green, which she later discovered was referred to as 'eau de sick'. Although everywhere was very quiet and the only person in sight was a tired-looking young woman in a white shirt and navy-blue tie who was sitting behind a desk, nevertheless the building had an air of occupancy, and Kitty was conscious of the fact that there were perhaps hundreds of people there. At that moment, two nurses came hurrying in and ran quickly up the stairs, their dark cloaks flowing, and she wondered if she would be given a cloak to wear.

The young woman smiled as Kitty approached. 'Can I help you, love?'

'I'm looking for Staff Nurse Bellamy.'

'She's in the basement, that's through the door in the corner over there. Turn right when you reach the

57

bottom of the stairs and you'll find her office at the far end of the corridor.'

'Ta.'

The basement was dimly lit by low-powered electric bulbs. Bottle-green iron doors, all firmly shut, lined the narrow corridor. The final door was open, and in a windowless room more like a prison cell than an office, a frowning nurse wearing a white lawn veil on the back of her head and a pale grey dress which had a little scarlet-trimmed shoulder cape was bending over a desk containing a large chart on which she was writing.

'Staff Nurse Bellamy?'

The woman looked up, frowning even more deeply. She looked more like a farmer's wife than a nurse, with a shiny face, red apple cheeks and a little round chin, which all contrasted rather oddly with her cool, regal dress. 'Who are you?' she demanded in a loud voice.

'Kitty Quigley. I'm the new auxiliary nurse.'

'That's right, so you are. Well, if you'd like to go in the room next door and find yourself a uniform, I'll put you to work.'

Kitty struggled for ages with the handle of the door trying to get it open, until an impatient voice shouted, 'You turn the handle up, not down.'

Once inside the dark room, Kitty groped the walls but was unable to find the light switch. She was close to despair – Nurse Bellamy would think her dead stupid – when something knocked against her forehead, a cord with a knob on the end. She pulled the knob with a trembling hand, praying it wouldn't bring something down on top of her, and the light came on.

There were uniforms, stacks of them in several different colours on the shelves lining the room. Kitty sorted through a heap of well-starched pale grey frocks until she found one that looked about her size. She hung her coat behind the door, removed her own frock and was buttoning up the grey uniform when an amused

58

voice said, 'You're only supposed to collect your uniform here, not change into it. And if Staff sees you in that get-up she'll bust a gut.'

A woman of about fifty was standing in the doorway. She was thin to the point of emaciation, with a deeply lined humorous face. Her brown eyes danced with amusement behind her rimless glasses.

'I thought I was supposed to wear one the same as hers,' Kitty stammered.

The woman laughed. 'Did you now! Here five minutes and you're already a State Registered Nurse. No, dear, it's green and white stripes for the likes of you. They're over there.' She nodded towards a shelf behind Kitty. 'The aprons are on the shelf below, along with the caps. Mind you, it wouldn't have hurt Staff to let you know what you were supposed to wear. She seems to expect everyone to read her mind, then blows her top if we read it wrongly. That said, Bellamy's okay deep down at heart. Her bark's ten times worse than her bite.' She smiled briskly. 'Here, give me that dress and I'll fold it whilst you put your own clothes back on. After you've collected your serf's uniform, I'll show you where to change.'

'Me serf's uniform?'

'You'll feel like a serf after you've been here a while. This hospital is run on a strictly hierarchical system. Right at the top there's God and the Apostles, in other words, the Chief Medical Officer and his various assistants. Then there's Red Cross nurses, Queen Alexandra nurses, plain ordinary nurses, SBAs, non-medical staff – mainly Wrens. Right at the very bottom of the shitheap, there's us, the auxiliaries.'

It was only then Kitty noticed the woman was wearing a green and white striped coarse cotton dress, a long white apron and a white cap consisting of a stiff band with a soft gathered crown over her short, greying-brown hair. She looked quite good-tempered whilst she

59

spoke, as if she wasn't particularly bothered at being regarded as a serf.

'I'm Harriet, by the way. Harriet Mansell, spinster of this parish. You're Kathleen Quigley, so I'm told.'

'Everyone calls me Kitty.'

'Mansell, Quigley,' a voice bellowed. 'What's going on in there?'

'Quigley's just finding a uniform to fit, Staff,' the woman called back.

'This is a hospital, not a mannequin parade.'

'Coming, Staff.' Harriet Mansell turned to Kitty, who was putting her coat back on. 'Ready?'

Kitty nodded and was about to leave, when Harriet said, grinning broadly, 'You've forgotten your uniform, which was the whole point of this rather elaborate and useless exercise!'

Nurse Bellamy was still studying her chart when they went in. 'Has Peterson turned up yet?' she enquired without looking up.

'I think I saw her upstairs, Staff,' Harriet Mansell replied.

'Really?' the Staff Nurse said sarcastically. 'In that case, she's forgotten to report in.'

'I'll remind her when I see her.'

'You do that, Mansell. Well, you know where to start; the corridors, the sluice room, then the wards. Show Quigley here what to do. She's taken over from Caldicott.'

'Rightio, Staff. I'll keep an eye on her. Come on, Kitty.'

Once they were outside in the corridor, the older woman said, 'We'll collect the buckets now, rather than come all the way down again when you've changed.' She led Kitty back along the corridor to a room where there was a large brown earthenware sink at floor level. Two women were already there, each filling a metal pail with water.

'Morning, ladies,' Harriet said cheerfully.

'Morning,' one replied. The other looked half asleep and didn't answer. As soon as the pails were nearly full of soapy water, they each collected a mop and shuffled out, yawning.

Harriet put three pails in the sink and sprinkled suds in each. 'I'll take two buckets with me, one for Lucy. She's late again. Staff's already noticed she's not here. Poor Lucy has a terrible job getting out in the mornings. Find three decent mops, there's a good girl. Some are so badly worn they're useless.'

Kitty sorted through a row of mops which were standing upside down against the wall and selected the best three. Although she said nothing, she felt more than a little dismayed at the idea she was expected to do cleaning. She'd thought she'd be tending to sick and injured sailors by now, though in what way, she wasn't quite sure.

They struggled up two flights of stairs. Water sloshed over the top of Kitty's bucket, soaking her leg, so she changed the bucket to her other hand and nearly dropped her cap in. She glanced surreptitiously at her companion to see if she'd noticed, but Harriet was slightly ahead and unaware of the fact the new auxiliary couldn't even carry a bucket of water without spilling it. When they reached the first floor, Harriet stopped outside a door.

'This is the auxiliaries' rest room. Change your clothes and I'll start on the floors.'

'You're not going far, are you?'

'Don't worry, I'll be right here.'

The rest room was scarcely bigger than a cupboard, a miserable place with a small table underneath the tiny barred window and wooden chairs pushed against the walls. There were several bags on the chairs and a pile of coats hung behind the door.

Kitty quickly got changed, wishing there was a mirror

so she could see what she looked like in the green and white striped dress and apron. Although she pulled her cap down as far as it would go, it sprang off her wild curly hair immediately she let go. She hung up her coat, rolled her clothes into a ball and left them with her bag on a chair, then went out to find Harriet, who was cleaning the floor outside and hooted when she appeared.

'That cap looks like a pimple on an elephant's arse! You'll never get it to stay on without a hairclip. Have you got one with you?'

Kitty shook her head numbly. She'd scarcely been there a quarter of an hour and so far had done everything wrong. She squirmed with embarrassment, imagining Staff's reaction if she'd turned up in the wrong uniform. Merely thinking about it seemed to sap every bit of confidence she might have had.

'I'll lend you one of mine, but I'd like it back, please. Hairclips are like gold dust these days.' Harriet removed one of the clips from her cap. 'We serfs must stick together, eh? On no account must we let the bastards get us down.'

Kitty wasn't entirely sure if she liked Harriet Mansell, although she was undoubtedly friendly and very helpful. She'd never known a woman swear before, apart from mild words like 'bloody' and 'bugger' which almost everyone used. She even came out with the occasional 'damn' herself, but it seemed odd to hear proper swearwords coming from a respectable middle-aged woman, particularly one who spoke so well, not posh, like Miss Ellis, but in a nice cultured, well-modulated voice. In fact, she wondered what someone so clearly well-educated was doing cleaning hospital floors.

Harriet was regarding her critically. 'I think you'll do. At least the cap won't fall off. Now, we really must get on with some work. We're already miles behind.'

Just then, a young girl in an auxiliary's uniform came skidding around the corner, carrying a coat over her arm. She opened the door of the rest room and chucked the coat inside.

'Harriet, you've brought me a bucket! You're a dead good sort,' she panted. 'I felt sure Staff would nab me before I could get upstairs.'

'Don't worry, I covered for you. I said I'd already seen you around.'

The newcomer seized a mop, dipped it in a bucket and began to clean the tiled floor where Harriet had left off. She was a plain girl, almost ugly, with an unnaturally narrow face and odd eyes – one seemed to be set at a slightly different angle from the other. There was a yellowing bruise on her right cheek.

'Me dad came home pissed as a lord last night,' she explained. 'I knew there was no way he'd get our Hazel and Benny off to work. I virtually had to drag the pair of them out of bed, else they'd have still been there by midday.' She suddenly became aware of Kitty's presence. 'Oh, hello,' she smiled. 'You're new, aren't you? I'm Lucy Peterson, the worst nurse in the world.'

'I'm Kitty Quigley. You won't be the worst nurse now I've started. I've done nothing right so far.' Kitty wet her mop and began to dab at the floor, and Harriet did the same as they talked.

'Well, this isn't exactly an efficient use of labour, three of us cleaning the same little bit of floor,' Harriet said crisply. 'You stay here, Kitty, Lucy, you take the far end, and I'll do the corridors leading to the wards.'

'Do we have to do the whole hospital?' asked Kitty. If so, they'd be cleaning for hours.

'No, just this floor. There's four auxiliaries on each level. Watkins, the fourth, is helping with the breakfasts.'

The hospital was gradually coming to life. As Kitty mopped and dried the floor, more nurses appeared, most of whom totally ignored her and left footprints all over the wet tiles which meant she had to do them again. She could hear dishes rattling and the smell of food being prepared. A young man in a short white coat came walking towards her, whom she assumed must be a doctor.

'I hope you don't mind if I spoil your nice clean floor, but I have to go downstairs,' he said jovially.

Kitty wondered what his reaction would be if she said she did mind. 'Of course not,' she mumbled.

'Are you new here?'

'I only started this morning.'

'Finding it all a bit strange, I suppose.'

'A bit,' Kitty whispered.

'You'll soon get used to it,' he assured her.

Will I, wondered Kitty after he'd gone and she wiped away the marks left on the tiles. I hate the building, for one thing, it's every bit as horrible inside as it is out, dead gloomy. The bare red-painted bulbs in the high ceiling cast a ghostly light over the sickly-coloured walls. A weak sun was beginning to glimmer around the edges of the black blinds on the narrow windows. A nurse, scarcely out of her teens, emerged from a room further along the corridor and said irritably, 'Why on earth don't you pull the blinds up?'

'I didn't know I was supposed to,' Kitty stammered.

'For God's sake, girl, if you see anything that needs doing, just do it!'

Kitty abandoned the floor and began to struggle with the blinds, feeling as if she'd never get the hang of things. Why hadn't she asked Miss Ellis if she could work in a factory? Eileen Costello had really enjoyed working at Dunnings in Melling, and Kitty would like to bet she'd never felt like a serf.

She'd only managed to pull one blind up, with some difficulty, and was trying to untangle the cord of the second, when Harriet Mansell appeared with her bucket and mop. 'You've done a lot,' she said sarcastically. 'You're scarcely any further than when I left.'

'People kept walking on it and I had to clean it again, then I was told to pull the blinds up and I've got this cord in a ravel.' Kitty was close to tears. To think she'd been longing to work for years, yet at that moment, she would have given anything to be home with her dad.

Harriet, though, looked entirely unperturbed. 'As long as you clean yesterday's dirt, it doesn't matter about today's. You'd be cleaning the floor till kingdom come if you worried about fresh marks. As to the blinds, leave them, that's the porter's job. He's the only one who can do them without getting the cords all tangled up. You help Lucy in the sluice room, and I'll finish the floor.'

As Kitty picked up her bucket and began to hurry away, Harriet said, 'Before you go, don't you think it might be a good idea if I told you where the sluice room is?'

'Oh, yes please.'

'Turn right, then right again, and it's the first door on the left.'

Lucy Peterson was already hard at work emptying a row of bedpans which had been left on the sluice-room floor. Kitty gritted her teeth and tried not to look at the contents as she joined in.

'Rinse them in the sink,' directed Lucy, 'the pee bottles, too. I've already filled it with disinfected water. Then lay them upside down on the ledge to dry. Make sure you wash your hands well when you've finished, 'case you catch something or pass germs to one of the patients. In fact, every time you go near a sink, it's wise to wash your hands – that's the very first thing nurses learn to do.'

'Is it? Until now, I've only been in hospital as a visitor. I've made a right old mess of things so far,' Kitty confided. 'I can't do anything right.' Lucy seemed more on her level than Harriet Mansell, who was a strange sort of person altogether.

'Everyone makes a cock-up of their first day. I know I did.'

'Have you been here long?'

'Three months. I hated it at first, but now I wouldn't be anywhere else. Trouble is, when I'm on the morning shift it's awful hard getting me brother and sister up for work – me dad's useless, he's hungover most of the time.' She suddenly grinned. 'The thing is, the Labour Exchange have caught up with him. They want to see him on Friday. It'll do the lazy ould sod a power of good to do a job of work.'

'Is your mam dead?' Kitty asked sympathetically.

'No, she did a bunk when us three kids were only nippers, which me dad seems to regard as our fault, not his.'

The bedpans and bottles were finished and laid neatly in rows on the slatted ledges which ran the full length of the walls on two sides of the room. Lucy quickly mopped the floor. When Kitty tried to help, the mops collided, so she edged to the corner, feeling useless.

'Now it's time to do the wards,' Lucy said, squeezing the water from her mop and putting it over her shoulder like a rifle. 'Come on.'

Kitty felt overwhelmed by the barrage of admiring comments which greeted them when they entered the ward.

'Well, there's a sight for sore eyes. Two beautiful young ladies come to spruce us up.'

'Good morning, me lovelies.'

'Someone take me temperature, quick. I reckon it'll bust the thermometer. Lucy, gal, you set me blood boiling, you really do!'

'A new one! What's your name, darlin'?'

Kitty blushed and dropped her mop in embarrassment, taken aback at the sight of about twenty men all in their striped pyjamas, some still in bed, some already up and wandering around on crutches in their dressing gowns, all obviously more than pleased to see them. Their happy young faces glowed the very warmest of welcomes.

'I'm Kitty,' she croaked shyly.

'Come on, youse lot, get your feet off the floor, we're in a hurry,' Lucy said sternly, but she smiled as she spoke. 'Go right under the beds with the mop,' she told Kitty, 'and move the lockers and do there. If Staff finds you've just gone round them, she'll have a fit. I'll do the window side, and you take the other.'

'Right.'

Every man had something to say when Kitty reached him.

'Are you married, luv?'

'Do you come from Liverpool, Kitty?'

'Me sister's got lovely pink cheeks like yours. I thought it was her for a moment when you first came in.'

'I bet you're Irish, Kitty. You're a real wild Irish rose.' He was as Irish as they come, this particular sailor, with a boy's skin and a wispy stubble of hair on his childish chin. Kitty noticed both his hands were heavily bandaged. He began to sing 'I'll take you home again, Kathleen,' and the whole ward joined in.

'Sing before breakfast, cry before tea,' yelled Lucy.

Kitty had almost reached the end of her side when she noticed the final bed was curtained off. She peered through and saw a figure covered entirely in bandages, from the very tip of his head down to where the bedcovers began at waist level. His arms lay like two white logs beside him.

'Oh, dear God!' she whispered. What unspeakable thing must have happened to this poor young man?

'Am I supposed to clean in here?' she asked the man in the next bed.

He nodded. 'Yes, luv. That's Geordie.'

Kitty worked as silently as she could, lifting the locker rather than sliding it along the floor as she'd done with the others. The figure didn't move, apart from a slight breathing movement of the chest. She'd almost finished when a husky voice said painfully, 'Who's that?'

There were tiny apertures in the bandages on his face where a nose and mouth should be, and two others for the ears. There were none, Kitty noticed, for the eyes.

'I'm the new auxiliary,' she said gently. 'Me name's Kitty.'

'What time is it, Kitty?'

'I'm not sure. About seven o'clock, I think.'

'Is that night or morning?'

'Morning.' Never, in her entire life, had Kitty felt so moved. She sat on the edge of the bed, a lump in her throat, wanting in some way to touch and comfort the young sailor whom she didn't know from Adam, to hold his hand or stroke his cheek.

'What sort of a morning is it?' Talking was clearly an effort. The voice sounded rusty, unused, an old man's voice.

'The sun keeps coming out, then going back in again.'

'Patchy?'

'That's right, patchy.'

He didn't speak for a while. Kitty stayed where she was, work forgotten, wondering what he looked like, or *had* looked like before it had been necessary to blot out his face and body with bandages.

His voice came again, a faint rustle. 'Are you still there, Kitty?'

'Aye, I am. What's your name, luv?'

'Everyone calls me Geordie.'

'I meant your real name.'

There was a long pause and she wondered if he'd

68

heard. Perhaps he'd gone to sleep? But no. 'Martin,' he whispered. 'Martin McCabe.'

'Martin's a nice name, much better than Geordie,' Kitty said. She smiled at him, though the smile was wasted. She forgot he couldn't see.

'It's the one me mother gave me.'

'*Quigley!*' The curtains of the cubicle were abruptly drawn back and Staff Nurse Bellamy stood there, her white veil quivering. She glared at Kitty, outraged. 'We've been searching for you everywhere. What on earth are you doing, tiring out this patient when you should be working? They're waiting for you to serve the breakfasts. Get to the kitchen this very minute. Come on, girl, *move!*'

Kitty picked up her bucket and mop and stumbled out of the ward feeling totally humiliated, though several men gave her a sympathetic wink as she went by, and as she began a frantic search for the kitchen, the young Irish lad began to sing again, '. . . And when the hills are fresh and green, I'll take you home again, Kathleen.'

'I'm sorry, Kitty, but by the time I'd finished my side, you'd completely disappeared. I thought you'd gone. I didn't realise you were in Geordie's cubicle.' Lucy was full of apologies. Then she giggled. 'Harriet and me thought you were fed up and had gone home.'

'As if I would!' Despite her humiliation, Kitty felt slightly better about everything. Those sailors had been thrilled to bits to see them. 'This has made my day,' one said, and she was convinced Martin McCabe had appreciated the few words they'd managed to exchange.

They took the breakfasts round on a trolley, collected the dirty dishes and washed them, cleaned more bedpans, gave each man a clean white towel. The soiled towels were removed for washing, and Harriet took

Kitty down to the laundry so she would know where it was in future.

On the way, Harriet explained there were two wards on the first floor with beds for twenty men in each. 'General Medical,' she said, 'which means it can be anything from getting over a ruptured appendix to exposure and frostbite.'

'I noticed some patients had their hands bandaged,' Kitty remarked.

'Poor young men, their feet are bandaged, too. You don't stand a chance if you're pitched into the freezing waters of the North Atlantic. Five minutes, that's all, and then you're dead. Even if you're picked up almost immediately, you've lost your fingers and toes.' Harriet's voice was devoid of the humour Kitty had come to expect. It throbbed with sympathy and not a little anger. 'Wars are the most stupid thing imaginable, such a terrible, tragic waste of life. At least our young men are still alive, some only barely, though their bodies will be blighted for ever.'

'What's wrong with Martin – I mean, Geordie?'

'He's dying,' Harriet said tightly. 'His ship was torpedoed and he leaped into the ocean with the rest of the crew. Unfortunately, a slick of burning oil washed over half a dozen men. Geordie was the only one to survive. It destroyed his face and body and there's scarcely anything left of his lungs. The shock to his system has severely damaged his heart. Under normal circumstances – if you could call any such circumstances normal – he would have been sent to the burns unit in Yorkshire, but it would be a waste of time with Geordie. Anyway, he's not up to the journey. I suppose some people might think he's better off dead, considering what he must look like underneath those bandages.'

Kitty sighed. 'Would it be all right if I went and talked to him after I've finished work?'

'I reckon so. He hasn't any family, so friends are what

he needs. The nurses are kind, but they're too rushed off their feet to stop and talk. The other men see Geordie as what they might have been themselves. I think he frightens them a bit.' Harriet glanced at Kitty, her face serious. 'You must never become emotionally involved with the patients, Kitty. Never, never, let them see you cry or be upset. They need you to be strong; not hard, just strong. All of them will leave us sooner or later, some in coffins. You must learn to accept that as part of the job.'

'I'm surprised you're not a nurse yourself, Harriet – I mean a proper one.' She was awfully wise, thought Kitty, as well as being remarkably knowledgeable.

Harriet smiled. 'As far as I'm concerned, I *am* a proper nurse. Us auxiliaries have far more to do with the patients on a day to day basis than the SRNs. Now, come with me, Kitty, and I'll show you how to make the beds ready for the MO's inspection. Once the great man's on his rounds, us serfs can disappear into our cubbyhole for a welcome cup of tea.'

Chapter 4

Jimmy Quigley was sitting up in bed reading yesterday's paper for the second time and feeling intensely sorry for himself. The wireless was on and he'd already listened to *Up in the Morning Early*, and been told to fetch a chair and swing his legs back and forth as high as they would go.

'Both at the same time?' he enquired sourly of the presenter.

Then came *The Kitchen Front*, and Freddie Grisewood gave the recipe for a cake made out of grated carrots which he promised was delicious.

'Sooner you than me, mate,' said Jimmy.

Now the Radio Doctor was rabbiting on about the importance of regular bodily habits. 'There is nothing more effective than the humble black-coated worker,' he intoned, and Jimmy assumed he meant funeral directors, but it turned out to be prunes.

He switched the wireless off in disgust. They were women's programmes. Kitty listened to them sometimes when she first got up.

Kitty! He felt a surge of resentment against his daughter for abandoning her ould dad. Surely she could have pressed her case a bit more firmly at the Labour Exchange? Trouble was, the girl was dead soft. Anyone could twist her round their little finger. It didn't cross his mind that he was the most adept at this of all.

Jimmy couldn't stand to be alone. Whenever he was, his mind went back to the day when his entire life had changed for ever, the day Everton Football Club told him they didn't want him any more.

He was twenty-one, just married to Audrey, and until then, the future had been bright and full of promise. Footballers earned three, perhaps four times as much as the average worker. Not only that, they were respected, looked up to. Some became household names. Jimmy had hoped that one day he might be as well known as Dixie Dean or Ted Sagar were now.

Instead, he'd been told he wasn't good enough and forced to find a job, just like any ordinary man, and had gone into the Merchant Navy which was what virtually half the men in Bootle seemed to do. It wasn't a bad life, and visiting other countries gave him a hankering to emigrate as soon as the Great War was over; Australia, Canada, a place where there was a bit of adventure. Audrey was all for it.

Peace came at last in 1918, but then, as if Lady Luck had decided to turn her back on Jimmy Quigley altogether, the peace was shortly followed by Audrey's death and he was left with a four-year-old daughter to bring up on his own. He left the Navy and went to work on the docks, like the other half of the men in Bootle.

Jimmy felt bitter tears sting his eyes. He loathed manual work. It had almost come as a relief when both his legs were broken and he'd had to leave. There was no way the Dock Board could claim he was in the wrong place at the wrong time when the crate fell on him — in other words, it was all his own fault — something they usually did when a docker was injured, or even killed. Jimmy was exactly where he should be; it was the crane that was at fault. With the help of Jack Doyle, the unpaid union representative, he'd managed to wangle a pension out of the mean buggers when it seemed to all concerned that his legs would never mend.

According to Jack, conditions on the docks had

improved out of all proportion since the war began. 'We're essential workers now, Jimmy.' Younger dockers were regarded as so important they weren't called up. The iniquitous system whereby men had to wait outside the gate early in the morning in the hope of being picked for work by some snotty foreman in order to feed their families was no longer in force. There was work a'plenty, wages had gone up, the job was secure.

Jimmy sighed. He was already bored out of his mind and it was still very early. Kitty had taken the alarm clock into her room and it hadn't crossed her mind to fetch it back, but he could tell from the sounds outside what time it was. He heard Nelson's hooves clip-clop over the cobbles and the clink of milk bottles.

To his astonishment, downstairs the key was drawn through the letterbox and the front door was opened. At first, he thought it was Kitty; she was worried about him, she'd chucked in the job and come home.

Instead, a deep voice shouted, a woman, 'It's only me, Jimmy.' Footsteps came pounding up the stairs and the house shook.

Only who?

Jimmy cowered against the bedhead and clutched the eiderdown up to his chin, just as the bedroom door was flung open and Vera Dodds, the postwoman, came marching in, bringing with her a rush of fresh air.

'What the hell do you want?' Jimmy demanded through gritted teeth. The nerve of the woman, coming unannounced and uninvited into a man's bedroom! Women had started taking all sorts of liberties since the war. Vera was one of those who came into the King's Arms *on her own*! Some of the chaps seemed to regard this as an improvement on their normally all-male preserve – Dai Evans, for one, who chatted Vera up all night long. But Jimmy couldn't stand women who thought themselves equal to men. If his Kitty ever got such ideas, he'd soon put her straight.

'I've brought your *Daily Herald*.' Vera threw the paper onto the bed.

'Ta.'

'Y'look like Funf, peering over the eiderdown like that.'

Jimmy angrily pushed the cover down to his waist. 'Thanks again for the paper,' he said pointedly.

'That's all right.' She smiled showing a row of huge white teeth. 'Any time.'

He waited anxiously for her to leave, and was taken aback when she took her bulging postbag off her shoulder, put it on the floor and approached him. He shrank back and she laughed uproariously.

'I'm not going to eat you. I'm going to get you downstairs.'

'I don't want to go downstairs.'

'Of course you do,' she said witheringly. 'It's not good for a man to be stuck in bed all day when there's no need.'

She yanked the covers back and Jimmy hastily covered his private parts with both hands, in case they were showing through the gap in his pyjamas.

Vera laughed again. 'You haven't got anything I haven't seen before, Jimmy Quigley. I'm in the St John's Ambulance, aren't I? I've been helping out in Bootle Hospital for the past two years.'

He thought she was going to help him out of bed and was stunned when she bent down, put her arms around his waist and effortlessly hoisted him over her shoulder.

Jimmy screamed.

'Be quiet,' Vera said brusquely, 'else you'll have the neighbours wondering what we're up to.'

She managed to carry him down the stairs with little difficulty and deposited him in the armchair underneath the window.

'There!' she said with a quiet air of triumph and only slightly out of breath.

75

Jimmy was too traumatised to speak, particularly when Vera clutched both his ankles and began to bend his legs as if he were a machine.

'Does this hurt?' she demanded.

He stared at her with glazed eyes, unable to answer.

'Because it shouldn't. If you exercised your legs every day, you'd soon be back on your feet. Fact, you should have been up and about years ago. You only broke 'em, after all. Now, I'll put the kettle on, then fetch your clothes, and you can make yourself a cuppa tea and get dressed after I've gone.'

She went into the kitchen, then disappeared upstairs and came back with her postbag over her shoulder and his clothes. 'Will you be all right?' she asked.

Jimmy nodded dazedly. He still couldn't quite believe what had just happened.

'I'll come back tomorrow with the paper and bring you down.'

'There's no need.' Jimmy found his voice. 'Just pop the paper through the door. I was just about to come down the stairs when you appeared.'

Vera regarded him suspiciously. 'Your Kitty said you couldn't manage 'em.'

'I was going to have a go for the first time on me own,' he replied defensively.

'In that case, I'll look in and make sure you're all right, just in case you're in a heap at the bottom.'

Vera Dodds departed, chuckling, to get on with her round. Jimmy got dressed, and had just finished when the kettle boiled. He fetched the teapot from the back kitchen, feeling resentful. It wasn't right, a man having to do menial tasks like this for himself. Not that he'd wanted Vera Dodds to do it for him, he wanted Kitty, his own flesh and blood. He couldn't recall when he'd last made a cuppa. He wondered what Kitty was up to. Taking it easy, he'd like to bet, flirting with the sailors and gossiping over nothing with the other nurses, which was all women seemed to do when they got together.

He'd just poured the tea when he realised the *Daily Herald* was still upstairs. It must have got mixed up with the bedclothes and Vera had forgotten to bring it down when she fetched his clothes.

'Stupid cow!' he cursed.

Jimmy looked right, then left, as if hidden eyes were watching from inside the chimney or the back kitchen, then ran upstairs for the newspaper.

It wasn't that he'd *meant* to fool his mates and the neighbours, even less his dear Kitty, but having the accident had made him feel important, the centre of attention for a while. Once his legs began to feel better, he couldn't bear the idea of going back to the docks. He liked being at home and the sole object of his daughter's attention. It made him feel rather like a king with his own tiny kingdom to rule. Somehow, he managed to convince both himself and everybody else that he was still an invalid, because he *wanted* to be an invalid. He felt happier that way.

Now, he thought drily as he returned downstairs with the paper, he was a king without a subject and a woman in trousers had just carried him downstairs as if he was a sack of coal. He shuddered at the memory. Tomorrow when she came, he'd be in the chair, tea made, and tell her it was sheer willpower that had done it, a victory of mind over matter.

He was just reading how the Russians were fighting back, defying the Germans every step of the way, and thinking admiringly, 'the stubborn red devils,' when the front door opened again and this time it was Aggie Donovan who came in, a bottle of milk in her hand.

'Oh, so you're up,' she remarked in surprise.

'Vera Dodds helped me down,' Jimmy explained somewhat unwillingly.

'Did she now!' Aggie looked slightly aggrieved, as if

she would have carried him down herself given half a chance. 'I've brought your milk in. Would you like a cup of tea?'

'I've already made one,' Jimmy said curtly. If she expected him to offer her some, she had another think coming.

'Wonders will never cease! Would you like a bite of breakfast, then?'

'No, ta. I intend making meself something in a minute.'

'Your Kitty will have a heart attack when she comes home.'

'Our Kitty cosseted me too much,' Jimmy said traitorously. 'She wouldn't let me do a thing for meself.'

'Pull the other one, Jimmy, it's got bells on. Oh, well, I'll love you and leave you. Tara.'

'Tara.'

Jimmy returned to the paper. He'd cut the key off the string in a minute, otherwise the house would be like Exchange Station all day long.

A few minutes later, the back door opened, and Dominic Reilly, Sheila's eldest boy, came in with a bowl of porridge.

'Me mam said she couldn't spare the milk and sugar. You'll have to use your own.'

Jimmy was about to tell Dominic what he could do with his porridge when he remembered he quite liked the lad. He was a splendid little chap, eight years old, clean-cut and with a pleasant open face – the image of his dad, Calum Reilly. Not only that, he was a good, keen footballer. Jimmy often observed the lads playing footy in the streets, goalposts chalked on the railway wall. Dominic stood out from the others with his speed and nifty footwork.

'Ta,' he said, doing his best to sound gracious.

'Me mam said you'd be in bed and I was to put the sugar and milk in and take it up to you.'

'Well, I'm not in bed, am I? I'm up, and I can put me own sugar and milk in, thanks all the same,' Jimmy said tartly. It was one thing having your own daughter waiting on you hand and foot, but another thing altogether for heavyweight postwomen and little boys to behave as if you were totally helpless.

Dominic looked at him with interest. 'You used to play footy for Everton, didn't you?'

'That's right. Only the reserves.'

'Still.' The lad seemed impressed and Jimmy preened himself. 'Did you know Dixie Dean?'

'He was after my time, I'm afraid.'

'He scored sixty goals one season,' Dominic said reverently, 'more than any other footballer in history.'

'I know.' If Jimmy had been standing, he would have genuflected.

'We've got a big match at school soon,' Dominic said proudly. 'I'm team captain. It's some sort of cup thing,' he added vaguely. 'We're already through the first round.'

'What position do you play?'

'Centre forward, same as Dixie. It's me favourite.'

'It was mine, too. You feel like you're king o'the pitch.'

They stared at each other, eyes aglow with mutual understanding.

'Look, I'd like to know how you get on.' Jimmy genuinely meant it. 'In fact, pop in after school some time and I'll give you a few tips.'

'Honest? I'll come today. I'll have to go now, else I'll be late.' Dominic was halfway down the yard when he shouted, 'I forgot to say, me mam'll be in later to make you a cup of tea.'

'Tell her not to bother,' Jimmy shouted, but the back door had already closed. He groaned. Dominic almost certainly hadn't heard.

★

It was almost six o'clock by the time Kitty arrived home, all dolled up in a green and white striped frock and her own clothes rolled up underneath her arm. 'Where on earth have you been?' he demanded indignantly. 'You've been gone more than twelve hours!'

'We don't finish till four, do we, Dad? Before I left, I had a little chat with one of the patients, then I decided to walk home. I was really in need of some fresh air to clear me head.' She could still smell the hospital even now, a mixture of disinfectant and urine.

'You had a little chat, then you walked home? But what about me?' Jimmy regarded his tired, flushed daughter with mounting irritation.

'What about you?' she frowned.

'As far as you were concerned, I could have still been in bed, waiting for you to help me downstairs. It seems to me you forgot your ould dad's existence. What's he like, this Jack Tar you were chatting to? Handsome, is he?' He was terrified he would lose her, that she'd fall in love with someone else and Jimmy would no longer be the centre of her universe.

She made a funny little movement with her mouth that he'd never seen before. It could almost have been contempt. 'I don't know what he looks like, Dad. He hasn't got a face.'

With a pang, Jimmy knew that she was already partially lost. It was nothing to do with love. She'd discovered there were other people in the world who needed her more than he did.

'How did you get on in the job?' he asked grudgingly.

'Oh, Dad!' Jimmy jealously noticed the way her face lit up and her eyes shone. 'I made a right ould mess of things at first.' She explained about the uniform and the floors. 'But once I got the hang of it, well sort of, I really enjoyed it. Guess what me and Harriet did just before we left? *We took the temperatures of one entire ward!* Harriet read the thermometer, and I wrote it on the chart. Oh, I love it there, Dad, I really do. I can't wait to get back tomorrow.'

'Well, I'm glad you like it, luv.' He told himself he was glad, even though her happiness was at his expense.

'Here's me,' she said suddenly, 'been home nearly ten minutes and I haven't even started on your tea.'

'It's all right, luv, I'm not hungry.' She'd left a vegetable casserole in the oven for his dinner, and on top of that, people had been bringing him food all day long. In the end, he'd begun to feel a bit like a stray dog.

'How did you manage the stairs, anyroad?' she asked. If the truth be known, she'd scarcely thought about her dad all day. Strangely enough, she didn't feel all that guilty.

'Vera Dodds helped me down.' Never, in a million years, would he reveal she'd carried him.

Later on, when he announced he was going to the King's Arms for a pint, Kitty said, 'Y'won't be back late, will you, Dad? I want to get to bed dead early tonight. I feel fair whacked.'

Jimmy took a deep breath. 'You go to bed whenever you like, luv. I'll see to meself, even if I have to crawl upstairs.' In response to her startled expression, he added, 'Well, I'll have to start learning to manage on me own, won't I? You're doing a good job in that hospital.' Now he thought about it, he felt quite proud. Fancy her taking temperatures, just like a proper nurse! He couldn't wait to tell his mates in the pub. He thought about the sailor without a face and felt more than a little ashamed of the way he'd behaved when she first came home.

Unfortunately, Jessica's plans for earning a living with the van came to naught. Offering a small delivery service had seemed a perfect way to make a living. As Penny loved going for rides, she could have taken her daughter with her. Jessica knew the haulage business inside out and had numerous contacts; old rivals of Hennessy Removal & Haulage Company, who, she felt sure, would be only too willing to pass on a small load that they might otherwise have had to turn down because it wasn't worth the petrol. It meant they kept the good will of the customer who might well turn to them again when they had a larger load that needed shifting.

The first inkling she had that there would be difficulties was when she bought a fireguard, which turned out to be a problem all in itself.

'Folks hand them in for scrap metal when they don't need them any more. I haven't had a fireguard in ages,' she was told again and again.

She walked for miles with Penny in the pushchair before she found a nice smart brass one in a shop at the far end of Stanley Road.

'I'll send the lad round with it Sat'day on the handcart,' the proprietor told her.

'Saturday! But I need it now.'

'I'm sorry, lady, but the lad only comes Sat'days. It'd mean closing the shop if I brought it before then.'

'Haven't you got a van?' It was a large shop and there was none of the usual rubbish for sale. Everything was good quality and she recognised a few valuable antiques. She vaguely remembered this was where her father used to bring the odd bit of porcelain and silver which he'd picked up for a song – making about one thousand per cent profit at the same time. Surely, a place like this didn't function with merely a handcart?

'I'm not using the van to deliver a fireguard, lady, not when petrol's so scarce. If I did that, me month's ration'd be gone in a few days.'

'Don't you get extra if you're in business?'

The proprietor took offence, apparently thinking Jessica was arguing for an early delivery, rather than asking the question out of real interest. 'Only for essential purposes,' he snapped, 'and I doubt if the Government would consider delivering a fireguard essential, not when the petrol's needed by the RAF to fight the bloody war.'

'I was only asking! I'll take the guard with me.' Both ends folded so it shouldn't be too difficult to carry. She bestowed upon him a brilliant smile. 'Thanks very much. I've been looking for one of these all over.'

Feeling placated by the smile, the proprietor offered her a piece of string so she could make a handle.

A few days later, Jessica telephoned Mappin's Nationwide Removals and asked for the manager.

'Charlie? It's me, Jessica Fleming, Bert Hennessy's daughter,' she said when an old voice quavered 'hallo'.

'Jessie! I thought you went to live in the States when war broke out?'

'I don't know where you got that idea from, Charlie. Arthur and I have been living in the Lake District.' The idea had in fact come from Jessica herself. When the axe of bankruptcy had fallen, she'd told all their old friends she and Arthur were moving to America, because she was too ashamed to reveal their real destination was Bootle.

She explained her proposed business plan to Charlie Mappin, but was dismayed by his reaction, even though, by now, it was half expected.

'You'd never be allowed the petrol, Jess, luv. I've already put three of me lorries into mothballs, and if I didn't have a Government contract which means I get an essential allowance, I doubt if I could keep the other four going.'

'What sort of Government contract?' Jess demanded. Perhaps she could get one for herself.

'Carrying troops, always at very short notice. I keep a couple of drivers on standby twenty-four hours a day.'

'Just a minute, Charlie, the pips are going.' Jessica fed more pennies into the box, but the extra money was

wasted. Charlie Mappin could offer no further encouragement. He was, he told her, even thinking of going
back to a horse and cart for local jobs.

'Ask the Kellys next door if they can get petrol for you
on the black market,' Sheila suggested when Jessica
explained her predicament. 'Though whatever you do,
don't mention it to me dad. He's never approved of the
Kellys. Faily got me a valve for the wireless the other
day. Me dad would have a fit if he knew.'

May Kelly and her brothers, Fintan and Faily, had
once done a roaring trade in shoplifting, occasionally
interrupted when one of the lads spent a short term in
jail. Since the war began, they'd turned their talents to
the black market, though they were hopeless spivs,
easily moved by a hard-luck story and often persuaded
to give their stuff away or, at the very least, sell it at the
price they'd paid themselves.

But the Kellys were unable to help Jessica when she
called.

'The cheapest I could get petrol for you,' announced
Fintan, a pale ginger-haired man in his early forties, 'is
six and six a gallon.'

'Six and six!' gasped Jessica. 'But it's only one and
eightpence from a garage.'

'It's going up to two and a penny-halfpenny shortly,'
said May. Slightly older than her brothers, she ruled
them both with a rod of iron.

'Even so, it's still three times as much.' She'd never
make a profit if she paid so much for petrol. Sadly, she
decided to give up the idea of starting a business with the
van.

'Sorry, Mrs Fleming, but that's the best I can do,'
Fintan said regretfully. 'Would you like a lipstick?' he
added, as if by way of compensation.

'What make?' enquired Jessica.

'Coty.'

'Yes, please,' she said eagerly. 'A nice bright red if

you've got it.' She was down to using a matchstick to apply the final remains of the only lipstick she had left.

'You can have it for nothing,' said May. 'Seeing as how we can't help you out with the petrol.'

Jessica wrote to Arthur and brusquely told him he could have the van, just in case he bought one himself. *You'll have to collect it, as I have no plans to drive up there at the moment.*

He replied by return of post. *I intend to visit you and Penny at Christmas. I'll come by train and drive the van back.*

'I'm not entirely sure if I *want* you for Christmas, Arthur,' Jessica said crossly when she read the letter. She rather liked living alone with just Penny for company. She walked far and wide with the pushchair or caught the train into town and wandered round the shops, or what remained of them after the Blitz. The city centre throbbed with life and was always packed with servicemen and women in a dazzling variety of uniforms. At night she sat up in bed reading library books and old magazines till the early hours, something Arthur couldn't stand as he couldn't sleep with the light on. Of course, all this would change when she got round to making a living, something she'd have to do if she wanted to be independent. If she didn't support herself, it would mean living off Arthur's money, and he didn't earn enough to keep two households going permanently. She felt doubly cross with Arthur, thinking of the money coming in from the rents of twelve houses. If the business hadn't gone bust, she could have lived on that. Instead, it was going to pay off debts *he* had accrued. It didn't cross her mind to stop the payments, keep the money for herself and let Arthur get on with clearing up his own mess. She'd given her word and she would stick by it. She visualised the horror, if all else failed, of having to go back to the Lake District to live.

'I *won't*!' she vowed. If it hadn't been for Penny, she

would even have taken a job, though she hated the idea of being told what to do. She was a capitalist, not a worker. There were jobs galore at the moment, but she wasn't prepared to leave her daughter with another woman for eight or more hours a day. Sheila Reilly, who was longing to get her hands on a baby, had already offered.

Whilst she wrestled with the problem of how to make a living, Jessica enjoyed what she hoped were her last few days of freedom, by familiarising herself all over again with the city she had deserted for far too long.

One Saturday, she walked the entire length of the Dock Road as far as the Pier Head, then caught the ferry to Birkenhead. The Dockie, the main target of the German bombs, had been bloodied and bludgeoned, and some of the landmarks she remembered were no longer there, yet it seemed busier than ever, as if every single aspect of the war at sea was being run from this very spot. Merchant seamen and sailors of all nationalities thronged the pavements in their colourful and often outlandish outfits. The noise of the traffic was deafening; trains thundered along the overhead railway, lorries and cars crawled along impatiently behind the occasional horse-drawn cart.

Behind the high dock walls, the tops of cranes could be seen, twisting and turning, stooping and lifting, never ceasing as ships were on-loaded or off-loaded with all possible speed, so more vessels could take their place and the cranes could start all over again.

'This is where I belong,' Jessica whispered. 'This is where we both belong. You were born here, Penny. It's in your blood, like it's in mine.' She patted her daughter's head. Penny, fascinated with everything, waved her arms in delight.

Later, they sailed across the Mersey. Jessica had never seen the river so crowded. There were ships of every conceivable shape and size, though apart from the aircraft carriers, the tugboats and a single ocean liner, she had no idea what types of ships they were. Here and there the topmost parts of sunken vessels protruded through the grey waters, and warning buoys indicated where others had gone to a deeper watery grave.

She stayed on the ferry when it reached Birkenhead, then caught the train home from Exchange Station. Penny fell asleep and for some reason, Jessica's mood changed and she felt slightly depressed. She worried that she might have done the wrong thing by uprooting them both from the security of the flat over the museum and Arthur's monthly salary, but by the time the train reached Bootle, she'd managed to convince herself that what she'd done was right. For the last year, she'd been merely vegetating. Now, she felt truly alive. She remembered that tomorrow she was going to see her friend Eileen in Melling. A lot had happened to Eileen since they'd last met, and she wondered how she'd coped with the traumatic events of the last year.

'I may as well use the bloody van seeing as how I've got it,' Jessica said to herself when she got ready the next morning.

Sheila, who was coming too, along with the children, was delighted to discover they didn't have to catch the usual two buses to go and see her sister. 'Y'can never be sure of the buses on a Sunday. Many's the time I've hung around for ages getting home.'

The children were all in their best clothes, having been to early Mass, and were even more delighted than their mother as they piled into the back. Sheila sat in the passenger seat with Penny on her knee. 'It feels dead funny, a woman driving,' she remarked when they set off.

It was a dull October day. Bulging black clouds chugged across the ashen sky and it looked as though it could well rain, but this did nothing to quench the spirits of the children. Sheila made a vain attempt to play 'I Spy', but they were too enamoured with their first journey in a van to co-operate.

When they reached the isolated cottage where their Auntie Eileen lived, they poured out of the back and ran whooping into the garden.

'They need a man's hand to keep them under control,' Sheila said. 'Poor Cal, he's hardly seen his kids over the last two years.'

The small house looked lonely and very small in its big garden, surrounded by trees. Sheila shuddered. 'I hate the idea of our Eileen living here all by herself, particularly in the winter.'

Jessica was shocked by how much Eileen had changed. When she first emerged from the house to greet them, she looked just the same; a tall graceful young woman with a luminous tranquil beauty, her butter-blonde hair dead straight and cut in a fringe. Closer, Jessica observed a deep well of sadness in the blue eyes which were so much like her father's, as though Eileen spent much of her time weeping for Tony, her lost son. It was as if someone had switched a light off inside her. She wore a simple blue jumper and navy-blue skirt.

She smiled though when she saw Jess, and the two women embraced warmly. Then they compared babies. Penny had been born almost exactly twelve months before five-week-old Nicky.

'Oh, I'd love another one,' breathed Jess as she picked up the tiny white-clad baby, who yawned extravagantly and immediately fell asleep in her arms.

'So would I,' Sheila echoed.

'I'm not too old, am I, at forty-five?' Jessica asked anxiously.

'There was a woman in Beryl Street who had a baby when she was forty-eight, though she had one up on you, Jess.'

'What's that?'

'A feller!' grinned Sheila. 'There'll never be a bun in your oven if Arthur's living in one place and you're living in another, unless you do it by post, or something.'

'Don't tease,' Eileen chided her sister. She glanced at Jess. 'You'd better get a move on, all the same. Now, let me take a look at Penny.'

Penny was reluctant to be looked at by a strange woman just then. She was anxious to get out into the garden with the other children. She allowed Eileen a cursory cuddle, before struggling out of her arms and making her unsteady way outside. Sheila shouted to Dominic to keep an eye on her. As the eldest of six, Dominic had been obeying the same instruction for years. He nodded obediently. 'All right, Mam.'

'She's beautiful, Jess,' Eileen said quietly. 'I reckon you must have looked like that when you were a little girl.'

'But don't you think, Eil,' Sheila said eagerly, 'that there's a touch of our Siobhan about her, round the chin and the eyes, like?'

'Perhaps, but nature's strange. Look at our Sean! He's not the least like anyone in our family.' She turned to Jessica. 'You must come to Sean's wedding, Jess. I think I told you he's getting married in December.'

Sean Doyle, their younger brother, was a charming gypsy of a boy, with olive skin, dark mischievous eyes and coal-black hair.

'I'd love to.'

'Shall we have our tea now in peace? We can feed the children later.'

There was only one downstairs room in the cottage. Low-ceilinged and thickly beamed, it was about twenty feet long and stretched from front to back. The table at the far end was already set with cutlery and side plates.

'I've brought you some cold ham, sis.'

'Here's a bunloaf and three hardboiled eggs, Eileen. Sheila said you'd be making salad.'

Since rationing began, no-one went to tea without bringing a contribution towards the meal. Eileen accepted everything gratefully.

'Have your hens laid yet?' asked Sheila.

'Not yet. I hope they're not all – what do you call men hens?'

'Cocks,' Sheila giggled.

'I hope they're not all cocks,' Eileen said gravely. 'I'll just go and put the kettle on.'

Sheila turned to Jessica the minute Eileen disappeared. 'She never laughs!'

'Since Tony was killed?'

'No, since Nick went away. He left for Russia the minute little Nicky was born. Eileen's convinced, more than she's ever been convinced of anything before, that he's not coming back.'

'Oh, God, that would be so unfair,' Jess said passionately. She remembered Boxing Day, the first Christmas of the war, when she'd gone over to Eileen's house in Pearl Street and found her black and blue, her neck raw, after Francis, her first husband, had tried to strangle her. He was a beast, Francis Costello, and Jessica wasn't sorry when she learnt he was dead. But for Eileen to lose her son, then Nick, the husband she loved so dearly, well . . . Jess was lost for the words to express how she felt.

'Death isn't doled out fairly, is it?' Sheila said acidly. 'There's no judge up there to say, "Well, we've taken one off her, let's take some other woman's son or husband now."'

'I feel terrible.' Jess's voice shook. 'I missed the raids and ever since I came back, I've been revelling in the war, walking up and down the Dockie thinking how exciting it all is.'

'It's not exciting, Jess. It's too bloody tragic for words.'

The children had eaten. Sheila went with them into the garden to supervise a game of rounders and Eileen and Jess stood by the window watching. The baby had just had his bottle and lay on his mother's shoulder whilst she rubbed his back.

'Penny's very anxious to join in,' Eileen remarked.

'Isn't she?' Each time someone hit the ball, Penny staggered after it, but before she was even halfway there, the ball had been picked up and thrown elsewhere.

'She's a lovely little girl, Jess, ever so sturdy. Going to be a tomboy, I reckon.'

'Tony was a lovely little boy,' Jess said softly. 'I haven't seen you since he was killed, Eileen, and somehow you can't express exactly how you feel in a letter, but I'm terribly sorry. I cried for days, he was such a gentle boy, very wise and knowing for six.'

'He was a daft lad, our Tony,' Eileen smiled. 'His dad used to get impatient with him because he wasn't good at football and he never cared about winning or coming first. Nick understood him better than Francis ever did. Tony really loved Nick.'

'I've never met Nick,' Jess said.

'Would you like to see his picture? It's on the sideboard. It's only a snapshot taken at our wedding that I had enlarged.'

'You're not on it!' The photo was of a smiling young man in an RAF uniform standing in the garden outside. He had a wide mobile mouth and a mop of dark curly hair.

'I was nine months pregnant, wasn't I? Nicky was born the night I got married. I kept well away from the camera.'

'He's got a slightly Latin look,' Jess said, examining the photo keenly.

'His parents were Greek. Their name used to be Stephanopoulos.'

'He looks as if he laughs a lot.'

'He does.' Eileen took the photo. She stared at it, her head on one side. 'Isn't it strange, the way two people manage to find each other out of all the other men and women in the world? Somehow, some way, they get thrown together and that's it, there'll never be anyone else. I met Nick, our Sheila met Cal, you met Arthur.'

'Sometimes we find the wrong one, though, like you found Francis – or he found you.' Jessica was unsure whether Arthur was the right man or the wrong one for her. Perhaps he'd been right at the time.

'I don't suppose fate always does it properly first time round. As long as she gets things right in the end, that's all that matters.'

Nicky burped and Eileen glanced at Jess triumphantly. 'What a welcome sound that is! They get more wind with powdered milk. I wish I could have breastfed him like I did Tony, but I lost all me own milk.' She closed her eyes briefly and held the baby's cheek to hers. 'I usually put him to the breast once he's had his bottle. I think we both find it a comfort.'

Outside, the black clouds were bunching together threateningly. Rain looked very close. A gust of wind shook the trees and leaves fluttered down. The children stopped playing and ran to catch them.

Eileen, watching, jerked her head suddenly and gasped.

'What's the matter?' asked Jessica.

'Sometimes I think I see Tony in the garden, just a flash of his fair hair underneath the trees.'

Jessica looked at her, alarmed. 'Do you think it's wise, love,' she said carefully, 'to stay here alone? It's awfully isolated.'

Eileen looked at her as if she was mad. 'As if I'd ever leave the cottage! Anyroad, I'm not alone. I've got Nicky. And I've got Nick. This is where we used to make love. His spirit is everywhere. Sometimes, late at night, I imagine we're all here together, the four of us, a proper family.'

Chapter 5

Jessica bought the Liverpool *Echo* on Monday and pored through the businesses for sale. There were only a few and all were quite beyond her means. As she had only fifteen pounds left of the housekeeping she'd managed to save whilst she was away, this was only to be expected.

'I wonder if I could rent a shop?'

There were three; a haberdashery, a newsagent's and premises which were empty, but although the rent for the first two was low, they wanted a hefty sum for the stock and goodwill. The third was 'in need of extensive renovation', and miles away on the other side of Liverpool, though Jessica cut the advert out, just in case.

She bought the paper every day, but by the end of the week she was as far away as ever from earning her own living and the fifteen pounds was down to thirteen pounds seven and threepence. The Lake District loomed ominously ahead.

'That would be unfair on Arthur. I'd only be going back because I can't live without his money.'

On Saturday, she managed to buy a piece of haddock for their tea. The fishmonger wrapped it in an old piece of the *Bootle Times*. After they'd eaten, when Jessica was clearing up, she was about to fold the paper up and put it neatly with the others ready to take to Aggie Donovan, who was the official waste-paper collector for the street, when she noticed it was a page containing the small ads and one immediately caught her eye.

'Garage to Rent,' it read, and in brackets underneath, 'Linacre Lane.'

It was a small advert outlined in black. At first, Jessica assumed it was someone renting out a place to store a car, just as she'd rented somewhere for the van. Nevertheless, she read on, 'One pump, small workshop. £5 a week for the duration.' This was followed by a telephone number.

Excitement mounting, Jessica searched for the date at the top of the paper. The excitement fled when she saw it was dated the end of August. Two months ago.

Still, it was worth a try. She took Penny along to Sheila's. 'Do you mind looking after her for a minute? I want to make a phone call.'

'Of course I don't. She loves being with her Auntie Sheila, don't you, Penny, luv?'

The number was answered by a woman who sounded as if she kept a special voice for the telephone, a rather exaggerated falsetto. When Jessica told her the reason she was calling, she lapsed into a normal Liverpudlian accent. 'The garage? I'd almost forgotten I'd put an advertisement in.' She put the emphasis on the third syllable, adver*tise*ment. 'She's common,' thought Jessica. 'Is it still available?' she enquired.

'I suppose so. I'd more or less given up on the idea. Me husband's in the army and I can't get anyone to work here. That's why I thought of renting and letting someone else take the bloody place off me hands.'

'Can I come and see it?'

'You? For your husband, like?'

'No, for myself. Can I come or not?' Jessica demanded impatiently.

'Well, if you like.' The woman sounded dubious. 'I hope you're not wasting me time. I've got friends in at the moment. You do realise it's a garage we're talking about; y'know, a place where you mend cars?'

'I know what a garage is,' Jessica said coldly. 'If I could

have your name and address?' She felt certain Sheila wouldn't mind looking after Penny for a while longer.

'The name's Mott, Mrs Rita Mott. I'm directly opposite the football ground by Linacre Bridge. You can't miss us.'

It was a relatively modern building, with double doors and living quarters above, the windows of which were adorned with frilly purple net. There was a single petrol pump in the small forecourt.

Jessica knocked on the side door as she'd been instructed and was pleased to notice a small, untidy garden at the rear where Penny could play. She could hear music from within and the sound of men's voices. After quite a while, the door was opened by a small skinny woman of about thirty with hair a far more brilliant red than Jessica's. She wore a purple scarf which looked as if it might have been made out of leftover curtains turbanwise on top of her head, and tied in a huge bow which made her look rather like a startled rabbit. She had on a tight-fitting black crepe dress with sequins on the shoulders, and a cigarette protruded upwards like a chimney out of the corner of her bright scarlet mouth, which had been painted slightly larger than it actually was.

'That much lipstick would last me a week!' thought Jessica. 'I wonder where she gets it from? And the pancake's plastered on.'

Rita Mott's eyelashes were little sticks of knobbly mascara. She fluttered them in shock when she saw Jessica, in her smart camel coat with a silk blouse underneath and brown alligator shoes with matching handbag.

'Are you sure about this?' she asked doubtfully.

'Dead sure. May I take a look around?'

Rita Mott opened the double doors with a key. The workshop was big enough to hold four cars at a pinch.

There was a pit at the back, a small half-glazed office in the far corner, and the place appeared adequately equipped with tools.

'It was Den's pride and joy, this garage.' Rita pursed her lips in a wry sort of way, as if she wasn't entirely sure if that had been a good thing or not. She had the ability to puff in and out on the cigarette without removing it from her mouth. She screwed up her eyes to escape the smoke. 'He skimped and scraped for years to get it off the ground. It was showing a good profit and he'd even taken on a mate from school to lend a hand, when not long after both of 'em were called up. Den's in India now, stationed in some place with a dead peculiar name.'

Jessica made sympathetic noises and Rita shrugged. 'Mind you, trade was already beginning to drop off a little bit by then. Quite a few cars have been taken off the road since petrol rationing started, but I'm sure there's still enough to keep one person busy. Anyroad, I promised Dennis I'd keep the place going while he was away so's he wouldn't lose the goodwill he'd built up, but although I manage the pump meself, I can't get a good mechanic for love nor money. I did have this old geezer for a while, but people kept bringing their cars back to complain they weren't fixed proper.'

'I suppose the good ones have gone into factories.'

'And what makes you think you're a good one – mechanic, that is?' Rita stared at Jessica somewhat belligerently. 'I still can't believe you're serious. One of me friends upstairs suggested someone's playing a joke, having me on, like.'

'It's no joke. My father had his own removal and haulage business,' Jessica explained. 'I used to help maintain the lorries when he first started. I know engines inside out.'

'All the same, it's a funny job for a woman to want to do,' Rita remarked.

'I like being my own boss – I take it there wouldn't be any interference from you?'

Rita sniggered. 'You can bet your life there wouldn't. I don't know one end of a car from the other. As long as no-one brings 'em back to complain, I'll be happy. Oh, you'd have to look after the pump, too. It's a bloody nuisance most of the time. It means I can never go out during the day.'

'That's all right. I take it the profit from the pump would be mine?'

Rita looked nonplussed for the moment. She puffed on her cigarette whilst she thought. 'That'd be only right, wouldn't it?' she said eventually. 'You don't make much on petrol, but it wouldn't be proper, you working it in on my behalf, as it were.'

Jessica decided Rita Mott was a fair-minded woman and she quite liked her, despite her ghastly appearance. 'Shall we shake hands on it, then?'

To her surprise, Rita looked more reluctant than Jessica had expected. 'Well, let's give it a month, see how you get on, like. I'm not sure how Den's old customers'll take to a woman.' She shook hands all the same. 'I'd better get back. I've got a party going on inside, and me friends'll be wondering where I've got to. You can pay the five quid at the end of the first week. When can I expect you to turn up?'

'Monday,' said Jessica. 'You can expect me on Monday, nine o'clock sharp.'

'Den always opened up at eight.'

'Eight o'clock, then. No!' Jessica remembered she was her own boss. It was *her* garage and Rita had promised there would be no interference. 'Half past eight. I'll see you at half past eight on Monday.'

A terrible thing happened that weekend. The air-raid siren wailed, as it still did occasionally. No-one took much notice, convinced it was another false alarm. They didn't rush to their shelters, but waited instead for the sound of planes overhead, a signal this was a real raid after four and a half months free from attack.

The planes seemed to appear out of nowhere and took everyone by surprise as all of a sudden, to their intense horror, bombs began to fall.

Sheila Reilly frantically dragged her children from their beds and ushered them under the stairs. Doors slammed throughout the street as people quickly made for the public shelter around the corner. Scarcely anyone in the King's Arms moved; if they were going to die, then what better way than with a pint of bitter in their hand and surrounded by all their old mates, though one or two men left to be with their families.

In number 1, Nan Wright was woken by the strange howling sound and wondered what it was. She couldn't be bothered getting up to find out. It couldn't be anything important, not in the middle of the night. Nan spent all her time indoors lately and her concerned neighbours kept coming in to see how she was. 'Ould Jacob Singerman hasn't been in a long time,' Nan thought. 'I wonder if he's all right?' She turned over and fell asleep and dreamt of Ruby, who was out in the street beckoning to her and calling, 'Come on, Mam.' 'Come on where, girl?' Nan cried. 'Come on where?'

Jessica Fleming stood mesmerised in the middle of the bedroom, Penny clutched to her breast, unsure what to do or where to go. The ground shook as one explosion was followed by another. Planes growled overhead, there was the sound of ack-ack fire from the guns on the ground, and missiles hurtled towards the earth with a hideous cruel whine. There would be a pause, then the ground would shake again.

She crept under the stairs and sat on the floor surrounded by the feather duster and the broom and boxes of Miss Brazier's old dishes. It hadn't crossed her mind to prepare the cupboard as a shelter.

'And to think I regretted missing all this!' she whispered. 'Penny, love, your mother must be mad!'

There were more victims of German bombs that night than on any other, even in the very worst of the Blitz, 109 casualties altogether.

Pearl Street remained untouched. The worst damage was concentrated on Surrey Street, where two bombs fell close together.

For days, weeks afterwards, everyone was petrified the whole terrible business was about to start again.

But that October night was the last time the German Luftwaffe were to target their bombs on the small town of Bootle.

Dominic Reilly swung his gas mask around in a wide circle above his head. At the same time, he began to run, hollering a war chant like the Red Indians he saw at the pictures on Saturday afternoons.

'Mind where you're going, lad,' an old man muttered as he dodged out of the way of the lethal weapon. 'You could knock somebody's block off with that.'

Dominic put the gas mask over his shoulder and galloped instead, slapping his hip to urge himself onwards. He stopped hollering and made a clip-clop noise with his tongue. He was Wild Bill Hickok chasing after the baddies.

His brother Niall caught up with him, panting breathlessly. 'You're daft you are, you nearly killed that ould man.'

'He was a baddy.'

'No he wasn't, he was an ould man.'

Niall, a year younger than Dominic, wasn't sure whether to be proud or jealous of his brother that day. St Joan of Arc's football team had just won their second-round game and Dominic, the captain, had scored the only two goals. Although Niall enjoyed basking in a certain amount of reflected glory, he would have liked to have been in the team himself and subject to the wild adulation of his team mates for having been responsible for his side's win. This was merely wishful thinking. Niall was built more like his mam than his dad, with pale, soft skin and narrow shoulders. He had no aptitude for games of any sort, yet he was brighter than his brother, a fact no-one had remarked on as yet, he thought resentfully.

'Me mam'll have a fit when she sees your jacket,' he said, to try and bring his brother down a peg or two.

'What's wrong with me jacket?'

'The pocket's nearly off, that's what. You must have done it when you got in that fight outside the gates.'

Dominic glanced down at the pocket of his tweed jacket which was hanging on by a few threads. He wasn't in the mood to be brought down the merest fraction of a peg. He pulled it off and put it in his other pocket. 'Now she won't notice,' he said airily.

As far as Dominic was concerned the world was almost perfect. The one thing that would have made it complete, was his dad being home when he got there so he could tell him about his win. Next best thing would be telling Mr Quigley, who'd been giving him a few tips on how to play.

When the boys arrived home, their mam was in the kitchen getting the tea ready. Dominic sniffed. Scouse, his favourite meal of all.

'We won the match, Mam.' He puffed his chest out and his face glowed with achievement. 'I scored the only two goals.'

Sheila, who was stirring the pan to make sure the suet dumplings didn't stick, her face red with perspiration, glanced across at her eldest son. 'Where's your pocket?' she snapped.

'In the other one,' Dominic snapped back, irritated that she showed no interest in his glorious success. 'I'm going to write to our dad tonight and tell him.' He knew the mention of his dad would have a beneficial effect.

It did. Sheila's expression softened. 'That's a nice idea, luv. Perhaps youse kids could all do a letter together. We'll get Ryan and Mary to put kisses at the end. Your dad might find it waiting for him when he gets to America.'

Niall was hanging back, feeling overshadowed by his brother, and was pleased when his mam ruffled his hair and said, 'And what did you do today, son?'

'I got all me sums right, even the multiplication.'

'Did you now! Your dad'll be pleased when he hears about that, too.'

Just as if the two achievements were equal, Dominic snorted inwardly. His dad was mad about football, same as every other man in the world.

'I'm going to see Mr Quigley,' he told his mam.

'Your tea'll be ready in a minute,' Sheila said sharply. 'Anyroad, I'm not sure if Jimmy Quigley'll be all that pleased if you turn up. He's more than a bit off-putting whenever people call to help.'

'I'm not going to help him, I'm going to see him,' Dominic said huffily. He still felt cross with her for not being more impressed with his win.

'Two-nil! That's dead good, that is. Two-nil! And you scored 'em both, eh?'

At last, someone who could appreciate the awesomeness of Dominic's achievement! Mr Quigley wasn't just impressed, he wanted to know the full details of each goal, each attempted goal, each goal the other side had tried to score but hadn't, the precise ability of each player and his height and approximate weight, the nature of the play and the standard and impartiality of the refereeing.

'What does impartiality mean?' asked Dominic, only too pleased to go through the entire match kick by kick.

'Was he fair?'

'Not so bad. I reckon he favoured the other side a bit more than he did us.'

'That's always the case,' Jimmy said sadly. He regarded Dominic with a proprietorial air, as if he wouldn't have won if it wasn't for him. 'Did you work out who their best player was, like I said, and shadow him whenever he went in your half?'

'You bet! I never let him out of me sight for a mo. Every time he got near our goal, I was there.'

'And did you shoot low, like, when you scored the goals? Remember, it's much easier for a goalie to jump up to stop the ball, rather than bend down to it – unless they've got a midget in the goal.'

'I remembered,' Dominic nodded. 'We've got another match in two weeks' time. Sister Gabriel said there's only sixteen teams left. There was over sixty to begin with.'

'Who's Sister Gabriel?'

'The games teacher.'

Jimmy said nothing, but was shocked to learn they were being taught football by a nun. 'That means if you win the next match, you'll be in the quarter finals. What is it you're playing for?'

'Some Merseyside junior cup thingy.'

'It would be dead good for Pearl Street if St Joan of Arc's won, you being the captain, like.'

Dominic glowed. 'I suppose it would.'

'Do you know about nutmegging?'

'Isn't that what you put in Christmas puddings?'

'No, you daft bugger. I'll show you what nutmegging is. Let's see, what can I use for a ball?' Jimmy snatched the knitted teacosy off the teapot. He threw the cosy on the ground and stood up. 'Get to the far side of the room,' he instructed. 'Now, look. I've got the ball and you're coming straight towards me ready to tackle. Come on, lad, tackle!'

He began to dribble the tea cosy across the floor. Dominic reached for it with his foot, but suddenly, the tea cosy was nowhere to be seen. Mr Quigley chuckled. 'It's behind you. I shot it between your legs. That's nutmegging.'

'I thought you couldn't walk proper?' said Dominic.

Mr Quigley sat down abruptly. 'Well, me legs have started loosening up a bit lately. Someone told me to do exercises and I've been doing them every day. It's made quite a bit of difference. I already manage as far as the King's Arms with only one stick.'

Dominic wondered why he needed a stick at all after all that fancy footwork. 'That's good,' he said, 'because perhaps you could come outside into the street and show me how to do nutmegging with a proper ball, like?'

'Perhaps I will, lad, one of these days.' Jimmy nodded. 'Aye, one of these days I will.'

The German onslaught on Russia continued unabated. They advanced like a typhoon destroying everything before them; everything, that is, that hadn't already been destroyed by the retreating army and the Russian people. The Russians were looked upon by the invaders as *untermenschen*, sub-humans, which boded ill for the three quarters of a million troops they'd captured by the time hordes of Panzer tanks were a mere fifty miles from Moscow. The citizens of Moscow, including the women and the children, began to build defences around their city and a few days later a state of siege was declared. Odessa fell, shortly followed by Kharkov, and in Leningrad the people starved to death on the streets.

The Germans were desperate for victory before the cold set in, but snow had already fallen in the Caucasus and frost was gripping the Russian Steppes, heralding the onset of their terrifying winter. And, ominously, the Soviet T34 tank was proving to be far superior to the German Panzers; the shells just bounced off.

The leaf which Adolf Hitler had boasted would fall so quickly was tougher than he thought. The leaf hung on, refusing to budge, no matter how frenziedly the tree was shaken.

If the Germans didn't win soon, if their massive army became bogged down in the raw bleakness of a Soviet winter, ice-bound and snowbound, without the proper equipment and in uniforms unsuitable for such perishing cold, then political commentators predicted it could prove a turning point for the war. The people at large took this with a certain amount of scepticism. So many turning points had been predicted over the last two years, that they were beginning to think they were going around in circles.

In Liverpool, the autumn saw a rush of distinguished visitors who came to express their thanks to the city for the efforts being made to bring about victory and in appreciation of the suffering that had been endured.

King George VI and Queen Elizabeth paid their third visit to the port, followed shortly afterwards by Winston Churchill who spoke to the dockers. The men, all left wing, wouldn't have given a Conservative politician the time of day under normal circumstances, but circumstances were no longer normal. Left wing, right wing, everyone was now united against a common enemy. They cheered their Prime Minister and he took off his hat to them. 'I see the spirit of an unconquered people,' he told them.

Count John McCormack, the great Irish tenor, gave a concert to the workers at Gladstone Dock, and the American Ambassador to the British Isles, John Vinant, came personally to watch cargoes from his country being unloaded. America had not joined in the war officially, but they knew whose side they were on.

Kitty Quigley bade a cheerful 'Good morning' to the

Wren on duty at the reception desk. The young woman smiled a tired greeting in return. She'd been on duty all night and still had two hours to go.

Kitty ran down into the basement, reported in to Nurse Bellamy, filled a bucket, collected a mop and carried them upstairs. Harriet Mansell and Lucy Peterson were already hard at work.

'You're early, Luce,' she remarked. She noticed the girl was sporting a whopping black eye. 'Don't tell me your dad's been at you again?' she groaned.

Lucy's dad turned violent when he was the worse for drink, which seemed to be most of the time. He lashed out at his three kids, as if it were their fault life hadn't turned out the way he'd hoped.

'You should see what he did to our Hazel!' Lucy said. 'I had to take her to the 'ossy on Saturday night. Near broke her arm, he did, though she's all right now.'

'Something should be done about that man, Lucy,' Harriet said grimly.

'What?' demanded Lucy. She'd lived with the violence her entire life and accepted it with surprising equanimity. Indeed, she always appeared happier than most people; a cheerful, outgoing girl whom only the most churlish person could dislike.

'Tell the police, gang up on him. There's three of you and only one of him.'

'I couldn't clat on me own dad, and I couldn't hit him, either. He doesn't mean any harm, Harriet, honest. He loves us in his own peculiar way.'

'Huh!' Harriet snorted.

They finished the corridor, emptied the bedpans and cleaned the sluice room. When she and Lucy entered the ward to clean, Kitty braced herself for the usual hearty greeting. She still felt slightly embarrassed, even after two weeks, by the eager vocal welcome bestowed on them each morning, though she had learnt to make a few comments back.

'Get away with you!' she joked, when one young sailor demanded to be kissed – 'Me mam always kisses me in the morning.'

'I'm not your mam, I'm your nurse.'

The young men regarded the auxiliaries as nurses every bit as much as they did the SRNs who'd spent years in training. They formed closer relationships with the women who cleaned their ward, checked their temperatures, made their beds, bathed them, fed them, tidied up their lockers when the MO's inspection was due, and provided them with bedpans.

Kitty had thought she would die when she was first asked to take a bedpan to a young man with two broken arms.

'Where do you want it?' Her voice was so choked up at the back of her throat, it would scarcely come out.

'Where do you think?' he grinned. 'Under me bum, of course.'

Kitty slid the bedpan under the sheet and tried not to look.

'It might help if you pulled me pants down. I can't do it with me feet, and as you can see, me arms aren't exactly in good working order.'

Fitting the urine bottles was even worse. She was all thumbs and on the first occasion the patient grumbled, 'Hurry up, nurse. I'm bloody busting here.'

'I didn't realise men were so hairy down there,' she said to Lucy later.

There was another cubicle on Kitty's side which had the curtains drawn that morning. When she reached it, she saw a man and woman sitting on each side of the bed in which a new patient lay, a young man as white as a ghost, breathing in a hoarse laborious way. Each time he let a breath out, he seemed to pause for a fearfully long time, and she saw the man and woman tense and glance at each other, before, suddenly, out came the breath and they relaxed.

'I'm sorry,' she whispered, 'but I've got to clean the floor.' It would be more than her life was worth to skip round it. Nurse Bellamy would skin her alive if she found out. 'I'll be as quick as I can.'

'I understand.' The woman's eyes were red-rimmed with tiredness. 'I used to be a nurse myself.' She patted the pale cheek of the young man. 'Your dad and I won't be a minute, son.'

Hospital regulations were rigid. The floors had to be cleaned, every single inch of them, no matter what obstacle might be in the way, such as very sick patients and grieving parents. Everything had to be done at a certain time in a certain way, and woe betide anyone, high or low, who broke the rules.

'Some of them seem silly,' Kitty complained to Harriet one day. 'Like having to hang the towel dead centre on the rail of the locker before the MO does his rounds.' The men's slippers had to be placed neatly under the bed about fourteen inches from the wall. Kitty had been called to account for hanging a dressing gown up by the collar.

'Hang it by the hook, nurse, the hook!' she was sternly told.

'The patients don't realise, but they appreciate a sense of order,' Harriet, who seemed to have an answer to everything, explained. 'They'd be unhappy if the place was untidy, if they fell over slippers and couldn't find their towel. Cleanliness really is next to godliness in a hospital, Kitty, which is why the floors have to be done each day. The medical staff are dealing with people's lives, every action they take is of critical importance. It helps if an atmosphere of discipline is maintained throughout the entire hospital, from God and His Apostles right down to us serfs.'

'I suppose you're right,' said Kitty.

'I *am* right, there's no suppose about it.'

Perhaps she wouldn't have felt like a serf if Harriet

hadn't mentioned it, but outside the wards and away from the men, the auxiliaries seemed to be at the beck and call of everyone, whether it be nurses, doctors or SBAs – sick bay attendants, mainly young men, who'd joined the Navy and had been allocated to sick bay duties because they'd done a Red Cross or St John's Ambulance course. Some days, Kitty found herself growing dizzy, as she ran upstairs and downstairs, fetching and carrying and taking messages. People were mostly too busy to ask her name. If they did, it was Quigley they wanted, not Kitty, and even that they didn't remember when next they wanted something done.

But whatever resentment Kitty might feel fled immediately she entered the wards, where she felt every bit as important and needed as the Chief Medical Officer himself as she mopped a patient's brow or opened his letters for him. Sometimes she even read them aloud if the young man felt too tired.

She finished cleaning the cubicle. The man and woman were talking to Brendan, the Irish boy in the next bed.

'It's all done,' she said and drew the cubicle curtains when they returned to their vigil at the bedside of their son.

Brendan was rather subdued that morning and didn't burst into song immediately she began to clean around his bed. He jerked his head in the direction of the curtained cubicle and whispered, 'He's not going to make it, Kathleen. He's already had the Last Rites.'

'What's wrong with him?' Kitty whispered back.

'Pneumonia.'

'Poor lad.'

She felt subdued herself. If the young man died, it would be the first death she'd experienced since coming to work at the hospital. She forced herself to be cheerful when she entered the cubicle where Martin McCabe lay encased in white bandages, still hanging grimly onto life.

'Is that you, Kitty?'

'Yes, luv, it's me,' she said tenderly, bending over the bed. Oh, if only she could touch him, stroke his hand, his cheek.

His next words made her shiver. 'There's someone dying, isn't there?' he said weakly.

'I'm not sure,' she stammered.

'I'm sure. I can sense it.'

'Y'shouldn't think like that,' she said uselessly.

'It's all I can do, isn't it, think, till I die meself?'

'Martin luv, don't talk like that, either.' Kitty tried to sound stern, but failed. She began to mop the floor around and underneath his bed. She was terrified Nurse Bellamy would find her talking to him again when she should be working.

'Will you miss me?'

'You know I will. I'll miss you something terrible.'

'You're the only one.'

Kitty moved his locker. It was light compared to the other men's. There were no books or magazines, no gifts from loving relatives or wives. One patient had even been sent his baby teddy bear by his anxious mother. Martin's parents were both dead and he'd been raised in an orphanage. He hadn't a single relative left in the world.

'One's enough to be missed by,' Kitty chided. 'Me dad's the only one who'd miss me if I died.'

'That's not true. I missed you yesterday.'

'It was Sunday, me day off.'

'Have you finished, Kitty?' Lucy called.

'I'm just coming.' She bent over Martin's bed. 'I'll come and see you when I've finished work, as usual.'

'Don't forget.'

'As if I would!'

Kitty was just leaving when one of the men called, 'Nurse?'

'What can I do for you, luv?' she enquired, approaching his bed.

'I thought you'd like this. I didn't realise I had it until I looked through me wallet for something yesterday.' He handed Kitty a small snapshot. 'That's Geordie on the right. We were both on the same ship together when we first joined up.'

Three young sailors leaned against the rail of the ship, their arms draped around each other's shoulders, all grinning broadly and apparently without a care in the world. No matter how hard she tried, Kitty found it almost impossible to relate the happy smiling sailor with his round hat perched rakishly on the back of his curly head with the still, bandaged figure in the corner bed. He wasn't exactly good-looking, but he wasn't plain, either. Just an ordinary young man with indeterminate features, who, at the time the snapshot was taken, thought he had his whole life ahead of him.

'What colour's his hair?' she asked.

'Plain brown, a bit like yours. He was a nice lad, Geordie. A bit shy, that's all.'

'Can I keep this?'

'You're welcome to it, love.'

Kitty put the photo in her pocket. 'I'll treasure it,' she said.

'Kitty!' Lucy called impatiently from the door.

They took the buckets and mops down to the basement, where they washed their hands and returned to the kitchen to distribute the breakfasts.

Clara Watkins, the fourth auxiliary, gave them a scathing look when they went in. 'You two took your time, and there's still no sign of Mansell.'

'Well, if she didn't have to clean the ward all on her own, she'd be done in half the time,' Lucy countered scornfully.

Watkins, a gaunt, sandy-haired woman with pale eyes, had worked there the longest, which she seemed to think gave her some authority over the other three. Somehow, she managed to avoid the hardest and most unpleasant jobs, as well as disappearing frequently into the rest room for a ciggie which she rolled herself, cadging the tobacco off the patients who received a plentiful allowance from the Navy. Whether these facts were noticed or unnoticed by Staff Nurse Bellamy, the other women weren't sure. They only knew that Watkins subjected the nurses, Bellamy in particular, to the most intense and embarrassing flattery that, for all their obvious intelligence, they fell for, 'Hook, line and sinker,' as Harriet put it. 'It's awfully difficult to resist a compliment.'

However she did it, whether by flattery or sheer cunning, plus an ability to turn a deaf ear when anything needed doing, Watkins got away with murder. Privately, when the four auxiliaries were in their own little room, she had nothing but contempt for the senior staff. 'She's a stupid ould cow, that Bellamy,' she would say contemptuously, when only minutes before she'd been buttering the woman up so comprehensively, that anyone listening would have felt their flesh crawl.

'Be careful what you say in front of Watkins,' Lucy had warned Kitty on her first day. 'If she can get you into trouble, she will. She thrives on trouble, that woman.'

'Come on, get a move on,' Watkins snapped. 'Else the breakfasts'll get cold.'

Lucy tossed her head derisively. While Harriet affected to ignore Watkins's frequent jibes and heavy-handed hints that she wasn't pulling her weight, Lucy was unable to resist responding in kind. 'Don't tell me what to do, Clara Watkins,' she snorted. 'There's enough people already pissing me around, so I'm not prepared to be pissed around even further by another bloody auxiliary. Come on, Kitty.'

Kitty felt dead on her feet by the time her shift was finished at four o'clock, but she still went to see Martin McCabe as usual. She felt a terrible rush of sadness as she drew the curtain and sat on his bed, thinking about the happy young man in the snapshot in her pocket.

'Kitty?'

'I'm here, luv.'

'I've been counting the seconds and the minutes waiting for you to come.' The voice from behind the bandages was as heavy and slow as sludge.

'Don't tire yourself out, now, or you'll get me into trouble.'

His next words took her by surprise. 'I want you to get something from me locker.'

'But your locker's empty, luv.'

'There's something,' he persisted. 'Open it.'

Kitty pulled open the door of the rather battered little cupboard. All it contained was a brown envelope on the top shelf. She took it out. It seemed to contain official papers relating to his service in the Royal Navy.

'Would you like me to read you something?'

'No.' His head moved and she realised he was becoming agitated. 'The ring, me mother's ring. It should be there.'

Kitty pulled the papers out and a thick black ring fell onto the bed. When she picked it up, she saw it was silver, heavily engraved, and in need of a good clean. 'I've found it,' she told him. 'It's beautiful.'

'That went with me to the orphanage after me mother died. It was her wedding ring. They couldn't afford gold.'

'Do you remember your mother, Martin?'

'Hardly a bit. Try the ring on, Kitty. I used to wear it on me little finger.'

Feeling slightly uncomfortable, Kitty slid the ring onto the third finger of her right hand.

'Does it fit?'

'It's a bit small.'

'Have you tried both hands?'

The ring fitted the third finger on her left hand perfectly, though Kitty felt even more uncomfortable when she put it on. It didn't seem right, wearing a dead woman's wedding ring.

'I want you to keep it,' Martin whispered.

'But, Martin, I couldn't possibly . . .' she began.

'*Please listen!*'

Kitty fell silent, conscious of the frustration in the smothered voice. How galling it must be, to have unseen strangers attending to your every single bodily need! He was fed by tube and the food was removed by tube. All he could do was speak and then only in a laborious whisper, yet most people were too busy or too impatient to listen to what he had to say.

'Go on, luv,' she said gently.

'I always thought I'd have a wife and family one day,' he said. 'There was a girl once, but nothing came of it. I lie for hours, thinking there's no-one to grieve when I go.'

Kitty opened her mouth to speak, to say she'd grieve, but thought better of it and let him continue uninterrupted.

'It makes me feel as if me whole life's been a waste of time, but if you take the ring, Kitty, keep it, be my girl for a little while, then you'll never forget me, will you?'

She knew she had to take the ring. 'I'll be your girl, Martin,' she vowed. She leant over and kissed the gap where his mouth was.

'I felt that.'

'I'll have to go now, luv.'

Martin didn't answer, and she realised after a while that he'd fallen asleep.

Chapter 6

The young man with pneumonia died during the night. His bed, stripped and re-made by the night staff, lay empty when the two auxiliaries entered the ward the next morning. The other patients were unusually buoyant, seemingly unaffected by the death of their comrade. Kitty was to discover this phenomenon always occurred when a young man died, as if the rest drowned their grief by celebrating their own good fortune in still being alive.

'Are you wearing me ring?' Martin breathed when Kitty entered his cubicle.

'Of course I am. I'll always wear it.'

'Good.'

Later, as the Chief MO began his rounds, the four auxiliaries made a cup of tea and retired to their rest room for a welcome break. Lucy and her sister had been to the pictures to see Ginger Rogers in *Fifth Avenue Girl* the previous night. 'It was worth standing in a queue for nearly an hour just to see the clothes she wore!' she sighed blissfully. 'We're going to see *Lady Hamilton* on Saturday, with Vivien Leigh. Did you see her in *Gone With the Wind*?' she asked Kitty.

'Not yet,' Kitty mumbled, too ashamed to admit she hadn't managed to get to the pictures since the days of silent films, and had only vaguely heard of Ginger Rogers and Vivien Leigh.

'I've already seen it twice, but I wouldn't mind seeing it again. Perhaps we could go one night, Kitty,' Lucy suggested. 'Saturday'd be best, when we don't have to come to work next morning. It's bound to be on somewhere in town.'

'That'd be nice.' Dad seemed much better lately and had even walked as far as Marsh Lane shops the other day when he'd heard Ernie Robinson had cigarettes in stock. Kitty felt sure he wouldn't mind if she deserted him one Saturday.

'I wouldn't mind coming with you,' Harriet put in. 'I prefer the theatre to the cinema, but I'd make an exception for *Gone With the Wind*.'

'It's all right for some people, isn't it?' Clara Watkins drew heavily on her cigarette and flicked the ash on the floor. 'I wish I could flit off to the pictures whenever I felt like it, but then some of us have got responsibilities, such as a husband to look after.' Clara could never resist pointing out that she was the only one who was married. 'Anyroad, my George considers pictures are a waste of time and money. Some of the nurses virtually live there when they're off duty; either that or they're out bloody dancing.'

'It's what's called enjoying yourself, Watkins,' Harriet said mildly. 'Films are a brief escape from reality, and reality can be pretty bleak these days.' She winked at Kitty. 'That's a pretty ring, I've never seen you wear it before. Don't tell me you got married overnight?'

Kitty looked down at the engraved band on the third finger of her left hand. She'd cleaned it the night before with silver polish until it sparkled. There hadn't been the opportunity to tell Harriet and Lucy about the ring that morning and she had no intention of doing so just yet, not with Watkins present.

'I got it off a friend,' she said, wondering why Clara Watkins was eyeing the ring suspiciously as she rolled herself yet another cigarette.

'Well,' Harriet sighed, looking at her watch. 'The great man has done his rounds by now and we'd better get back to work. The patients will have been holding themselves in all this time, so there'll be a rush on bedpans.'

'I'll be along in a minute,' Clara Watkins said. 'As soon as I've finished this ciggie.'

At three o'clock each afternoon, the patients were served with a cup of tea and a slice of bread and butter. Harriet and Kitty were just about to leave with the trolley, when Nurse Bellamy came into the kitchen.

'Quigley,' she said quietly, 'as soon as you've finished, I'd like to see you in my office.'

'All right, Staff.'

'Have you done something wrong?' Harriet demanded.

'Not as far as I know,' said Kitty. 'Why?'

'I didn't like her tone of voice. She usually converses in a bellow. When she sounds normal I begin to worry.'

'Oh, Harriet, don't! Now you've got me worried.'

While they went round with the trolley, Kitty felt on edge. As soon as they returned to the kitchen, Harriet said, 'Go and see what Bellamy wants. I'll collect the dirty dishes.'

Nurse Bellamy was sitting behind the desk in her little dungeon in the basement when Kitty arrived.

'Shut the door,' she snapped.

Kitty obeyed and stood in the middle of the room, feeling uncomfortable and wondering what on earth to do with her hands.

'Where did you get the ring?'

The question took her so much by surprise, that Kitty jumped. 'Off a friend,' she stammered in reply.

'I'd like a more specific answer if you don't mind. Which friend?'

'Martin McCabe. He gave it to me yesterday afternoon.'

Nurse Bellamy pursed her lips and her little chin

tightened into a ball. She said nothing for several seconds and, picking up a pencil from the desk, began to twist it between her fingers as if she were weighing up what her next words should be.

'Have you any idea what a serious offence you have committed?' she asked eventually.

'Offence?' gasped Kitty, startled.

'You have taken an item of jewellery from a seriously ill – no, from a terminally ill patient, and you don't regard that as an offence?' The woman's voice was stark with contempt.

Kitty felt her blood run cold. 'I never *took* it! In fact, I didn't want it. It's his mam's wedding ring and it made me feel uncomfortable putting it on, but Martin insisted. In fact . . .' She paused, embarrassed at the thought of conveying to this unsympathetic person the words Martin had spoken to her in confidence. 'I promised to be his girl. He's terrified no-one will miss him when he dies.'

'Twaddle!'

'It's not twaddle.' Always slow to anger, even more so over the last ten years when she'd required never-ending patience with her dad, nevertheless Kitty felt a stir of resentment curl in her breast. The more she thought, the more the resentment grew, until she could contain it no longer. 'How dare you call it twaddle?' she exploded. 'Martin McCabe is dying and he wants me to be his girl. What's wrong with that?'

'Because you're not his girl, you're his nurse.' Nurse Bellamy seemed remarkably unimpressed by Kitty's show of rage. 'I also understand you've been visiting this young man out of working hours?'

'So what?' Kitty jutted out her chin aggressively.

'It's entirely against hospital rules, that's what.' The older woman pushed back her chair and stood up. 'I've no time to waste arguing with you, Quigley. We'll pay you until the end of the week, but I don't want to see you on these premises again. Please arrange for your uniform to be returned.'

'You mean you're sacking me?'

'I am.' Nurse Bellamy thrust out her hand. 'Oh, and I'd like the ring, please.'

Kitty put her hands behind her back. 'What are you going to do with it?'

'That's none of your business.'

'It is my business,' Kitty cried, 'because if you're going to give it back to Martin, that would be cruel beyond words.'

A flicker of a frown appeared on Nurse Bellamy's face. 'I shall discuss the matter with Sister Naughton in due course,' she said crisply. Sister Naughton was second only to Matron in authority. 'Just give me the ring.'

'No! Not till I know what you're going to do with it. Another thing,' Kitty continued as the full horror of what had happened began to sink into her brain. 'What will Martin think if I just disappear? He'll be heart-broken.'

'If he is, Quigley, then it will be entirely your fault. You had absolutely no right to build up a relationship with a patient which causes him to be heartbroken if you're no longer here. Say if you had to leave for some other reason – if you'd been knocked down by a car, for instance? It's unprofessional to say the least, and foolish in the extreme.'

Kitty's anger dissipated completely. Nurse Bellamy was right. 'I'm sorry,' she said abjectly. She put the ring on the desk.

'Thank you, Quigley. Now, if you don't mind, I'd like to get on with some work.'

Harriet and Lucy were in the rest room and in the process of putting on their coats to go home when Kitty returned. Immediately she saw them, she burst into tears. 'I've been sacked,' she sobbed. She explained why, finishing, 'I know I shouldn't have taken the ring. It didn't seem right at the time, but I didn't like to refuse.'

'I did warn you, Kitty, that nursing is for kindhearts, not softhearts,' Harriet said gently. She sat on the chair beside Kitty and stroked her hand.

'I know you did. Oh, I wish I'd taken notice, it's just that I felt so sorry for Martin.'

'That's understandable. We all feel sorry for him, but in a way, love, you're preying on his emotions by allowing yourself to get carried away, taking his ring and letting him think of you as his girl. They're terribly vulnerable, our poor young men. We're the only women in their lives during this frightening period and they fall in love with us so easily. Even I once had a proposal of marriage from a sailor half my age. Geordie – Martin – could have given his ring to any one of us.'

'I've been an idiot,' Kitty wept. 'I wish Bellamy would give me another chance.'

Harriet put her finger to her lips. 'Just a minute. I'll see what I can do.'

She left the room. Lucy took her place on the chair beside Kitty. 'I bet it was Clara Watkins who told Bellamy about the ring,' she said. 'She's forever rooting through the patients' lockers on the look-out for tobacco. She probably recognised it when she saw it on your finger.'

Kitty remembered the way Clara Watkins had stared earlier on. 'I'll never forgive her if it was,' she said.

Harriet was gone for ages. After half an hour, Lucy said she had to go home to get the tea ready. 'Me dad's quite likely to blow his top if his meal's not on the table. Since he started work, he seems to think the whole world circles round just him.' Lucy's dad had been deployed to help repair houses damaged in the Blitz.

It was almost five o'clock by the time Harriet returned. 'Nurse Bellamy would like to see you in her office, Kitty,' she said.

'She's not going to tear me off another strip, is she?'

'Just go and hear what she has to say.'

'After considerable thought, I've decided to give you one more chance, Quigley,' Nurse Bellamy said glacially. 'Not for your sake, mind you, but for the sake of the hospital. Putting aside the foolishness concerning the ring, you have the makings of a good nurse. But one chance you're getting, that's all.'

'Thank you. Oh, thank you.' Kitty was about to burst into tears again when she remembered Harriet. Nursing held no place for softhearts.

'As to the patient concerned,' Nurse Bellamy continued, 'thinking about it further, I realise it would indeed be cruel to sever the relationship you have so unwisely formed. You may continue seeing him for a short period once you have finished your duties, but you must never become involved with a patient again, Quigley. Never again.'

'I won't, I promise.'

'Good. Regarding the ring, it seems to have been given and taken in good faith. Keep it. Seaman McCabe has no relatives. It will only be returned to the Admiralty when he dies.' She glanced at Kitty. 'And he will die very shortly, Quigley. I hope you are prepared for that eventuality?'

'Yes,' Kitty said simply. 'I'm quite prepared.'

It wasn't until a still shaking Kitty was in bed that night that she began to wonder about Harriet Mansell. It seemed very odd that she, a mere auxiliary, had been able to persuade Nurse Bellamy to think again. She felt too relieved to wonder about the matter too deeply. All that mattered was she still had her beloved job.

At the end of Jessica's first week as the proprietor of a garage, she was beginning to feel glad that Rita Mott had insisted the arrangement be for only a month initially, because she hadn't even taken the five pounds required for the rent.

On the first day, she cleaned the office thoroughly and settled Penny with her toys on an old blanket she'd brought with her. Then she placed the metal OPEN sign in the forecourt and waited for Dennis Mott's old customers to return to the fold.

Plenty of motorists stopped for fuel, but as the petrol ration ranged from four gallons a month for a tiny Austin Seven, up to a maximum of ten gallons for larger cars, the amounts she sold were small. Several auto-bike riders bought only half a coupon's worth for their tiny engines. As the fuel had already been bought by Rita Mott, they'd have to come to some sort of arrangement as to how the money would be shared out.

Mid-morning, a man drove his Ford Eight onto the forecourt and drew up outside the workshop leaving the engine running. Jessica wiped her clean hands on a rag and tried to look busy as she approached him, smiling brilliantly. She was well aware of the effect her smile could have on most men.

'Can I help you?' she enquired.

'There's a funny knocking noise coming from the engine,' the man complained. 'It's been going on for a week or more.'

'There could be all sorts of reasons for that. At worst, your big end's gone. On the other hand, it could be something simple like a frayed fan belt. I'll take a look, shall I?'

The man's jaw dropped several inches. '*You'll* take a look? You must be joking. Isn't there a proper mechanic about?'

'I am a proper mechanic.' The smile having had no apparent effect, Jessica decided to look grave instead.

'I'll take a peek under the bonnet and see if there's anything obviously wrong.'

'No thanks, lady,' the man snorted contemptuously. 'There's no way a woman's going to peek under *my* bonnet, thanks all the same.' With that, he got back into the car and drove off.

'Horrible man!' Jessica cursed. She went over to the office. 'Wasn't he a horrible man, sweetheart?'

Penny's face was screwed in an expression of earnest concentration as she placed one wooden block on top of another. Jessica held her breath when she reached four, but Penny decided she'd done enough and swept the whole edifice away with a squeal.

'Dada!' she cried.

Her first word!

Jessica knelt on the blanket and gave her daughter a tearful hug. 'You clever girl! But why dada? Why not mama?'

Just then, Rita Mott came wandering into the workshop wearing a vivid flowered dressing gown, a cigarette poking out of her unpainted mouth and a tumbler of what looked like whisky in her hand. Without her garish make-up, she looked considerably younger. Her hair was looped in big sausage-like curls. Having taken out her curlers, she'd not yet combed it.

Jessica went out to meet her.

'How are you getting on?' Rita asked.

'Not so bad. I've sold a lot of petrol.'

'It was lovely having a lie-in and not having to do it meself. It's a bind, having to make yourself respectable so early in the morning.' She eyed Jessica, in her navy-blue slacks and oldest jumper, up and down. 'You look smart, I must say. I was thinking of buying a pair of slacks meself, they're all the rage since the war, but I'm not sure I'd suit them, being small. They suit you a treat. You've got the figure for them.'

'Thanks.' Jessica had bought the slacks on Saturday,

feeling rather daring when she tried them on. She'd never worn trousers in her life before, and they felt rather peculiar.

'There's a pair of clean overalls in the locker in the office for when you have dirty work to do. My Den's not exactly Mr Universe, so they should fit you.'

Penny, bored with the blocks, came crawling out of the office in search of her mother. Rita Mott watched astounded as she used Jessica's leg to pull herself to her feet.

'You've got a kid!' she said in a shocked voice. 'Christ Almighty, a kid could get into all sorts of trouble here. It's dangerous. What if she falls down the pit?'

'She won't. I've tied a length of rope to her reins and the other end's attached to the desk in the office. See! She can't reach the pit.'

'Even so!' Rita didn't look very convinced. 'I would have thought a kid'd be bored witless, stuck in this filthy hole all day.'

'She might if she was older.' Jessica did her best to keep the impatience out of her voice, feeling this wasn't any of Rita Mott's business. 'If I was home, all she'd do is play with her toys. When she needs a nap, I'll put her in the pushchair. I thought she might play in the garden later on.'

'I suppose you know best, being her mother.' Rita was staring at Penny as if she was a creature from another planet. 'I don't know nothing about kids. Me and Den never had any, and I'm not sure if I'd've been all that keen if we had. What's her name?'

'Penny,' said Jessica, adding, 'She's nearly fourteen months old,' to save Rita from asking.

'Hallo, Penny,' Rita said awkwardly.

Penny had inherited her mother's smile and gave Rita the full benefit as she tottered towards her, grabbed her legs and looked up at her appealingly.

Rita asked nervously, 'What does she want?'

'She wants you to pick her up, but you don't have to. She's a terrible weight.'

A horn honked and Jessica hastily left the workshop and served a customer with petrol. The man was unusually garrulous and wanted to know where Rita was and how was Den getting on in the army.

Jessica explained about Rita, but expressed total ignorance about her husband's progress in the military. 'If you and any of your acquaintances need work doing, the garage is open for business again,' she told him.

'So she managed to get a mechanic, after all?' he remarked.

In view of her previous experience, Jessica felt it wise not to say the mechanic was herself. 'A very good mechanic,' she said.

'I'll bear that in mind, though I don't have any acquaintances who own a car. This isn't mine, it belongs to me boss who just sent me out in search of petrol. You don't get many car owners in Bootle.'

This was something that had already begun to dawn on Jessica when she noticed the singular lack of traffic in the road – and most of that was commercial. She went back into the workshop, where Rita and Penny were sitting on the blanket playing with bricks.

'Where did Den get his work from?' she asked.

Rita thought hard. 'I never took much interest in the business meself, but I know he had a contract with the GPO in Balliol Road. He used to maintain all their vans. Oh, and he used to do work for Mersey Cable Works, as well.'

'I suppose I could get in touch and inform them the garage has re-opened.'

'You'll have a job. Both the GPO and Mersey Cable Works were bombed. I've no idea if they've opened up again. Come on, Penny, put another block on, then you'll have five.'

'Oh, no!' Jessica groaned.

'By the way, a letter came for Den this morning. I don't suppose the Ministry have caught on he's been called up.' Rita produced a creased letter out of the pocket of her dressing gown.

'Oh, no!' Jessica groaned again as she read the contents. From this month, November, spare parts for vehicles could only be obtained by the production of a certificate from the Ministry of War Transport. Tyres could be replaced if an official inspector confirmed the existing ones had worn out. It meant that even if she could persuade motorists to allow her to mend their cars, obtaining the spare parts could prove rather difficult to say the least.

'Aren't you glad we only shook hands on a month?' Rita said with a grin. 'Mind you, I wasn't expecting that letter. Eh, your Penny's dead smart. Going to be a bricky when she grows up, aren't you, luv? Where's her dad, by the way – if you don't mind me asking?'

'Up in the Lake District. I've left him.'

'Have you now?' Rita's eyes narrowed. 'On the market again, are you? Well, you shouldn't have too much difficulty finding another feller. Is your hair natural red, or is it hennaed?'

'Natural,' lied Jessica. It was only a partial lie; the henna merely hid the few grey hairs that had begun to appear over the last few years.

'I dye mine.' Rita touched her bouncy curls. 'Den'd have a fit if he could see me. I was plain brown when he left.' She drained her glass and got to her feet. 'Well, I think it's time for a cuppa. D'you fancy one yourself? I've got some lemonade for Penny.'

'I've brought tea and milk with me.'

'Well, it's no use down here, luv, there's nowhere to boil water.'

'In that case, I'd love a cuppa,' Jessica said gratefully. 'Take my tea. I don't want to make you short.'

'There's no need. I've stacks of tea. In fact, you can have a packet if you like.'

Rita left and came back about ten minutes later with a tray set with a frilly cloth and tea things, including a cup and saucer for herself, along with a glass of lemonade. She'd started making up her face which was covered with bright orange pancake.

Throughout the morning, she kept appearing, each time having done something more to prepare herself for the day ahead. Her lips were painted, her eyes made up, her hair arranged in a daring and rather elaborate style that must have taken ages to do and she'd changed into a skimpy crepe de Chine frock patterned with scarlet poppies. She brought two packets of tea and a tin of corned beef on one occasion and flatly refused to take the money for them.

'I got them for nothing. It wouldn't seem right, taking money off me friends.'

Despite the in-built snobbery that still persisted, Jessica felt rather touched that she was already regarded as Rita's friend.

Next time Rita arrived with something black over her arm. 'What size are you?'

'Forty inch hip,' replied Jessica. She knew she was large, but she also knew she was shapely with it.

'Perhaps this skirt'll fit you. One of me friends brought it for me, but it's miles too big. It's good quality. I think it dropped off the back of a lorry.'

The skirt, straight, with a kick pleat at the back, had a Gor-ray label. Jessica was instantly enamoured.

'It's lovely, but this time I insist on paying you.'

'Don't be silly. I told you, someone gave it to me. It's been hanging in me wardrobe for ages.'

'What did your husband do to make you leave him?' she asked on another occasion.

Normally, Jessica would have resented such a question, but she was still too pleased about the skirt to mind.

'He didn't do anything. He's a very nice man, Arthur. We got on very well.'

Rita stared at her blankly for a moment, as if trying to understand. Then she nodded, 'I know, but you were bored. Strange, isn't it, how the nicest men are always boring?'

'I suppose it is.' Jessica decided Rita was remarkably astute.

'You must come to one of me parties some time. I always have at least one a week, usually on Saturdays.'

'Thanks all the same,' Jessica said hastily, 'but I couldn't, not with Penny.'

'Well, if you can get someone to look after her, you're always welcome.'

The telephone in the office went around one o'clock and Jessica nearly jumped out of her skin. She ran to answer it, desperately trying to remember the number, but when she picked it up she heard Rita give it in her funny special voice. There must be an extension upstairs.

'Rita, gal,' a man's voice boomed, 'it's Larry, your favourite man in the world.'

Jessica hurriedly replaced the receiver, feeling disappointed. She'd rather hoped it was someone wanting their car fixed.

'Well, Penny, I reckon it's time we had our lunch. We've not been exactly busy, this morning, have we?'

'Dada,' said Penny.

An hour later, Rita appeared dressed in a royal blue coat with a little veiled hat over one eye. 'I'm off to the pictures,' she announced, 'to see Cary Grant in *His Girl Friday*. I often used to go to a matinee performance until I had to look after that bloody pump. You'll probably be gone by the time I get back, so tara.'

'Cheerio.'

Lucky old Rita, Jessica thought gloomily as she watched her trip away rather unsteadily on her high heels. She supposed she too could have gone to a matinee if she'd stayed with Arthur, but she hadn't, and some way, somehow, she had to support herself, which meant getting the garage off the ground.

How? she wondered, after having served several more customers with petrol. One man, who turned out to be a doctor on his rounds, asked if he could make an appointment to have a new clutch fitted.

'Only when you get a licence from the Ministry of War Transport,' Jess said sadly. 'It's a new regulation, starting this month.'

'Good gracious me! They do make things complicated, don't they?'

'Would you like our mechanic to take a look at the clutch you've got?' Jessica suggested hopefully. 'It might stand tightening.'

'No thank you, dear. It's already been adjusted as far as it will go. I'll just have to get a dratted licence.' He got into the car, grumbling. 'I wonder if the Government realises how difficult they make it for me to look after my sick patients?'

Perhaps I could get some business cards or leaflets printed and distribute them around, Jessica thought as she watched him drive away. Then she remembered there was a paper shortage and it was difficult enough trying to find a writing pad in the shops.

'I've bitten off more than I can chew,' she said to herself. 'Even if someone came in with a simple job that didn't require spare parts, they mightn't be prepared to let me do it because I'm a woman.'

A few nights later, she aired her grievances when she went over to Brenda Mahon's with some of her old clothes which she wanted bringing up to date, particularly the turquoise bouclé suit which she intended to wear at Sean Doyle's wedding. Business had definitely not picked up as the week progressed. She'd cleaned an old man's plugs for sixpence and offered to de-coke the engine of a van that was puffing clouds of black smoke, but had been huffily rejected. 'We've already got a mechanic at the factory. He's been meaning to do it for ages. Anyroad, what the hell do you know about engines?'

Brenda Mahon was a dressmaker patronised by some of the wealthiest women in Liverpool. Since clothes rationing had been introduced, she made her living re-modelling outdated outfits, turning two suits into one, adding padding to unfashionable drooping shoulders, taking hems up, turning long dresses into short ones and making sleeves from the surplus material. She still turned out some new garments, but with material at two coupons a yard, these were few and far between.

A nondescript little woman wearing nondescript clothes because she was always too busy to make anything for herself, she usually sat in the middle of her parlour working away furiously on her treadle sewing machine, her mouth full of pins. Hanging from the picture rail on all sides of the room were an array of beautiful outfits in various stages of completion. Not all were expensive; Brenda's friends and neighbours paid a mere fraction of what she charged her wealthier clients.

Sheila Reilly was already there when Jessica arrived, as well as Kitty Quigley, a pretty, timid girl with lovely skin whom she scarcely knew. Although Kitty had apparently been in the same class at school as the two other women, she looked years younger than them both. Sheila was standing on a chair in a half finished frock while Brenda crawled round the floor, her mouth full of the inevitable pins, adjusting the hem.

'That's smart, Sheila,' Jessica said. The dress was pale grey heavy wool, completely plain with a straight skirt.

'It's got a matching three-quarter-length jacket,' said Sheila, 'with a shiny collar and cuffs.'

'Grosgrain,' Brenda said through the pins. 'It's nice to make something new for a change.'

'It's for our Sean's wedding, a present from our Eileen. I could never have afforded it meself. It was supposed to be for her own wedding originally, but then Nick turned up out of the blue armed with a licence, and she got married at a few hours' notice, didn't she? Mind you, it was a lovely wedding, wasn't it, Bren?' Sheila's blue eyes turned dreamy, remembering.

Brenda nodded, 'Dead lovely. Ever so romantic, just like a novel.'

'It's a pity you couldn't have been there, Jess, but there wasn't time to tell you. Fact, there wasn't time to tell half the street.'

'It's what I missed the most when I was away, the weddings and all that sort of thing,' Jessica said.

'Aye, but don't forget you missed quite a few funerals, too.'

'Even so, I'd sooner have been here for them.' Jessica turned to Kitty, who'd not spoken a word since she arrived. 'Did you go to Eileen's wedding?'

'No, I couldn't leave me dad. He's an invalid, y'see,' the girl said nervously.

'Was!' Sheila said sharply. '*Was* an invalid. Since you started work, Kitty, I've seen him bobbing up all over the place. He was in Ernie Robinson's the other day buying ciggies.'

'He's much better than he was,' Kitty conceded. 'It's just sheer willpower on his part. He's determined to get better so's I won't worry about him when I'm at work.'

Sheila made a face, as if she didn't believe a word of it.

'Kitty works in the Royal Naval Hospital in Seaforth,' Brenda explained out of the side of her mouth that wasn't full of pins. 'She's a nurse.'

'Only an auxiliary,' Kitty said, blushing.

'That sounds awfully responsible and important,' Jess said warmly.

'Oh, it is!' Kitty launched into a vivid description of the job she obviously loved. 'I wouldn't mind training to be a proper nurse once the war's over,' she finished.

'I think that'll do, Sheil.' Brenda got to her feet, groaning. 'Now, Kitty, perhaps you'd like to try your coat on. I won't be long, Jess. Is Penny by herself?'

'Yes, but she was fast asleep when I left and she rarely wakes up.'

'How are you getting on with the garage?' enquired Sheila.

'Abysmally,' Jessica sighed. 'I'm glad I only took it on for a month. I can't see me getting it off the ground. There's all sorts of rules and regulations, and even if there weren't, no-one's willing to let me fix their cars because I'm a woman – not that there's many cars about to fix.'

Sheila wrinkled her nose dubiously. 'You must admit, Jess, it's a dead scream, a woman running a garage.'

'I can't see why.' Jessica felt defensive. 'Your Eileen became a centre lathe turner and we've got a woman delivering the post. There's women in the forces and working on the buses and the trams. Women can do anything men can do as long as they're properly trained.'

'But, even so, Jess, a garage?' Sheila shook her head. 'I'm not sure I'd leave my car with a woman to mend, not that I'm likely to have a car in a million years.'

'Well, if women don't have faith in each other, there's not much chance we'll get anywhere,' Jessica said testily.

Support came from an unexpected quarter. 'Xavier couldn't even change the gas mantle,' Brenda Mahon said as she turned Kitty round and began to pin the collar on her blue velour coat. 'It was always me who had to put a new one in. And it was me who fixed the lavatory when the chain wouldn't work and screwed the latch on the back door that time it fell off. And I put the shelves up in the kitchen. Xavier wouldn't know what a screwdriver was if you shoved it up his arse. It would never have crossed the girls' minds to ask their dad to do anything for them. No, I reckon Jess's right, Sheil. Women can turn their hands to most things if given half a chance.'

Xavier Mahon was in the army and had been posted somewhere up in the wilds of Scotland. According to Sheila, Brenda had decided she and her daughters, Muriel and Monica, could live quite well without him. Xavier was no longer welcome in Pearl Street when the army allowed him leave.

'I'll have your coat ready by the end of next week.' Brenda patted the collar. 'Pop over for a final fitting on Monday.'

'Ta,' Kitty said gratefully. 'It means I can wear it for *Gone With the Wind*. I'm going a week on Saturday with a couple of women from the hospital.'

Brenda turned briskly to Jessica. 'Now, what can I do for you, Jess?'

'I just want this suit and the two dresses bringing up to date, the shoulders squared and the hems taken up a bit. And perhaps you could take a bit of material out of the skirts so they're not so full.' Fashions were becoming more utilitarian and less feminine. Frills, flounces and bows were considered a waste of material. Straight skirts were 'in', as well as tailored suits and neat, unadorned blouses. Although Jessica preferred the old, more glamorous, styles to the new, she couldn't stand the idea of looking old-fashioned.

She wondered where the money would come from to pay Brenda. Sadly, she supposed it would have to come from Arthur, who'd already sent a cheque, though she'd not banked it yet. There was only about ten pounds left from the housekeeping, and half of that would go when she paid Rita Mott tomorrow – and pay Rita Mott she would, on that she was determined, despite the fact she'd already said on several occasions to leave the rent

133

till business picked up. 'It's nice having you here just for the company.'

Jessica was not prepared to trail all the way up to Linacre Lane every morning just to keep Rita company. Somehow, she had to make that garage work.

Each day, Jessica found herself closing the place down earlier than the day before as there seemed little point hanging on. Penny, normally so good humoured, was becoming tetchy by then and in need of a proper nap somewhere more comfortable than the pushchair.

By Friday, she was about to lock the doors at half past four, her coat on ready to go home, when a little battered Austin Seven drove onto the forecourt and stopped by the pump. Jessica almost contemplated turning it away, the profit on a couple of gallons of petrol was scarcely worth putting herself out for, when she remembered something her father used to say all the time. 'Look after the pennies, girl, and the pounds will look after themselves.'

She approached the pump and was surprised when the driver got out of the car and turned out to be a woman, a tall emaciated woman of about fifty in rimless glasses with short untidy brown hair turning grey. She wore an expensive fawn trenchcoat over some sort of uniform, a green and white striped frock.

'Just a gallon, please,' she said in a pleasant, well-modulated voice, 'and a tin of engine oil, if you've got any.'

'I've one tin left.' She'd sent off to the supplier for another dozen tins but had no faith that she would get them. Jessica had no faith in anything to do with garages at the moment.

After putting in the petrol, she screwed the cap back on, and went into the workshop. The woman followed.

'You're Jess, aren't you?'

Jessica stopped short as she was reaching for the oil. 'I'm terribly sorry,' she said politely. 'Do I know you?'

The woman laughed engagingly. 'Not from Adam. Kitty Quigley told us all about you this morning. I work with her at the hospital. My name's Harriet Mansell.'

'I think she mentioned you last night.'

'According to Kitty, you're an emancipated woman. I thought it only proper that I purchase my final gallon of petrol from someone who's fighting for our cause.'

The mention of emancipation and causes made Jessica's lip curl. She wanted no truck with such left-wing rubbish. Like her father, she'd voted Conservative all her life and would never vote anything else. Nevertheless, this was a customer and she didn't want to rub her up the wrong way.

'I'm not fighting for a cause,' she said lightly. 'I just want to fix a few bloody cars.'

Harriet Mansell recognised a subtle snub and her brown eyes danced with amusement behind her glasses. She put out her hand for the oil and Jessica noticed she was wearing a pair of beautiful pale kid gloves.

'I'll wrap it in a bit of newspaper,' she said, 'else it might stain your gloves.'

'Thank you.'

There was an awkward silence as Jessica searched for paper. She racked her brain for something to say. 'Why is this your final gallon of petrol?' she asked eventually.

'I'm laying my car up for the duration this weekend. It seems the patriotic thing to do, let the RAF have the petrol instead of me. I understand you need a drop of engine oil in each cylinder.'

'That's right.' The paper found, there was another silence as Jessica wrapped up the tin and Harriet Mansell rooted through her leather handbag for her purse. 'Do you live far?' Jessica asked.

'In the wilds of Ince Blundell, I'm afraid, down a long winding lane far off the beaten track.'

Ince Blundell! That meant the garage was miles out of her way. Jessica wondered if she'd made a special journey as a tiny gesture of support. She felt her conscience prick. 'Do you know the proper procedure for laying cars up? It's rather complicated.'

'More or less. You're supposed to drain the radiator, aren't you, and mount the car on its axles on blocks of wood?'

'Yes, and let the tyres down to half pressure, then remove them.'

'Bloody hell! That sounds a bastard to do, though I'll manage it somehow. If a man can do it, I can do it, too.'

Jessica blinked. She agreed with the sentiments expressed completely, but Harriet Mansell didn't look the sort of woman who swore.

'How are you going to get to work without a car?' she asked.

'I've bought a bicycle. Had a helluva job finding one, though. I suppose everyone's after bikes these days. I shall cycle as far as the station and leave it there.'

Penny had been tucked in her pushchair in the corner of the workshop all this time expecting to be taken home. She was hungry, cold and tired, and began a cry of protest, quietly at first, swiftly raising the tone until it became a bawl.

'You poor dear child, I didn't notice you there!' Harriet Mansell's face broke into a wide smile of delight. 'What a beautiful little girl! Kitty didn't mention you had a baby. How brave you are, struggling to get a business going with a child to take care of at the same time.'

She chucked Penny under the chin and said soothingly, 'Don't cry, love. Mummy'll be taking you home soon.' Somewhat surprisingly, Penny stopped crying immediately. Harriet looked at Jess. 'How many children do you have?'

'Just the one. How about you?'

'I'm not married. I suppose it must have felt like a miracle, having a first child at your age.'

Jessica had a secret dread that one day someone would assume she was Penny's grandmother. It was almost as bad to be told it was a miracle she'd had a child. 'I'm only thirty-nine,' she lied stiffly.

But Harriet Mansell didn't appear to notice Jessica's ruffled feelings. 'I tell you what,' she cried. 'I'll give you a lift home. After all, I've held you up all this time.'

She positively refused to take no for an answer. They said little to each other on the short journey home, Jessica appeared lost in thought and merely pointed out which way to turn when asked.

'There's no need to come down the street, it's a cul-de-sac and you'll have difficulty turning round,' she said briefly when they reached the King's Arms.

Jessica was just about to open the door of number 10, when she glanced sharply back to see if the car was still there. She couldn't remember whether she'd thanked the woman or not. But the car had gone.

'Damn!' she muttered, irritated at her own rudeness.

The trouble was, she'd just had the beginnings of another great idea.

Chapter 7

Jack Doyle had never wanted anything more from life than to earn a decent wage for himself and his family, which was the basic right of all men throughout the world. He'd fought for his country during the First World War, the war to end all wars — so it was said at the time — and was lucky enough to emerge unscathed. He then proceeded to fight for the rights of his comrades on the docks, to gain for them what it was only proper every man have; sufficient wages to pay for a decent roof over your head, food for your table, clothes for your back, and the same for your wife and children.

It riled him to the point of apoplexy on occasion that there were a handful of people who seemed to think it acceptable that a large mass of the population went without the basic necessities of life, the roof, the food, the clothes, and equally acceptable to rake in massive profits from their sweated labour. Not only that, they were happy to see a million men go without a job at all so they could have their pick of a dispirited and servile workforce.

But that was before the war. Now, there were more jobs than men to take them. The boot was on the other foot for a change, which made Jack Doyle a happy man.

He was also an uncomplicated man. He'd taken the death from breast cancer of his wife, Mollie, with quiet stoicism. These things happened. Not every couple were destined to grow old together. Eileen and Sheila were of an age when they could look after him and little

Sean, who was only two at the time, as good daughters should. Life had a pattern; babies were born, they grew, got married, had children of their own and one day they died. One day, their children would die, and so on. The day would come when Jack would die, something of which he was unafraid, because it was all part of the pattern. It was nowt to do with God or religion, neither of which he believed in. He believed in simple truths which you didn't need to learn from a catechism or a Bible; goodness, being straight and honest, standing by your mates and helping your neighbours out when they were in trouble.

Sometimes things went wrong, spoilt the pattern, like his Eileen getting stuck with Francis Costello who'd turned out to be a bad 'un, but now Eileen was all right, married to Nick. Sheila had a dead good bloke in Calum Reilly, and his Sean would be getting married soon to Alice Scully.

There were events outside your control, such as wars, which in his case meant the death of Tony, the dearest grandson a man could have, as well as the loss of his good friend, Jacob Singerman. But even these tragedies Jack accepted as unavoidable and therefore exterior to the course of his own destiny.

So why then, with the pattern of his own life rolling so smoothly before him, did he feel so agitated and on edge?

If he believed in being straight and honest, then he should be straight and honest with himself, Jack thought drily. It was Jessica Fleming who'd disturbed his uncomplicated life, turning up when he thought he'd never see her again, filling his head with all sorts of disturbing nonsense which made him feel ashamed.

As long as he lived, he would never forget the night he'd gone into number 5, and there she was standing in the bath in front of the fire, red hair streaming down her back, and without a stitch on. When she saw him she held out her hand, inviting him to take it. He'd struggled with himself for what seemed like eternity at the time, willing himself to resist the hand, to turn on his heel and go. But something within him, some wicked imp in his brain, wouldn't let him. He took the hand, then he took the woman, and the memory made him shiver with a mixture of disgust and a terrible desire to do it again.

It was better than it had ever been with Mollie, wild and uninhibited, which made him feel like a traitor. He'd kissed Jess . . . Jack caught his breath when he remembered where he'd kissed her whilst she cradled his head in her strong white hands. Moll would have been sickened if he'd done anything like that to her.

Now, when he thought there'd merely been a little crinkle in the pattern, Jess was back. She'd left Arthur, and although she hadn't made any sign, always treating him coolly and politely when they met, he had a feeling she was waiting for him to make some sort of move.

And did he want to make that move?

Christ Almighty, yes! There were nights when he was doubled up in agony in the bed where he'd slept alone for sixteen years, thinking about the soft body that could be his. He imagined exploring it with hands, putting his . . .

'Jaysus!' he groaned.

'What's the matter, Grandad?'

Jack felt his sleeve being tugged. He looked down. His grandson Niall was looking at him strangely. 'What made you think there was something the matter?' he asked. Even to himself, his voice sounded as if it came from somewhere far away.

'You made a funny noise, like you were snoring.'

'Perhaps I'd gone asleep. This match is bloody boring.'

He'd entirely forgotten where he was, which seemed to be happening quite often lately. He stamped the earth with his size twelve boots, as if trying to re-establish contact with reality. It was Saturday morning and they were at Linacre Lane football ground where Dominic, Sheila's eldest lad, was playing in some sort of match, an important one according to Jimmy Quigley. If they won, St Joan of Arc's would go into the quarter finals. Jimmy was running up and down the edge of the field like a maniac yelling instructions to Dominic. You'd never think he'd needed two sticks to get as far as the King's Arms less than a month ago.

'Shoot, lad,' Jimmy screamed. '*Shoot!*'

There was an appreciative burst of applause from the small crowd lining the pitch, composed mainly of other lads from the two schools concerned and quite a few parents, as well as half a dozen of the nuns from St Joan of Arc's. One of them was waving her fists and jumping up and down like a Jack-in-the-box which had gone completely crazy.

'Did it go in?' Jack asked vaguely. He'd already begun to return to the world occupied only by himself and Jessica Fleming.

Niall said scathingly, 'Of course it went in, Grandad. That means we're winning three–one.'

'Good.'

Part of the problem was he didn't like the woman. In fact, he couldn't stand her. Bert Hennessy, her dad, had been the epitome of a scavenging capitalist, earning his living by taking from the poor to make himself wealthy, and just as Jack's daughters had inherited his blue eyes, Jessica had inherited Bert's rotten philosophy. Not for her an honest day's work in a factory or a shop. No, she had to start her own business. Embracing Jessica was like embracing everything he had fought against over his entire life.

'Fine match, eh, Jack?' Jimmy Quigley came up, rubbing his hands together with enthusiasm.

'Excellent,' Jack said, doing his best to equal Jimmy's

enthusiasm. The crowd were dispersing so he assumed the match was over. 'Are we going home now?'

'As soon as your Dominic's got changed. You want to keep an eye on that lad, Jack. He could become a professional one day.'

Jack nodded. 'I'll do that.'

Jimmy began to chat about the game. He seemed to have memorised every single kick and assumed Jack had done the same. Jack managed not to disgrace himself; after all, Dominic was his eldest grandson and entitled to have his grandfather taking an interest. Apparently, he'd scored two of the goals and been responsible for the other. Jack made appropriate approving grunts from time to time.

'D'you mind walking home with the lads, Jimmy?' he said when the man paused for breath in the middle of his eulogy. 'There's someone I'd like to have a word with.'

'Of course not, mate. I'll see you in the King's Arms tonight.'

The garage which Jessica Fleming had taken over was directly opposite the football ground, and the workshop doors were wide open as Jack Doyle crossed the road towards it. There was a large notice attached to the petrol pump, BICYCLES FOR SALE AND WANTED. He wondered if it had always been there, or was this some daft idea of Jessica's?

There was the sound of women's laughter coming from the back of the workshop where Jess was kneeling on the floor beside an upturned bike cleaning the rusty spokes with emery paper and another woman with unnatural carrot-coloured hair and still in her dressing gown was watching.

Neither noticed he was there for several seconds as he stood looking at the woman who disturbed him so greatly. She wore a pair of navy-blue overalls which were too short in the leg, exposing slender ankles. Although she'd tied a scarf around her red hair, little tendrils lay against her long white neck which moved gently as she rubbed the spokes. She was clearly putting every ounce of energy into the task.

'Oh, we've got company!' The other woman was the first to become aware of his presence. She looked at him coyly, pouting her lips in what she must have assumed was a seductive manner. 'And what can we do for you, luv?'

Jack felt uncomfortable. He could have sworn the words held a double meaning.

'Hallo, Jack,' Jessica said sedately.

'I just came to see how you were getting on, like,' he mumbled.

'In that case, I'll love you and leave you.' The top of the woman's flowered dressing gown had fallen open, revealing a black lace nightie underneath. She paused too long before clutching the front together and giving Jack another coy look. 'See you Monday, Jess.'

'Have a nice weekend, Rita,' Jessica said. The pair were obviously great mates.

'Where's Penny?' Jack asked when the woman had left.

'Asleep in her pushchair in the office,' Jessica shifted her position, twisting her shoulders as if they were hurting.

Jack gestured around the workshop. 'This is no place for a baby.' He was angry with her for no reason he could think of, though perhaps the mere fact he was there was enough. He felt, unreasonably, that she'd drawn him into the place against his will.

'Penny's okay,' Jessica said brusquely. 'She's happy anywhere.'

'It's not right,' Jack burst out. 'Why don't you leave her with our Sheila and get a proper job like other women?'

'Because Penny's my child, not Sheila's. It's not right, shifting the responsibility onto someone else.'

143

'In that case, why don't you go back to Arthur?' he said crossly. That would be the solution to everything. If she were out of his sight for ever, perhaps the longing for her soft white body would lessen. He'd forget her and life would return to its inevitable and predictable pattern.

Jessica stopped work and looked at him with a mixture of amusement and outrage. 'You've got a nerve, Jack Doyle,' she snorted. 'I've already told you once, it's none of your business how I conduct my life. Did you come all this way just to tell me to go back to Arthur?'

'I happened to be in the vicinity.'

She tossed her head and he noticed, fascinated, the way the little red curls on her neck fluttered wildly. 'The trouble with you, Jack,' she said hotly, 'is you and your ilk can't stand the thought of a woman being independent. It makes you feel scared, seeing one of us making a living on her own, particularly when she's doing a man's job. Perhaps I should have taken up dressmaking like Brenda Mahon and no-one would have minded so much.'

'It's nowt to do with that,' he said, equally hotly. 'I was thinking of Penny, that's all.'

'Penny's none of your business, either.' She squatted back on her heels and began to rub her right shoulder.

'What's the matter?'

'My shoulder's hurting a bit, that's all.'

Despite himself, Jack's innate chivalry came to the fore. 'Here, let me do that for you. It's no job for a . . .' He bit his lip as he shoved her to one side, removed his jacket, and began to rub the spokes with a fresh piece of emery paper which was lying on the floor. 'What are you up to, anyroad? I thought this was a garage, not a bike shop.'

'It'll be both from now on.' She was behind him and he couldn't see her face, but her voice was full of determination. 'Someone mentioned how hard it was to get bikes nowadays. I drove round all the second-hand shops and pawnshops this morning and managed to get three.' For the first time, he noticed two more bikes leaning against the wall, both in better condition than the one on which he was working.

'I suppose you'll sell them at a profit,' he said sarcastically.

'There wouldn't be much point in doing it otherwise. I shall put an advert in the *Echo* this weekend.' No, two adverts, thought Jessica; one under Articles for Sale and the other for Articles Wanted – and she'd put them in the *Bootle Times* as well. She'd left the telephone number of the garage with the shops that morning with the request they kindly let her know if they got more bikes in, and had written to Arthur and told him that, if things went the way she hoped, she would need the van, after all.

'And if someone who's hard up for a few bob offers you a bike, you'll tell them it's worth nothing, but you'll take it off their hands for peanuts, just as a favour like.' Jack could scarcely hide his contempt. 'That's what your dad used to do.'

'I shall drive an honest bargain,' Jessica said coldly.

'Huh!'

'I'm offering a service, Jack, a selection of bicycles all under one roof.' She knew he didn't like her, the attraction between them was purely physical, and she wasn't prepared to change in order to alter his opinion – he had to take her as she was or not at all. Nevertheless, she felt uneasy that he seemed to think what she was doing was somehow dishonest. 'Every time you buy a packet of cigarettes or a pound of sugar someone makes a profit. It's the way of the world.'

'Shopkeepers get their goods fair and square, not like your dad. The way he conducted business was little short of highway robbery.'

Jessica had reached the same conclusion herself some while back. She recalled when Bert Hennessy used to come home to their house in Pearl Street crowing over the fact he'd persuaded some poverty-stricken old women to part with a family treasure; a dish, a statue or a painting, which had perhaps been a wedding present and worth little when given, but become valuable with the passage of time. She'd crowed with him, particularly when the item was sold at a vast profit. She was an adult and Bert was dead before, looking back, she realised it was neither an honest nor an honourable way to make a living.

'My father was wrong,' she conceded briefly. 'I shall offer everyone a fair price for their bikes.' She'd only feel uncomfortable if she didn't.

Jack turned, eyebrows raised. To admit, to him of all people, that Bert Hennessy had been wrong, in other words a crooked, twisting bastard of the worst sort, must have taken some courage. He couldn't help but admire her. She might well be thoroughly irritating, but she was tough and a fighter. 'As long as you do, I'll come and give you a hand from time to time.'

He regretted the offer the minute he'd made it. It wasn't that he minded the work, but he did mind helping to make a profit in a way he still felt wasn't entirely above board, all of which only made him feel angry with Jess again, as if she'd forced the offer out of him against his will.

'There's no need,' Jess said haughtily. 'The whole thing's my idea. I don't expect help from anyone.'

'There might be odds and ends you find hard to do, rusty bolts for instance,' he argued – why was he arguing when he'd just regretted offering to help? 'You haven't got the strength to move this saddle, it's completely rusted in.'

'If there's something I can't do, I'll just have to find a way to do it,' Jess argued back, somewhat illogically. She noticed the spokes were gleaming on one wheel and he'd already nearly finished the other, whereas she'd spent all morning cleaning only a few. He stood up, turned the bike upright and clutched the saddle in his big hands. It twisted slightly one way, twisted more the other, and gradually began to move freely as he kept on. His shirt-sleeves were rolled up and she saw the muscles in his arms ripple. The coarse working trousers tightened over his thick haunches as he put his entire strength into removing the saddle, which must have been fixed on for years.

A shiver of desire passed through Jessica's body which left her gasping, and it was a physical effort not to reach out and touch the broad taut neck which was so close. She made a sound and quickly put her hand to her mouth to prevent the sound from being heard.

Too late. Jack glanced in her direction. 'Did you say something?'

Jessica shook her head numbly. Their eyes met and slowly, very slowly, his face flushed as he read the message in her eyes and on her face. Very carefully, he laid the bike on the floor and came towards her. She felt as if her insides had turned to liquid and could scarcely breathe as he approached . . .

At that moment, Penny decided to wake up. There was a whimper, followed by a gurgle and a slight crash as she attempted to scoot the pushchair out of the office, which was something she'd lately started to do.

The spell was shattered. 'I'm coming, sweetheart.'

Jessica rushed into the office and picked her daughter up. Still shaking, she buried her face in the plump body.

'Is she all right?' Jack was standing in the doorway, his own face expressionless. The last few minutes might never have occurred.

'She's taken to regarding her pushchair as a scooter. I daren't leave her outside shops any more, even with the brake on she manages to get a few yards.'

'I'll tighten the brake up for you. By the way, I've still got our Tony's scooter in the washhouse. I made it for him when he was two. She may as well have it. I'll bring it round one day.'

'Thanks.'

Penny beamed at Jack. 'Dada,' she cooed.

'She calls everyone that,' Jessica said quickly. 'Me, Rita, everyone. Do you mind holding her for a minute whilst I take these overalls off? It's one o'clock, I'm going home.' It wasn't fair on Penny to work six full days a week. She'd take her into town that afternoon to see the decorations which were already up for Christmas – and deliver the advert for the *Echo* at the same time.

If only Penny hadn't woken up, thought Jessica in the office as she struggled out of Dennis Mott's overalls. Even so, it only brought the day when they'd make love again closer. She knew without a doubt that it was bound to happen some time, the sooner the better as far as she was concerned.

Outside the office, Jack Doyle wiped his brow with his free hand. 'Jaysus!' he muttered. 'What's got into me? If the baby hadn't woken up . . .'

'Dada,' said Penny. She arched her spine and suddenly swung herself backwards as far as she could go, as if daring him to drop her. Jack managed to catch her before she slipped out of his arms.

'You little bugger! You nearly went flying then,' he said, frightened.

Penny pursed her lips and regarded him wisely. She clutched his ears and pressed her nose against his so he could scarcely breathe.

'You're a handful, Penny Fleming,' he managed to splutter. 'Just like your bloody mam, if the truth be known.'

'Dada.' She released his ears and laid her head on his shoulder. He glanced down fondly at the round curve of her cheek. Dada, she'd called him. He'd always loved

148

children. It would have been nice if he and Mollie had had more.

Jack suddenly felt his blood run cold! Dada!

Sheila was always on about the similarity between Penny and Siobhan. 'You'd think they were sisters. Wouldn't you say so, Dad?'

He couldn't recall having answered. Women always seemed to be seeing a likeness between people who couldn't possibly be related. It hadn't crossed his mind to do so before, but he began to work out the length of time between the night he'd found Jessica in number 5 – January, it was, the snow was thick on the ground – and when Penny had been born, which was September.

Nine months!

And Jess had spent more than twenty barren years with Arthur.

Penny raised her head and looked at him sleepily. Her blue eyes blinked with tiredness. Jack saw his own face staring back at him, just as he remembered doing when Eileen, his first-born, was the same age. Sheila had taken after Mollie. He knew without a doubt that this was his child.

Jessica emerged from the office dressed in a royal-blue jacket, slacks and jumper. She had removed the scarf and her long hair was held back with a slide.

'Ready?'

He looked at her stupidly, his mind in a turmoil, until he realised she was waiting for him to put Penny in the pushchair.

It seemed only natural that they should walk home together. Jack was too dazed to speak for most of the way. Jess mustn't want him to know the truth, else she would have said something. Knowing her independent ways, perhaps she thought she'd be exerting pressure if she told him Penny was his child.

Exerting pressure to do what?

Christ knows, thought Jack, his thoughts wild. Even

walking beside the tall, vibrant woman, their child in the pram, felt odd. It didn't seem right, it didn't fit in, it wasn't proper. He was a widower and had no plans to be anything different until the day he died. Not only that, he was fifty-three . . .

His thoughts veered crazily and he imagined them a couple, a couple with a young child, living in the same house together, Jess's pliant body his to take night after night, but even that seemed wrong. What had happened between them wasn't natural. Men and women weren't supposed to act that way. But if that was the case, why was he aching for it to happen again?

Harriet Mansell snapped her fingers in front of Kitty's eyes. 'Come on, Kitty, back to the land of the living.'

'Leave me alone,' Kitty groaned as Lucy began to drag her along Lime Street. 'I want to stay where I am, in the pictures still watching *Gone With the Wind*.' At least, that's where her head was. She resented being jolted into the present.

'It was the gear, wasn't it?' Lucy said with smug satisfaction. She considered herself entirely responsible for Kitty's state of euphoria. Going to the pictures had been her idea.

'The gear! That's an understatement. It was wonderful, it was breathtaking. It was an experience I'll never forget.' She'd completely forgotten where she was during nearly four hours of total enchantment.

'I must admit it was very enjoyable,' conceded Harriet. 'Certainly not something that could have been done in the theatre.'

Lime Street was crowded with the post-cinema crush. For some reason, voices always sounded muffled in the blackout. A few cars crawled by, slits of headlights glinting weakly. It was a terrible anticlimax, Kitty thought, after the colourful glory of the American Civil War.

'Would you two girls like a drink?' Harriet asked.

'I'd love one,' Lucy said. 'Shall we go to Lyon's for a cup of tea?'

'I meant something stronger. It'll be my treat.'

Harriet plunged into the first pub they came to. The place was packed. To Kitty's relief, she noticed there were plenty of women there, many in uniform. She'd never been in a public house before and had always assumed it was just not done for women to go in alone – except women who were no better than they should be, of course – but it seemed that this was one of the numerous customs that had changed since the war.

They found three empty stools and put them in a corner and Harriet asked what they would like to drink.

'Shandy,' said Lucy.

'I'll have shandy, too.' The only alcohol Kitty had ever consumed was a small glass of sherry at Christmas. It all felt very daring; her first pub and her first talking picture, both on the same night. Then she remembered Scarlett O'Hara, and it didn't seem daring at all, not compared to the things she'd done.

Harriet was ages getting the drinks. She returned eventually with them on a tray, having bought herself a pint of beer.

'I haven't had a beer in ages. We used to drink it by the gallon when I was a student.'

'Did you go to university, Harriet?' Lucy asked in surprise.

'Yes,' Harriet said briefly. She didn't elaborate further and looked as if she regretted what might have been a slip of the tongue. 'I see there are some SBAs from the hospital at the bar.'

Both Kitty and Lucy turned to look, just as the three young men turned to look at them. They spoke briefly to each other and came across. Sick bay attendants wore a different uniform from ordinary sailors; a peaked cap and navy-blue serge suit.

'So, you three girls are out on the town, eh?' one said jovially.

'We've been to see *Gone With the Wind*,' Lucy explained. 'Poor Kitty still hasn't come down to earth.'

One of the men crouched down beside Kitty. He was the one who'd walked over her clean floor on her first morning at the hospital. Larry Newell had turned out to be an SBA, not a doctor. She'd come across him often since and he was always friendly and one of the very few who remembered her name. He was handsome in a suntanned, open-air way, with straight fair hair which fell in a little careless quiff over his forehead, and nice brown eyes.

'Good, was it?' he asked.

'Very good,' Kitty stammered awkwardly. She'd learnt to talk quite easily to the patients, but wasn't sure if she could cope with a healthy man who wasn't in pyjamas. She wished he wouldn't stare at her so keenly, as if he was genuinely interested in what she had to say. 'Oh, yes, it was very, very . . . good,' she finished, blushing.

'That's a nice coat. Blue suits you.'

Kitty blushed even more. 'It's new. Me friend made it for me.'

'Go to the pictures often, do you?' he asked conversationally. 'I often wonder what you get up to out of working hours when I see you rushing round the hospital.'

'Not really. This is the first time in ages.'

'Fancy us going together next Saturday? *The Road to Singapore*'s on across the road, with Bob Hope and Bing Crosby.'

'I can't,' Kitty gulped. 'I'm on afternoon shift for the next month. We don't finish till ten o'clock.'

'Of course, I forgot. I'm on afternoons, too. In that case, we can go on Sunday, a week tomorrow.'

Kitty glanced across at her friends. Harriet looked

quite content, sipping her beer and listening to what was going on, and Lucy was laughing uproariously at something one of the other SBAs had said. She might be plain, almost ugly, but Lucy had enormous confidence and was popular with everyone, particularly men. She always knew exactly what to say and when to say it and was forever ready with a quip or an encouraging word. Unabashed by authority, she'd been known to pass the time of day with Matron if she came within earshot. The only thing that worried Lucy was losing her job for being late. 'If only I could be like that,' Kitty thought enviously. 'She's eight years younger than me and she's got more confidence in her little finger than I've got in me whole body.'

Lucy would know how to deal with the young man crouched on the floor beside her waiting for an answer.

'I suppose so,' Kitty said eventually.

'You don't sound very enthusiastic.' He looked hurt.

'Oh, I am,' Kitty lied. 'It's just that I have stacks of work to do on Sundays. I was just wondering if I could fit it in, like.'

'I'll find out the time of the performance and we can arrange when and where to meet next week.'

The three men left shortly afterwards. 'I'm seeing Bob tomorrow for a drink,' Lucy said with an air of satisfaction. 'I've always fancied Bob Morrissey.'

'You look as if you've lost a pound and found a sixpence, Kitty,' Harriet said with a grin. 'What's the matter?'

'Nothing,' Kitty said gloomily.

'Yes, there is. Come on, love, what's wrong?'

'It's just that I've been asked out, too, and I'm not sure if I want to go.'

'That Larry Newell's a bit of a dark horse. I've never known him ask one of the nurses out before,' remarked Lucy. 'You've scored a hit there, Kitty.'

'She shouldn't go if she doesn't want to,' Harriet argued. 'Just because a man asks a woman out, she doesn't automatically have to say yes.'

'But she'll never gain any experience with men, will she, if she refuses every time because she's scared?'

In the confines of their cubbyhole, when Clara Watkins wasn't around, the three women had shared confidences and knew a great deal about each other's lives. Harriet's fiancé, Hugh, had been killed in the last great war, and Lucy felt deeply hurt that her mother had walked out on the three children when they were small, leaving them with a violent father. Both Harriet and Lucy were aware of the sheltered life Kitty had led so far, and her dad's subsequent miraculous recovery was discussed in detail from time to time.

'I don't know what to do,' Kitty said miserably.

'I think you should go,' Lucy declared firmly.

'And I think you shouldn't,' Harriet declared just as firmly.

'You're a lot of help, the pair of you.'

'Let's have another drink,' said Harriet. 'We'll discuss it further over a liqueur.'

In the end, it was Kitty herself who decided she must go. Because of the war, the warm, comfortable life closeted with her dad had come to an end, a life which she'd secretly resented for most of the time. She'd always been shy, and ten years of virtual isolation from company her own age had done her no good at all. Now she must learn to live as other young women did. She'd got a job she loved, made new friends, bought new clothes. The nurses in the hospital were forever giggling over the dates they'd been on the night before.

It was time Kitty Quigley went on a proper date with a man.

Larry Newell was waiting outside the Palais de Luxe, a

navy raincoat over his arm. He was close to the front of the long queue, which meant he must have been there quite some time.

'Hallo, there,' he smiled when Kitty arrived. 'I thought I'd come early so we'd get good seats.' He caught her arm and pulled her protectively inside the queue so she was against the wall. 'You're wearing lipstick. I've never seen you with lipstick on before.'

'It's black market,' she said. She'd got it off the Kellys the night before.

He seemed to think this amusing and laughed heartily. Kitty noticed there were little shreds of orange and gold in his brown eyes.

'These are for you.' He handed her a box of chocolates. 'I hope you like dark chocolate.'

'I love Black Magic,' Kitty gasped gratefully. She'd keep the nuts for her dad – unless Larry would like them, of course.

The supporting film had already started by the time they went in. The usherette showed them to a row near the back, the most expensive seats. Kitty found the film very disappointing. Not only was it in black and white, but the actors seemed strangely wooden after *Gone With the Wind*.

During the interval, conversation turned out to be easier than she'd thought because they had something in common to discuss, their work.

'So, you're under Bellamy, are you?' he said with a shudder. 'I must say I don't envy you.'

'She's all right once you get to know her,' Kitty assured him. 'Her bark's worse than her bite.' Since her sacking and swift reinstatement, Kitty had begun to establish a wary sort of friendship with Nurse Bellamy. 'Would you like a chocolate?'

'I wouldn't mind a nut if there is one.'

The Road to Singapore was thoroughly enjoyable; Bob Hope was a scream, and Bing Crosby sang in a voice like velvet. Dorothy Lamour drifted in and out looking serenely beautiful.

'Would you like a drink? We could go to the same pub as last week,' Larry asked when they emerged into the darkness.

Kitty ordered a shandy again. By now, she was beginning to feel exhilarated. Her first date, and it was all going so smoothly. She felt as if she'd known Larry for ages. He was incredibly easy to talk to. She watched as he stood at the bar waiting for the drinks, for the first time seeing him properly as a man, her date.

He was very good-looking, as Lucy had been saying enviously all week. Quite tall, he wore his uniform smartly and the jacket fitted perfectly across his shoulders. His thick blond hair gleamed under the lights from the bar. Kitty felt a pleasant little thrill. They got on so well, she felt positive he'd ask her out again. If so, she'd definitely say yes. Her mind drifted to the future, with Larry as her permanent boyfriend, then her fiancé. She visualised them getting married in St James's Church – wartime weddings were so romantic. She wasn't sure where they'd live, perhaps with Dad until the war was over . . .

She already had two children, a boy and a girl, by the time he arrived with the drinks, and blushed furiously, worried he might read her thoughts. 'Ta.' She took a long mouthful to calm herself.

He began to tell her about himself. Before the war, he'd helped his father run the family roofing firm in Dorset. 'The business will be mine one of these days.' He wrinkled his rather fine nose. 'Not that I'm much interested.' He preferred sport, boxing mainly. 'The school insisted we take a course in first aid, which is why I was made an SBA when I was called up. I was the Southern Middleweight Champion at nineteen,' he added proudly. 'One of these days I'd like to start my own gymnasium.'

'Me dad's interested in sport. He used to play for Everton.'

Larry was impressed. 'Everton! I'd love to meet him some time.'

'You can come to tea next Sunday if you like,' Kitty suggested shyly, the sound of wedding bells beginning to ring in her ears – until she remembered church bells had been banned and were only supposed to ring if an invasion was imminent.

'I'd like to very much. Do you want another drink?'

'No, ta. I think I'd better be getting home.'

'To your dad?' he smiled.

'That's right.'

'We can get the train together. You get off a few stops before I do.'

He linked her arm companionably when they got outside the pub and began to stroll through the black streets in the direction of Exchange Station. Kitty doubted if she'd ever felt so happy. She had a young man and it had all happened so quickly. Wait till she told Sheila Reilly, and Harriet, and Lucy . . .

'You know,' Larry said huskily, 'I've been dying to ask you out for ages, but you always seemed to be on some terrifically important errand, whizzing round all over the place.'

'Have you really?' Kitty had always found him pleasant, but had never even remotely regarded him as a future husband before tonight.

'Did you notice me?' he asked in the same husky voice.

'Of course. You spoke to me, didn't you, on me very first morning?'

'So I did. I walked over your nice clean floor.'

They bumped into another couple walking in the opposite direction. There was no moon that night and the blackness was total. One or two trams and buses lumbered past, their headlights scarcely visible.

'Where are we?' Kitty asked nervously. The footsteps of the couple they'd bumped into faded into the distance and she could hear no others.

'By St George's Hall – I think.'

'It's funny to think you could get lost in the middle of Liverpool. I know these streets like the back of me hand in daylight.'

Larry put his arm around her and squeezed her tightly. 'You're safe with me,' he said. He began to lead her up some steps.

'Where are we going?' cried Kitty. 'This isn't the way to the Exchange Station.'

'Don't worry, Kitty. You'll be all right.'

She felt his other arm snake across her front, pressing heavily against her breasts. 'Larry!' she said indignantly. 'What are you doing?' She was unable to work out what was happening. Was he sick or something?

Suddenly, she felt herself being pushed against something hard and cold and Larry was kissing her, hot dry kisses from which she seemed unable to escape.

'Kitty, oh, Kitty,' he groaned and thrust his tongue into her mouth.

'No!' She almost choked and tried to wriggle out of his grasp, but remembered he was a boxer and his strength was far greater than hers. She felt her coat being unbuttoned whilst he pinned her painfully against the hard wall with one hand. His other hand began to fumble underneath her jumper with her breasts.

Kitty struggled harder, but the harder she struggled, the more he seemed to groan and pant, as if she was egging him on, not trying to escape. She felt his hand run down her hips and he was pulling at her skirt.

'Aargh!' His whole body shuddered when he touched the flesh between the top of her stockings and her pants. 'Kitty, my lovely, lovely Kitty!'

'*Stoppit!*' Kitty screamed. 'Go away! Leave me alone!' She managed to free her arms and beat his face with her fists, which only seemed to inflame him more and before she knew it he was kissing her again. She felt his teeth grind against hers.

Kitty twisted her head and bit his nose, hard. He yelped, stepped backwards and released her. She heard him swear as he lost his balance, but by then she was, somewhat miraculously, down the steps and already on the pavement. As she began to run through the darkness in what she hoped was the direction of Exchange Station, a cry of pain came from somewhere behind her. He must have fallen down the steps.

She paused briefly, but decided she didn't care, not even if he'd broken his neck!

Chapter 8

The atmosphere in the hospital on afternoons was entirely different to mornings. The floors had been done hours ago, the wards tidied, the men bathed and the Chief Medical Officer had already been on his rounds. At two o'clock, the afternoon shift arrived and there was a wild flurry of activity during which the kitchen, the sluice room and the toilets were scrubbed from top to bottom with disinfectant and the morning women stopped for a belated dinner break. They then prepared the patients' tea before going home. After they'd eaten, the men sat quietly in the dimly lit wards listening to the wireless, playing cards or reading. It was the time for visitors, some of whom had travelled long distances to spend a few hours at the bedside of their loved ones.

At the beginning of Kitty's second week on afternoons, the day after her date with Larry Newell, the weather had turned wild and stormy. A gale blew in from the River Mersey, rattling the windows of the old building. Rain had fallen in a steady downpour all day long, with thunder rumbling in the distance and occasional flashes of lightning.

At half-past eight, after the patients had taken their medicine and drunk their cocoa and all the visitors had gone, Kitty entered one of the wards to tuck them up in their beds and say goodnight.

'Sing us a lullaby, Kitty,' one man pleaded.

Kitty smiled and began to sing softly, 'Rock-a-bye baby, in the tree top.'

'That's nice.'

She patted his face and moved on to the next bed, still singing.

'Goodnight, Kitty, luv,' the man said contentedly.

'On nights like this, me mam always used to say a prayer for the sailors out at sea,' said another.

'I'll say a prayer later,' promised Kitty.

Martin McCabe was fast asleep when she went into his cubicle. He was heavily sedated and she'd hardly spoken to him since she'd started on afternoons.

'Goodnight, luv,' she whispered.

A few minutes later, she switched off the main light, leaving only the red-painted bulb above the clock on the far wall. She paused at the door. It was strange to see the ward so still and peaceful, every man tucked in his bed. Most were already asleep, though a few were watching, waiting for her final 'goodnight'. The wild noises coming from outside, the lash of the wind, the rain, the trees whipping back and forth, seemed to belong to a different world altogether.

What was it Miss Ellis had said when she was at the Labour Exchange? 'Working for one's country during a war is a privilege, not a chore.' Kitty caught her breath, as a feeling almost of exultation swept over her. She felt privileged beyond words that she'd been allowed to help take care of these young men during this terrible period of their lives, a period when some had to come to terms with the fact they'd never walk again or that parts of their once healthy bodies were no longer there. Others knew they would recover and be expected to return to another ship, where once more they'd be at risk of injury or death from every direction. It might come from the sky above, from the sea around them or the waters underneath.

'Goodnight,' Kitty mouthed, and the men who were watching closed their eyes and went to sleep.

★

Half a dozen nurses, as well as the auxiliaries, were standing round the kitchen drinking tea. The air was thick with smoke. Unless one of the patients called out, there was little to do in the final hour before the night shift took over. Sometimes, even one of the MOs popped in for a cuppa.

'There's tea in the pot, Kitty,' one of the nurses said.

'Ta.' Kitty poured herself a cup. She'd been surprised at how friendly the nurses turned out to be when they weren't rushed off their feet and could relax for a while. They transformed from stiff, starched individuals snapping out orders into ordinary young women with all the problems young women often had. Few came from Liverpool. They lived, far away from their hometown, in a hostel along the road in Waterloo. Some were homesick, others yearned for their husbands or boyfriends who were away in the forces. They worried about their job, their patients, their looks, their clothes. They were upset if Matron or one of the sisters spoke to them sharply.

'I understand you're responsible for the plaster on Larry Newell's nose,' one remarked to Kitty, grinning.

Larry Newell had avoided Kitty's eyes when she passed him briefly that afternoon. 'Yes, but not the bruise on his forehead,' she said. 'He must have got that falling down the steps of St George's Hall.'

Everyone laughed. 'I wish I'd known you were going out with him, Kitty,' remarked Jenny Downing, a pretty young nurse with short crisp curls peeping out from underneath her lawn veil. 'I would have warned you off. Dirty bugger, he can't keep his hands to himself.'

'What I can't understand,' Kitty said, 'is why he wouldn't stop when I asked him to.' She'd been wondering about it ever since it happened. How could a man enjoy doing things to a woman who was trying to fight him off?

'Because men are so bloody conceited, they can't

imagine there's a woman alive who'd turn their advances down.'

'Either that, or in their own twisted way they think "no" means "yes".'

Kitty began to doubt if she'd ever learn how to cope with men, particularly when one of the nurses said, 'You want to steer clear of men like Newell in future.'

'But he seemed very nice,' she cried. 'How am I supposed to know which men to steer clear of?'

There was silence until Lucy piped up, 'I suppose you've got to play it by ear. Being very nice is often a sign they're up to no good. Mind you, most men'll have your knickers off given half a chance.'

'But I didn't give him the least chance,' Kitty said indignantly. 'All I did was let him walk me to the station. What's wrong with that?'

There was another silence, as if Kitty had posed an unanswerable question. 'If, as Lucy says, most men are like that,' Jenny Downing said, frowning, 'it means that most women end up marrying them.'

'Perhaps most men don't behave that way with the women they fall in love with,' another nurse suggested hopefully. 'One of these days Larry Newell might turn out to be someone's perfect husband.'

There was a united groan at this. One of the older nurses spoke up, a woman with several grown-up children. 'I didn't like to say anything before, but Newell's already married. I once heard him mention he had a wife to another SBA.'

'Do you mean to say I've been out with a married man?' said Kitty, horrified.

'I'm afraid you have, dear.'

'That means Newell's turned out to be anything but the perfect husband,' commented Lucy. 'Jaysus, how's a girl supposed to know about these things? Perhaps it would be best if we all stayed spinsters and let men stew in their own juice.'

'If we did, the human race would die out altogether.'

Harriet Mansell spoke for the first time. 'You just have to accept the fact that men are very different from women,' she said sensibly. 'They have different needs, different priorities. Sex is all-important and few will turn it down when it's on offer, nor hesitate to try their hand if they think there's the slightest opportunity, as Newell did with Kitty. This doesn't mean they don't love their wives, or their future wives, deeply.'

'How the hell would you know,' Clara Watkins sneered, 'when you've never been married yourself?'

'I may not have been married,' Harriet replied, unfazed, 'but I know quite a lot about love.'

'Well, my George would never even look at another woman,' Clara said huffily.

'I suppose we just have to accept what Harriet said is right,' Jenny Downing said with a sigh. 'Anyway, who are we to criticise? Most of us have boyfriends, even husbands, yet we go out with other men. Somehow, it doesn't mean anything, particularly when there's a war on. I know it sounds stupid, but I even feel as if I'm doing my bit, particularly if I let them kiss me. Charlie, my boyfriend, would have a fit if he knew.'

'Charlie's probably doing the same thing down in Portsmouth.'

'I suppose so,' Jenny said gloomily.

'If it doesn't mean anything to you, then it won't mean anything to Charlie, will it?' Harriet put in. 'As you said, there's a war on. None of us can be sure we'll be alive this time next week. We all should live life to the full whilst we have the opportunity.'

There was a chorus of agreement, and Lucy said, 'Do you realise, we would never have had this conversation if Kitty hadn't bitten Larry Newell's nose?'

Everyone burst out laughing, though the laughter quickly subsided when Staff Nurse Bellamy appeared in the doorway. Staff normally did a quick round of the first-floor wards alone before finishing her shift. She beckoned Kitty outside, looking grave.

Perhaps it was second sight, but Kitty knew immediately what she was about to say.

'I thought it best to tell you this privately, Quigley, though it's not something I would usually do. When I checked on Seaman McCabe, I found he had passed away peacefully in his sleep.'

'May I see him one last time?' Kitty asked, her voice devoid of emotion.

'I'm afraid not,' Bellamy said crisply. 'I want the other patients disturbed as little as possible. Two SBAs are already in the process of removing the body to the morgue.'

'I see. Thank you for telling me,' Kitty said politely. 'It was very kind of you.'

'Kindness didn't come into it. I just didn't want you making a scene if you found out in public.'

'I wouldn't have done, but thanks all the same.'

Instead of catching the bus, Kitty walked home that night along Liverpool Road with the sound of the waves crashing against the shore. She shed no tears for the poor young sailor whose face she'd never seen except in a photograph, though she knew she'd never forget him as long as she lived. When she got home, she'd put the ring and the photo underneath her handkerchiefs in the dressing table drawer. She'd always felt uneasy wearing another woman's wedding ring.

Instead of crying, Kitty cursed. She cursed Hitler for all the misery he'd brought onto the world, for the terrible waste of young men's lives, men who'd done harm to no-one and wanted only to grow old in peace, for the loss of children like Tony Costello, scarcely old enough to have had any life at all, and all the ordinary men and women who'd been blown to smithereens during the Blitz.

When she got in, her dad was sitting at the table where

twenty-two matchsticks were set out in the pattern of two football teams, eleven dead matches, eleven live. He was moving them about, lips pursed, practising manoeuvres for the game on Saturday, too engrossed to notice his daughter's wild appearance. Kitty's hair was matted to her head and her coat was soaking.

' 'Lo there, kiddo,' he said without looking up. 'I'm dying for a cup of cocoa.'

'In that case, you'll just have to make it yourself,' snapped Kitty. 'I'm not in the mood for making cocoa just now.' With that, she placed her squelching shoes in the oven and marched upstairs to bed.

Jimmy stared after her resentfully. He wasn't sure what had got into his Kitty lately, but she seemed to be looking after him less and less.

St Joan of Arc's won their quarter final match on Saturday. Dominic Reilly played a superb game. He had the ability to visualise several strikes ahead of the other players. A goal had been scored in Dominic's head long before it thudded into the net of the other side. Jimmy Quigley knew it was a rare ability, one that only the finest footballers had.

When the game was over and the boys had gone to get changed, Sister Gabriel, the games mistress, approached Jimmy. They resisted the urge to throw their arms around each other triumphantly, and allowed themselves a sedate handshake. 'We never dreamt we'd get as far as the semi-finals, Mr Quigley,' Sister Gabriel said gleefully. She was a wiry, pugilistic woman in her sixties with a lively face and enormous energy.

'Well, it's all thanks to Dominic Reilly, Sister. You've got a cracking player there,' Jimmy said modestly. There were times when he felt as if he'd invented Dominic all on his own.

'It's thanks to you, too,' Sister Gabriel said warmly. 'Your support has been very evident and Dominic said you've been coaching him. In fact, I wondered if you wouldn't mind coming into school before the next match to coach the entire team?'

'I wouldn't mind a bit,' Jimmy agreed, chuffed out of all proportion.

'As long as it doesn't overtax your legs.'

'I'll be careful,' promised Jimmy, wondering where he'd left his stick. He still used one occasionally, just to remind people it wasn't long since he was an invalid.

A young woman with a large chest came up. Jimmy had noticed her at previous matches. She was the mother of one of the centre backs, a solid little chap who did his best with two left feet and was in the same class as Niall Reilly.

'Ah, Theresa,' Sister Gabriel beamed. 'They're nearly changed.' She turned to Jimmy. 'Mrs Beamish has kindly offered to wash the kits for us.' She wandered off in the direction of the changing room.

'That's a task all on its own,' said Jimmy. The kits were sort of new, having been run up out of old sheets, some dyed blue, by one of the nuns. Until the quarter-final, the team had been playing in a collection of scarcely matching odds and ends. Now, they wore the same colours as Everton, and in Jimmy's eyes looked almost professional, especially since the nuns had organised a raffle to raise the funds to purchase footy boots, so the team no longer had to use their own shoes.

'I don't mind. I like hard work,' Theresa Beamish said seriously, 'particularly washing and cleaning.'

'You sound like a woman after me own heart. I like everywhere to look spick and span meself. Unfortunately, since me daughter took up nursing a couple of months ago, the house has gone to rack and ruin.' Jimmy entirely overlooked the fact that although the place looked the worse for wear by the end of the week, poor Kitty spent every Sunday cleaning it from top to bottom – and doing his washing.

Theresa tut-tutted. 'Your lad's a fine player,' she said in her rather flat voice. 'Takes after his dad, I reckon. Someone said you used to play for Everton.'

'He's not my lad, though I wish he was. I would have loved a son. No, he's a neighbour's. His dad's away in the Merchant Navy. Hasn't been home in months.' Jimmy felt flattered to be taken for the father of an eight-year-old.

'Me husband, Frank, was in the Merchant Navy. His ship went down with all hands in the first month of the war.'

'You're awful young to be a widder.' She was a rather plain young woman, with an enormous square white face, an even more enormous chest and short brown hair cut in a sensible style. Her eyes were like wet stones, a dark unsmiling grey, and her clothes were as sensible as her hair, a brown belted gaberdine mackintosh and flat, lace-up shoes.

'I'll be thirty soon,' she said grimly.

A boy of about five came running up and grabbed her arm. She shook him off impatiently. 'What do you want?'

'I wanna go home, Mam,' the boy whined. 'I'm cold.'

'We'll go home as soon as Georgie's got changed and Sister's given me the clothes to wash. Now, go away. Can't you see I'm talking to someone?' The boy obediently departed.

'How many kids have you got?' asked Jimmy.

'Just the two. Billy's six and Georgie's eight. They're a handful, the pair of them, I can tell you, particularly since we moved in with me mam and dad after we lost our house in Tennyson Street in the raids.'

'Here we are.' Sister Gabriel came panting towards them with a large, bulging drawstring bag.

'Well, I'll be off,' Jimmy said with alacrity, worried he might get landed with carrying the bag. 'Dominic's grandad is working in the garage across the road. I'll pop in and let him know what the score was.'

'Tara, then,' Theresa said laconically. Her lads had both appeared as if by magic at her side and were quietly waiting for her to leave. They seemed to be well-disciplined boys, Jimmy thought approvingly, and anything but a handful, unlike Dominic and Niall who were swinging on a goalpost.

'See you at the semi-final in two weeks' time,' he called to Theresa as he went to collect them.

'D'you think he'd like to come to one of my parties?'

Rita Mott stared at Jack Doyle's retreating back. He was giving Niall a piggy-back and Dominic was hanging onto his arm describing the match they'd just won.

'I doubt it very much,' said Jessica. 'He's not the partying type.'

'Are you sure he's not your feller?'

'I've told you a dozen times, Rita, he isn't. I haven't got a feller – I mean, a fellow.'

'I wouldn't want to make a move on a mate's feller, like, it wouldn't be nice,' Rita said virtuously. 'I don't half fancy him, though. Has he ever mentioned me?'

'Not that I can recall.' If only the poor woman knew, thought Jessica. Jack loathed Rita Mott. He considered her a bad influence on Penny. They'd discussed her the previous Saturday morning when he'd turned up to help as promised and Rita had gone off to lunch in Chester with a flash-looking individual in a red sports car.

'She's got a husband away fighting in the war,' Jack spluttered, outraged, 'yet she flaunts herself around the garage in that negligy thing . . .'

'Négligé,' corrected Jessica.

'Whatever,' Jack said impatiently, 'and she goes out with other men. It's disgusting.' He unscrewed the rusty top off a bicycle bell and poured oil inside.

'Don't be such a prude. Not everyone's got such high morals as you, Jack.' Jessica looked at him sideways and was pleased when she saw him go red. Jack Doyle could

169

be a tiny bit hypocritical at times. 'Rita's terribly lonely.'

'A lot of women must be lonely with their men away,' he said testily.

'Maybe they've got families, children. Rita's got no-one. All she wants is friends.'

'Friends!' Jack guffawed. Penny, sitting on her blanket outside the office, guffawed with him. 'That chap in the red car looked a bit more than a friend to me.' The man had slapped Rita's bottom as she got in. 'It's not good for Penny being stuck with a woman like that all day.'

'Penny and Rita love each other,' Jessica said calmly, 'and personally, I like Rita very much. She's generosity itself, and you know what they say, "Generosity covers a multitude of sins".'

'Since when have you been so understanding?'

Jessica pumped up a tyre and looked deliberately vague. 'I'm not sure. There was a time when I would have disapproved of Rita, but perhaps as you get older you learn to accept people's weaknesses as well as their strengths, particularly when you discover yourself to be far weaker than you thought.'

Jack went even redder. Jess saw and smiled – if she was weak, then so was he. She sensed he felt resentful that she was making herself out to be a better, a more understanding person than he was. He must have decided to change the subject. 'How many bikes have you got now?' he asked.

'Ten,' Jessica replied proudly. 'I sold three last week – and I did a few small car repairs. I made enough for the rent and nearly four pounds over.'

'That's good,' Jack said sarcastically.

'I wonder what Den would say to all these bikes?' Rita mused. She was sitting on an upturned box in her flowered dressing gown and her legs were clearly visible through the diaphanous lilac nightie underneath. On her feet, she wore a pair of purple fur slippers as big as cats. She was smoking, as usual, and spat out a shred of tobacco in a delicate, ladylike way.

Jessica blinked herself back from last Saturday morning to this one. It hadn't crossed her mind to discuss the subject of bicycles with Rita before she'd gone out and bought them several weeks ago. 'Do you think he'll mind?'

'I'm not sure. This garage was his life. He might think bikes are a good idea or he might think they stink.'

'Perhaps you should write and tell him,' Jessica suggested.

'On the other hand, perhaps I shouldn't. It would be best if he didn't know, 'case he's against it. I'd hate it if you weren't here, Jess, and I'd really miss Penny.' Penny was fast asleep upstairs in Rita's bright pink bedroom.

'In that case, don't mention it,' Jessica said hastily. She'd hate it if she had to look around for another site from which to sell her bikes.

'I won't, though I usually write to Den every Monday regular and tell him everything that's going on.'

'Everything?' Jessica enquired with a twinkle as she levered a tyre onto a rear wheel. She was making one decent bike out of two old ones.

'Well, no, not everything,' Rita conceded. She took a deep puff on her cigarette and blew the smoke out slowly. 'I suppose you think I'm a dead horrible person, going out with other chaps when me husband's in the army.'

'It's none of my business what you do with your life, is it?'

'That doesn't stop you from having an opinion though.'

'I don't know what my opinion is,' Jessica said thoughtfully. She was still not sure what Rita got up to with her numerous manfriends, but suspected the relationships weren't platonic. 'I've never met Den,

171

have I? I don't know what sort of person he was – is.' There was a photo of Dennis Mott on the sideboard upstairs, a quiet looking young man with prematurely receding hair.

Rita sniffed. 'He's ever so nice, is Den.'

Jessica glanced at the woman. Without her tawdry make-up, Rita had a curiously innocent face. 'In that case . . .'

'I suppose now you think the worst,' Rita said gloomily.

'Not necessarily. I reckon there's something you haven't told me.' Jessica began to wonder why Rita seemed so eager to confide such intimacies to another person.

'I was ever such a little mouse in those days, Jess,' she said in a rush. 'I had brown hair, I never wore make up, I didn't smoke and I only owned one frock. I spent all me time cooking and cleaning, yet Den'd only been gone a week, when this chap drew in for petrol and asked me to go to the pictures with him and I said yes.'

'Really!'

'Really. We saw this dead romantic picture with Joan Crawford in. She was having an affair with a married man. Afterwards, the chap – I think his name was Johnnie – brought me back to the flat and we . . .' Rita paused and gave an embarrassed grin. 'We, you know what, on the mat in front of the fire.' She lit another cigarette from the stub of the old one. She grinned again, no longer embarrassed. 'It wasn't half good. I'd always wondered what it would be like with another feller. After all, they write books about it and make pictures about it, so I reckoned there must be more to it than I knew.'

'What do you mean?' asked Jessica, fascinated.

'Do you mind me talking to you like this?'

'I don't mind at all.' Jessica was anxious for her to continue.

'The thing is,' Rita went on, 'when you've only known one feller, how are you supposed to know what's normal? With Den, it was five minutes once a month if I was lucky. I usen't half to feel fed up, as if I could bust, sometimes. I'd go to the pictures, and there'd be people fighting for it and killing for it, and I'd think, "What's all the fuss about?" Then Den went away and I couldn't wait to find out for meself.' She sighed contentedly. 'I discovered it was worth it, after all. I realised Den had all the right equipment, but he never learnt how to use it, not properly. That's why we never had kids.'

'I suppose everyone has a right to a healthy sex life,' said Jessica.

Rita giggled. 'That's a funny way of putting it. One of me chaps said I was a nympho . . . nymphy . . .'

'A nymphomaniac.'

'Is that good or bad?' Rita asked anxiously.

Jessica wrinkled her smooth white brow. 'I'm not sure. Probably it's only good if you're married to another nymphomaniac, otherwise you'd spend your life in a constant state of frustration.'

'Do you still think I'm a terrible person?'

'I never did in the first place.'

'Are you sure, Jess?'

Rita had obviously been suffering from a guilty conscience and was anxious for Jessica's blessing or seal of approval on her rather unconventional lifestyle.

'I'm positive,' Jessica said firmly. 'A person's morals are entirely their own affair, no-one else's.' Which was, she thought, a surprising statement from someone who wouldn't have passed the time of day with Rita Mott only a few short years ago if she'd even suspected the way she carried on.

Rita looked relieved. 'Anyroad,' she said, 'I thought if I crammed as much of the "you know what" into the time Den's away, I'd get enough to last the rest of me life.'

'I doubt it,' said Jessica. She glanced at her watch. It was nearly one o'clock and she had two bikes to see and make offers for that afternoon. She began to tidy the workshop.

'I doubt it, too,' Rita said with a coarse laugh. 'Though you never know, Den might learn a few tricks while he's away.'

'What happens if he doesn't?'

'Christ knows! I'll just have to try and teach him a few tricks meself, won't I?'

Sean Doyle, Jack's son, got married on the first Saturday in December. He came home from the RAF camp where he was stationed in Lincolnshire on a forty-eight-hour pass, along with six of his mates who formed a Guard of Honour when the newly married couple left St James's Church.

Brenda Mahon had done wonders with five yards of cheap taffeta lining to make a dress for the bride. Alice Scully, a tiny waif of a girl with pale fair hair and huge blue eyes, was determined to have a white wedding. Her borrowed veil was held in place with a red velvet band and she carried a small bouquet of red roses. The hem of the dress trailed the floor in order to hide the ugly boot which Alice was forced to wear to disguise her deformed leg.

'I hope you know what you're doing, son,' Jack Doyle muttered to himself as he stood outside the church whilst the photographs were being taken. Alice was an orphan with five younger brothers and sisters she was determined to take care of. Despite her delicate appearance, inside she was as hard as iron. It meant his Sean, only nineteen, was taking on a wife and five growing children. Even so, Sean looked serenely happy throughout the ceremony. Jack had never dreamt his charming, idle son had so much character.

'Aren't they a proper picture, Dad?' His daughter,

Eileen, squeezed his arm. 'Alice looks like a fairy off the top of a Christmas tree.'

'They make a lovely couple,' Jack said gruffly. 'How are you, luv? You're looking a bit pale.'

'I'm fine.'

'Where's Nicky?'

'Our Sheila's got him. You know what she's like the minute she sets eyes on a baby.'

'I'll be along to the cottage tomorrow to tidy up the garden and take a look at the Brussels sprouts,' Jack promised. He went most weekends, mainly to keep an eye on her. 'They should be ready in time for our Christmas dinner.'

The reception was held in Sheila Reilly's house. After a quick sandwich and a fairy cake, most of the men departed to the King's Arms. Despite the cold, Sheila left the front door wide open so the neighbours could pop in for a glass of sherry and a piece of wedding cake – seeing as virtually everyone in the street had contributed something towards the cake, this seemed only fair. Aggie Donovan, in her element, was put in charge of the cake to make sure it went round.

Guests spilled out onto the pavement. It was a brilliant December day with a touch of frost in the air, but the clear yellow sun seemed to convince everyone it was not really all that cold.

Nan Wright, her dress on back to front, dragged her old body as far as the front door and found she could go no further. She sat down on the step, enveloped in a hazy, happy dizziness and wondered what was going on. 'Is the war over?' she asked when the lovely red-haired lady from across the street whose name she couldn't remember brought her something to eat.

'Not yet, dear,' said Jessica Fleming.

Paddy O'Hara was yanked from the pub and pressed to play his harmonica for the ever-increasing crowd outside the Reillys'. Paddy didn't need much persuading. In fact, he would have felt hurt if no-one had asked. He tapped his way outside with his white stick, his dog Rover faithfully at his heels. Paddy was part of the ritual; the sweet quivering notes of his harmonica had accompanied every celebration which had been held in the street over many years. The men came out of the pub and stood listening, joining in the singing when it was something they knew. Nan Wright sipped her sherry and ate her cake and thought it was the most beautiful sound she had ever heard.

At half past twelve, Jimmy Quigley came round the corner waving his stick in the air. 'We won,' he shouted jubilantly. 'We won two–nil.'

'Won what?' folks demanded.

'The bloody semi-final, that's what.' Dominic and Niall Reilly followed behind Jimmy. If everyone hadn't known better, they would have said all three of them were drunk, even the little lads. They were grinning stupidly, as if they'd just won a hundred quid each on the pools.

'What bloody semi-final?'

'The semi-final of the Merseyside Junior Football Cup. It means St Joan of Arc's are in the final in two weeks' time.'

'St Joan of Arc's, in the final?'

'I've been telling you for weeks, but no-one's taken any notice,' Jimmy said impatiently. 'And you'll never guess where they'll be playing – Everton Football Ground. All the junior schools have been invited.'

'Can we come?'

'Can the street come?'

'Are we invited?'

'The whole of Bootle's invited as far as I'm concerned,' cried Jimmy.

'I'll just go and tell me mam,' Dominic said blissfully. His mam had tried to insist he and Niall stay home for his

Uncle Sean's wedding and had been taken aback when both boys had adamantly refused.

'I can't let the side down, Mam,' Dominic said in a horrified voice.

'And he needs me to cheer him on,' Niall assured her.

The house was packed with people when Dominic went in. Uncle Sean was in the parlour, looking incredibly grown up in his uniform with his new wife hanging onto his arm. He spoilt this impression rather when he noticed Dominic in the doorway and squinted his eyes and made a horrible face. Dominic made an even more horrible face back and went in search of his mam. He found her in the kitchen where she was hurriedly cutting sarnies. 'We won again, Mam,' he announced grandly.

'That's good, luv.' Sheila glanced at him vaguely. She patted his head. 'That's good. Would you like something to eat?'

Women, thought Dominic disgustedly. They didn't seem to know what was important in the world. He helped himself to three sarnies and a big chunk of wedding cake when Aggie Donovan wasn't looking and went to join the men outside the King's Arms where he knew he'd be appreciated.

'Jess, I'd like you to meet Kate Thomas.'

Jessica Fleming turned swiftly at the sound of Eileen's voice. Kate Thomas was the woman Sheila had described, albeit jokingly, as her father's 'girlfriend'. Jessica was aware she looked her very best that day, in her turquoise suit and matching pillbox hat with a little veil. She'd put her hair up for a change and wore the marcasite and mother-of-pearl earrings and pendant set which Arthur had bought her on their honeymoon in Paris – all her good jewellery, as well as her furs, had gone the same way as the house in Calderstones, to pay off the firm's debts.

'How do you do?' she said with a vivid smile. No

contest, a voice inside her said when she saw the tiny drab woman in her forties wearing a moth-eaten fur coat and a battered old hat. She had a nice face, shiny, as if it had just been scrubbed very hard, and clear hazel eyes. She shook Jessica's extended hand firmly.

'Kate's the women's overseer at Dunnings, the factory where I used to work,' Eileen explained. 'She gave me loads of legal advice when I had that trouble with Francis. Now, if you'll both excuse me, I'll take Nicky upstairs and put him down for his nap.'

Kate Thomas smiled at Jessica. She had a lovely smile which reached her eyes and made them sparkle. 'Eileen makes me sound very knowledgeable. It's just that I was married to a solicitor and picked up bits and pieces of information over the years.'

For some reason, Jessica had got the impression she was an old maid, and was slightly put out to discover she'd been married. She felt certain a man would find a widow a more attractive proposition than a spinster.

'Have you been widowed long?' she asked politely.

'Oh, dearie me, I'm not a widow, more's the pity,' Kate said with a laugh. 'I left my husband a long while ago. To be blunt, he's an even more unattractive character than Francis Costello was. That's why I found it so easy to relate to Eileen's troubles.' She began to chat eagerly about her eldest daughter who was in the WAAF and stationed in Chester. 'We normally meet on Saturday afternoon if she can snatch a few hours away. This week it will have to be Sunday.'

Kate Thomas was gradually transforming in front of Jessica's eyes, from an old maid who went to political lectures into a woman with three children and a lovely smile who'd actually had the guts to walk out on her solicitor husband. As if eager to assist in the transformation, Kate snatched off her hat and shoved it in her pocket, muttering, 'I don't know why I'm wearing that in here,' revealing short, if untidy brown curls

Suddenly, she looked not just nice, but pretty. Jessica began to feel alarmed, particularly when Jack Doyle appeared and put his arm around Kate's shoulders and led her away without even noticing Jessica was there.

'I want you to settle an argument,' she heard him say. 'What was Woolton's job before he was made Minister of Food . . . ?'

They had things in common, Jessica realised with a pang; politics, for one, whereas all she and Jack did was argue. They agreed about nothing. Still, she squared her shoulders and went in search of Penny, whom she found underneath the table in the living room, playing house with Sheila's three girls. She had no intention of changing and pretending to be someone else just to catch Jack Doyle, no matter how much she wanted him.

At half past four, the bride having changed into a blue suit, the newly married couple left on their honeymoon, a single night in a hotel in New Brighton, a wedding present from Eileen to her little brother and his new bride. Sean's friends were being accommodated in various houses in the area and would all return to Lincolnshire together next morning.

It was not quite dark, not quite time for the blackout, as everyone gathered outside to see Sean and Alice off. For a few precious moments, it was possible to imagine there was no such thing as a blackout as shafts of pale orange light fell across the cobbled street from the open front doors.

'Tara, Sean. Don't do anything I wouldn't do.'

'Tara, Alice.'

'Good luck the two o'yis.'

Suddenly, the pair were gone, accompanied by a gang of other young people who were going with them on the train into town to finish off the celebrations there. Darkness fell, doors were closed, curtains drawn and everywhere fell silent. It was difficult to believe the black, empty street had been full of noisy, laughing people such a short while ago.

Inside Sheila Reilly's house, bedlam reigned. The women were sitting in the parlour, six of them, finishing off the sherry, whilst elsewhere the children noisily ate the remainder of the food.

'The divil's got into our Dominic today,' sighed Sheila. 'There's no controlling him. He's infected all the other kids. They've all gone wild.' Her eldest son had been responsible for all sorts of mischief ever since he'd come back from the football match almost out of his head with excitement.

'He needs his dad,' said Brenda Mahon.

Sheila winked. 'So do I!'

There was a crash from the other room and everyone jumped and waited for the ensuing screams. When none came, they decided to ignore it. Jessica worried briefly about Penny, but her daughter had been kept safely under Siobhan's wing all day, and anyway, she would never agree to stay quietly with her mother when she knew the other children were so evidently enjoying themselves elsewhere.

'I used to love weddings and parties when I was little.' Eileen transferred a sleepy Nicky to her other arm. 'All you cared about was having a good time. Although I enjoyed meself today, I kept worrying about our Sean. Where on earth will they live when he's home for good? I mean, there's no room for a young married couple in Alice's place in Miller's Bridge. They're already crammed like sardines in there.'

'Have some more sherry, luv, and worry about it tomorrer,' Sheila urged her sister. 'Anyroad, me dad's already keeping an eye out in case a house falls empty.'

'There'll be dozens already after it,' Kitty Quigley warned. She'd only recently arrived and was still in her striped nurse's uniform. 'Accommodation's dead scarce in Bootle with so many houses lost in the Blitz.'

'They'll be too much in love to notice where they're living,' said Kate Thomas, adding with a smile, 'At least for a while.'

'Who wants more sherry?' asked Jessica.

'Me,' everyone chorused.

'This is ever such a good make, Jess. Where did you get it?' enquired Eileen. Like the others, she was beginning to look ever so slightly drunk.

'Off Rita Mott who owns the garage. She gave me four bottles, all for nothing. She gets piles of stuff on the black market.'

'You should have asked her to the wedding,' said Sheila.

'It's a bit late to suggest that now. Anyway, your dad wouldn't have approved. He can't stand Rita.'

'Talking of Jack, where is he?' Kate Thomas demanded. 'Where are all the men, come to that? Why is it there's only women left?'

'Do you realise,' Sheila said slowly, 'there's six of us and not a single husband amongst us? Three are away in the forces, two have been done away with as it were, and in the case of Kitty, he hasn't yet arrived on the scene.'

'Xavier's in the forces *and* he's been done away with,' Brenda said sourly.

'Mine might have arrived on the scene,' Kitty hiccuped. 'I've got a date tonight with a sailor. In fact, I'd better go home and get washed and changed.' She got reluctantly to her feet.

'Keep your hand on your ha'penny this time,' Sheila said darkly. She turned to the others. 'She nearly came to no good on the steps of St George's Hall last time she had a date.'

There was a full moon that night. It hung, glittering, in the navy-blue star-powdered sky as Jessica Fleming made her unsteady way home some hours later with her daughter. She wasn't sure what time it was, but the sherry had all gone and Sheila's house had gradually grown quiet as most of the exhausted children became sleepy.

'It was a lovely wedding, Sheil,' said Brenda in an unnatural, high-pitched squeak. Her two girls were fast asleep on the landing. 'I had a lovely time.'

'Me, too, Sheila,' Jessica echoed. Dominic was teaching Penny how to play football with the teacosy. They were the only two left who were wide awake.

'Me house is wrecked,' groaned Sheila. 'Though it's all me own fault. I was enjoying meself too much getting pissed in the parlour.'

Kate Thomas was taking Eileen home in her car. 'Are you sure you're fit to drive?' asked Jessica.

'I drive better when I've had a few drinks, it gives me more confidence.' Kate swayed slightly. 'I'm only dangerous when I'm sober.'

Jessica gave Penny a cat's lick of a wash and put her straight down in her cot. Despite the fact she wriggled her plump body in protest, she fell asleep the minute her head touched the pillow.

'You're beautiful, sweetheart,' whispered Jessica. 'I'm so lucky having you.' She bent down and stroked the soft golden hair, noticing the way the slightly distorted jowels quivered with each swift intake of breath. She recalled all the weddings she'd gone to in the past when she'd been the only married woman present who was childless. No matter how well dressed she'd been, no matter how expensive the present she'd bought, she always felt inferior, second best.

She began to remove her clothes and sighed with relief when she peeled off the rubber corselette that had been digging into the top of her legs all day. She only wore it nowadays for special occasions. There were dents in her skin that felt red raw. She rubbed them, wincing painfully, and reached quickly under the pillow for her thick winceyette nightdress. There was no heating in the bedroom and it was freezing. Shivering, she took a final look at Penny as she put on her dressing gown and slippers.

'If only I could have another baby!' she said aloud. She went downstairs, removed the fireguard and knelt in front of the fire, stretching out her hands to warm them. She'd never blamed Arthur, not even in her mind, but if it hadn't been for him she might have had half a dozen children by now, like Sheila Reilly.

'Please God, don't let it be too late!'

Jessica stood up, feeling warmer. She noticed in the mirror that her hair was still pinned up and removed the combs and clips to let it down. It fell onto her shoulders in waves. She was still a good-looking woman. From time to time, Rita brought one of her 'friends' into the workshop, and Jessica was conscious of the way they looked her up and down appreciatively. What a pity she couldn't be like Rita and make love with any man who happened to be around! But Jessica knew there was only one man she wanted to father a second child.

Sighing, she took the kettle into the kitchen and filled it up with water. She was dying for a cup of tea. She'd just put the kettle on the hob when there was a knock on the front door and she went to answer it.

The moonlight fell like fine liquid on the street outside, illuminating everything with an unnatural, vivid clarity. Jack Doyle was standing there holding something in his hand. Perhaps it was because she was still a little drunk, but his entire body seemed to be surrounded by a narrow line of light, like a halo.

'I was helping our Sheila tidy up a bit, and we found this behind a chair in the parlour.'

Jessica regarded him wordlessly.

'It's your handbag,' he explained with a touch of impatience. 'Sheila thought you might be worried you'd lost it.'

'My handbag?'

'Don't tell me you're drunk, too,' he said disgustedly. 'Our Sheila doesn't know which way she's going.'

'Give it to me.'

Jessica took a step back when he handed her the bag. Before he could remove his hand, she caught it in her own. He looked at her, wide-eyed and slightly shocked.

'*No, Jess!*'

Jessica didn't answer, but began to tug him ever so gently into the house. She suspected there was nothing between him and Kate Thomas, but meeting Kate had made her realise she had to be quick, just in case . . .

'Oh, no, Jess,' Jack groaned.

Jessica placed the hand she had imprisoned on her hip and felt it rest there, comfortably, warmly. She reached for his other hand and when it was safely where it should be, her arms crept round his neck and she pulled his head down until their lips met.

'Yes, Jack,' she whispered after one long intoxicating kiss. He was in the hallway by now. He kicked the door shut with his heel.

Oh, yes, yes, yes!

Chapter 9

It was more like a carnival than a football match. Christmas was only five days away, the schools had broken up the day before and everyone was in the very best of spirits. Compared with the numbers present at a league game, the crowd was sparse, the Everton ground nowhere near full to capacity, but in fact there were more than a thousand people there, at least three-quarters of them boys from local schools. For some reason, many brought Union Jacks to wave. Several also brought ARP rattles which they whirled around with a tremendous clatter whenever it looked as if there might be a goal. Every able-bodied person from Pearl Street had come, and Brenda Mahon had been busy knitting blue and white striped scarves.

Sheila Reilly felt slightly overawed. She'd scarcely taken any notice of Dominic each time he'd come home and announced his team had won, and not only that, it was he who'd scored most of the goals. Yet over the last fortnight all sorts of people, including many she didn't even know, had approached her in the street and congratulated her on having given birth to such a fine footballing son!

'You must be very proud,' they said.

'Oh, yes, I am,' Sheila assured them, wishing Cal were home. Cal would have understood, offered encouragement, spurred Dominic on, instead of ignoring him as she had done – not that he needed much encouragement, the swollen-headed little bugger. He'd been unbearable for weeks.

The other finalists were Wilson Carlyon, a private school from Ormskirk. Their red and white kits were brand new. They fitted well, having obviously been bought in different sizes for each individual player, and had the position number sewn on the back. St Joan of Arc's kits were all the same size and fitted where they touched, if they fitted at all. A piece of paper was attached to each lad's back with several safety pins indicating the position he was to play.

'I wish I'd known, Sheil,' Brenda said when the teams ran onto the pitch. 'I would have sewn on proper numbers for them. Why do they need numbers, anyroad?'

'I dunno,' replied Sheila. 'Perhaps it's in case one of 'em gets lost.'

Wilson Carlyon were slightly older, slightly bigger and better nourished than the opposition. They were also very good. When the whistle blew for kick-off, they stormed as one man into the other half and scored a goal in the first minute.

Dominic Reilly's brain clicked into action. He felt annoyed that he'd been taken so much by surprise. He'd already managed to identify their best player, a knobbly lad on the left wing, a good head taller than himself, with wavy hair like a girl's. From then on, he stayed glued to his side. The trouble was, the knobbly lad had recognised Dominic as his equal and stayed glued to him. Dominic could get nowhere near the other goal with the ball. The play was lively, but neither team had much opportunity to score.

Just before half-time, Dominic saw an opening. Their side were taking a corner at the Wilson Carlyon end. Dominic rubbed his eyes, pretending to be temporarily distracted, and the knobbly lad relaxed. The ball came towards them and Dominic leapt forward and caught it between his feet. He dribbled it skilfully in and out of the players surrounding the goal, and suddenly, there he was, just him and the goalie facing each other. He drew back his foot, ready to thud the ball in low, when suddenly he felt his other foot being kicked from under him and he landed face down in the mud.

'FOUL!' screamed the crowd.

'Foul!' screamed Jimmy Quigley from the touchline.

Sister Gabriel did a maniacal Irish jig beside him. 'Foul!' she screeched.

But the referee had been looking the other way, and blew the whistle for half-time.

'Never mind, boy, you did your best,' Sister Gabriel said sympathetically when they were in the changing room. She was cleaning Dominic's grazed and bruised ankle with cotton wool.

'No he didn't, none of 'em did.' Jimmy Quigley regarded the eleven boys with utter contempt. 'You were dead lousy, all of you, Dominic in particular. You deserve to be one down. You deserve to lose. You'll all go home with your tails between your legs if you don't do better in the second half.'

Sister Gabriel looked dismayed. 'Now, now, Mr Quigley. There's no need to speak to the boys like that.'

'Yes there is. They played like little fairies when they should have played like men. Are you actually going to let this lot beat you?' He glared at the team. Apart from Dominic, they all regarded him fearfully. 'A private school, a shower of poncy little gits who think themselves too good to go to an ordinary school like you do?'

'Please, Mr Quigley!'

'I bet most of 'em still suck from their mammies' titties.'

'*Mr Quigley!*' Sister Gabriel crossed herself.

'So,' snarled Jimmy, 'what are you going to play like in the second half?'

'Men,' the boys quavered. Dominic curled his lip and said nothing.

'Right, then. Have you had your lemonade?'

'Yes Mr Quigley.'

'Off you go, then, and I want to see some proper football in the second half.'

'Yes Mr Quigley.'

'How's your ankle?' asked Jimmy in a normal voice as Dominic ran past.

'Not so bad.'

Jimmy had never committed a foul during his brief career as a footballer, nor had one done to him, but there came a time, and now was it, when such gentlemanly and sportsmanlike behaviour had to be put aside. As the Bible said, 'Do unto others as you would have them do unto you,' or something like that. From the side of his mouth, he hissed, 'If you can give that effing left-winger a taste of his own medicine, don't hesitate.'

'I won't,' vowed Dominic.

The players assembled on the field, the crowd cheered, the whistle blew and Dominic immediately captured the ball. He heeled it gently behind to his left-back, and the Wilson Carlyon players poured onto St Joan of Arc's half of the field. The knobbly lad seemed unsure whether to chase the ball or Dominic.

'*Give us it back!*' Dominic yelled.

The half-back was running around in circles with the ball. He looked only too relieved to be rid of it, and it landed with a thump at Dominic's feet. Apart from the goalkeeper, there were just two defenders left in the opposition's half. Dominic passed them easily. He knew, he just *knew* he was going to score. It was inevitable, it was an utter certainty. The goalie faced him for a second time, hopping nervously from one foot to the other. He dodged to the left when it looked as if the ball was coming that way. Dominic slammed the ball low into the right side of the net.

One all.

From then on, the knobbly lad never let Dominic get more than a couple of feet away. He was always there, nudging him, poking him, pushing him, knocking him and stamping on his feet. He even managed a few sly kicks on the already damaged ankle. 'He's not covering me,' thought Dominic in a rage, 'he's battering me. He's worse than a bloody German.'

The second half took on the pattern of the first, with neither team able to get close to the other's goal. If it was still a draw when the final whistle blew, the teams would have to play extra time.

Dominic felt as if he could play all day, but he knew most of his team would be exhausted by now. Not every mam fed their kids with plates of scouse and steamed puddings the way his did. Some kids were lucky if they saw a hot meal once a week. He had to get another goal before the whistle went. He had to win. He was determined to win, not just for himself, but for his mam and dad and Mr Quigley, for Pearl Street, St Joan of Arc's. For Bootle.

But how was he to get near that goal?

The ball was being knocked about in a desultory fashion mid-field. Dominic signalled to his inside left to let him have it. The knobbly lad immediately jabbed him aside with a vicious thrust of his elbow and went for the ball. For the first time, Dominic deliberately jabbed him back.

'Stay away from me,' he threatened, 'or I'll gouge your eyes out!'

The knobbly lad fell back, startled. Dominic scooped the ball between his feet and began to run with it towards the Wilson Carlyon goal. He had the same feeling as before. He was going to score, he knew it.

'Come on, lad,' a thousand voices yelled.

He reached the penalty area. The goalie was poised like a gorilla in the goal. Dominic had drawn back his right foot, knowing there was nothing that could stop him now, the goalie was wasting his time, when a leg appeared from nowhere and kicked the ball offside.

Dominic, his wits all about him, and remembering the goal he should have scored in the first half, flung himself over the outstretched leg, and began to roll on the ground, groaning in agony.

'FOUL!'

'Dominic! Are you hurt bad, luv?' Sheila called plaintively. 'I'd best go and see to him,' she said to Brenda.

'I wouldn't if I were you, Sheil. He'd never forgive you if you did.'

Jimmy Quigley was already kneeling beside the injured player. 'You okay, lad?' he whispered.

Dominic groaned dramatically. 'I've never felt better.'

'Just look at this ankle!' Jimmy said angrily when the referee came up. 'It's a miracle it's not broken.' Dominic gave another agonised groan.

The whistle sounded and there was a cheer from the crowd. 'What's happened?' muttered Dominic.

'We've got a penalty. Are you up to taking it?'

'Just try and stop me, Mr Quigley.'

It was obvious to all that Dominic was in great agony as he slowly and painfully got to his feet. The ball had already been placed invitingly in front of the goal. He limped towards it, remembering to grimace from time to time. The crowd fell silent, but as far as Dominic was concerned the crowd and the other players no longer existed. All that remained in the entire world were himself, the leather football at his feet, and the goalie in the net in front of him.

Dominic just knew he was going to score.

It seemed a bit anti-climactic to catch a tram back to Bootle after all the excitement. The gold-plated cup, which had been presented to Dominic, the team captain, by the Lord Mayor of Liverpool to wild cheers from the crowd, would be displayed in the window of a shop in Marsh Lane over Christmas, a symbol of Bootle's pride.

Sheila Reilly sat on the top deck of the tram watching her eldest son. He was kneeling backwards on the front seat, facing an adoring audience of schoolmates and neighbours. There was no sign of Jimmy Quigley, who was equally fond of the limelight, and Sheila noticed him a few seats behind sitting beside that horrible Theresa girl who'd been two years ahead of her at school and had the reputation of being a bully.

'Any minute now, someone's going to touch our Dominic's hem or kiss his feet and expect a miracle,' she thought to herself. She felt a little scared, as if she'd lost him, as if he no longer belonged just to her, but to all these other people. He didn't seem like *her* Dominic any more, but someone else much grander, a stranger who'd never need his mam again.

'They'll all go. One of these days, all my kids'll go. The time will come when none of 'em will want me.' She glanced at her dad who was sitting on the far side of the tram, staring out of the window as if he were miles away. She remembered when he'd been the most important person in her life, but although he was still dear to her, it was Cal and the kids who mattered most.

They got off the tram at the top of Marsh Lane and began to walk home, Sheila still full of dark thoughts. Then Dominic caught up with her and laid his head briefly against her arm. 'Me ankle isn't half hurting, Mam,' he complained.

'I'll bathe it with iodine the minute we get in,' she promised.

'Can we have chips for tea, as a special treat, like?'

'Y'can have home-made ones. I can't afford them from the chippie.'

'That's all right, Mam. I like your chips best, anyroad.'

Sheila breathed a sigh of relief. He was a little eight-year-old boy again who needed his mam – at least for now.

They went into the house the front way, Sheila first. Her heart nearly turned over when she entered the living room and a figure rose from the chair in front of the fire.

'I was beginning to think me family had all left home for good,' the figure said with a grin.

Sheila burst into tears. 'Cal! Oh, Cal!' She flung herself into his arms.

'Our dad's home!'

Calum Reilly fell back laughing in the chair as he disappeared beneath the weight of his tearful wife and six excited children.

'How long are you home for?' asked Sheila. They'd had their tea, Dominic's ankle had been bathed and bandaged, and the match described in detail.

Sheila glowed. Since the war, it was rare they had the chance to sit round the fireside together, Cal Reilly, his wife and his children. In fact, Mary, the youngest, born a week before the war started, had seen little of her dad, though you'd never think so. She was sitting on his knee, completely at home, as if it was something she did every day. Ryan was on his other knee and the other kids were draped around their dad so that in some way they could touch him. Dominic had managed to get behind the easy chair and was leaning on the back with his arms around Cal's neck.

'I'll be home till the thirtieth,' Cal replied. 'I'm changing ships.'

Niall did a quick calculation. 'That's ten whole days, Dad!'

'Ten whole days!' Sheila thought she could quite easily burst with happiness. It was the longest he'd been home in years.

'You'll be here on Christmas morning when we open our presents,' Siobhan sang happily.

'I certainly will, luv.'

At eight o'clock, with some difficulty, the children were persuaded to bed. Calum had a shave, changed out of his uniform and went along to the King's Arms for a quick pint – everyone would have been hurt if he hadn't turned up to say hello after so many months at sea. The neighbours had tactfully stayed away that night, but Sheila knew that tomorrow the deluge would begin and the world and his wife would be popping in to see Calum Reilly.

She put the iron on the stove to press her one and only nightdress. She used to have a best one, kept specially for when Cal came home, but it had been lost when number 21 was bombed.

'Still, it won't be on for long,' she thought. Her stomach gave a pleasant little lurch when she thought about making love with Cal. She felt just as thrilled as she'd done on their honeymoon ten years ago. That was a good thing about being married to a Merchant Navy man – perhaps the only good thing. It meant life was a whole series of honeymoons.

She finished the ironing, folded the nightdress neatly and placed it on her pillow upstairs. The children were still wide awake. She could hear them talking to each other, the boys in the rear bedroom, the girls all squeezed together in the double bed which took up the entire boxroom.

'Be quiet the lotta'yis,' she called.

They stopped talking for a few seconds, but by the time she was halfway down the stairs they'd started again. Now, if Cal were to say the same thing, they'd have stopped dead and not spoken another word, yet they knew he'd never lay a hand on them. He never had. There was just something about Calum Reilly that made everyone want to please him; a sort of quiet dignity that commanded respect despite the fact that he looked so youthful, almost boyish. He'd scarcely changed since they were first married.

Sheila returned upstairs to the front bedroom where she regarded her reflection worriedly in the wardrobe mirror. No-one would guess she was two months younger than Cal. She'd put on weight and her figure, what was left of it, sagged pathetically. She drew her stomach in and tried to hold it, but it burst out again of its own accord.

'I need a new brassiere. Our Eileen asked what I wanted for Christmas. I'll tell her I want a brassiere. And I'll eat less bread and less taters – as soon as Christmas's over, that is.'

Cal was coming in through the backyard when she went down again. She caught her breath. He wasn't exactly handsome, Cal, but as far as Sheila was concerned, his calm clean-cut features had a beauty and an integrity all of their own. He'd had his hair cut before leaving ship and it was clipped close to his neck. She noticed there were little arches of white skin where it had been shaved neatly around his ears. Somehow, it made him appear even younger and very vulnerable. She'd noticed the same thing with the boys after a haircut, as if some of their virility had been removed at the same time.

'You weren't long,' she said, taking off her pinny and smoothing down her skirt so she'd look her best for him. She patted her own hair, remembering she hadn't combed it since that morning.

'I was much too long.' It was the first opportunity they'd had to be alone. He caught her in his arms and they stood together, not speaking, for a long time. 'I've missed you, Sheil.'

'And as if I haven't missed you,' she answered shakily.

He began to touch her, but she stopped him. 'Not

here, luv. Wait till we're in bed. The kids are all wide awake. One of 'em might come down.'

'The little buggers,' he grinned. 'I'll go up and have a word with them.'

Sheila busied herself making tea. She could hear Cal's quiet voice upstairs, together with the ticking of the clock on the mantelpiece and the faint strains of music coming from the Kellys' wireless next door. This was all she'd ever wanted from life; herself, her husband and her children, all safe under the same roof.

'It's not much to ask, is it?' she murmured aloud, though she'd always accepted the fact Cal would never leave the Merchant Navy. He'd joined when he was thirteen and it was in his blood. She'd married him realising she'd be alone for most of the time, that she'd be worried for his safety, but never dreamt it would turn out to be so dangerous. Ever since the war began she'd been petrified he'd be killed. She was convinced she would die herself if anything happened to Cal.

During the Blitz, the boot had been on the other foot for a while, and it was Calum's turn to be petrified he'd lose his family. 'If we hadn't gone to Eileen's cottage that night in May, we'd be dead, all seven of us,' Sheila thought in horror for the umpteenth time.

'We'll have to keep an eye on our Dominic,' Cal said when he returned. 'He's growing far too big for his boots.'

'We?' Sheila raised her eyebrows as she handed him a cup of tea.

'You, then. It's our Niall I'm worried about. He's a bright little chap and I don't want him growing up in the shadow of his big brother.'

'Perhaps you should have a few words with Dominic before . . .' Sheila paused. She'd nearly said, 'before you go back,' but she didn't even want to *think* about him going back, let alone mention it, not when they had ten blissful days ahead. She intended to enjoy every single minute. 'Oh, I wish you were home more often, Cal,' she burst out. 'I mean, when the hell's this war going to be over? Nothing seems to be happening . . .'

'Nothing's happening!' Cal's voice was mild, but Sheila could tell he was annoyed and wished she'd kept her big mouth shut. 'Nothing's happening! Don't you listen to the wireless or read the paper, Sheil? Don't you know about Pearl Harbor? There were more than two thousand American seamen killed. Two weeks ago, America entered the war.'

'I know that, Cal, but what difference will it make? They'll only be fighting the Japanese.'

'I think you'll find it'll make quite a bit of difference, luv.' He smiled tolerantly, as if she were a child. 'And that's not all that's been happening – or not happening, as you seem to think. The *Barham* was torpedoed only recently, and over six hundred crew were lost. The *Prince of Wales* has gone, as well as the *Repulse*. The Japs are attacking in the Philippines, Hong Kong may well fall soon. All of a sudden, we're at war with Hungary, Romania and Finland . . .'

'Finland! I thought we were on the same side?'

'We were – once.'

Calum recalled, yet again, the incident which had occurred only hours before the Japanese attack on Pearl Harbor, although he hadn't known that then. There'd been a full moon that night and the seas were friendly, flat and glistening like the smoothest of silk. He was on the night watch and several ships in the convoy were clearly visible, including one of their naval escorts. The dark vessels sped silently through the water spurting silver froth in their wake. He used to love the midnight watch, just him, the helmsman, the silence and the sea, but no more. These were the hours when danger most threatened. The scene might look peaceful, but beneath the friendliest of seas German U-boats lurked, like sharks in search of prey.

Less than half a mile ahead of the *Chrysalis*, slightly to port, sailed the *Magnolia*, a freighter with a mainly Canadian crew. Cal had become friendly with a few of the men last time they docked in Malta. One had six children about the same ages as his own. He trained his binoculars on the ship, but there was no sign of life, which was only to be expected. Cal's hands were hot and sweaty inside his thick woollen gloves. He felt nervous, on edge. In fact, he felt terrified. He tried to think about Sheila and the kids. When the war was over he'd get a shore job. He was no longer in love with the sea.

Apart from the monotonous hiss of the waters breaking as the ship thrust through the gentle waves, there was not another sound to be heard. Jocko Dougall, the helmsman, was a taciturn man who scarcely spoke a word once he got behind the wheel. Jocko preferred his pipe to human company. He was puffing away, his dark silhouette wreathed in clouds of smoke. Cal wished he was more communicative. He would have rather liked someone to talk to just now.

Suddenly, without warning, the *Magnolia* erupted in front of them. It exploded like a firework, showering sparks and flames. Cal quickly went outside. He could hear the crackle of burning and the sizzle of red-hot metal as parts fell back in the water. He could hear men shouting and screaming for help.

'Oh, Jesus Christ!' he groaned aloud. He returned to the bridge. 'Jocko?' he whispered hoarsely.

Jocko shook his head slightly. 'No, mate. Y'know what the orders are.'

The orders were not to stop for any reason, no matter what emergency might arise or tragedy occur. The *Chrysalis* forged ahead at ten knots. Some of the men down below must have heard the explosion and had come up on deck. By now fifty or more stricken seamen could be seen struggling in the water, several directly in their path. Cal watched helplessly as they seemed to bounce on the bow-wave of the *Chrysalis* before being sucked towards the propellers at the stern.

The ship sailed onwards. Still watching, Cal saw the bodies in the water gradually disappear from sight. He noticed a lifeboat emerging from behind the burning wreckage of the *Magnolia*. It must have been thrown off, apparently undamaged. He looked through his binoculars. 'Please, God,' he prayed. 'Please God let there be someone on it.' To his relief, there were at least a dozen men on board. They were searching the water for mates who might still be alive.

Soon, there was nothing left to see. The convoy sailed onwards, every ship at the same speed. The sky began to lighten in the east and the smooth waters below were tinged with gold, heralding the rising of the sun. It was going to be a lovely day.

'What are you thinking about, luv?' asked Sheila.

'Nothing,' smiled Cal. How could he tell her, when he knew she was already worried sick? But it dismayed him when she said there was 'nothing happening'. It had been the same in the pub, where all the talk was of the football match that afternoon, as if they'd grown so used to their country being at war, it was so much part of their everyday existence, they no longer took any notice of what was going on elsewhere unless tragedy hit their own particular family.

Cal held out his hand to his wife, thinking how remarkable it was that she hadn't changed a jot in ten years. She was still his pretty Sheila, the only girl he'd ever loved, the only girl he'd ever wanted – and he wanted her right now more than he'd ever done before.

'It sounds as if the kids have dropped off. Come on, luv. Let's dampen down the fire and go to bed.'

'I suppose,' said Jack Doyle, 'folks are mainly concerned with their own particular struggle. The fighting's in the background, yet they never forget it's there. They're grateful, Cal. They couldn't possibly be more grateful for what you and your like are doing.' He lit one of the cigarettes which Calum had brought home from America. Cal wished he'd given him only half the hundred pack and kept the other half till Christmas. At the rate he was going, five ciggies during the short time Cal had been there, the whole lot would be gone by Christmas Day.

'I know,' murmured Cal. 'I was just surprised last night in the pub when everyone seemed to think a football match more important than Pearl Harbor.'

'They don't,' Jack assured him. 'The match merely took their minds off things a bit, that's all. It's like the pictures, not that I ever go meself, but there's queues a mile long of people trying to escape the war for a few hours. Same with the wireless. We all look forward to programmes like *ITMA* with Tommy Handley. I mean, I bet it's not gloom and doom on the ship all day long, is it?'

'No,' Cal conceded. 'We have a good laugh mostly.'

'There! As regards our Sheila,' Jack went on, 'she has enough on her plate trying to keep six kiddies fed and warm as well as worrying about you. She hasn't the time to bother her head with what goes on outside Pearl Street.'

'I weren't criticising,' Cal said quickly. As far as he was concerned, Sheila was darn near perfect. 'I was just surprised when she didn't seem to know what was going on.'

'It probably went in one ear and out the other,' Jack remarked comfortably. 'She was never much for thinking deep, our Sheila. Now our Eileen's a different kettle o'fish altogether. She listens to every single news bulletin on the wireless as well as reading the paper from front to back. 'Fact, I miss having our Eileen around to talk to. We used to have some good old barneys about the war.'

Cal had called on his father-in-law on the way back from Mass, leaving Sheila and the kids to go on home. Jack Doyle was someone he could talk to, explain his feelings to and get a straight answer. He felt better for the talk, but there were still things he wanted to get straight.

'I can't get the picture of those men out of me mind,' he said in a low voice. 'I keep thinking of them struggling in the water and the ship going right through them as if they didn't exist, yet they were our own men. They were on our side.' It made human life seem worthless.

'I know, lad. I witnessed sights in the Great War, sights I'll never forget.'

'Never?'

Jack shook his head. 'Never,' he said emphatically. 'The picture fades, you stop thinking about it so much, but it's always there, ready to be dredged up if something reminds you.'

'It's a terrible world, Jack.'

'It's only terrible at the moment, lad. That's what this is all about, isn't it? That's the reason for all the loss of life, the sacrifices, the rationing – to make it a better world in the future.'

'You're right, Jack.' His father-in-law always seemed very wise. Cal couldn't imagine having a problem that Jack couldn't solve. 'This is the first time I've come back,' he said, 'when I haven't felt at home straight away. Everywhere looks a bit disjointed and I still haven't got me land legs. I felt as if I was rolling all over the place on me way to Mass.'

'You'll feel better in a couple of days,' Jack assured him. 'Now, how about a pint before we have our dinner?'

'I wouldn't say no, but I'd better tell Sheila first, else she'll be worried where I am.'

'I'll just get me best coat, seeing as how it's Sunday.' Jack disappeared upstairs.

Cal stood up in readiness to leave. His legs were a trifle unsteady, so he stamped his feet until they felt slightly better. For the first time, he noticed the familiar shabby Christmas tree on the wireless. The small tree was home-made, the branches wound with green crepe paper, fringed at the edge. It was decorated with straggly woollen pompoms and cardboard stars and moons which had been covered in silver paper. The knitted fairy on the topmost branch wore a dress made from a scrap of lace curtain and held a matchstick for a wand.

'I suppose you think it's daft, a man on his own having a Christmas tree,' Jack said from the doorway, 'but Mollie made that the first Christmas we were married. I could never bring meself to throw it away. Anyroad, the girls'd kill me if I did.'

'I don't think it's daft, not a bit. I remember the tree meself from when I first started courting Sheila.' The room was full of things Mollie had made; patchwork cushion covers, lacy crocheted runners, a rag rug. There was a photo of Jack and Mollie's wedding on the sideboard, the smiling bride the absolute image of Sheila.

'The little 'uns used to get dead excited each Christmas when Mollie brought the tree down. The girls used to fuss over that little fairy, rearranging its frock. The place seems very quiet now compared to then.' There'd been no-one around when the tree was brought down this year, not even Sean to comment it was about time his dad got a new one. 'Sometimes,' Jack said in a strange, tight voice, 'things change so much you can't bear it.'

Cal glanced sharply at his father-in-law. It wasn't like Jack to sound depressed. He always appeared to be completely in control of his life, an indestructible rock able to take everything thrown at it. He recalled it was only two weeks since Sean, his only son, had got married and returned to the RAF – and Eileen was living in Melling. There was just Sheila left close at hand. Not only that, both his sons-in-law were involved in dangerous occupations and could be killed any minute.

Jack must have noticed Cal's worried glance. He said, 'Don't take any notice of me, lad. It's just that I always particularly miss Mollie when it's Christmas.'

As the two men made their way towards the King's Arms, Jack Doyle knew he had just told a terrible lie. It wasn't missing Mollie that so disturbed him, it was having Jess. He couldn't keep away from her. Since the day of Sean's wedding, he'd called in every night on his way home from the pub. Lying was so alien to Jack, he could feel himself trembling, but the woman had jolted his brain, made him think of what life could be like, when he'd been quite content with the way it already was. When he brought the Christmas tree down, it wasn't Sheila and Eileen he thought about as he attached the fairy to the top, but Penny, imagining her chubby little hands playing with the lacy frock. If he wanted, he could start all over again. It mightn't even be too late for Jess to have another baby.

The trouble was, it spoilt the pattern he had ordained for himself. He wished he could talk about it to someone, the way Cal had just confided in him, but that seemed weak, almost degrading. A man should be capable of sorting out his own destiny when provided with a choice. Anyroad, he'd feel embarrassed.

Perhaps that was it! It was nothing to do with patterns and that sort of rubbish. It was all to do with embarrassment. Jack had done nothing deliberately to foster the image people had of him, but he was vain enough to realise he was looked up to as a man of character, a strong man, a man who spoke his mind without fear or favour. Maybe he was worried what folks would think if he took up with Jessica Fleming in public.

'Oh, bloody hell!' he groaned aloud.

'What's the matter, Jack?' Cal asked, concerned.

'I've got a stone in me shoe, just a minute.' As he removed an imaginary stone, Jack thought to himself, 'another lie,' and wished Jess was somewhere on the other side of the world.

Chapter 10

After the recent sinking of so many ships, the Royal Naval Hospital in Seaforth was crammed to capacity during November and December. More beds had to be brought up from the basement storeroom, and where there had been twenty patients to a ward, there were now twenty-six. As Christmas approached, however, the staff worked like Trojans to ensure every man fit enough would be home for the holiday, even if it meant some might have to return at a later date to have their splints, plaster casts and dressings removed or changed.

Ambulances came and went, private cars arrived to whisk away beloved sons and husbands so they could spend Christmas with their families. Gradually, the wards began to thin out. Nurses scratched their heads over railway timetables and tried to work out if they could get to and from home during the few days they had off. On the Monday beforehand, Staff Nurse Bellamy told the auxiliaries that only two of them would be required on Christmas and Boxing Day, and to sort it out between themselves.

'Shall we draw straws?' suggested Harriet when they stopped for their tea break. 'The two who pick the long straws have Christmas Day off.'

'That seems the fairest,' Lucy agreed. 'I hope I get a long one. Me dad'll do his nut if he's got to wait for his dinner till after four o'clock.' They'd been on the morning shift again during December.

Clara Watkins watched closely, as if worried Harriet

might cheat as she tore a piece of paper into four strips. She shortened two, and tucked them all inside her palm leaving four ends the same length showing.

'You first, Clara.'

'I might have known I'd get a short one,' Clara said bitterly after she'd drawn. 'The thing is, we were going round to me in-laws for the day.'

'You can still go. It'll just have to be later than planned,' Harriet said blithely. 'Who's next?'

Both Kitty and Lucy drew long straws.

'That means it's just you and me, Clara.' Harriet looked quite content. 'I don't mind in the least,' she said. 'I love hospital Christmases. This year, there's going to be carol singers in the morning and a comedian from the Empire to entertain the men in the afternoon.'

'That's pathetic, that is,' Clara Watkins sneered. She was clearly still smarting after drawing a short straw. 'Most people prefer to be with their family on Christmas Day, not spend it with a crowd of strangers.'

'You're a cruel bitch, Watkins,' Lucy spat. 'Harriet can't help not having a family.'

'Shush, Lucy.' Harriet patted Lucy's hand affectionately, though she looked shaken. 'I can fight my own battles, though in this case, the enemy isn't worth fighting.'

'What's that supposed to mean?' Clara demanded belligerently.

'Isn't it time we started work?' Kitty was anxious to get away in case a full-scale row broke out. Lucy was forever threatening that one day she mightn't be able to help herself and could well tear Watkins' hair out. 'The MO will have done his rounds by now.'

'I'll be along in a minute,' Clara Watkins said as the three other women prepared to leave. 'As soon as I've finished this ciggie.'

'I've got Christmas Day off, Dad,' Kitty said delightedly

when she got home. 'We can have our dinner at one o'clock, then listen to the King in the afternoon the way we always do. I've ordered a chicken from the butcher's, and Sheila Reilly's given us some lovely Brussels sprouts from their Eileen's garden.' She'd already made a cake and a Christmas pudding, though both were sadly short of dried fruit. Yesterday, she'd unearthed the decorations and the living room had paper chains hanging from each corner, though the imitation tree on the sideboard was beginning to look the worse for wear.

'Actually, kiddo,' Jimmy said casually, 'I've already made arrangements to have me dinner elsewhere.'

Kitty looked at him in astonishment. He was standing in front of the mirror over the fireplace, rubbing brilliantine into his hair. He brushed it flat, took a step backwards and regarded his reflection with approval. 'Where's the clothes brush?' he enquired, as if unaware he had just dropped a bombshell.

'Elsewhere?' Kitty couldn't believe her ears.

'That's right, with a friend. D'you know where the clothes brush is?' He sounded a touch impatient.

'In the left-hand drawer of the sideboard. What do you mean a friend? Which friend?'

He looked vague. 'It's someone you've never met.'

'You mean you're leaving me all on me own on Christmas Day?' She still couldn't believe it.

'I thought you'd be working, didn't I?' He leaned forward and examined his teeth in the mirror.

'Seeing as how I'm not working after all, can't you tell this friend your daughter will be home and you've got to have dinner with her?'

Jimmy turned, eyebrows raised. '*Got* to?'

Kitty felt herself grow cold. She thought of the numerous times over the last ten years when she'd been asked to places and refused because she'd felt obliged to stay in. She hadn't gone to work, she hadn't gone to

206

dances, to weddings, to the pictures. You never know, she might even have been married if it wasn't for her dad. Yet the minute he was better, he didn't give a damn about her. She sat down, feeling suddenly scared. She'd always been there for him, had always put him first, and assumed the feeling was reciprocated. Instead, he was putting this mysterious 'friend' first. It didn't bother him that Kitty would be all alone for the first time in her life on Christmas Day.

It was only then that Jimmy noticed his daughter's white face. He felt, very slightly, guilty. 'Someone's bound to ask you to have dinner with them as soon as they realise you'll be by yourself,' he assured her.

As if I'd tell them, thought Kitty. I'd look a proper fool if folks found out. She visualised their pity, their knowing looks. 'That poor girl, stuck by her dad she did for all those years, yet we always knew he was having her on.'

'I'll be all right, Dad,' she told him gaily. There was no way she was going to sound sorry for herself as he used to do with her. 'We can have the chicken for tea, instead. It means you'll have two Christmas dinners.'

'I'm not sure if I'll be back for tea, luv. I might stay out the whole day.'

So, even if she'd been working, the house would have been empty when she got home.

Jimmy did a little pirouette. 'Well, I'll be off now.'

'You're going out already?' Kitty said weakly. 'It's only five o'clock. The King's Arms won't be open yet.'

'I thought I might go to the pictures for a change. Are you seeing your sailor tonight?'

'No, it's Monday, isn't it?' She hadn't liked to leave her dad by himself more than one night a week.

'I just thought, being Christmas week like . . .' Jimmy shrugged and grinned. 'I was wondering if it was getting serious. After all, you've seen him three Saturdays in a row.'

'It's not the least bit serious, Dad. Anyroad, he's going back to Plymouth in the New Year.' Stan Taylor was a pay clerk in the Navy who'd been temporarily transferred to Seaforth. He'd asked Kitty out purely for company and spent the entire time telling her how much he missed his fiancée who worked in London.

'Tara then, kiddo.' Jimmy preened himself for one last time.

'Tara, Dad.'

Jimmy went out whistling, leaving his daughter feeling totally betrayed.

Next day was Christmas Eve, and the hospital buzzed with excitement. The nurses rushed around, bright-eyed, even the ones who weren't going home. There were all sorts of parties taking place tomorrow. After work, Harriet was going to the staff bar, nicknamed the Mortuary Arms because of its situation, then to the nurses' home for tea, followed by a party in the evening.

The patients on the first floor had been squeezed into a single ward which was decorated with branches of holly from the trees outside. One of the men had obtained a sprig of privet which he proclaimed to be 'wartime mistletoe', and Kitty found herself kissed again and again as she did her rounds. She affected to ignore the bottles of spirits which were being surreptitiously passed from bed to bed.

Kitty was aware of the excitement, but she felt excluded. She still hadn't got over the shock of being deserted on Christmas Day by the one person in the world she thought she could rely on.

'I'm all on me own now,' she kept reminding herself. She wondered if Stan Taylor might welcome being asked to Christmas dinner, but when she could spare a minute to go down to the office on the ground floor, the big room, normally a hive of activity, was almost empty.

'Stan managed to get a forty-eight-hour pass,' she was told. 'He's gone to London to see his girlfriend.'

If it had been Lucy on duty the next day Kitty would have offered to swop. 'Then there'd be two old maids together, me and Harriet,' she thought bitterly. But there was no way she'd swop with Clara Watkins after that business with Martin McCabe's ring. Anyroad, she'd want to know why Kitty was suddenly free and when she explained, Clara might declare her too to be 'pathetic'.

Later, when she went round with the trolley to collect the afternoon tea dishes, she wished everyone a Merry Christmas from the door.

'Does that mean you won't be in tomorrow, Kitty, luv?' a chorus of voices demanded in dismay.

'I'm afraid you'll just have to manage without me,' she told them with a forced smile. Her head had begun to ache in sympathy with her misery and between her eyes throbbed painfully.

'Excuse me, miss?' one of the men called.

'Yes, luv?'

Glyn Thomas had only arrived at the hospital the day before. His arms and chest had been badly scalded in a boiler-room accident when his ship was docked in Liverpool. He was older than the average patient, thirty-eight, Lucy had established, declaring herself to be thoroughly smitten by his captivating, all-embracing charm, a view already shared by half a dozen other nurses. A typical Welshman in appearance, he was small-featured, with dark wavy hair, thick dark eyebrows and roguish eyes which sparkled like black diamonds.

'Are there any books around?' he asked Kitty.

'I'll try and find you a few novels before I go,' she promised.

He shook his head, which must have hurt his chest because he winced painfully, though the wince was

209

quickly followed by a brief, sweet smile. 'Not novels; political books, biographies, that sort of thing.'

'I'm sorry, luv. There's none of those sort of books.'

'Never mind, it's just that I miss reading.'

Kitty remembered Jack Doyle had a whole shelf of books, all of which were political. 'I know someone who'll lend you some. I'll bring them in on Boxing Day.'

'Pity it won't be tomorrow,' he said, eyes twinkling mischievously, 'and it's nothing to do with the books.'

Used as she was to compliments by now, for some reason Kitty flushed bright pink.

As she wheeled the trolley back to the kitchen, she thought, 'I'm cutting off me nose to spite me face by not offering to swop with Clara. I'll be dead lonely tomorrow stuck at home by meself. I'd be far happier here at the hospital.'

There was no sign of Clara in the kitchen, and by the time Kitty had washed and dried the dishes and put them away and been wished a Merry Christmas by a score of nurses and SBAs, it was a quarter to four before she was able to set out in search of her.

She found Harriet alone in the empty ward, making up the beds with fresh linen. 'She's gone,' she said when Kitty asked if she knew the whereabouts of Clara. 'She had a bit of a headache, so seeing as how Bellamy's not around, she went home early.'

'Oh, dear,' sighed Kitty. Her own headache had become worse over the last half-hour.

'I would have thought that news was a cause for rejoicing, not sighs. What did you want her for, anyway?'

'Nothing,' said Kitty.

'In that case, why did you say "oh, dear"?' smiled Harriet. 'Did you have a big expensive present for her?'

Kitty started to help with the beds. 'Not likely,' she said. She flung a sheet over a thin, rather lumpy palliasse, and tucked it firmly underneath. She shrugged two pillows into their cases, plumped them up and placed them at the head, flung on another sheet . . .

'What's the matter, Kitty?' Harriet asked gently.

'Nothing,' Kitty said again as she grabbed two blankets.

'You know, I have a strong desire to hit you with this pillow.'

Kitty wrinkled her nose disparagingly. 'It's just that I discovered me dad's going out for the day tomorrow, that's all, and I thought I'd swop duty with Clara.'

'I see,' said Harriet, and Kitty could tell from the tone of her voice that Harriet saw everything.

On Christmas morning, Jimmy Quigley spent an hour getting ready. He cleaned his teeth both before and after breakfast and spent an age having a shave and doing his hair in the living-room mirror, humming carols under his breath. He wore the maroon and yellow Paisley tie Kitty had given him that morning, and requested that she iron his best shirt again as she hadn't got all the wrinkles out of the cuffs.

'Where's the clothes brush?' he demanded, straightening his collar as he took a last pleased glance at his reflection.

'In the same place as it was last time you asked,' replied Kitty. She'd been watching the proceedings, doing her best not to look as miserable as she felt, which was difficult because her headache was worse today than yesterday. Not only that, her limbs throbbed painfully and felt too heavy to move. She was determined not to enquire again the identity of the 'friend' who'd invited him to dinner, though she was dying to know who it was. 'If he wanted me to know, he'd tell me,' she reasoned.

'I'd've thought you'd have the chicken on by now,' Jimmy said.

'I might have dinner later.' If the truth be known, Kitty didn't feel the least bit like eating. Even the thought of the smell of roasting chicken made her feel slightly nauseous.

'Does this mac look all right, luv?' her dad asked when he was ready to go. 'I haven't worn it in years.'

She resisted the urge to say he looked a bit like the gasman in the navy-blue belted raincoat, and it definitely didn't go with a brown felt hat. Instead she said, 'It looks fine.'

'I might take a look in Burtons after the holidays and buy meself an overcoat, one of those loose tweed ones. After all, now you're working, we're not short of a few bob, are we?' He readjusted his hat. 'Have you got a bag, luv?'

'A bag? What sort of bag?'

'A shopping bag, a big paper bag. Anything'll do.'

'You don't get paper bags from the shops since the war. There's a string bag hanging behind the door in the kitchen.'

'Ta.'

He went upstairs and returned with the string bag bulging. Before Kitty could see what it contained, he was gone.

She made herself a pot of tea, recklessly strong in view of the fact there wasn't much left. As soon as she'd finished the pot, she made another, took three aspirins for her headache and turned the wireless on. Later, she'd pop over and see Nan Wright. Nan was going funny lately and kept calling her 'Ruby', the name of the daughter who'd died long before Kitty was born. Still, she'd make sure Nan had something proper to eat, though Aggie Donovan or someone else had probably done so already.

The key was drawn through the letterbox and Kitty prayed it would be Eileen or Brenda, even though she hadn't wanted them to know she was by herself, but it was Vera Dodds, the postwoman, who came in, looking majestic in a black coat with an astrakhan collar, her hair set in rigid waves especially for Christmas. She looked slightly disappointed when she saw only Kitty was there.

'Your dad hasn't turned up at the ale house,' she said brightly. 'I just wondered if he was all right, like?'

'He had to go out for a while, something to do with football,' Kitty lied.

'Will he be along later?'

'We'll be having our dinner as soon as he gets back. I reckon it won't be till tonight.'

Vera looked unaccountably shy. She put a little box beneath the tree on the sideboard. 'I've brought him a little prezzie. It's only a pair of cuff links.'

'I'm sure he'll be dead pleased.' She's after him, thought Kitty in astonishment.

'Well, I'll be getting back. Are you all right, Kitty? You don't half look pale.'

'I'm just tired. We were terrible busy yesterday at the hospital.'

'I'll love you and leave you, then. Merry Christmas, luv.'

'Merry Christmas, Vera.'

Vera hadn't been gone long, and Kitty was still feeling stunned at the idea of a woman chasing her dad, when she began to shiver uncontrollably; despite the blazing fire, her entire body felt as if it were encased in ice. She went upstairs and fetched an eiderdown, legs almost too stiff to move. Halfway down again, she felt the urge to vomit, and reached the kitchen just in time to throw up her breakfast in the sink.

'Oh, God!' she groaned, as she wrapped herself in the eiderdown and curled up in the chair. 'If only me dad was here.'

The objects in the room turned hazy and began to float away. Then they became very clear again, but seemed unnaturally large. They turned hazy, grew large, turned . . .

Kitty began a bizarre journey. She swooped crazily through the hospital wards where the patients were all lying face down beneath their beds. Huge grinning faces kept looming in front of her and she punched them out of the way. The faces looked vaguely familiar, and she realised they were people she knew; Harriet, Lucy, Clara, Nurse Bellamy.

She came to every now and then, still shivering though by now she was covered in perspiration and boiling hot.

'I should be in bed,' she told herself during one of her lucid moments. She managed to struggle as far as the stairs, but her legs and her mind gave way, and she sank to her knees at the bottom where she was carried away in another nightmare. This time she was in the hospital entirely alone. There were no patients, no nurses, no doctors, just Kitty wandering through the empty building which seemed to be ticking like a bomb about to explode. Then the trees began to tap against the window as if they wanted to come in. Tap tap, tap tap . . .

Kitty woke up again, heart racing. The hallway was pitch dark and someone was knocking on the door, which meant it wasn't anyone from the street, else they would have let themselves in.

'The key,' she called weakly. 'Use the key.'

The knocking continued and eventually the letterbox flap was lifted and someone peered inside. 'The key's behind the door,' Kitty sobbed.

A few seconds later, the door opened and a dark figure stepped inside. Kitty had no idea who it was until the figure stood on her foot, uttered a yelp of alarm and shone a torch in her face.

'Kitty! Oh, what a good job I came,' cried Harriet Mansell.

*

Harriet helped her upstairs, tucked her into bed and placed a wet flannel on her forehead. She made a hot water bottle and a cup of tea and doled out three more aspirins. As soon as Kitty was half sitting, half lying against her own pillows and the two off Jimmy's bed, Harriet emptied her handbag on the counterpane, rummaged through the mess, found a thermometer, shook it, and stuck it in Kitty's mouth.

'I think I'm going to die,' groaned Kitty after a while.

Harriet removed the thermometer. 'High, but not dangerously so,' she said briskly. 'I think you'll live. You've got three-day 'flu. You'll be as fit as a fiddle by Saturday. Scores of nurses have come down with the same thing, including poor Clara Watkins. She still came in, the brave soul, despite feeling as ill as you do, though she was despatched home pretty damn quick in case the patients caught it.'

'You mean you had to manage on your own?'

'We were under-staffed all round, but everyone mucked in cheerfully and some of the walking wounded gave a hand. In fact, we all enjoyed ourselves tremendously.'

'How did you know I was ill?' Kitty asked. She was beginning to feel slightly better, not solely due to Harriet's tender ministrations, but for knowing that someone cared about her.

'I didn't. I remembered you'd be alone. I'm here to invite you to a party.'

'I'm afraid you'll have to go by yourself.'

Harriet looked shocked. 'As if I'd leave you like this! I'll stay and keep you company.'

'But . . .' began Kitty.

'There's no buts about it,' Harriet said firmly. 'Do you want to sleep or talk? I'll go downstairs and listen to the wireless if you prefer, and you can call out if you need anything.'

'I'd sooner talk, but I might well fall asleep in front of your eyes. I feel a bit dozy.'

'I shan't be offended if you do. What time will your father be home?'

'I've no idea.' Kitty felt strangely embarrassed and ashamed of having been let down so badly.

'I suppose you feel deeply hurt,' Harriet said intuitively.

'Not just hurt,' Kitty replied. 'All of a sudden, I knew I could never rely on me dad again. I was on me own from now on. It was a dead horrible feeling.'

Harriet nodded understandingly. 'I felt the same when Hugh was killed. My parents were dead by then, my brother worked in the Foreign Office and I scarcely ever saw him. It was a scary sensation, realising I was totally alone.'

'What did you do?' whispered Kitty.

'What else was there to do except get on with my life? I threw myself into my work, made friends, nearly got married on two occasions.'

'What stopped you?'

Harriet shrugged and pulled a face. 'They were good, decent men, both of them, but I would have been marrying for companionship, not love.'

'You mean you turned them down because you preferred being by yourself?' said Kitty in astonishment.

'I did,' smiled Harriet. 'I wasn't prepared to be stuck for ever with someone I didn't sincerely care for. I've enjoyed my life, Kitty. It's not a tragedy to live alone – most of the time I've been quite happy. It's other people such as Clara Watkins who poke fun and make snide remarks and tell me I'm pathetic. I could have had a husband and children if I'd wanted, but I decided I didn't, not if the husband couldn't be Hugh.'

'It's not fair,' Kitty burst out. 'Everyone feels sorry for spinsters, yet never for bachelors.'

'That's because they assume spinsters haven't been

able to catch a man, and bachelors were clever enough to escape a woman's clutches,' Harriet laughed. 'They can't visualise a woman living contentedly alone without a man's support. Spinsters are automatically deemed second-rate citizens – what an ugly word spinster is, and "old maid" is even worse.' She patted Kitty's hand. 'Whatever you do, Kitty, don't marry the first man who proposes just so you can have "Mrs" in front of your name.'

Kitty shook her head tiredly. 'I won't.'

Harriet removed the flannel from her forehead and said, 'Lie down and sleep for a while. I'll go downstairs and make myself something to drink. Is there any more tea? I used the last of the packet.'

'You'll have to borrow some from number sixteen.' Kitty slid underneath the clothes.

'I might well do that. I'm aching for a cuppa.'

'Have some Christmas cake,' Kitty muttered just before her eyes closed.

'I'll do that, too,' said Harriet.

It was past midnight by the time Jimmy Quigley arrived home, whistling 'God Rest Ye Merry Gentlemen' and feeling extraordinarily pleased with life, to find a strange woman sitting in the living room and no sign of his daughter.

'Where's our Kitty?' he demanded. The woman was as thin as a rake and as plain as a pikestaff and he disliked her instantly.

'Kitty's very ill,' the woman said crisply. 'Very, very ill.'

'Where is she?' Jimmy, alarmed, realised he hadn't given a thought to Kitty all day.

'In bed. It was fortunate I dropped by, else the poor girl would have still been lying in the hallway.'

'In the hallway! Jaysus! I'd best go and see to her.'

As Jimmy made to go upstairs, the woman said in a

217

voice like ice, 'It's rather late for that. Anyway, there's no need. She's fast asleep and you'll only disturb her.'

'Did you fetch a doctor?' Jimmy wondered who the woman was. She had an air of authority which made him feel rather small as well as guilty for having been out enjoying himself all day. From the way she spoke, he sensed she disliked him as much as he did her.

'No.' She smiled sardonically. 'There's nothing a doctor could have done for her that I couldn't do myself. She's got a severe dose of 'flu and will need to spend the next two days in bed.' She picked up her coat. 'I'd better be getting home. I expect it will be difficult to find a taxi at this time of night.'

'There's never taxis round here, luv.' Jimmy bit his lip. The woman didn't look the sort to be called 'luv'.

'In that case, I suppose I'll just have to walk.'

'Have you got far to go?'

'Ince Blundell.'

Jimmy gasped. 'But that's miles away!'

The woman frowned. 'Yes, and now that I think about it, I'll have to take Kitty's place tomorrow, which means I'd scarcely be home before it would be time to leave.'

'You work at the hospital?'

'I'm Harriet Mansell, one of Kitty's colleagues.'

Jimmy recognised the name. She was only another bloody auxiliary like Kitty. He felt slightly less small and slightly less guilty. 'Y'can sleep in the chair, if you like?' he said magnanimously.

Harriet Mansell curled her lip. 'In the chair!'

She might be only a bloody auxiliary, but the curled lip made Jimmy Quigley squirm. 'I'd offer you me bed,' he said quickly, ''cept I don't know where Kitty keeps the clean sheets.'

'That's all right,' Harriet said just as quickly. 'I'll sleep on top of the covers.'

★

Jessica and Arthur Fleming lay side by side in bed, not touching.

'I'm glad I came,' said Arthur. 'It's been a lovely day.'

'I'm glad you enjoyed it,' said Jessica. They'd gone to Melling for their Christmas dinner, along with all the Reillys and Jack Doyle.

'Remember all those pre-dinner and after-dinner drinks parties we used to be invited to at Christmas?' Arthur mused. 'I never enjoyed a single one. It was all business, never friendship. We went to the ones we thought it wisest to be seen at.'

'I think I enjoyed them at the time,' Jessica conceded, 'but not in retrospect.' She'd enjoyed showing off her latest outfit, her newest fur, telling everyone what presents Arthur had given her – which she'd usually chosen and paid for herself.

'It was entirely different today at Eileen's,' Arthur said contentedly. 'We wanted to be there and they genuinely wanted us. You could sense the goodwill and affection. Penny almost seemed like part of the family.'

As if she'd heard her name being mentioned, Penny uttered a huge sigh and turned over in her cot beside the bed.

'I've missed Penny.' Arthur turned on his side and laid his hand on Jessica's stomach. 'And I've missed you too, Jess. I've missed you terribly.'

Jessica froze. She'd been hoping all along he'd change his mind and not come, but he'd turned up early that morning, having travelled all night, and seemed so pleased to see her that it was difficult not to be nice. Even though she'd prepared the bed in the other room, she hadn't the heart to tell him when he'd automatically assumed they would be sleeping together. As far as he was concerned, they were still man and wife. He couldn't read her mind and know that she considered the marriage was over.

'Have you, dear?' she said with as much sincerity as she could muster.

He began to stroke her breasts. Jessica caught his hand in both of hers and held it still. She knew she wasn't perfect, that she had many faults, but the idea of letting Arthur make love to her whilst she was having an affair with Jack Doyle seemed dishonourable in a crazy sort of way.

'You know, Jess,' he said quietly, 'I'm beginning to realise what a useless life I lead, messing about with fossils and old bits of tile in that museum. I'm cut off from the real world up there.'

Jessica held his hand and said nothing. She'd used virtually the same words herself when she'd explained why she wanted to leave. She prayed Arthur wasn't intent on making the same decision.

'Today,' he went on, 'the cottage seemed so charged with emotion that you could almost touch it. Sheila and Calum couldn't take their eyes off each other and the sad expression on Eileen's face made me want to weep. Even Jack Doyle seemed different, more subdued. I felt like a gatecrasher, not in person, but in spirit, as if they, and you, Jess, all belonged to a club I'm not a member of. My life, my job, both are entirely unaffected by the war.'

'But it's a job in a million, Arthur,' Jessica said inadequately. 'It's what you always wanted to do.'

'You sound as if you're worried I might give it up and want to live with you.' His voice was a mixture of amusement and resentment. He removed his hand. 'You can't even bear for me to touch you, can you?'

Jessica sighed. 'I don't know, Arthur,' she said. She couldn't bring herself to tell him bluntly, 'No.'

'Does that mean we're finished?'

'I suppose it does.'

They lay, not speaking, not touching, for a long time.

Eventually Arthur asked conversationally, 'Have you taken up with him again, Penny's father?'

'I'm not prepared to discuss it,' Jessica said flatly. She loathed hurting him. He was a good man who loved her and although he was weak, he'd never intentionally harmed anyone in his entire life.

He turned his head away. The bedroom door was open slightly and the gaslight had been left burning low on the landing because Penny was afraid of the dark. Her face was just visible in the yellow light, long lashes quivering, lips pouting. The sheer miracle of Penny hit Jess with such force that she almost gasped. Her heart hardened against Arthur. He hadn't deliberately denied her children, but due to him she'd had to wait until she was forty-three, and it was another man who was the father.

'Jess.' His voice was barely audible.

'Yes, Arthur?'

'You know, if it's another child you want, then I could accept it. I've always loved Penny as if she were my own. I would love a second just as much.' He began to cry. 'You've no idea how much I miss my family, Jess.'

'Oh, my dear!' Jessica's heart softened instantly and she took him in her arms. It had almost killed him when he discovered she'd been unfaithful, yet he loved her so much he was willing to let it happen again. She began to cry with him. 'It's no use, Arthur. It's no use.' She convinced herself he would be all right once he was back in the museum and immersed in his beloved artefacts.

They fell asleep and although Jessica didn't move away deliberately, when they woke, they had their backs to each other and there was a space between them like a barrier that would never again be breached.

Next morning, Boxing Day, they strolled up Linacre

Lane with Penny in her pushchair, so he could see for himself the garage he'd heard so much about. They were scrupulously polite to each other, like strangers who had barely met.

Jessica unlocked the workshop and showed him the bikes she had in stock. 'I've got fourteen at the moment. They'll be gone in a week. I could sell two, three times that many if I could get my hands on them.'

'What's this for?' Arthur pointed to a little Austin Seven tucked in a corner.

'An old man offered to sell it to me for fifteen pounds. I couldn't resist. You know, Arthur,' Jessica said, eyes shining, 'once the war's over it'll be years before they start producing cars again. If only I had the space to store them, I could make a fortune. People will be desperate to buy second-hand.'

Arthur shook his head in admiration. 'I might have known you'd do well, Jess. You never really needed me, did you?'

'Don't be silly, dear,' she chided. 'You need people for all sorts of different reasons, not merely financial.'

'You didn't need me for another rather important reason, either.'

'Arthur!'

Penny was clamouring to be released from her pushchair and he lifted her out. 'Don't take any notice of me, Jess. I'm just feeling rather superfluous all round at the moment.'

'I said once before, we'll always be friends. You can come and stay with me whenever you like.' Jessica genuinely meant it. Now they'd sorted their relationship out, she didn't want to cut him out of her life completely. 'Penny will always think of you as her father.'

'That's right, so she will.' He regarded Penny fondly. 'She called me dada yesterday.'

'She recognised you, that's why.' Jessica didn't mention it was what Penny called every man she met.

'I thought I heard voices!' Rita Mott came into the workshop wearing the inevitable dressing gown, a georgette scarf tied around her curlers and an equally inevitable cigarette poking out of her mouth. She eyed Arthur up and down speculatively. 'And who's this?'

Jessica introduced them. 'I've heard a lot about you,' Arthur said as they shook hands.

Rita giggled. 'Not all bad, I hope.'

'No, but not all good either, which makes you that much more interesting,' he answered with a smile.

Jessica had forgotten how charming he could be. She'd also forgotten how attractive he was in his quiet, gentle way. Eileen always claimed he looked a bit like Leslie Howard. Rita was instantly enamoured. She invited them upstairs for a glass of whisky and a turkey sandwich.

'Turkey!' exclaimed Jessica. 'Where on earth did that come from?'

Rita winked. 'Don't ask! It didn't exactly fall off the back of a lorry, but the Christmas dinner it was meant for wasn't mine.'

'That sounds very mysterious,' said Arthur.

'I'm a very mysterious woman.' Rita rolled her eyes.

'Just the sort of woman I like.'

As they went upstairs, Arthur some distance behind helping Penny, Rita whispered, 'He's so gorgeous, Jess, I could eat him. You must be mad, ditching a man like that.'

'I probably am – mad, that is.'

'This is cosy,' Arthur remarked when they entered Rita's living room which Jessica had always thought was in execrable taste, with its purple net curtains and brightly flowered chintz three-piece which clashed with the wallpaper and geometric patterned carpet which clashed with just about everything. It looked even worse now, positively drenched in Christmas decorations. She recalled how well Arthur had settled when they moved from the detached house in Calderstones to the tiny one in Pearl Street. He'd made friends with incredible ease, despite the fact he'd never mixed with working-class people before. He took folks for what they were with an almost breathtaking non-judgemental innocence – which was the reason the business had gone bust, because he was too trusting.

Jessica realised with a flash of insight that in his own way, Arthur was a better man than Jack Doyle would ever be. Yet she didn't love him, which was sad.

Rita put a record on the gramophone. She had quickly removed her curlers, combed her hair and put lipstick on, and was flirting with Arthur outrageously, and Arthur, clearly enjoying himself, was flirting back. When she went into the kitchen to fetch biscuits for Penny, he said to Jessica, 'She's fun. I really like her.'

'She's a genuinely nice person,' Jessica declared.

'But not the sort you would have liked once?'

'No, but we all change.'

'Not necessarily. You might never have changed if our lives hadn't gone a certain way.'

Rita returned and refilled their glasses before Jessica could think of an answer. She noticed with alarm the way Arthur drained his whisky in a single swallow and held the glass out for more. He used to drink too much in Calderstones when everything had got on top of him, but a glass of beer had been his limit since then.

'Well, what do you think of the garage now your Jess has taken it over?' Rita asked coquettishly.

'She's done wonders, but then I wouldn't have expected anything else She's a businesswoman to the core, is Jess.' Arthur's voice was becoming thick and unsteady. I'll make sure he doesn't have any more to drink, Jessica decided.

'We're becoming quite famous,' Rita continued. 'A chap came all the way from Blackpool for a bike the other day, though lord knows what Den, that's my husband, would say if he knew his garage had become a bike shop.'

'But we still sell petrol, Rita,' Jessica protested, 'and I never turn away anyone who wants something doing on their car. The trouble is, most of them won't let me touch it because I'm a woman.'

'Perhaps you should pretend it's Jack who's the mechanic,' Rita laughed coarsely. 'He looks as if he's got a particularly safe pair of hands. I'd trust my chassis with him any day.'

'Jack?' Arthur frowned at Jessica.

'Jack Doyle,' she explained easily. 'He usually gives me a hand on Saturday mornings.'

'You never said so before.'

'It never crossed my mind, that's why.'

'I see.' He leaned back in the chair and was quiet from then on. When Rita spoke, he responded with a brief, polite smile, as if he hadn't taken in a word she'd said. Jessica glanced at him worriedly from time to time to find him staring intently at Penny, who was playing with a set of blocks which Rita kept especially for her. Next time Jessica looked, he was staring at her instead. Their eyes met. Jessica dropped hers immediately.

He knows!

He asked Rita for the bathroom and, once there, Jessica heard him retching, but she stayed glued to her chair, too scared or possibly too embarrassed to face his misery. His wife had betrayed him with the man he admired most in the world. Rita, snapping her fingers to a Carmen Miranda record, was too engrossed to hear.

When Arthur emerged, white-faced, he said, 'I think I'll go home. I feel a touch unwell.'

'I'll come with you.' Jessica jumped to her feet.

'I'd sooner go on alone.' He picked Penny up and hugged her fiercely. 'Goodbye, sweetheart.'

'Dada!' She banged his cheeks.

'Goodbye, Rita.' He bowed courteously. 'It was nice meeting you.'

'You too, Arthur.'

The door closed. In the ensuing silence, Rita asked, 'Is there something wrong?'

Jessica nodded. 'I'd better go.'

'Was it my fault?'

'No, it's mine.'

'He's a lovely chap, Jess.'

'I know.' Jessica bundled Penny into her coat and carried her downstairs. Arthur was already out of sight by the time she set off along Linacre Lane, and when she arrived in Pearl Street, there was no sign of him or his suitcase in the house.

Jessica had almost forgotten about him when, four weeks later, she received a short letter. '*I've joined the Royal Artillery as a driver. Surprisingly, they seemed quite happy to take an old man of forty-five. I'm unsure where they'll send me, but then I scarcely care. Please never let Penny forget me. With love, Arthur.*'

Chapter 11

Calum Reilly stayed glued to the wireless for most of Boxing Day. The grim news was what he'd been expecting. Hong Kong had fallen to the Japanese the day before and 12,000 British troops, the entire garrison, had been taken prisoner.

'Nice Christmas present they got,' he muttered.

'What's that, luv?' asked Sheila.

He told her what had happened. 'And the Japs are advancing in the Philippines. Manila has just been declared an open city.'

'What does that mean?'

'It means there'll be no more fighting because the Americans have given up. It's a world war now, Sheil. It's no longer just Europe and Africa. Our lads are being driven back in Malaya. I bet you a pound to a penny that Singapore will soon go the same way as Hong Kong.'

The names meant nothing to Sheila, but she was alarmed by the glum look on Calum's face. 'We're not going to lose the war, are we, luv?'

'Christ Almighty, Sheil, I hope not.'

'You mean there's a chance?'

Cal pulled her down onto his knee. 'Of course not, luv.' He couldn't reveal to her his worst fears, but all the victories so far had been on Hitler's side. The monster merely had to glance in the direction of a country and it was his – though the Russians were still putting up a helluva fight. Even in Africa, where the Brits had wiped the floor with the Italians, as soon as the Germans arrived under the leadership of their brilliant general, Rommel, the whole British front had collapsed. Now the Japs were on the scene with an equally efficient and ruthless fighting machine, and the same thing was happening in the Far East; defeat followed by defeat. What if the unthinkable happened and Britain lost?

That's what it was, Cal told himself angrily, unthinkable. If you started to believe you might lose, then you might as well give up the ghost right now and save thousands, if not millions, of lives. They *had* to win, in order to save not just his own country, but the entire world from Fascism.

'Conquer or die,' Churchill had said, and whilst Cal had never believed a word that came out the mouth of a Conservative politician in the past, he believed that much. They'd conquer Germany or die in the attempt, because he himself would sooner be dead and his whole family along with him, than live under a Fascist dictatorship.

Sheila was saying something in his ear. 'What, luv?'

'I said, would you like to go upstairs for a while? The kids are all out and we'd soon hear if one of 'em came in.'

He grinned at her, his good humour restored. It helped to lose himself in Sheila. 'I wouldn't say no, but you're wearing me out, girl. I'll be no use for a week after I'm back on board ship.'

To his surprise, she didn't move off his knee straight away. 'Cal,' she whispered shyly, 'do you have to use one of those precaution things? I want another baby, luv, I really do.'

He shook his head firmly. 'I told you, Sheil. Once the war's over we'll think about more family.'

'But there'll be such a big gap. Our Mary's nearly two and a half, and Churchill said it won't be over until nineteen forty-three.' She kissed him beseechingly. 'I'd love a baby, Cal. I feel dead empty if I'm not expecting or I haven't got one to feed.'

He looked down at her exasperatedly. 'But you're only twenty-seven, Sheil, and we've already got six kids. We'll end up with a couple of dozen at the rate you're going.'

'A couple of dozen'll do me fine.' She stroked the back of his neck, where the hair already felt slightly longer. 'Please, Cal!'

'What about the last time when you had a miscarriage?' he asked sternly.

'The baby was growing outside me womb. The doctor said it would be a miracle if it happened a second time. But I'll go to the clinic and be examined regular, I promise.'

Perhaps it wouldn't do any harm, thought Cal. After all, the bombing seemed to have stopped, his family would be safe. And if it made his darling Sheila happy . . .

He pushed her off his knee. 'Come on, then. Let's go upstairs.'

Lucy Peterson called in to see Kitty on her way to the pictures on Saturday night. She was all dolled up in a teddy-bear jacket and a bright red dress which her dad had bought her for Christmas. 'He was in ever such a nice mood over the holiday. I think the job's doing him good. Anyroad, how are you feeling?' she asked.

'Absolutely fine,' Kitty assured her, ''cept me legs are a bit weak. I would have gone back to work today, but Harriet said she'd kill me if I didn't wait till Monday.'

'The last few days have been really the gear,' Lucy said happily. 'I never thought working in a hospital over Christmas would turn out to be so much fun. That Glyn Thomas bloke is a dead scream. He had the entire hospital singing "Men of Harlech" on Boxing Day.' She looked at Kitty slyly. 'He kept asking about you.'

'I promised to bring him some books,' Kitty explained.

'He didn't mention anything about books, but when he learnt you were ill he looked dead upset. I told him I was coming to see you and he sends his love. I reckon he's interested. Oh, and Stan Taylor came searching for you yesterday. He was in a right ould state. His fiancée's given him his marching orders and he wants to talk to you. He said only you would understand.'

'Honest?'

Lucy giggled. 'He must think you've got a sympathetic ear.'

'Actually, he was dead boring. I only went out with him because I felt sorry for him.'

'Well, you'll feel even more sorry for him now. They're the most dangerous, men you feel sorry for. You might end up marrying him on the rebound – his rebound, I mean.'

'There's not much chance of that,' Kitty said disparagingly. 'We'd spend the entire honeymoon talking about Daphne, his fiancée.'

'Can I have him?'

Kitty burst out laughing. 'What do you mean, can you have him? He's not mine to give.'

'I think he's quite good-looking in a mangy sort of way.' Lucy pursed her lips speculatively. 'What he needs is his mind taking off things. I'd look upon it as a challenge.'

'You can have him with pleasure.' Kitty clapped her hand over her mouth. 'Gosh, I'm being dead cruel. He was madly in love with Daphne.'

'She obviously wasn't madly in love back.' Lucy frowned severely at Kitty. 'You shouldn't give a toss about being cruel to men. They won't hesitate to be cruel to you if it suits them.'

With that, Lucy left. She'd scarcely been gone a

minute, when Sheila Reilly came in through the yard with a bowl of jelly and custard.

'But I'm an not invalid,' Kitty protested. 'I've completely recovered. I can make jelly and custard for meself.'

'Stop complaining and eat it,' Sheila ordered. 'It'll do your throat good.'

'There's nothing wrong with me throat.'

'I made the custard with that new household milk. Have you tried it yet?' Tins of dried skimmed milk powder had only just become available. Each family was allowed one tin per month to supplement their meagre weekly milk ration of two and a half pints.

'Yes, but it's horrible in tea.'

'It's only good for cooking.' Sheila fetched a spoon from the kitchen and watched as Kitty ate. 'What does it taste like? It's no good asking Cal and the kids, they'll eat anything.'

'Why are you asking me? Haven't you had some yourself?'

Sheila shrugged dismissively. 'I didn't really feel like any.'

'Oh, Sheil,' Kitty said in dismay. 'You've given me your share.'

'I told you, I didn't feel like any.'

'Fetch another spoon and we'll share.'

The two women sat down at the table, taking turns to have a spoonful each.

'It's all right, isn't it?' said Sheila, pleased. 'I declare household milk a great success. Y'know, this brings back memories of when we were kids and we'd try and raise a penny between us for a bag of chips.'

'Whoever had the first go always picked the biggest chip!'

'And we'd end up fighting over the crispy bits.'

When they'd finished, Sheila washed the dish ready to take home. 'By the way,' she said coming in from the back kitchen, 'who do you know in Flint Street?'

Kitty shook her head. 'No-one,' she said. 'Why?'

'It's just that your dad asked our Dominic to take a note round to number twenty-two on Boxing Day.'

'I wonder if that's where he went for his Christmas dinner? He stayed in looking after me all Boxing Day. Perhaps he'd arranged to go again. Perhaps that's where he is now!' From yesterday, since she appeared to be on the road to recovery, there'd been scarcely any sign of her dad.

'Maybe he's got a woman!' Sheila suggested with a grin.

'Never! On the other hand – promise not to breathe a word to a soul, Sheila – Vera Dodds bought him a pair of cufflinks for Christmas.'

'She didn't!' Sheila's mouth fell open in astonishment.

'She did!'

'That's odd, because according to Aggie Donovan – this is in the strictest confidence, Kitty – Vera's got something going with Dai Evans on the quiet.'

Kitty hooted with laughter. 'They're both taking a risk, aren't they? Ellis'll kill them both if she finds out.'

'Anyroad, what did your dad have to say about the cufflinks?'

'He pretended to be annoyed, but I could tell he was secretly chuffed. He said she's always making eyes at him in the King's Arms.'

'It's hard to imagine people their age fancying each other, particularly if one of 'em's your dad. I mean,' Sheila said emphatically, 'there's no way *our* dad would become involved with a woman. I know we make jokes about Kate Thomas being his girlfriend, but that's merely to get up his nose. In actual fact, they're just good mates. Oh, well,' she sighed, 'I'd best be on me way, I don't like leaving Cal for long. He's going back the day after tomorrer.' She could almost hear the minutes ticking away before he left her. 'Is your doctor friend coming to see you today?'

'Who do you mean?' Kitty frowned.

'The doctor who borrowed tea off us on Christmas night.'

'Harriet! She's not a doctor, she's an auxiliary, same as me.'

'She may be an auxiliary now, Kit, but she used to be a doctor. Remember when I had that miscarriage? Oh, it must be eighteen months ago now. After the man doctor had seen to me, dead impatient he was, she came in and told me everything was going to be all right.'

'Are you sure, Sheila?' Kitty pressed.

'Dead sure. I'll always remember her. She was ever so kind.'

It explained a lot of things which had puzzled Kitty. Harriet's knowledge of medicine and hospital practice had always seemed surprising for someone who'd only started as an auxiliary a few months before. 'I love hospital Christmases,' she'd said only the other day – and she'd accidentally let slip she'd been to university. There was also the thermometer in her handbag which Kitty had felt too ill to remark on at the time. Harriet had always been extremely unforthcoming about her past.

Kitty resolved the secret would remain safe with her. She'd never reveal it to another soul, not even Lucy, though it all seemed very mysterious. Why should a trained doctor take a job as an auxiliary? No wonder Harriet regarded herself as a serf.

'Have we got much food in, kiddo?' Jimmy asked the following morning as they were on their way home from Mass. The sky was heavy with grey clouds which threatened snow, and a freezing wind howled in from the River Mersey.

'A little bit of boiled ham and some leftover chicken

which I was going to do with 'taters for our dinner,' Kitty told him. 'Why, are you hungry?'

'Is that all? Is there nothing in the store cupboard?'

'Since when have we had a store cupboard, Dad? There was never enough money to have more than a couple of tins put away, and no-one has a store cupboard since the war.'

He looked dismayed. 'Y'mean, we've got nothing 'cept a bit of boiled ham and leftover chicken?'

'There's a tin of beans for our tea and mince for tomorrer. Oh, and there's plenty of Christmas cake and I've still got the Christmas pudding.' Kitty wondered why on earth he was showing a sudden interest in the contents of the larder.

'It's just that I've invited someone for tea.'

'Oh, Dad, why on earth didn't you tell me before?' she cried. 'I might have been able to get something special yesterday. It's too late now.'

'Never mind, you can probably knock up a meal for five out of that lot,' he said, 'though forget about the mince.'

'Five!' Kitty said weakly.

'Morning, Mr Quigley.' Dominic and Niall Reilly pushed through them kicking a tin can to each other, their cheeks flushed with cold.

'Morning, lads,' Jimmy replied jovially. As soon as the boys were out of earshot, he said, 'Scallies! You'd think Cal Reilly'd keep his kids in hand while he was home. It's a disgrace the way that lot behave.'

Kitty immediately leapt to the defence of her friend's family. 'They're just high spirited, that's all. Anyroad, I thought you really liked Dominic.'

'He's a good footy player, that's all. He needs disciplining. A good hiding wouldn't do him any harm at all,' Jimmy said harshly.

'You never hit me when I was little.'

'You behaved yourself, that's why. You'd have got

the back of me hand if you'd carried on like the Reillys.'

'Dad!' She decided she far preferred him ill. Lately, she'd been noticing quite a few aspects of his personality which she found unpleasant.

When they reached Pearl Street, he said, 'Actually, kiddo, I don't think I'll come back with you. I'll be home about five o'clock for me tea. Don't forget, there'll be five of us including you.'

Kitty made herself a jam butty for her dinner so as not to use any of the more precious food, and afterwards set the table in the living room with special care, using the best white cloth which hadn't seen the light of day since the previous Christmas. It was too cold to use the parlour and it seemed a waste of coal to light a separate fire.

She spread the ham and chicken onto five plates, putting the inferior meat on her own, cut several rounds of bread and margarine, peeled the potatoes and put them on a low light to boil, along with the Christmas pudding. There was a packet with just two paper doilies left in the sideboard cupboard, and she cut the cake into dainty little fingers and arranged them in a pattern on the plate.

'Custard for the pudding! I'll have to make it out of that dried milk. Oh, I do hope I don't burn it!' She discovered there was enough jam left to make a tart, though it meant using the last of the flour and she'd intended making a pie for tomorrow with the mince.

As she worked, she wondered who on earth were the three people who'd been invited to tea? Three people seemed a strange number to ask. She could understand one, but three!

Once the table was set, it looked quite sumptuous. Kitty trailed two pieces of tinsel in and out of the plates in what she hoped was an artistic fashion.

She was a bag of nerves when five o'clock approached. Promptly on the hour, the front door opened and Jimmy entered. Kitty stood in the middle of the living room smiling a welcome, and tried to contain her astonishment when her dad was followed by a young woman about the same age as herself and two young children.

'Kitty, luv. This is Theresa Beamish and her lads, Georgie and Billy. Theresa, pet, meet me daughter, Kitty.'

Theresa Beamish didn't smile when they were introduced. 'How do you do?' she said sourly. She was verging on ugly, with a great white face and cold grey eyes. Her gaberdine mac was buttoned severely up to the neck and tightly belted.

'Shall I take your coat, pet?' Jimmy asked in an unctuous voice which Kitty had never heard before.

Theresa removed the mac, to reveal a plain navy-blue jumper and pleated skirt. Kitty noticed her dad's eyes flicker to her massive bosom.

He fancies her!

She wasn't sure if the realisation made her want to laugh or cry. 'Would you like to sit down?' she said.

'This looks nice, kiddo.' Jimmy rubbed his hands together approvingly. 'Come on, lads, take a seat.'

Neither child had spoken so far. They were solid, well-built boys, neatly dressed, with broad white faces like their mother, and appeared more sullen than shy, keeping their eyes fixed firmly on the floor. Once seated, they waited to be told to eat, hands folded obediently on their laps. When Theresa nodded they began to devour their food slowly and methodically until every bit had gone.

'Now have some bread and margarine,' she commanded and they obediently took a slice each. She rubbed at a tiny stain on the cloth which Kitty hadn't managed to get off in the wash.

When they reached the pudding stage, Kitty apologised for the lack of fruit. 'I'm afraid there's not much in the cake, either.'

'Well, it's hard to get, isn't it?' said Theresa. She seemed to have found something on her spoon and was scraping it with her nail.

Jimmy finished his pudding and put his elbows on the table. 'Is there a cup of tea, luv,' he asked Kitty, 'to have with the cake?'

'The kettle's already boiled. I won't be a minute making it.'

Theresa leaned across the table, lightly tapped one of Jimmy's elbows and gave him a sullen nod. He hastily removed them. 'Sorry, pet.'

Pet! Wait till I tell Sheila, thought Kitty in the kitchen as she hastily examined the cups to make sure they were clean.

When the meal was finished, to Kitty's surprise, Jimmy stood and tapped his cup with his spoon. 'I've got an announcement to make,' he said importantly.

Kitty felt her spirits wilt. 'Oh, no!' she thought. She had a horrible feeling what the announcement was going to be.

Jimmy coughed. 'I've asked Theresa here to marry me and she's agreed. We're getting wed at the end of February after a short engagement.' He clapped Kitty on the shoulder. 'So, kiddo, you'll soon have a stepmother.'

Georgie and Billy glanced at each other surreptitiously and looked disgusted. Theresa's sour expression didn't change.

'Congratulations,' Kitty said with a warmth she didn't feel. She kissed her dad on the cheek and shook hands with Theresa, convinced he was making a terrible mistake. Why on earth didn't he take up with Vera Dodds, who was more his age and far more fun and whom she'd much prefer to have as a stepmother? Still, maybe Theresa would turn out to be less surly and more friendly once she got to know her.

'Now that's over, pet, I'll show you round the house,' Jimmy said.

'You mean you'll be living here?' Kitty tried to keep her voice steady.

'Of course, where else would we live? This is my house, isn't it?'

Kitty swallowed. 'I just thought you might move in with Theresa, that's all.'

'We're living with me mam and dad and it's cramped enough already,' Theresa said in her dull, rather grating voice.

'But . . .' began Kitty. She wanted to know what was to happen to her. Perhaps they expected her to move out. Where will I go? she wondered in a panic. I really will be on me own then.

Jimmy apparently sensed what she was about to say. 'Of course there'll always be a place for you, luv. You can stay where you are, and the lads'll sleep in the box room, but Theresa will take over the running of the house, which should suit you down to the ground, seeing as how your job takes up so much of your time. You'll be our lodger,' he finished with a chuckle.

'Thanks,' said Kitty.

Sheila Reilly heard the clip-clop of Nelson's hooves as he began the day's rounds. 'I must ask Bill Harrison for more cobbles,' she thought. They'd been burning fuel like there was no tomorrow over Christmas and what with Cal being home as well. Doors slammed as people began to go to work and someone whistled 'Auld Lang Syne'. Of course, it was New Year's Eve tomorrow.

'If only Cal could be here. If only . . . oh, God!' She was going to cry again, which only upset him. She took a deep breath and blinked furiously in an effort to hold back the tears. She'd cried for hours in his arms the night before, unable to contain her grief. It was their last night together. This was their last morning. In a few hours he

238

would be gone. It was bad enough him going and having to live without him, but knowing he could be killed at any time was just too much to bear.

She turned to look at him. He was fast asleep and she held out her hand and left it an inch from his face. 'I won't touch him. I'll let him sleep on. It might be tomorrow till he gets to bed again.'

'I love you, Cal,' she whispered. She loved him so much it hurt.

'Hallo, Sheil.' He woke up and reached for her. They made love silently and feverishly. 'This might be the last time ever,' Sheila kept thinking. 'We might never make love again.' She wondered if Cal was thinking the same. She could barely see his face with the blackout curtains drawn, but he seemed less gentle than usual, as if driven by a quiet rage.

'Oh, Cal!' she shouted when they came, together as always.

'Christ, girl, I can't stand to leave you.' His naked body, poised over her, glistened dully with perspiration. He collapsed beside her. 'Jaysus!'

But there was to be no more time alone. There were footsteps on the landing and the door opened. Cal managed to struggle into his pyjama pants and Sheila pulled her nightdress down, as six children poured into the room and threw themselves en masse onto the bed.

For they also knew that this was the last morning in a long time they'd spend with their dad.

Someone had the kind idea of organising a New Year's Eve dance in the assembly hall for the nurses and Wrens who worked in the hospital. The trouble was, they hadn't thought to ask any men. The women, giggling helplessly, danced with each other, and ended up having a riotous time. Kitty, however, in one of the two new frocks she'd recently had made, a fine pale blue woollen crepe with a fitted bodice and skirt and long tight

239

sleeves, found herself monopolised by one of the few men there. Stan Taylor, anxious to unload his tale of woe and clearly oblivious to Lucy's desire to take him on as a challenge, pinned Kitty in a corner and bared his soul. Every now and then, she glanced enviously across the room where everyone else was doing the Hokey-Cokey or Knees Up Mother Brown or stamping out a vigorous Gay Gordons. She wondered where Harriet was. She hadn't turned up for work that week, and when Lucy asked Nurse Bellamy for her address in case she was ill so they could visit her, Bellamy had churlishly refused to let them have it.

'I expect she wants her privacy,' she said gruffly.

She and Stan danced the occasional waltz, which was apparently Daphne's favourite, and when the clock struck midnight, he pecked her cheek and burst into tears. Kitty was forced to take him home to his lodgings and deliver him into the hands of his landlady, who promised to put him to bed.

Then she went home herself, thinking what a washout New Year's Eve had turned out to be.

'What's that doing there?' Nan Wright stared down at the glass of stout in her hand. She racked her brains and vaguely remembered someone had just been in and given it to her, that busybody of a woman from across the road whose name she couldn't recall. It was to toast something with.

Nan drank the stout and licked round the edge of the glass where there was still foam. 'Ruby,' she called. When her daughter didn't come, Nan stared deep into the dying embers of the fire and could dimly see Ruby there.

'Your ould mam wants to go to bed, girl.' But Ruby was playing with a ball and didn't seem to hear. The glass slipped unnoticed from Nan's hand onto the floor. 'I'm dead tired,' she complained. The busybody woman hadn't helped her upstairs to bed as she usually did. Nan couldn't move from her chair nowadays without help.

'I'll be back next year,' the woman had said in a joky voice. That's right, it was New Year's Eve. But which year?

'What date is it, Ruby?'

Ruby's face grew large amidst the glowing ash. 'It's eighteen ninety-nine, Mam.'

'I'm not half tired, luv.'

'Then come and sleep with me, Mam.' Ruby held out her hands.

'Can I, luv?' Nan said eagerly.

'Yes, Mam. It's time.'

With a superhuman effort, Nan managed to ease her massive frame out of the chair.

'Come on, Mam,' urged Ruby.

'I'm coming, luv,' said Nan.

At the Reillys', the New Year, the third since the war began, was greeted with slightly less jubilation than the previous two when everyone had managed to convince themselves that it would soon be over, that war was merely a temporary aberration. But now, what with rationing set in and shortages of virtually every basic necessity, as well as the fighting expanding throughout the world, war seemed here to stay.

The house was subdued. It had become a tradition, with Sheila having got married first, that the family gather there to let the New Year in. Brenda Mahon usually came, even if only for half an hour, along with one or two other people from the street. Aggie Donovan was there, but this year Nan Wright was housebound and unable to get as far as her front door. Jess Fleming popped in just before midnight. Jess had been very quiet since Arthur had returned home. Jack Doyle arrived, as he always did, as soon as the King's Arms closed its doors for the night, bringing Paddy

O'Hara with him. Rover immediately settled himself in front of the fire as soon as he was assured his master was comfortably seated.

They sat quietly around the wireless waiting for Big Ben to chime.

'Happy New Year!' Sheila said on the first stroke of twelve. Everyone stood up and kissed each other dutifully. Sheila noticed her dad kept well clear of Jess, and wondered what he had against the poor woman.

'Happy New Year, Dad.' She kissed him on the cheek.

'Same to you, luv,' said Jack. 'Though it doesn't seem the same without our Eileen, does it?'

'She wouldn't come, even though Jess offered to put her up for the night in her spare bedroom. She said she preferred to be alone.'

'If that's what she wants, luv!' Jack shrugged. He never ceased to worry over his eldest daughter. 'I'll be along to see her as soon as I've got a spare minute.'

'You'd better propose the toast, Dad.'

Jack raised his glass. 'Here's to the ones who can't be with us tonight; our Sean, Cal, our Eileen's Nick, Xavier.' At this, Brenda made a face at Sheila. For all she cared, Xavier could stay away for ever. 'At the same time,' Jack went on in a sombre voice, 'let's not forget those who'll never be coming back; me little grandson, Tony, Francis Costello and that fine ould man, Jacob Singerman, and all the other men and women whose names we'll never know who've lost their lives in this senseless war.' He bowed his head. 'May God rest their souls.'

The final words didn't sound all that strange from the mouth of someone who was an atheist through and through.

Sheila's bottom lip trembled. 'Jaysus, Dad! What a dead miserable toast. You've made me want to cry.'

'I'm sorry, luv, but that's the way I feel.'

'I'd better get back to the girls,' said Brenda.

'And it's time I put Nan Wright to bed.' Aggie Donovan bustled out.

Everyone left, and as Sheila washed and dried the glasses, she became aware of a familiar sensation between her legs.

'Bloody hell!' she groaned. She'd started a period, yet she'd felt convinced she would conceive when Cal was home. Perhaps her body had all closed up by now. In the past, there'd scarcely been time between babies for things to shrink back to normal. Listlessly, she went upstairs and had just tucked a folded sanitary rag inside her knickers, when the front door opened and Aggie Donovan came rushing in to say she'd found Nan Wright dead on the mat in front of the fire.

'Oh, but she looked ever so happy, Sheila,' Aggie sobbed. 'You know, there was a smile on the ould biddy's face wide enough to split the flags.'

Jessica Fleming had only been home a few minutes when the light, familiar tap came. She opened the door, but shrank back when Jack immediately took her in his arms and began to touch her.

'It's the wrong time of the month,' she said.

'Oh,' he said, embarrassed.

She wished she could tell him, tell someone, how bitterly disappointed she'd felt that morning when she woke up to find she'd started a period. It had only taken one single time to produce Penny.

'You can go home if you like,' she said in a hard voice. 'After all, that's all you come for, isn't it?' She knew it was unfair to take her disappointment out on him. It wasn't his fault she hadn't conceived.

'That's not true, Jess,' he protested, though he wondered if it was.

'It is.' She turned away and went into the living room. 'We've got nothing in common.'

He followed. 'Yes we have.'

'What? All we do is argue.'

'We've got Penny.'

'Oh, God!' She sat down, looking dazed. 'How long have you known?'

'A few weeks, months. What does it matter?' Perhaps he shouldn't have admitted he knew he was Penny's father. She might want something off him, a promise for the future which he didn't, which he didn't *think* he wanted to give.

'I never want that fact to go beyond these four walls, Jack.'

'I wasn't thinking of telling anyone,' he said stiffly.

She smiled obliquely. 'Because you're ashamed?'

'Of course not,' he said irritably, and turned the question back on her. 'Are you?'

'As if I'd be ashamed of Penny! But I'd sooner people didn't know I was unfaithful to Arthur.'

He stared at her. She looked tired and drawn, which was unusual for her, normally so full of energy and enthusiasm. It only seemed to add to her beauty, giving her a heartstopping air of frailty which made him want to take her in his arms and comfort her. He reminded himself that they were two opposites, that she stood for everything he hated, that he was drawn to her solely by a hungry need for her soft, luscious body. But how long would she be prepared to carry on the way they were? Women weren't like men. They didn't like being dangled on a string. They wanted proper relationships, commitments . . .

'Would you like to call it a day, Jess?' He half wished she would say 'yes', then, almost immediately, wished he could unsay the words in case she agreed because he knew he would be bereft without her. She'd brought excitement into his life, re-awakened urges he'd never expected to feel again – and stirred some he'd never known he had.

'*No!*' She was off her chair like a shot, kneeling before him, cradling his head in her hands. 'Oh, no, Jack!' She kissed him passionately and, unable to help himself, he began to kiss her back. Gradually, she drew him down until they were lying on the floor.

'But I thought . . . you know,' he stammered, heart pounding with desire as she undid the buttons of her blouse. He buried his face in the frothy cream lace of her petticoat and could feel her nipples, as hard as buds, through the thin material.

'Don't worry, Jack,' she whispered, 'there's other things we can do.'

Jessica had no idea where she'd learnt the things she was about to do to Jack Doyle. They just seemed to come naturally once they were together. But she knew one thing with utter certainty, and that was that she hadn't come back to Bootle just for him. It was when he'd suggested they call it a day that the pieces of the jigsaw had fallen into place, neatly and perfectly, until the picture was clear. She'd come back solely because she wanted another baby. Jack had given her one, which meant he could give her another. She was using him, just as she'd used Arthur and other people in the past. If she became pregnant, she would let Jack down gently and as soon as the war was over she'd be on her way to a bigger house in a better part of Bootle. Shortly, she'd look round for a site and buy every secondhand car she could get her hands on so that she could raise her children in comfort.

Jack groaned as she ran her hands over his broad, muscled body. In the meantime, the achievement of this ambition was proving to be highly enjoyable.

Dear Kitty,

Your friend recognised me, didn't she? Yes, I used to be a doctor in Walton Hospital. I was struck off the medical register a year ago because I carried out an abortion on a twelve-year-old girl who'd been raped by her father. Since then, I've been rather cowardly, unwilling to give up my comfortable home, yet needing to be involved in medicine in some way.

I was always worried I might meet an old patient and now it's happened, and if it can happen once, it can happen again. I can't stand the idea of someone like Clara Watkins finding out. Can you imagine the cracks she'd make THEN!

So I'm leaving. I've been to see my good friend and confidante, Joyce (Nurse Bellamy), who has always been supportive, and handed in my notice. I'm off to America to be a doctor there, that's if they'll have me. If not, I'll wander down south where I'm sure I can put my skills to good use amongst the poor. I doubt if they'll care if I've been disowned by the stuffy authorities in this country.

Anyway, having given orders all my life, I could never get used to taking them.

Look after yourself, Kitty, dear. Be confident, be self-assured. Don't take shit off anybody. You're a lovely person and deserve the happiness I'm convinced you'll one day find.

I've also written a farewell letter to Lucy, but of course haven't mentioned the things I've told you.

Goodbye, Kitty.
Your good friend,
Harriet.

The hospital would never be the same without Harriet. The young woman who took her place, Valerie Simmonds, had dark smooth hair parted in the middle and the face of a saint. Clara immediately took her under her wing and the two quickly became firm friends. As Clara seemed to thrive on trouble, a miniature war developed, with Kitty unwillingly drawn in on one side. Without Harriet's calming influence, Lucy and Clara almost came to blows at times over the sharing out of the work. An atmosphere of confrontation reigned whenever the auxiliaries retired to the rest room for a break.

Meanwhile, winter set in and bleak skies daily

threatened snow which never came, and the carnage at sea continued unabated. Young men continued to arrive at the hospital with pneumonia, frostbite, burns, broken bones and missing limbs. Occasionally there'd be quite ordinary complaints, such as a burst appendix or a minor illness like mumps or German measles. Some men died, leaving anguished relatives for whom the nurses would make cups of tea and offer meaningless words of comfort.

Glyn Thomas, the dark-haired Welshman, quickly read the books which Kitty had borrowed from Jack Doyle and asked for more. 'Tell him this one's a load of rubbish,' he said, pointing to a paperback entitled *The Achievements of Communism in Russia*.

'How would you know?' demanded Kitty.

'I've already told you I lived in Russia for nearly three years. There were achievements, there's no doubt about it, but this book doesn't mention the costs.'

'I'll tell him,' promised Kitty.

Glyn winked. 'What are you doing tonight?'

'Me and Lucy are going to the picures to see *Fantasia*. It's a full-length cartoon.'

'Seen it,' Glyn said promptly. 'The music's first rate.' He was the most knowledgable and well-travelled man she'd ever met, having spent his entire life since leaving school working his way slowly around the world. He'd washed dishes, worked as a chef, a fieldhand, driven lorries, shod horses, built cars for the Ford Motor Company in Chicago, and taken numerous other jobs to support himself in his travels. When the war began, he'd joined the Royal Navy. 'I didn't fancy the Army or the RAF,' he told Kitty. 'I might have ended up being stationed in the one place.' His appetite for books was insatiable. When some old yellowing *National Geographic* and *Antique Collector* magazines had been found in a dusty cupboard in the basement, Glyn had eagerly read them from cover to cover. He still kept them in his locker to re-read when there was nothing else available. When not reading, he kept the ward amused with anecdotes of his adventurous past and frequently led them in a singsong in his fine baritone voice.

Even Nurse Bellamy was captivated, though Kitty was the one who appeared to have stolen Glyn's heart, much to the envy of other nurses, particularly Lucy. Kitty felt flattered, because she found his rather raffish charm disturbing and had to keep reminding herself that he was a patient, and patients frequently fell in love with their nurses.

'I've decided to settle down once the war's over,' he had said only the day before.

Kitty was mopping the floor beneath his bed. 'You'll be dead bored.'

'Not if I settle down with the woman I love and start a family,' he replied, his dark eyes twinkling.

'You've got to find her first, haven't you?'

'I think I already have.' There was no mistaking the meaning behind his words.

Kitty said awkwardly, 'Everything will seem different once you leave the hospital.'

'No it won't.' His expression became serious for once. 'Think about it, Kitty. Would you fancy living in the Welsh valleys with a wild Taffy who'd wake you up every morning with a cup of tea and "Men of Harlech"?'

'Get away with you!' she muttered.

'I mean it!'

'You can't possibly mean it,' she said, doing her best to sound scathing. 'You don't know anything about me.'

'I know everything there is to know. They say the face is the window of the soul, and that's definitely true in your case, Kitty, my darling. It's obvious to all and sundry that you're beautiful inside and out. In fact, I'm surprised you haven't been snapped up years ago.' He gave an impish grin. 'I reckon fate has been saving you just for me.'

By this time, Kitty was cleaning underneath the neighbouring bed and the young sailor there was listening to the conversation with interest. 'You'd make a handsome couple,' he said.

'Is this some sort of conspiracy?' Kitty asked, exasperated.

'I'm going to get the entire ward on my side,' Glyn vowed.

In the end, she told him she might, just might, go out with him once he was discharged and able to think more clearly.

'But I can think clearly now.'

Kitty recalled Martin McCabe and the trouble she'd got into. 'I can't promise any more than that,' she said firmly.

Stan Taylor sought her out that afternoon to apologise for his behaviour on New Year's Eve. 'It dawned on me how kind you've been all this time, Kitty, letting me pour my troubles out on your shoulder. Daphne would never have done anything like that. Let me take you to the pictures on Saturday, and this time we'll talk about nothing but you.'

'Why wait till Saturday?' Kitty said gaily. 'I don't have to stay in with me dad any more. He's found company of his own.'

Chapter 12

'He what?' said Jack Doyle, shocked to the core.

Kitty had called round to the house in Garnet Street after tea to return his books. She placed the bundle on the table and repeated, 'He said the top one's a load of rubbish – and he'd like to borrow some more.'

'You mean he implied Communism was rubbish?' Jack sat down suddenly. He couldn't have looked more stunned if he'd been told the world was going to end.

'He didn't just imply it, Mr Doyle, he said it outright.'

'Yet you say he's lived there, this bloody know-all Welshman?'

'For three years,' said Kitty. 'Can I have a few more books, please?'

'I'm not sure.' Jack put his arms around his books protectively. 'Not if he's going to tear them to pieces.'

Kitty smiled. 'He was just expressing an opinion, that's all.'

'Is he allowed visitors?' Jack asked suddenly.

'Of course, afternoons and evenings.'

'In that case, I'll take the books meself and have it out with him. A load of rubbish, if you please.'

Jack Doyle was nearly ejected from the hospital when the sound of shouting reached the nurses who were having a quiet cup of tea and a ciggie in the kitchen.

'He said Stalin's a monster!' Jack was standing at the

foot of Glyn Thomas's bed, on the verge of apoplexy, when half a dozen scared young women reached the ward.

'Now, now, sir,' one said in an attempt to pacify him.

'Bugger off! A monster! Stalin's a hero. He's converted his country from stultifying serfdom into an efficient industrial economy within a generation!'

'And personally ordered the murder of millions of peasants in the process!' Glyn shouted from his bed. His face was red with anger and he was clutching his scalded chest painfully.

'That's a lie!' yelled Jack.

'I've seen the bodies.'

'Stalin's the saviour of his country!'

'That's what they said about Hitler!'

Jack turned to the ward, where the men and a few other visitors were listening open-mouthed to the argument. 'Did any of you ever think you'd see the day when Stalin was compared to Hitler?'

Half shook their heads and the other half nodded.

A nurse nervously took Jack's arm. 'I think you'd better go, sir.'

'I don't want him to go!' Glyn yelled. 'Let him stay and listen to the truth. What about the labour camps?' he sneered at Jack. 'I suppose you're going to say they don't exist?'

'What labour camps?'

'See!' Glyn glanced around the ward for support. Unsure what was expected of them, everyone again responded with a shake of the head or a nod. 'The labour camps in Siberia, where the dissidents are dumped to die; the writers who dare criticise, the politicians unwise enough to ask an awkward question, the ordinary people who for no reason at all find themselves dragged out of their houses in the middle of the night by the Russian equivalent of the Gestapo and are never seen again by their families.'

'You don't know what you're talking about,' Jack said, disgusted.

'Have you lived there?' challenged Glyn.

'No, but . . .'

'Well I have,' Glyn said triumphantly. 'I've seen it with my own eyes. They're fine people, the Russians, it's their leaders that let them down.' He shrugged. 'But then, that's the case everywhere. It's the scum that rises to the top, and only occasionally the cream.'

'That's something I can agree with.' Jack returned to sit beside the bed. 'Have you been to America?' When Glyn nodded, he asked with genuine interest, 'What's it like there?'

When the bell went to signal it was time for visitors to leave, Jack growled, 'D'you want me to come again?'

'How about tomorrow?' said Glyn.

Two weeks later, Glyn Thomas was well enough to leave hospital, but still in constant pain and certainly not fit enough to return to his ship. He was put on sick leave, and as he had no family and no home to go to, it was suggested he stay in a convalescent home for a few weeks until his health improved.

When Jack Doyle heard this, he said casually, 'You can stay with me if you like. I've got a spare room as me son's married and left home. You'll have plenty of peace and quiet there.'

'Well, I wouldn't mind,' Glyn said equally casually. 'I suppose you get lonely stuck on your own.'

'One thing I never am is lonely. I was just doing you a favour.'

'I don't need favours, thanks all the same.'

'In that case, don't come.'

'Don't worry, I wouldn't come if they paid me.'

It was snowing hard the following Saturday when an ambulance took Glyn to Jack's house in Garnet Street.

From then on, when he wasn't involved in a fearsome argument with Jack, Glyn began to court Kitty Quigley with a fervour that left her breathless.

Kitty was on the late shift. On the first Saturday when she arrived home at half-past ten, she found him sitting on her doorstep in the freezing snow, slightly inebriated, and singing 'Men of Harlech' at the top of his voice. He was wearing civvies; a pair of thick corduroy trousers, a polo-necked jumper topped by a duffel coat. He had no hat, and his dark wavy hair was flecked with ice.

'You're supposed to be convalescing!' she said, aghast. 'You should be in bed by now – and where's Jack Doyle? He promised to look after you.'

'He's gone somewhere. We had a few drinks in the pub, then he took me home, but I came out again to look for you – someone told me where you live.' He did a little jig on the pavement. 'I came to arrange for that date you promised.'

Kitty pursed her lips angrily. 'Oh, this is disgraceful, it really is. I'll wipe the floor with Jack Doyle when I see him. Come in and I'll make you a nice hot drink, then I'll take you home again – but this time you're going to bed and staying there.'

'Yes, ma'am.' Glyn grinned and saluted as she unlocked the front door. 'Has anyone ever told you, you look even more beautiful when you're angry?'

'I'm too angry to listen to that sort of nonsense! Get indoors this minute and sit yourself by the fire.'

She pulled out the flue on the grate and coaxed the glowing coals into flames, then she took his coat and laid it on the hearth to dry. 'Now, get warm!' she commanded. 'I've a good mind to report this to Nurse Bellamy on Monday. She'd have you in a convalescent home before you could say "Jack Robinson" if she knew what was going on.'

Glyn looked oblivious to the threat. When she

fetched the water to make cocoa, he began to sing, 'Yours till the stars lose their glory, yours . . .'

'I love that song!' said Kitty.

'Dance with me.' He took her in his arms and began to whirl her around the room.

'Glyn!' It was difficult to stay angry with him for long. Laughing, she tried to push him away. 'You're not up to this. You've only just come out of hospital. You should be resting.'

'I've never felt better. Ouch!'

'What's the matter?' she cried.

'Just a twinge across my chest,' he said dismissively. 'It's nothing.'

He stopped dancing, but remained holding her. Suddenly, the room seemed very quiet. He wasn't tall, and his dark eyes were level with her own. Kitty's arms were resting on his shoulders and his were linked around her waist. His dark dancing eyes glistened as he leaned towards her and kissed her lightly on the lips. 'I love you, Kitty.'

'No, Glyn.' She tried to push him away, but he kissed her harder. Kitty waited for something to happen inside her, some sort of magical awakening, rising passion, a faster beating heart, but nothing did. It was nice, but that was all.

She was too engrossed in her first real kiss to hear the door open, and Jimmy Quigley came in just as Glyn had embarked on a second. He was wearing his new overcoat, a chunky herringbone tweed with the collar turned up in the manner of American film stars.

'Oh, hallo, Dad,' she said, breaking away from Glyn's arms and feeling more than a little embarrassed.

'Hallo,' he said acidly.

Kitty introduced Glyn to her father, then made them all a cup of cocoa. Despite Glyn's best efforts to be friendly, Jimmy positively refused to be friendly back. In fact, he was almost rude, grunting scarcely audible replies when asked a question and adopting an expression of studied indifference to anything Glyn had to say.

At half past eleven, Kitty took the invalid home to Garnet Street, where Jack Doyle was about to go firewatching and was startled to discover his visitor wasn't in bed and fast asleep. When she got back, Jimmy was still up, waiting for the midnight bulletin on the wireless.

'Well, I didn't think much of *him*,' he said dismissively.

'I doubt if he thought much of *you*!' Kitty said crossly. 'You were dead rude, Dad. I felt ashamed.

'He was too mouthy for my liking. Had too high an opinion of himself. I'm not bound by law to like the men me daughter goes out with.'

'No, but you're bound by good manners to treat them with civility when they're guests in your house. I'm always nice to Theresa.' Theresa Beamish and her children had been round to the house on several more occasions since they first came to tea.

Jimmy bristled. 'Does that mean you don't like her?'

'I never said that, did I, Dad? I meant I'd still be nice even if I didn't.' In fact, Kitty couldn't take to her dad's fiancée. No matter how friendly she tried to be, Theresa always shrugged her away, as if she were incapable of any warm feelings. Even towards Jimmy, her soon-to-be husband, she appeared cold and unaffectionate, and wasn't much different with her children.

'Dad?' she said quietly.

'What?' He was pulling apart some cigarette stubs which he'd collected in his pocket, and placing the shreds of tobacco onto a paper to make a whole one.

'Are you sure you're doing the right thing?'

He turned on her, ready to tear her off a strip, to say of course he was, and what business was it of hers, anyroad, when he saw her wide hazel eyes were anxious. She was anxious for him, her dad. 'I'm sure, kiddo. Don't worry about me,' he replied kindly.

Jimmy had managed to convince himself that his entire life had been a tragedy, particularly the last ten years, when he'd been tied to a chair, unable to walk, living on a pittance of a pension. He wasn't quite sure whose fault it was, but it certainly wasn't his. Now he was about to marry a woman over twenty years his junior and his mates in the King's Arms were green with envy because Jimmy Quigley was about to achieve the happiness he so richly deserved and which had been unfairly denied him up to now. Theresa made him feel young again, rejuvenated, as if he was making up for lost time. He admired the way she kept her two lads firmly in line. She might be a bit low on imagination and short on conversation, but sometimes she took him into the parlour of her parents' house in Flint Street and allowed his hands to stray underneath her jumper and caress her breasts and Jimmy would feel re-born, as if he'd been allowed another chance to have a go at life. He couldn't wait to get her into bed. It was a bit disconcerting to have a father-in-law scarcely older than himself and a mother-in-law a year younger, but once Theresa and her lads were ensconced in Pearl Street, Jimmy wouldn't have to make the comparison so often.

Glyn took Kitty for a drink next day to the Adelphi, the poshest hotel in Liverpool. Although badly bombed the year before, the place continued to function. Kitty had a Pimms No 1 which made her head spin. Afterwards, they went to see *Citizen Kane* with Orson Welles, though it was Joseph Cotton whom Kitty found the most attractive. When they came out, she insisted they went home immediately so Glyn could go to bed early.

'I'd be failing in my duty if I let you stay up late,' she said virtuously when they were on the train.

'I wish you weren't a nurse.' He looked aggrieved. 'I'm fed up being bossed about.'

'If I wasn't a nurse, we'd never have met.'

Glyn smote his brow dramatically. 'Of course! I was forgetting. And the course of my life would never have changed.'

'Please, Glyn!' It frightened her that he seemed to have made the assumption they'd get married.

He raised his dark eyebrows. 'Am I rushing you?'

'Yes.' She scarcely knew him.

'I'm sorry,' he said penitently, but even so, he put his arm around her shoulders and drew her to him. 'Let's see, what can I do within the next few weeks to persuade Kitty Quigley I'm the man for her? I've got savings, you know, quite a bit in fact. I'd come with a dowry.'

She dug him in the ribs with her elbows. 'Shurrup, you!'

'We could live in the Welsh valleys as I've already suggested, or we could go to Australia and farm sheep. We'll stay in Bootle if you prefer. Alternatively, how about the States?'

'I don't know, Glyn, I need time.'

A telegraph boy called at the house at ten o'clock the next morning. Mystified, Kitty tore open the bright orange envelope. *I love you, Kitty Quigley*, the message inside read. There was no signature, but Kitty had no doubts who it was from.

'Who was it?' Jimmy asked when she returned inside.

'It was a telegram from Glyn,' she replied, smiling.

'Daft git,' Jimmy said sourly.

Another telegram with the same message arrived an hour later, and a further one at midday. Kitty went round to Jack Doyle's house. Jack was at work and Glyn was in the kitchen. There was a delicious smell of cooking.

'There won't be any dowry left if you carry on with

257

this nonsense,' she admonished, waving the telegrams. 'If you send one to the hospital this avvy, I'll kill you. I'd never be able to live it down.'

'I was wondering how many I'd have to send before you came,' he said, his face gleeful. 'Look, I've got some wine.' He pointed to the table, which she was surprised to see was nicely set with a vase of paper flowers in the middle, a bottle of red wine and two glasses. 'And I've made moussaka.'

'Wine, at this time of the day!' Kitty said weakly. 'And what on earth's moussaka?'

'Greek scouse. I managed to buy some herbs. I did enough for Jack, but I doubt if he'll appreciate it.'

'You should be in bed, resting.'

'Stop being a nurse, for God's sake. Take your coat off and sit down.'

'But I'm in the middle of making dinner for me dad!'

'He'll just have to wait till you've had yours.'

The meal was delicious, though it was only mince and potatoes with a few chopped vegetables. It tasted like no scouse Kitty had ever eaten before. 'It's lovely,' she said when she'd finished every mouthful.

'See, it's not just a husband you'd be getting, but a cook as well.'

Kitty went off to work that afternoon, heady with wine and flushed with Glyn's kisses, though the first had had more effect than the second. She wished she could respond with more vigour, but the fact was he left her cold, which was a pity, because he would make an exciting husband. Life would never be boring or dull married to Glyn Thomas.

When she entered the ward where he'd been, each man solemnly handed her a note. *Glyn Thomas Loves Kitty Quigley*, each one said.

'Oh! I bet he put you up to this!' she cried.

★

From then on, Kitty found him waiting for her at the bus stop every night. He would take her to Jack Doyle's for a candlelit supper which he'd cooked himself – Jack was always mysteriously elsewhere. One Sunday, they caught the train to Southport where they strolled, window-shopping, through a snowstorm and Glyn tried to coax her into choosing an engagement ring from a jeweller's window. The following weekend they went to Chester and ate lunch in such a grand hotel that Kitty was the only woman not wearing a fur coat. When she pointed this out, Glyn immediately offered to buy her one. Occasionally, they caught an early train into bomb-scarred Liverpool or wandered along the busy Dock Road. Glyn seemed to see the world as a more vivid, interesting place than most people, pointing out sights and sounds that Kitty would never have noticed on her own. Whatever they did, wherever they were, he always managed to turn it into an adventure.

'I hardly ever see you,' Jimmy complained to Kitty.

'He'll be gone soon and everything will be back to normal,' she replied, half dreading the return to her usual humdrum life.

Three weeks later, after the most strenuous convalescence anyone could have had, Glyn returned to the hospital and was pronounced fit. He was ordered down to Chatham in two days' time where he'd be found another ship. That night, wearing his sailor's uniform for the first time, and looking even more devil-may-care than usual in the round hat, he took Kitty to a dark little pub just off Lime Street which they had decided was their favourite, and formally proposed marriage. 'There's just time for us to get a twenty-four-hour licence.'

Kitty was sorely tempted to accept. Six months ago, she might well have done, but she recalled Harriet's advice: 'Whatever you do, Kitty, don't marry the first man who proposes just so you can have "Mrs" in front of your name.' It was unlikely that she would ever meet anyone else like Glyn again. She hoped she wasn't making the greatest mistake of her life by turning down this extraordinary man. 'I'm sorry, Glyn, but I don't love you,' she answered sadly.

'But I've enough love for both of us.' He'd never looked more serious. His face was grave, almost tragic, as if he had already known what her answer would be.

'But that wouldn't be fair, either on you or on me,' she cried. 'We'd both be missing something.'

'Oh, damn this bloody war,' he cursed. 'I've been waiting for a girl like you all my life. If only we'd had more time!'

Kitty felt her heart could easily break when she saw the bleak expression on his normally cheerful face.

'Could you grow to love me, Kitty?' he pleaded.

She couldn't bear to hurt his feelings. She liked him more than any person she'd ever known. She might even love him, but not in the way he wanted, at least not yet. 'Possibly,' she whispered.

'Does that mean we could get engaged?' he said eagerly.

Kitty's heart fell. She didn't want to raise his hopes, then dash them later. 'I'd sooner not, Glyn. Let's be friends, good friends. We'll write to each other – and see each other when you get leave. You can always stay with Jack.'

He sighed and made a face. 'I suppose that'll just have to do.' He stroked her cheek and kissed her softly on the lips. 'I still think you're the only woman for me, Kitty Quigley.'

'Perhaps I am, Glyn,' she replied shakily. 'You never know, the time might come when I'll realise that for meself.'

She genuinely hoped it might one day turn out to be true.

★

Singapore fell, as Calum Reilly had predicted it would, in the middle of February, when the British general went out with a white flag and surrendered to the Japanese. Eighty-five thousand Allied troops were either lost or taken prisoner. Across the Pacific, Australia and New Zealand trembled.

On the BBC that night, Winston Churchill told the nation, 'So far we have not failed. We shall not fail now. Move forward steadfastly together into the storm and through the storm.'

'What does he mean, we haven't failed?' Jack Doyle demanded in the King's Arms. 'What's the fall of Singapore if it isn't a failure?'

'I dunno, Jack,' Paddy O'Hara said gloomily. 'Seems to me, we're failing all round at the moment.'

Jack wished Glyn Thomas were there because he would inevitably provoke an argument and somehow prove they were winning, which was what everybody desperately wanted to believe. Jack really missed Glyn.

So did Kitty. She felt as if a light had gone out of her life, a brilliant, dazzling light that would never be switched on again. When Stan Taylor asked her out – his transfer back to Plymouth had been delayed a further three months – she spent the entire evening trying to explain how she felt.

'There'll be another light, Kitty,' he comforted.

'Will there?' she asked plaintively. 'Perhaps I should have agreed to marry him if I miss him so much.'

'I don't think so. You wouldn't have had doubts if you really loved him. You'd have snapped up his proposal like a shot.'

'I suppose so,' Kitty sighed. 'It's dead stupid, isn't it, getting all upset after you've turned someone down.'

'You'll get over it.'

Kitty managed a smile. 'I tried telling you that when you split up with Daphne. You didn't believe me.'

'I do now,' he said firmly.

'Do you?' She glanced at him in surprise. He was a tall, lean man with scarcely an ounce of spare fat on him. His hollow cheeks and deep-set eyes gave him a gaunt, hungry look which many of the nurses found attractive. His skin had a slight yellow tinge as a result of jaundice as a child, making him appear as if he had a permanent tan. This had precluded him from active service in the Navy and left him bound to a desk which he hated. 'Don't tell me you've got over Daphne already?

'Already! It's nearly two months since she ditched me. You can't stay brokenhearted for ever, particularly when there's a war on.'

'I'm ever so glad, Stan.' She was beginning to like him as a friend. There'd never been the slightest hint of romance between them. 'I really hope you meet someone else you'll love as much as you did Daphne.'

'I already have, someone much nicer than Daphne ever was!'

Although she pleaded with him to reveal who it was, he adamantly refused. 'I haven't told her yet. When the time's ripe, Kitty, you'll be the first to know.

Jimmy Quigley married Theresa Beamish at half-past two on a cold wet Saturday when there were still dirty clumps of frozen snow on the ground and the sky was black enough for midnight.

Only a few people from Pearl Street braved the icy winds to see the newly married couple emerge from the church and the single photo taken of the wedding showed an unsmiling bride with her two sulky children, though the bridegroom looked as if he'd just scooped the pools. Kitty Quigley was obviously doing her best to appear happy for her dad, and the best man, an unwilling Jack Doyle, would clearly have preferred to be somewhere else. Only the bride's parents beamed cheerfully at the photographer the way proper wedding guests were supposed to do.

'Perhaps they were only too glad to get rid of her,' Sheila Reilly suggested when Kitty showed her the photo a week later.

'I wouldn't be surprised,' Kitty said miserably. 'Honestly, Sheil, I feel ashamed. She's cleaned the house from top to bottom since she moved in. You'd think she'd found it filthy dirty, or something. We're not even that clean in the hospital. And the washing! She's forever washing, I don't know where she finds it. Thank God she has a job in the evenings, so we can have a bit of peace.' Theresa had a part-time job in a fish and chip shop in Marsh Lane.

'What does your dad think?'

'Oh, he thinks it's the gear. He keeps pointing out how much better Theresa does his shirts compared to me; they're whiter and she irons them without a single crease.'

Sheila was doing her own ironing, despite the fact it was Sunday and supposed to be a day of rest. She paused and said thoughtfully, 'I must say, he looks dead pleased with himself when I see him out. He's like a new man altogether.'

Kitty thought about the nights when she lay with her head beneath the covers trying to shut out the noise of the bedsprings creaking in the front bedroom and her dad's anguished groans. It seemed to go on for ages and ages and she felt like an eavesdropper. She was neither disgusted nor shocked, more embarrassed at this highly vocal evidence of passion on the part of her dad, whom she'd thought long past it. It was too intimate to tell Sheila, but she would have loved to know if the groans implied pleasure, not pain, and what was the meaning of the shrill little scream, the only sound from Theresa, which usually came just before the creaking of the bedsprings stopped?

'I don't know what I'm going to do with meself next week when I'm on afternoons,' she said instead. 'It wasn't so bad last week. I was only in an hour or so before Theresa took herself off to work. Today, for instance, I've been bored out of me mind, with madam cleaning all around me and refusing to let me lend a hand, pointing out it's *her* house now, not mine. I'm not even allowed in the kitchen.'

'Never mind, luv,' Sheila said sympathetically. 'You can always come here.'

'I know, Sheil, but I'm beginning to feel a bit like a stateless person. I've no real home. I don't belong anywhere.'

Jessica Fleming was the first to see one; two, in fact, both emerging out of Rita's flat one blowy morning early in March. They were tall fair-haired, athletic young men, as alike as brothers, with bright eyes and healthy sunburnt complexions. The well-tailored uniforms fitted their broad-shouldered frames to absolute perfection; more beige than khaki, the material had a silky, expensive sheen.

Americans! The men touched their caps and bade her 'Good morning, ma'am,' with a confident, easy-going charm. They beamed at Penny, and one murmured she was definitely going to be a heartbreaker when she grew up. Penny beamed back, already well aware of her own charm.

Jessica returned their greetings politely and was conscious of the fact that both had turned to eye her up from behind as she unlocked the garage door and went inside.

She was wheeling the bikes outside to be displayed on the stand which Jack Doyle had knocked up out of an old plank of wood, when Rita appeared carrying a paper bag, eyes aglow with excitement. 'Did you see them? Oh, aren't they gorgeous? Look what they gave me!' She opened the bag and Jessica peered inside. It was full of small bars of toffee and chocolate. 'Sweets, but they call it candy.' She insisted Jessica take the lot. 'I've still plenty upstairs. You can give some to the kids in your street if there's too much for Penny.'

'Thanks, Rita.' Jessica always felt uncomfortable taking gifts from Rita when she considered the way she'd earned them.

'That's not all!' Rita's eyes glowed even more. She took a cellophane packet out of the pocket of her dressing gown. 'Nylons! This pair's for you. They're a size ten.'

'Nylons!' Jessica said weakly. She'd felt a bit low over the last few days because she was in the middle of another period and her forty-sixth birthday rapidly approached. Not only that, on the news that morning it had been announced that the basic petrol ration would disappear altogether at the end of July, which meant even more cars would be laid up for the duration so there'd be little use for the garage as a source of petrol and the repair side of the business would dry up completely. Even worse, she wouldn't be able to use the van. But all this was forgotten when she took the cellophane packet and stared in awe at her first pair of nylons. They were like glass, with stark black seams. 'They're completely sheer!' she gasped. 'I bet you couldn't tell you had stockings on from the front.'

'They're the gear, aren't they?' Rita said smugly.

'Oh, Rita,' Jessica cried emotionally. 'You're ever such a kind person, you really are. Where did you meet the Americans?'

'The Yanks? Some pub in town. I was with this chap, Tommy, and they were with two girls. We all came back together and had a party, though the girls had to leave early for work. They're coming again this weekend with a few of their mates. Why don't you come, Jess?' Rita offered generously for the umpteenth time.

Jessica once again refused, saying she couldn't leave

Penny, and anyway the men had looked very young. 'I'm old enough to be their mother – well, almost.'

People began to remark, some bitterly, that you'd think there'd been an invasion. American tanks rolled triumphantly off the ships in the Dockie, along Miller's Bridge and onwards to the main camp at Burtonwood and other sites in Liverpool, whilst a section of the population, consisting mainly of young children, lined the route and welcomed them with the soon-to-be-familiar cry of, 'Got any gum, chum?' Suddenly, everywhere you looked, there were brash, noisy, gum-chewing GIs in their expensive, well-cut uniforms – far superior to anything the ordinary British forces wore – acting as if they owned the place with their complacent and irritating self-confidence and automatic assumption that they were God's gift to women and the best buddy of every man.

'Overpaid, overfed, oversexed – and over here,' the men grumbled.

This was undoubtedly true, and all four facts were much appreciated by the young women. Yanks appeared to be made of money, though they made up for this by being generous to a fault. Their girlfriends were sure to be taken to the best restaurants, where they'd be bought the best food and the best wine, and end up being showered with gifts of candy, nylons or expensive scent. Many a father found his opinion of the Yanks altering rapidly when presented with an entire box of Camels or Lucky Strikes or a bottle of American whisky.

No-one did more to foster Anglo-American relations than Rita Mott. Jessica would arrive for work and find a party still in progress which would carry on all day, and the same party would still be merrily in force when the time came to lock up for the night.

GIs came down to see what Jessica was up to and frequently gave a hand. She got to know a few of the

266

regulars by name and when they returned they brought oranges and bananas for Penny, fruit which Jessica hadn't seen in years. They were nice boys, good-natured and eager to please, and seemed more appreciative of the fact that Rita was providing them with a home from home, rather than anything else she might be offering. None appeared the least bit surprised to see Jessica doing a man's job and to her delight, one actually paid thirty pounds for the Austin Seven she'd been hoarding till after the war, which meant she'd made one hundred per cent profit.

'I'd like my own transport,' he said, 'and there's plenty of gas available on the base.'

'I bet I could have my own garage in the States and they wouldn't blink an eye,' she said to Jack Doyle one Saturday morning. There was little to do and they sat talking in the office. Penny was fast asleep on Jack's knee. 'America's full of opportunities. No-one's ashamed of making money, not like here.' She knew this would irk him and didn't care. She was becoming increasingly fed up with their hole in the corner affair, though she was as reluctant as he to allow it to become public.

'They're not ashamed of folks dying with hunger on the streets, either,' Jack grunted predictably. 'It's each man for himself over there. You're either a winner or a loser, there's no in between.'

That would have suited Jessica down to the ground. She was a winner and always would be.

A man popped his head into the workshop at that moment to ask about the dark green racing bike outside. Jessica went to see to him and returned five minutes later with thirty shillings in her hand.

'Another sale!' she sang, though she was frowning. 'I haven't had any fresh bikes for a fortnight. I've only got ten left and I'm beginning to worry the market has dried up.'

'Oh, dear!' Jack said sarcastically. 'You'll just have to go to work like everybody else.'

Jessica ignored him. 'You know,' she mused, 'there's other things apart from bikes that there's a shortage of; prams, for instance. I bet all sorts of women have got prams and pushchairs tucked away that they'll never use again.'

'You'll end up a rag-and-bone merchant like your dad.'

She still took no notice. 'Toys are something else I could sell if I could get my hands on them; big toys, like scooters and pedal bikes. And I might advertise for cars – you never know, the Yanks might snap them up.'

'Yanks!' spluttered Jack with loathing. He couldn't stand the way they'd arrived, two years late as far as he was concerned, with the frequently declared intention of saving li'l old England from the Germans. 'I hope you don't intend fraternising with . . .' He paused, he'd nearly said the enemy. 'With that lot,' he finished lamely.

'Oh, don't start, Jack,' Jessica said impatiently. 'They're mostly young boys who are lonely and miss their moms and pops.' She felt unreasonably irritated with him, with herself, with bikes and cars, and with the world in general.

On Monday, she arrived at the garage to find the upstairs flat quiet for a change, and noticed the curtains were still drawn. There was no sign of Rita all morning and Jessica assumed she'd gone away for the weekend, which she did occasionally. The weather was springlike and Penny was able to play, well wrapped up, in the tiny garden. Jessica felt at a loose end, with nothing to do except sell the occasional gallon of petrol, keep one eye on Penny and the other on the forecourt in case someone wanted to buy a bike. Someone did, which left only nine. The telephone rang soon afterwards; a woman was moving from her house in Aigburth and had three rusting, ageing bikes in her cellar which she didn't like to leave for the new occupants.

'You can have them for nothing if you're willing to collect them,' she said. 'I just want them out of the way.'

Jessica promised to come that evening. Feeling slightly cheered, she decided to clean the office and give the workshop a good brush. She put Dennis Mott's overalls on over her clothes and tied a scarf around her hair. Penny came in to help and Jessica sang at the top of her voice; 'Red Sails in the Sunset', which had been her father's favourite. She really must find out about troop concerts, and now there was something else called Workers' Playtimes in which concert parties entertained factory workers during the lunch hour. She'd been too busy to do anything so far, but it seemed a shame to waste a voice like hers.

'Ma'am!'

Jessica jumped. A man was standing at the entrance to the workshop, glaring at her unpleasantly, a stocky American, powerfully built, and at least twice as old as the ones she'd met so far.

'Yes?' she said coldly. How dare he look at her like that, as if she was something the cat had just dragged in from the street? Penny clutched her mother's leg nervously.

'What went on here last night?' He was clearly unwilling to step inside, and was arrogantly waiting for her to approach him.

Jessica didn't move. 'I've no idea what you're talking about.'

'Don't give me that, ma'am.' The contempt in his voice made Jessica's blood boil. 'I've two men in hospital, so something pretty serious occurred in that apartment upstairs and I'd like to know what it was.'

'How do you know the men were in the apartment upstairs?'

'Because,' he said with forced patience, 'it's where our MPs picked them up after the local police were alerted that a fracas had occurred. The locals then contacted the base at Burtonwood.' Clearly frustrated at the idea of conducting a conversation from so far away, he came into the workshop and stood in front of Jessica, saying accusingly, 'It's no use trying to evade the issue, ma'am. I'm not trying to get you into trouble. I merely want to know what happened.'

'I wouldn't know,' said Jessica. 'I wasn't here.' She liked him even less close up. He had hard blue eyes behind rimless glasses, a tough mouth and smooth tanned skin with a suggestion of growth on his firm round chin, as if he needed to shave twice a day. His close-cropped hair, what she could see of it underneath his cap, was silver. His uniform was impeccable, his bearing stiff and formal. He didn't look capable of relaxing for a moment.

'Ma'am,' he said, and there was a steely edge to his deep voice, 'the men reported a red-headed woman was the hostess of the . . . the party last night.'

Jessica hid a smile. He would clearly have preferred to say 'orgy'. She was beginning to enjoy playing with him. She removed her scarf so he could see even more of her hair, fluffing it out with both hands tauntingly. 'I never realised you Americans were so uncivilised,' she said, pretending to yawn.

'I beg your pardon?'

'It's common in this country for people to introduce themselves when they first meet. Who exactly are you?'

His lips tightened. 'Major Henningsen, Provost Marshal's Office, Eighth Army Air Corps, Burton-wood,' he said stiffly.

Jessica stuck out her hand. If he didn't shake it, she'd hit him. 'Jessica Fleming, Bootle, proprietor of this garage, who doesn't live in the flat upstairs but some-where else, and has absolutely no idea what happened last night because she wasn't here – which she has already told you.'

He gave her outstretched hand a brief, hard shake. 'But they said a redheaded woman?' He obviously didn't believe her.

'There's more than one redheaded woman in Bootle. I think you may be looking for Rita Mott. She's not in at the moment. I'll tell her you called when she arrives.'

'I'll wait,' he said grimly.

'In that case, wait outside. I'm busy.'

'Don't like man,' Penny whimpered. 'Naughty.' She gripped Jessica's leg harder.

Jessica picked her up. 'Never mind, darling, he'll soon be going.' She turned to Major Henningsen and said tartly, 'By the way, don't bother to apologise. After all, maybe you Americans don't know what an apology is. In this country, it means saying you're sorry when you've made a mistake.'

'I made a mistake, I'm sorry,' he said in a clipped voice.

He didn't look particularly sorry, more irate that she'd dragged it out of him.

'Apology accepted, goodbye,' Jessica said sweetly.

Major Henningsen turned on his heel and marched out of the workshop without another word. A few minutes later she heard the sound of an engine starting up and went to look. A jeep was parked on the pavement outside and he drove away, tyres screeching. He must have decided not to wait for Rita. He was several hundred yards down the road, when he braked, reversed the jeep at top speed and backed into the forecourt.

'What does he want now?' Jessica asked Penny, who responded by hiding her head in her mother's shoulder when the uniformed figure got out of the vehicle and approached.

'I wonder if you would do me a favour?' he said.

Jessica took a step backwards. Although the Americans she'd met so far had been nice boys – apart from Major Henningsen, that is – rumour had it they were only after one thing. 'What?' she said warily.

He laughed for the first time, an unpleasant bark. 'Jeez, lady, don't worry, you're not my type.' Before Jessica could come up with a suitably crushing response, he went on, 'It's Mothers' Day on Sunday. A few of the boys, the very young ones, are pining for the home country. Would you be willing to have a few over for a meal? The food will be provided, of course.'

'I wouldn't mind,' Jessica replied through gritted teeth. She couldn't very well refuse. But not his type! What an arrogant, obnoxious pig! He was as far from her type as any man she'd ever met.

'Thanks.' He returned to the jeep and climbed inside. 'The boys only need a bit of motherly attention,' he shouted, 'and your granddaughter might remind them of the kid sisters they left at home.'

Jessica was still smarting when Rita came limping home, having spent the night in a police-station cell. She sported a magnificent black eye and her green silk dress was torn in two places.

'What happened?' Jessica demanded in a shocked voice.

'I met these two black Yanks and brought them home,' Rita explained tiredly. 'They were ever so nice, Jess, proper gentlemen. Then a crowd of white Yanks turned up unannounced and were as mad as hell to find the black ones there. They tried to throw them out, but I wouldn't let them, which is when I got this.' She pointed to her half closed eye. 'Someone passing called the Bobbies, one thing led to another, and they ended up arresting the lot of us.'

Jessica shook her head worriedly. 'Perhaps you should keep your head down for a while,' she suggested.

'Of course I will. I don't want anyone to see me looking like this,' Rita said indignantly.

'What I meant, Rita, is that if GIs are turning up unannounced, it looks as if your place is getting a bit of a reputation.'

'Do you honestly think so?' Rita looked so pleased that Jessica gave up. 'You've had a visitor,' she said, 'a major from the Provost Marshal's office in Burtonwood.'

'A major?' Despite her pitiful state, Rita perked up. 'Was he good looking?'

'I would have thought you'd be more interested in what he wanted, not what he looked like.'

'I merely wondered if he'd like to come to one of my parties, that's all.'

Jessica guffawed. 'Ask him and see!'

Chapter 13

Jessica asked Kitty Quigley if she would come to tea and help entertain the visitors on Sunday. 'You're young and single and used to dealing with young men. I won't know what to say.'

'I'm not sure if I will, either,' said Kitty. 'Would you like me to bring someone else from the hospital? There's this girl, Lucy. She'll soon make them feel at home.'

Lucy was aching to go out with a Yank. It was rumoured that hundreds of girls hung round on Central Station waiting to be picked up when the GIs poured in from Burtonwood, but Lucy didn't quite have the courage. 'If me dad found out, he'd kill me.'

She was thrilled to bits to be invited to tea. 'Tea sounds dead respectable. I won't tell me dad about the Americans in case he won't let me come.' She patted her dark hair and said thoughtfully, 'They like blondes best, don't they, Yanks?'

The GIs arrived in a jeep at four o'clock, Major Henningsen having telephoned Jessica at the garage to ask for her address. 'I forgot to ask where you live,' he said in his cold, clipped voice.

She told him, equally cold, 'How many are there coming? The house is rather small.'

'Will three be all right?'

'Yes. What time?'

'Four.'

'Right.'

'Goodbye.'

274

'Goodbye,' said Jessica, slamming down the phone.

'Jaysus, Mary and Joseph!' remarked Sheila Reilly who, in common with the rest of the street, was watching through the parlour window when the jeep drew up outside number 10 and three young lads alighted. 'They're scarcely out of nappies.' Her heart twisted when she thought about their mams, thousands of miles away in America and almost certainly worried sick about their boys. Dominic and Niall and a pile of other kids were hanging starry-eyed around the jeep. Say if the war continued another ten years and they were called up! 'I couldn't bear it,' she whispered.

The driver of the jeep, a young man in his twenties with a fresh open face, was talking to the kids, chaffing them along, and they were all grinning. He handed them a little packet each.

'I bet that's gum,' thought Sheila. 'I hope they didn't ask, because I specifically told them not to. The Yanks'll think we're all beggars in this country!'

The driver leapt out and said something to three GIs who were standing mournfully on the pavement, and all four started to unload boxes from the back of the jeep.

'I wonder if that's the food?' Sheila's mouth watered. She'd been eating herself to death since Christmas, mainly butties, as bread was the only thing there was plenty of. The trouble was, food seemed a solace when Calum was away. She already couldn't fasten the brassiere which Eileen had bought her for Christmas. She watched as the lads returned to unload more boxes. 'There's enough there to feed an entire army.'

'We'll never eat all this!' gasped Jessica when every surface of the kitchen was covered with cardboard boxes. She opened one and found an entire leg of pork, already cooked. In another, a piece of ham as big as Major Henningsen's head. There was a catering-size tin of strawberries, another of cherries, a huge jar of fresh whipped cream, an equally huge fruitcake, boxes of biscuits, boxes of fresh fruit; oranges, bananas, pears. 'And peaches!' she exclaimed, close to tears. 'Look, Penny, this is a peach. Doesn't it feel beautiful?'

'Everything's ready to eat,' said the young man who appeared to be in charge. He'd introduced himself as Sergeant Dale Tooley, and the boys were Gary, Frank and Wayne. 'There's potato salad and some fresh greens in one of the boxes. Well, I'll leave you to it, ma'am. The boys'll help you set the table.'

'You're going?' Jessica felt alarmed. He was the only one who'd spoken so far. The others, looking extremely wan and miserable, were sitting dejectedly in the living room and hadn't said a word.

'I'd like to stay, ma'am, but I've things to do. I'll be back around seven thirty.' With a cheery wave, he was gone.

'Well,' said Jessica, rubbing her hands together with an enthusiasm she didn't feel, 'let's get that table ready, shall we?'

The boys mutely did as they were told and began to carry food into the parlour where the table had been opened to its fullest extent and was already set with cutlery. Jessica put Penny in her high chair so she'd be out of the way. She sat sucking her thumb and watching the proceedings with wide-eyed curiosity.

Kitty Quigley arrived, accompanied by a young peroxided blonde with her arm in a sling. 'I'm sorry I'm late, but I was waiting for Lucy,' Kitty said when Jessica thankfully opened the door.

'Me dad refused to let me out,' Lucy explained. 'I got me hair dyed yesterday, and you'd think I'd announced I was about to go on the game. Look what he did!' She held out her arm. 'It's me wrist, but it's only sprained, not broken. He locked me in the bedroom this morning and I ended up climbing out the window, which is not easy, I can tell you, with only one arm.'

'I see,' said Jessica faintly. 'They're in the parlour, and

I think they might all be dumb, because no-one's spoken so far.'

The boys perked up a bit at the sight of two young women, but only slightly.

'Christ Almighty, get a load of this grub!' Lucy set to with relish, but the three young boys picked at their food throughout the meal and the conversation was forced, despite Jessica's strained attempts to enquire about their families, their hobbies, their favourite sport.

'The USA,' Gary replied when she asked where he came from. He was a slight, white-faced boy with babyish fair hair.

'I know that,' Jessica said patiently, affecting not to hear Lucy's stifled giggle. 'I meant what town?'

'Houston.'

'Is it nice there?'

'Gee, I suppose it's okay.'

'And what about you, Frank?'

Frank had lovely soft skin and a slightly Latin look. 'Paris, Texas,' he replied.

'I didn't know there was a Paris in America,' Jessica remarked in surprise. 'I went to Paris, France, on my honeymoon.'

She rather hoped one of them would ask what Paris was like and the conversation would start rolling, but after a long pause, Kitty said politely, 'Did you, Jess?'

Jessica began to wonder, seeing as it was Mothers' Day, if she should have made herself look more motherly; put her hair in a bun, gone without make-up and worn her dowdiest frock, which might have made the boys feel more at home. Instead, in an effort to look glamorous for her youthful guests, she was dressed up to the nines in a purple two-piece, her highest heels, the treasured nylons and possibly two much jewellery and make-up. She racked her brains for something else to say. Even Penny was unusually silent and Kitty was staring shyly at her plate, as if as stuck for words as Jessica.

Lucy, for the moment at least, had abandoned her sling and was too busy attacking the food to be of much use.

'This isn't half the gear,' was the most Lucy had uttered on several occasions as she cut another slice of ham or pork and helped herself to more salad. Wayne, who had a faint hint of a moustache and seemed the most mature of the three, regarded her from time to time with surreptitious interest.

The main meal finished, Jessica opened the tin of strawberries which she served with lashings of cream. What on earth were they to do when they'd finished eating? She glanced at the clock. Only half four, which meant it would be another three hours before Sergeant Tooley returned. She imagined the three boys reporting back to Major Henningsen that they'd had a lousy time and come away feeling even more miserable than when they'd arrived.

Unknown to Jessica, in the street outside a crowd had gathered and unrest was stirring. 'She can't expect to keep them to herself the whole time,' complained Aggie Donovan. 'I mean, we're entitled to meet the Americans every bit as much as she is.'

'They probably haven't finished their tea yet,' said Sheila, though like Aggie, she was dying to meet the foreign guests. 'Maybe she'll invite us in later.' Little did she know, but this was the furthest thought from Jessica's mind.

'I've got a brother in America,' claimed Paddy O'Hara. 'You never know, one of 'em might have met him. He's quite well known in Boston,' he told the crowd.

'That's more than likely,' someone agreed.

'I'm going in,' Aggie said determinedly, and made for the entry which ran behind the houses. Jessie Fleming seemed to forget she was only a rag-and-boneman's daughter and didn't deign to hang her key inside the letterbox like other people, which meant Aggie would have to go in the back way. If she knocked on the front door, she ran the risk of being turned away.

'Oh, God!' Jessica groaned when she heard the back kitchen door open. If the neighbours arrived on the scene, the occasion would turn out to be a worse disaster than it already was.

'Hallo, lads.' Aggie Donovan appeared in the parlour doorway in the brown wool frock with the beads on the bodice which had been her best for over a quarter of a century. By now, half the beads were missing and the frock hung lankly on her skinny frame, which seemed to get skinnier by the year. 'Welcome to Bootle. How are you settling in, like? Poor little lambs, stuck in a strange foreign country at your age. I bet you don't half miss your mams and dads.'

To Jessica's astonishment, Gary burst into tears. 'Gran!' he bawled. He stumbled out of the chair into Aggie's arms.

'There, lad! Have a good cry on your ould gran's shoulder.' Aggie patted his back energetically and grinned triumphantly at Jessica.

At first, Jessica thought it was a reunion between two long lost relatives, but apparently Aggie was merely a substitute. 'I really miss my gran,' Gary sobbed.

'Never mind, lad, you've got a replacement for the duration. You can come and see me any time,' Aggie assured him.

'Can I hold Penny, Mrs Fleming?' Frank enquired tearfully. 'I've a kid sister at home who's not much older than she is.'

'Of course.' Jessica picked Penny out of the high chair and dumped her on Frank's knee. 'And please call me Jess, not Mrs Fleming.'

'Can Wayne plug his . . . what did you call it?' Lucy turned to Wayne, who had magically transported himself into the chair beside her the very second it was vacated.

'Phonograph.'

'Can Wayne plug his phonograph in? I think he means a gramophone,' she added in an aside.

'I've brought some records with me,' said Wayne.

'I'm afraid there's no electricity in the house,' gulped Jessica. Everything was getting beyond her. The tea party was totally ruined.

'Sheila Reilly's got electricity,' said Kitty. 'We'll take it there.'

Outside, the crowd were waiting for Aggie to establish diplomatic relations. If she didn't emerge soon, they'd all go in themselves. One or two had already moved in the direction of the entry, when the front door of number 10 opened and the three young soldiers came out. They almost disappeared beneath a deluge of delighted people anxious to make the lads welcome in their country.

Kitty and Lucy carried the gramophone into the Reillys', but the plug wouldn't fit the socket in the parlour. A distress alert was sounded for an adaptor.

'Go round to your grandad's,' Sheila instructed Dominic urgently, 'and tell him to fetch the box of plugs and things he keeps in the washhouse. He's a terrible magpie, me dad,' she explained to Jessica when Dominic scooted off. 'He collects all sorts of funny odds and ends.'

Jack Doyle came hurrying around the corner minutes later clutching a cardboard box. He found a suitable adaptor, Sheila opened the parlour window, and soon the sound of the Andrews Sisters' 'Boogie-woogie Bugle Boy of Company B' came blaring out.

Wayne began to dance with Lucy, a most peculiar dance, in which Wayne remained half crouched, kicking his legs in rhythm to the music and twirling his partner around like a top. Lucy quickly got the hang of it. Her sprained wrist forgotten, she twisted and turned and flailed her arms like a crazy windmill.

'That's a funny dance, lad,' Aggie remarked to Gary.

'It's called the jitterbug, Gran. Do you want to try it?'

'I'll have a go at anything. Come on.'

More people joined in the dancing, and suddenly a party was in progress. It was months since the street had had a party. At the sound of the noise, doors were flung open and those who'd been quietly reading the Sunday paper or preparing the tea, came out, took one look, and promptly joined in the festivities.

Jessica told Sheila on the quiet that there was plenty left to eat if she was hungry.

'I'm bloody starving,' said Sheila. Calum never seemed to be home when the street had a party and on these occasions she missed him more than ever. She turned to Paddy O'Hara who was blissfully tapping his stick on the pavement. 'Are you peckish, luv?'

'I'm always peckish, Sheila.'

Afterwards, Jessica was never quite sure how it happened, but her house was suddenly full of people after food.

'Pork!'

'Ham!'

'Jaysus, Mary and Joseph, is that peaches?'

'Help yourself,' Jessica called gaily. All of a sudden she didn't care. The meat wouldn't keep and it wasn't fair that she should be left with loads of cake and biscuits all to herself. If it hadn't been for the neighbours the tea party would have turned out to be a wash-out. As it was, Gary, Frank and Wayne appeared to be having a whale of a time.

Jimmy Quigley stood at the parlour window, watching. 'I think I might pop outside for a few minutes,' he called to his new wife.

'I'd sooner you didn't,' Theresa said primly from the other room where she was ironing. 'It sounds dead rowdy out there.'

'They're playing an Al Jolson record.' Jimmy sang

281

underneath his breath. 'Mammy, Mammy, the sun shines east . . .' He loved Al Jolson. 'We could dance together,' he called wistfully. 'I haven't danced in years.'

'In the street! Not likely.'

'Y'know, it wouldn't hurt to let Georgie and Billy out for a while. There seems to be plenty of food.' Georgie and Billy had, like himself, been stuck at the window watching the goings-on with longing. Theresa had sent them to bed, fed up with them nagging to be allowed to join in the party like the other kids. Jimmy didn't like to say anything, but he was beginning to feel concerned that the lads spent far too much time shut in their room.

Theresa didn't answer. Jimmy remained, as his daughter had so often done in the past, feeling slightly cut off from a world where everybody else seemed to be enjoying themselves. He sighed and returned to the living room where he picked up the paper and began to read. 'Never mind,' he muttered, half to himself, 'the King's Arms'll be open soon.'

'Me dad never drank on Sundays, nor me first husband.' Theresa ironed a cuff with careful precision. 'And I've been meaning to say this before, Jimmy, but I'm only home one night a week, and I'd've thought you'd prefer to stay in with me.'

'If that's what you'd like, luv.'

Theresa glanced at him with her wet grey eyes. 'It seems proper.'

Jimmy reached out and stroked her bottom. Her square face didn't change, but she must have liked it or she would have stopped him. He didn't want to stay in, but knew if he put his foot down and ignored her, she would deny him the privilege of her body that night, and possibly the next night if she thought the offence warranted sterner punishment. She enjoyed making love, but seemed to be able to turn herself on and off like a tap, lying with her back to him and positively refusing all his coaxings.

'How about . . . y'know?' He cocked his head upstairs. The lads knew what was good for them, so there was no chance of them emerging from their room without permission.

'Your Kitty might come in.'

'What would that matter? She won't come in the bedroom.'

'In a minute, as soon as I've finished the ironing.'

Jimmy pretended to read the paper, his body trembling with anticipation. Half an hour in bed with Theresa was better than a street party or a pint of ale any day.

It was still daylight when Sergeant Dale Tooley drove his jeep around the corner into Pearl Street. The peculiar habit the Brits had of fiddling around with their clocks had occurred a few weeks ago, which meant that darkness fell two hours later than it had done the day before.

He grinned with satisfaction. 'Gee, the boys sure seem to be having a great time.'

To the strains of a harmonica and a great deal of whooping and shouting, the entire street seemed to be involved in an exuberant Irish jig. His three young charges could be seen, jackets and caps removed, at the very centre of the riotous dance. To the sergeant's surprise, he felt homesick himself for the first time since he'd come to England several weeks ago. His folks were first-generation Irish immigrants, and he'd witnessed the same mad scene at Boston ceilidhs numerous times during his twenty-eight years.

He was rather pleased when he noticed the bar across the road open its doors for business. He climbed out of the jeep, went inside and ordered a pint of bitter ale. It was a strange old place, with sawdust on the floor and wooden benches and tables that looked a hundred years old.

283

'How much is that, pal?'

The landlord laid his hands flat down on the counter and beamed, 'It's on the house, mate.'

'Gee, thanks a million.'

Suddenly, as if would-be customers had been hiding close by down alleys and around corners, the bar was full. Dale Tooley found himself plied with pints of ale and double whiskies. The Brits certainly were a friendly lot.

'What did you do back in America?'

'I was a construction worker, like my pa before me.'

They asked where he came from and when he said, 'Boston, Massachusetts', someone shouted, 'Fetch Paddy O'Hara. He's got a brother in Boston, you might know him.'

'It's a big place,' said Dale Tooley.

A blind man was ushered into the bar leading a large friendly dog.

'Tell him about your brother, Paddy.'

'Boston's a big place,' the sergeant said again.

To his everlasting surprise, although he'd never actually met Donal O'Hara, Dale recognised the name. 'Didn't he lead a strike once?'

'That's right.' Paddy swelled with pride. Sometimes, he wondered if folks actually believed him when he told them he had a brother in the States who was a permanent thorn in the side of the establishment. 'He spent three months in jail.'

An hour later, the sergeant remembered he was there for a purpose and it wasn't to liquor up in a British pub, but to collect his three young comrades and take them back to Burtonwood.

Outside, the sky was slowly turning purple as dusk began to fall. It wasn't yet time for the damned blackout that caused such confusion and chaos, thank the Lord. Yellow light spilled from the open doors of the tiny cramped houses onto the shiny cobbles of the street.

They were dancing to a record now, the Andrews Sisters' 'Oh, Johnny, Oh, Johnny, Oh, Johnny, Oh . . .'

Dale Tooley leaned against the wall and took several deep breaths to try and clear his head. He reckoned he'd have a job dragging the boys away. Wayne was cheek to cheek with a cute blonde and the pair looked as if they were glued together. The Andrews Sisters finished 'Oh, Johnny' and began 'I'll Be With You in Apple Blossom Time'.

'I'll let this be the last waltz,' he thought. He paused at the edge of the crowd encircling the dancers and lit a cigarette to sober himself up. No-one had yet noticed he was there. He blew the smoke out slowly as his eyes searched for the other two boys. They were chatting away to a couple of women and looked as happy as larks. He was about to drop his eyes, when he saw the girl.

Jeez! She was Irish as the Pigs of Trogheady and the prettiest girl he'd ever seen, with a mass of brown curls and cheeks like roses. There was an innocence about her, a purity, that unexpectedly tore at his heart. She was totally different from the girls he'd come across so far in England, the ones who hung about the base, prepared to trade their bodies for a night out and a pair of nylons. This girl was one in a million.

He flicked his cigarette away, unaware that it was immediately picked up by a young boy who scurried into an entry to smoke it out of sight of the grown-ups. The girl was talking to someone, and she looked round, startled, when Dale asked, 'Can I have this dance?'

'Oh!'

Her eyes were hazel, wide apart and completely trusting. Dale felt his insides melt. Perhaps it was the drink, but he wanted this girl more than he'd ever wanted any woman before. She glanced around her wildly, as if searching for a means of escape, and when she saw there was none, she smiled, lifted her arms for him to take her, and Dale was lost.

Her hair was like wild silk fluttering against his face and her hand felt soft and small in his. 'What's your name?' he mumbled in her ear.

'Kitty. Kitty Quigley.'

'Hi, Kitty. I'm Dale Tooley.'

She smiled again, her face only inches from his, and he could almost taste the sweetness of her breath. It took a sheer physical effort on Dale's part not to lean over and kiss her pretty pink lips.

'Hi, Dale,' she said, and within that second, Kitty Quigley fell completely and totally in love with Dale Tooley.

Major Henningsen telephoned Jessica at the garage the next day. 'Thanks,' he said grudgingly. 'The boys had a great time.'

'Glad to be of service,' Jessica replied.

'No doubt you'll be pleased to hear the apartment over the garage has been declared a no-go area to the men from here.'

'I'm neither pleased nor sorry. It makes no difference to me what goes on up there.' There were plenty of Americans stationed elsewhere, and Jessica had no doubt that once Rita's black eye had faded, the shenanigans would continue in full force.

There was a pause, and she was about to say goodbye and put the phone down, when the curt voice said, 'I'd like to ask another favour.'

'Ask away.'

'The officers are holding a party a week this Saturday at the Dorchester Hotel in Rodney Street, and I wondered if you were free.'

Jessica held the receiver at arm's length and looked at it in astonishment. Just as if she'd go out with *him*! She returned the receiver to her ear, laughed incredulously, and said, 'I thought I wasn't your type.'

'You're not, dear lady, you're not. I merely asked if

you were free. I heard you sing the other day and you sounded like a professional. I was going to ask if you would entertain us.'

She felt as if she'd like to curl up and crawl into a hole after such a comprehensive misunderstanding. 'I'm not sure,' she said weakly, though she longed to start singing again.

'We'll send a staff car to collect you and take you home – and there'll be refreshments laid on.'

Jessica thought about the lavish food the day before. She'd been too wrought up to enjoy a bite herself, and by the time the neighbours had helped themselves, the parlour and kitchen looked as if they had been attacked by a plague of locusts. Paddy O'Hara had even taken the bones for Rover. It would be nice to have something to eat in comfort – and if they were sending a car!

'I don't suppose it would hurt,' she said with feigned reluctance.

'You can bring your granddaughter if you like.'

Jessica scowled and snapped, 'She's not my grand-daughter, she's my daughter.'

A funny little coughing noise came from the other end of the line, and she realised he was chuckling. 'I know. You're so alike she couldn't be anything else. I was just teasing.' With that, he rang off.

Brenda Mahon cut the sleeves and part of the bodice away from one of Jessica's old dance dresses and made two narrow straps instead to hold it up. The material was red, slippery satin, very heavy, and the dress was snugly form-fitting down to the hips, from where it swirled out in a great circle of material which fell against her legs in deep folds.

'The Yanks'll drop dead when they see you in that, Jess,' Brenda said admiringly when Jessica tried the finished garment on.

'Arthur thought I was wrong to wear red with red hair. He said it clashed.'

'It does, but it looks really striking.'

'Do you think so?' Jessica smoothed her hands over her hips with a satisfied sigh. 'Are you very busy? I might have a few more things altered.'

'I'm always busy.' Brenda explained that the Government had announced Utility clothes would be brought in that summer. 'Frocks'll all be virtually the same, like a uniform: much shorter, dead plain, no pleats, and they're cutting down on colours.' Appliqué would be banned and there would be no more lace on underwear.

'I don't see how that'll help us win the war,' Jessica remarked.

'It cuts down on manufacturing and imports,' Brenda said knowledgeably.

'In that case, you'll be busier than ever with women wanting to look different.'

Brenda shook her head. 'No, I'll be busy with women wanting their frocks altered to look the same. They'd feel unpatriotic if they looked different.' She giggled. 'It's not just us women. Even the men will have to go without turn-ups on their trousers and there'll be no more double-breasted coats or pockets on pyjamas.'

'Strewth!' gasped Jessica. 'Very soon, the Government will be asking us to go round stark naked in order to win the war.'

Later that night, Jessica tried the dress on again, twisting to and fro in front of the wardrobe mirror in the spare bedroom so as not to disturb Penny, who was asleep in the front. She had to wear her black strapless corselette underneath, which nipped her waist in so tightly she could scarcely breathe, though it was worth it, giving her an hourglass figure. 'I'm not bad for nearly forty-six!' she thought proudly.

The dress still on, she went downstairs and tried her

hair in a variety of different styles before the mirror over the fireplace. She'd just decided she'd wear it loose for the concert, with her marcasite and mother-of-pearl earrings and pendant, when Jack Doyle came in through the back door. He'd been coming that way for weeks, worried he'd be noticed waiting to be let in the front as the nights rapidly grew lighter.

He stood in the doorway, almost disgusted with himself as desire engulfed his body at the sight of her gleaming white shoulders which contrasted starkly against the scarlet thing she was wearing.

'What's that, a nightgown?' he growled.

She threw back her head and laughed at him in the mirror. 'Of course not. It's an old dance frock. Brenda just altered it for me.'

'You don't intend wearing it outside, surely?'

'I'll be wearing it a week on Saturday. I'm singing at a concert at the Dorchester Hotel.'

'Not in that. I won't let you.'

She turned and regarded him coldly. 'You can't stop me, Jack.'

Jack knew it would be a waste of time arguing. She was right. 'Then I'll come with you.'

'You'll do no such thing. The Americans will think you're my chaperon.'

'The Americans?'

'It's a concert for American officers.'

He could scarcely contain his rage. Americans! Officers! In that frock! He thrust his hands into his pockets, scared what he might do to her if she provoked him further. 'What's happening with Arthur?' he asked.

She shrugged, surprised. 'I don't know. All I've had is a letter to say he's joined the Army. Why?'

'I was just wondering if you intended breaking off with him legally like, that's all?'

'I hadn't given it much thought,' she said carelessly. 'Why?' she enquired a second time.

289

Jack emitted a deep breath and drew it in again like a gasp. He was on the verge of proposing, driven almost to distraction at the thought of her flaunting herself in that frock in front of a crowd of Yanks, yet knowing he had no power to prevent her.

'I dunno.' He took another deep breath. 'Will you . . . should we . . .' He paused, floundering, unable to put his tongue around the words.

She wasn't listening. Oblivious to his inward torment, she was undoing the fastenings down the side of the frock, her back still to him.

The moment was lost. She stepped out of the red satin. Underneath she wore a tight black boned thing with suspenders holding up her stockings. Mollie would have considered such a garment indecent, and there was a time when he might have done so himself. Jessica undid the suspenders and began to unpeel her stockings in a slow suggestive way, glancing at him from time to time in the mirror.

'Jaysus!' He put his arms around her, tore the black thing away from her breasts and cupped them in his large hands. He began to kiss her neck, her shoulders. 'Don't go to the concert, Jess,' he pleaded. 'Come out with me instead.' They could go somewhere in town where there was no chance of being seen together.

'Don't be silly, Jack. I've promised. I'd be letting people down.'

Niall Reilly, Georgie Beamish, and the entire third-year class of St Joan of Arc's made their First Holy Communion the following Sunday, Easter.

Jimmy Quigley doubted if he'd ever felt so proud in his life as he stood in the pew behind the row of youngsters in their gleaming white frocks and shirts – though none gleamed so brightly as did Georgie. It was twenty years since he'd stood almost in the very place and Kitty had gone through the same rigmarole. Never, in his wildest dreams, had he envisaged doing the same thing a second time around. It occurred to him that he felt younger now than he'd done then. There was a brief moment of regret when the ceremony was over, they went out into the churchyard, and instead of a bright, girlish face turning eagerly to kiss him, Georgie merely shrugged and twisted his lips churlishly when Jimmy tried to shake his hand, father to son, like. It was a pity the lads couldn't bring themselves to be a bit more friendly. Despite encouragement, they positively re- fused to call him 'Dad'. All Jimmy could do was hope they'd come round eventually.

He noticed that, unlike twenty years ago, there were scarcely any dads present. Those who weren't already in the Merchant Navy had been called up into the armed forces, though Cal Reilly had arrived home the day before. Cal, like dozens of other Bootle men, had been transferred to the Arctic convoys, the most dangerous route of all. Their ships turned into blocks of ice and the equipment froze solid to the decks. Last month, two hundred and seventy-three Allied merchant ships had been lost to German planes and U-boats.

Jimmy glanced across at Sheila. She was holding her sister Eileen's baby in one arm and hanging on to Cal like grim death with the other. Dominic caught Jimmy's eye and gave him a wide, cheerful grin. Jimmy pretended not to see and turned away. For the barest moment, he traitorously wished Georgie was a bit more like that scally, Dominic.

Afterwards, they walked home along the Dockie. Theresa liked a short stroll after Mass. 'That's where I used to work,' said Jimmy, pointing to the tall gates of Gladstone Dock.

'Y'said that last week,' grumbled Billy.

'Did I?' Anxious to please the lads, Jimmy kicked a tin can in their direction. Unable to resist, Georgie kicked it back.

'Jimmy!' Theresa exploded. 'You're making a show of us.'

'No-one's looking.' His attention momentarily diverted, Jimmy missed the can and it rolled into the road. He ran to fetch it and behind him a car came to a halt with a screech of brakes.

'Mind where you're going. I nearly ran you over,' a voice called irritably.

'Sorry, mate.' Jimmy tipped his hat apologetically at the driver, a posh geezer in a bowler and a pin-striped suit who looked vaguely familiar. The man stared back, as if he was trying to place him in turn.

'That'll learn you,' Theresa said nastily. 'If you're not careful, I'll end up a widow again.'

On the day Jess was due to sing at her concert, Jack caught the bus to Melling to see his daughter, Eileen, and his youngest grandchild. Spring had suddenly burst out with a vengeance. The hedges were covered with a spattering of green and the sun shone out of the milky blue sky with a welcome warmth.

'It's about time I started on the garden,' he grunted, and with barely a glance at Nicky and without even waiting for a cup of tea, he went straight outside.

He'd always wanted a garden. It was the only thing he'd missed throughout his entire adult life spent living in Bootle with only a tiny patch of yard. Now Eileen had an acre or more and Jack was in his element. No member of his family had wanted for basic vegetables over the past year, nor rhubarb and cooking apples – there'd even been strawberries in June. He thrust the spade fiercely into the ground. The soil was black and damp and soft. Immediately he began to feel at one with the earth and Jessica Fleming was forgotten, or so he told himself.

Eileen came out after a while and regarded him worriedly. 'Do you intend turning the entire garden over in a single afternoon, Dad? You'll have a heart attack at the rate you're going.'

She persuaded him to come inside for a drink and a smoke. 'I managed to get ten ciggies in the post office. Anyroad, I've got something to tell you.'

'Alice is expecting a baby in August,' Eileen said when they were seated in the living room and he was gratifyingly puffing on the first cigarette he'd had in weeks. Nicky, eight months old tomorrow, a handsome little chap who, unlike his dad, rarely smiled, stared at him solemnly from the playpen in which he was sat clutching a teddy bear.

'Our Sean, a dad!' Jack suddenly felt very old. It had always been a quiet dream that his three kids would end up settled with families of their own, but now he felt, unfairly, that he was being abandoned. He blamed it all on Jessica for upsetting the pattern he'd so carefully planned. He thought of Penny, still a baby. It would be many years before she'd grow up and get married.

'It's hard to believe, isn't it?' laughed Eileen. 'He was such a flirt, never out with the same girl twice until he met Alice.'

'How come you know, Eileen? Our Sheila didn't mention it when I saw her this morning.'

Eileen looked uncomfortable. 'Alice came all the way out here yesterday to tell me. She's convinced our Sheila doesn't like her.'

'Neither me nor Sheila liked Alice much at first,' Jack conceded, 'and even now I'd have preferred Sean to marry someone carrying a bit less baggage. Five kids, a wife, and now a babby on the way! It's a big responsibility for a lad of nineteen.'

'It's no good crying over spilt milk, Dad,' Eileen said flatly. 'They're married, Alice is expecting, and that's all there is to it. The thing is, how on earth are they all going to fit into that cramped little flat in Miller's Bridge?'

The problem drove Jack back into the garden, taking the ciggies with him, where he turned the black earth over and broke it into pieces even more energetically than he'd done before. Alice's place in Miller's Bridge was poky in the extreme, with just two tiny bedrooms, a living room and a basic back kitchen that could only be described as Victorian. The lavatories outside were shared with other families in the block. The Scully boys slept in one room, Alice and her two sisters in the other. He hated to think where Sean laid his head when he was home on leave, but presumed it could only be on the floor. Jack attacked a clod of earth with hatred in his heart for the property owners who fattened their wallets by cramming the poor into substandard accommodation that wasn't fit for animals – and for the politicians who allowed it to happen. If they'd let him, he would have built a house for his lad with his own bare hands.

He lit another ciggie and cut the grass on the small lawn with the ancient mower which the previous owners of the cottage had left behind. It was a waste of good growing space and he'd have liked to turn it over to vegetables, but Sheila's kids needed somewhere to play when they came, and Nicky would soon be walking.

When Nan Wright died at Christmas, he'd put in an application for number 1 on behalf of Sean and Alice, willing to pay the increase in rent out of his own pocket, but so many folks had lost their homes in the Blitz that his application had been just one of many, and some other family had been successful. According to Sheila, they'd paid the rent collector a few bob on the side as a bribe.

The lawn finished, he trimmed the hedges, pruned every bush in sight, and could only be persuaded to stop when Eileen announced Kate Thomas had turned up for tea. By then, all the ciggies were gone.

He liked Kate. They usually talked about politics, and

despite their totally different backgrounds, they agreed on most things. He eagerly went indoors.

'Hallo, luv,' he beamed. Her little scrubbed face and untidy hair posed no threat, unlike Jess Fleming who oozed danger from every pore. Little did Jack know, but Kate Thomas loved him far more deeply than Jessica ever had or ever would.

The lights in the ornate dining room of the Dorchester Hotel were dimmed except for the one over the grand piano. There were about seventy people there, more than half American officers, the remainder guests, both men and quite a few smartly dressed women. Against one of the walls stood several white-clothed tables laden with food and drink. The pianist, an elderly man in evening dress, had already agreed the programme with Jessica, who'd brought her own music with her. The colonel who appeared to be in charge of the proceedings banged on the piano with a glass tankard, the pianist winced, and everyone fell silent as Jessica was introduced as a British nightingale who was about to entertain them.

She sang 'We'll Meet Again', 'I'll be Seeing You', 'Yours', several Cole Porter songs, a few Irving Berlins, including her favourite, 'There's a Small Hotel'. Her voice, as dazzling and pure as clear crystal, soared upwards and outwards, intoxicating an already partly intoxicated audience with its beauty. After something patriotic for the British, 'The White Cliffs of Dover', she finished up with the American National Anthem. 'Oh, say can't you see, by the dawn's early light . . .' The uniformed men stood stiffly to attention, put their hands on their hearts, and joined in.

Between songs, she was cheered to the echo. When she finished, they threatened to lift the roof off with their shouts for an encore.

'I don't think I can manage any more,' she said to the

colonel when he came hurrying over to thank her. 'My throat's hurting.'

'That's okay, honey. They'll soon quieten down. Come and have a drink.' He snapped his fingers imperiously at the pianist to continue and the man began to play 'There'll Always be an England' with a slightly mutinous air.

Jessica had quite a long conversation with the colonel, who was a benign, middle-aged man with a shock of prematurely white hair. He led her towards some empty chairs in the corner where they discussed the war, and he told her that folks in the States had no idea the Brits were in such a bad way.

'This rationing, for instance, it's appalling how little you have to eat.'

'We have enough to keep us going,' said Jessica, 'and the Government is very sensible. They make sure what we eat is good for us.'

'And the Blitz!' He shuddered. 'How on earth did you live through it?'

Jessica thought of Jacob Singerman and little Tony Costello. 'Some of us didn't,' she said drily, and suggested that if he cared to travel as far as Exeter, York or Norwich or several other places, he could find out what the Blitz was like for himself. 'They've all had air-raids recently.'

'You're a brave little country, that's for sure.'

'We're little in size, but big in heart.' He was beginning to sound a bit patronising, she thought.

'You lost your big aircraft carrier, *Hermes,* off the coast of Ceylon last week, didn't you?' He shook his head ruefully, as if the ship wouldn't have been lost if he'd been there to protect it.

'I didn't lose it personally, but yes, I understand it was sunk by the Japanese.'

'Not only that, your troops are retreating on all fronts in the Far East. Never mind.' He slapped her thigh. 'The good ol' US of A will turn the tide. By this time next year, it will all be over.' He made no attempt to remove his hand. When Jessica tried to stand up, she found herself imprisoned on the chair.

'If you wouldn't mind!' She raised her eyebrows and glared at the hand on her thigh. The back was covered with white hairs.

'How's about we two take a room upstairs?' he whispered in her ear. He no longer seemed benign.

'How's about we don't!' She tried to prise the hand away, but it felt as heavy as lead and seemed to be permanently adhered to her leg. She didn't want to make a scene, but if he didn't let her go soon she'd be left with no alternative but to throw her drink in his face or scream for help.

She was contemplating which of the two would cause her the least embarrassment and had decided on throwing the drink when an unexpected saviour appeared on the scene.

Major Henningsen, whom she hadn't so far seen all night. He bent his broad, tough body over the colonel and said urgently, 'You're wanted in the lobby, Doug. Something important's come up.'

The colonel blinked and looked grave. 'I'll be there on the double, Gus.' He released Jessica's thigh and marched off in the opposite direction from the lobby.

'Is there really something important?' Jessica tried to smooth the creases the colonel's clammy hand had made in her frock.

'No, but he'd had far too much liquor and he'll have forgotten all about it if and when he finds the lobby.' He sat down in the chair the colonel had vacated.

'Thanks for rescuing me.' She felt genuinely grateful, but, true to form, Major Henningsen immediately put her back up with his next words.

'That's okay, but what do you expect men to do when you turn up looking like that?' he said curtly.

'Looking like what?' she gasped, enraged. 'I came as a singer, not a courtesan. Are you suggesting I should have dressed as a nun?'

He gave a fleeting grin. Without his cap, she noticed that his crewcut hair wasn't silver as she'd originally thought, but milk blond. 'I'm not sure if that would have caused more excitement or less.'

'Huh!'

'I see you didn't bring your little girl.'

'Penny? I left her with a neighbour.'

'Penny's a cute name.'

'I can't say the same for Gus. You definitely don't suit Augustus.' Attila, perhaps, or Genghis Khan.

'It's Gustav, actually. My folks were Danish.' He leaned back in his chair and regarded her disdainfully. 'Where's your husband?'

'In the army,' Jessica snapped.

'What regiment?'

'The Royal Artillery.'

'Stationed where?'

'I've no idea where he's stationed. We're separated.'

'I thought as much.' He nodded knowingly. 'A respectable married woman would never wear a dress like that.'

Jessica made a superhuman effort to retain her temper and think of a way of riling him as much as he riled her. 'I reckon the problem with my dress lies more with you than me.' She patted his arm understandingly. 'This is a perfectly normal evening dress that any woman with a decent shape and decent shoulders would wear. You may well say I'm not your type, but I reckon I'm very much so. You're attracted to me and it scares you stiff, doesn't it?'

He glared at her so balefully that she was worried he might strike her. Then his hard narrow lips twitched and suddenly he was laughing so much that he had to remove his glasses to wipe his eyes.

Jessica thought resentfully that as far as Major Henningsen was concerned, it was always *her* who ended up feeling discomfited. There was nothing more deflating than being laughed at, particularly by someone who looked as if they only laughed once a year. Perhaps, like the colonel, he was drunk.

'It's not fair,' she thought. 'I came to entertain them, not to be insulted.' She got up abruptly to seek some food, and was captured by another major who turned out to be delightful company. He showed her pictures of his wife and children and told her she had the most glorious voice he'd ever heard. 'Please come and sing for us again,' he pleaded.

'I second that,' said a captain, overhearing. 'I heard Helen Morgan sing once, and you were much better.'

The remark was enough to make the entire evening seem worthwhile. Helen Morgan was a famous, highly-thought-of nightclub singer in the States. Her ego had been fully restored and her stomach was pleasantly full, when she noticed it was nearly midnight and time she went home. There was no sign of the private who'd collected her, which wasn't surprising as he wouldn't be allowed into an officers' party. She wondered if he was waiting in the lobby and was about to go and look, when a voice said grimly in her ear, 'I've been delegated to take you home.' She turned to find Major Gus Henningsen at her side.

'Reluctantly delegated, I'm sure,' she said coldly. 'Is there no-one here who'll take me willingly?'

'If you would kindly collect your coat, ma'am, we'll get going,' he replied, ignoring her sarcasm.

They were halfway towards Bootle before he spoke. Jessica had taken a holy vow not to say a word before he did.

'I'm sorry about my behaviour earlier,' he said. His voice, for a change, was relatively pleasant. 'It was rude of me to laugh the way I did.'

'I consider you to be an utterly hateful person.' It wasn't just the laughing, but every single thing he'd done and said since they'd first met.

'*Utterly* hateful?' There was a catch in his voice, as if he might laugh again. She decided he was definitely drunk.

'Utterly!' Jessica said firmly. When you said the word more than once, it actually did begin to sound rather amusing.

'Utterly!' He whistled. 'Phew!'

They didn't speak again until the car drew up outside the King's Arms and he handed her an envelope.

'What's this, a billet-doux?'

'No, ma'am, it's your fee – for singing.'

'Thank you.' A fee was entirely unexpected. She bade him a frosty 'Goodnight,' and slammed the car door before he could reply.

Once home, she opened the envelope and found a cheque for fifteen pounds, which she stuck behind the clock on the mantelpiece. Instead of feeling pleased, a sensation of inexplicable sadness came over her and for some reason she thought about the flat over the museum and the desolate beauty of the view from the window. Perhaps it was because the view had always depressed her, though Arthur had loved it. If only things hadn't turned out the way they had and she'd felt able to settle in the Lake District! Arthur was a good man, yet she'd walked away from him, changed the entire course of her life, and here she was, a middle-aged woman with hennaed hair, all dolled up in a red dress singing for American soldiers. Major Henningsen had made her feel like a tart.

'Have I changed the course of my life for the better?' she asked herself in a whisper. She sat in front of the cold grate for nearly an hour, but was unable to provide herself with an answer. She longed for Penny to hug and kiss, but Penny was spending the night at Sheila's, and Jessica eventually went to bed alone.

Chapter 14

The bloke came in after the pub had opened its doors at half past ten one morning just after Easter. He wore a bowler hat, a pinstriped suit and carried a brolly over his arm. It was rare that the King's Arms had such a distinguished-looking customer, particularly one who talked dead posh, as if he had a plum in his gob. For a while, he was the only customer there.

He seemed very friendly. 'Have one yourself,' he said to Mack, the landlord, when he ordered himself a whisky and soda. He removed his bowler hat and placed it on the bar.

'Ta, mate, you're a king,' said Mack, helping himself to a pint of ale. 'You're not from round here, are you?'

'No, but I happened to be in the vicinity and I thought I'd look up an old friend, James Quigley. Do you know him?'

'Jimmy, sure I do, along the street, number twenty.'

'And how's Jimmy keeping?' the chap asked conversationally. 'It's ages since I last saw him.'

'Well, very well.' Mack grinned. 'In fact, he's just got married again to a girl young enough to be his daughter.'

The posh bloke grinned back. 'He always was a lad, was Jimmy.'

'Where do you know him from, like?' asked Mack. He didn't look the sort to have been a friend of Jimmy's.

'We were in the Merchant Navy together.'

'Ah!' That explained it. All classes of men joined the

Merchant Navy as a youthful fling. 'You didn't stick it out, then?'

'No, after a couple of voyages I decided it wasn't the life for me and I pursued a different career.' The man ordered a second whisky and told Mack to have another beer on him. 'I left at the same time as Jimmy. If I remember rightly, his wife died and he went to work on the docks. The last I heard, he'd just had some sort of accident. After that, we seemed to lose touch.' He shook his head sadly. 'I hope the accident wasn't a bad one.'

'Nah,' said Mack. 'Well, perhaps it was at first. He was housebound for a long time and his daughter, Kitty, looked after him, though we always thought that a bit of a joke. Since Kitty started work, Jimmy's been prancing round like a two-year-old.'

'That's good news, I must say.' The man looked dead pleased. 'Would you like another beer?'

'Wouldn't say no. More whisky?'

Paddy O'Hara and Rover came in through the swing doors. 'This chap's been asking about Jimmy Quigley, Paddy,' said Mack. 'He's an ould mate from the Navy.'

'Can I buy you a drink, Paddy?' Jimmy's ould mate enquired.

'I'll have a Guinness, ta.' Paddy tapped his way towards his favourite seat beneath the black-painted window.

'And what else has Jimmy been up to, apart from getting married, that is? He used to play football, didn't he?'

'That's right,' Mack regaled the stranger with the story of the Merseyside Junior Football Cup and how Jimmy had trained the winning team. 'He's lost none of his old . . .' He paused. From across the room, Paddy O'Hara was shaking his head and mouthing, '*No! No! No!*' Mack had an urgent desire to cut off his own tongue.

'None of his old what?' the bloke asked courteously.

'I can't remember,' Mack mumbled. 'You'll have to ask Jimmy that for yourself. Number twenty, just along the street, like I said.'

'You know,' said the stranger, 'I've spent so long enjoying myself in your fine establishment, that I don't think I've the time to squeeze in a social call, after all. I'll just have to send Jimmy a letter instead.' With that, he plonked his bowler hat on his head, swung his brolly over his shoulder like a rifle, and, with a cheery wave, was gone.

With the aid of several pints of Guinness, Mack managed to persuade Paddy O'Hara to promise, on Rover's life, that he'd never mention the visitor to a soul. 'I don't know what the hell he was after, but if Jimmy finds out it was me who clatted on him, he'll have me guts for garters.'

The letter landed on Jimmy's doormat three days later. When he opened the envelope, he recognised the headed notepaper straight away as that of the solicitors who had acted for the Dock Board at the time of his accident.

The message was short and to the point. He was advised that his invalidity pension was dependent on him being physically incapacitated and therefore unfit for work. It had come to their notice that this was no longer the case. *Under the circumstances, at the end of this month your weekly pension of twenty-five shillings will cease forthwith*. He could appeal if he wished, but should he choose to do so, *Evidence of your fitness for work can be provided*.

Jimmy sat on the stairs and read the letter again. They were taking his pension away! He would have to get a job! From now on, he would have to drag himself out of bed at some unearthly hour of the morning to be pissed around by some snotty foreman all day long. He couldn't stand it, not after ruling the roost in his own house for all these years. He noticed the neat signature on the letter: N. P. Norman, the same as on other letters he'd had from the solicitors in the past. In fact, Mr Norman had come round to see him when the pension details were finalised, bringing papers with him for Jimmy to sign.

The bloke in the car! He'd been wondering ever since where he recognised him from. Mr N. P. bloody Norman had nearly run him over last Sunday when they were on their way home from church.

'Aw, Jaysus!' Jimmy groaned. He felt as if he was entering a long dark tunnel which didn't have an end. It was just his sodding luck that, of all the cars in the world to kick a tin can under, he should pick the one belonging to the solicitor who dealt with his pension.

'Is something the matter, Jimmy?' Theresa called.

He staggered into the living room and showed her the letter. 'I suppose I could ask our Kitty to come up with a few more bob?' he said, his face ashen. Added to the pittance Theresa earned in the fish and chip shop, it might, just might, be enough for three adults and two kids to live on, though he'd have to cut down on the ale and the daily paper would have to go, as well as sweets for the lads on Sundays. He remembered they were still paying the tally man for Georgie's First Holy Communion clothes.

'No,' Theresa said promptly. 'I've no intention of allowing me and me lads to be kept by your Kitty. Apart from which, she already gives us thirty shillings, which is more than half her wages. It wouldn't be fair to ask for more.' Theresa had very strict ideas on what was right and proper. 'Anyroad, another few bob wouldn't be enough. I'll just have to get a full time job meself.'

'Oh, luv, would you mind, like?' Jimmy gasped, his heart overflowing with gratitude as a bright light gleamed at the end of the dark tunnel. Anything, anything, rather than go to work himself. 'I'll look after the kids, get them off to school, see to their meals and keep the place tidy the way you like it. You can do the main housework at the weekend same as our Kitty used to do. Of course, I'd go to work meself like a shot, but despite what the letter says, I still have terrible trouble with me legs.' He rubbed them piteously. 'I've never mentioned it before, 'cos I didn't want to worry you.'

He was a bit peeved when Theresa didn't look very interested. 'I'll pop round to the Labour Exchange once I've tidied up,' was all she said.

The following Monday, Theresa started on the production line in a munitions factory in Kirkby. It was shift work and her wages were an incredible four pounds, three and sixpence a week, plus bonuses, which meant that instead of Jimmy having to cut down on the ale as he thought he might, he began to consider buying himself a new suit.

'She loves hard work, does Theresa,' he explained, chuckling, to Kitty and the neighbours. 'She got bored at home without much to do.' He didn't add that the work was dangerous, involving as it did explosives, because it made him feel just a tiny bit ashamed.

Theresa was halfway through her first week, when the light at the end of the dark tunnel abruptly disappeared. They'd gone to bed early because she had to be up at half past five for work. To Jimmy's pleased surprise, she lay facing him, and he immediately placed his arm around her thick waist. Her body mechanism worked as regular as clockwork. Every fourth Wednesday she'd be out of action with what she called 'the curse' for the next five days. During that time, she usually turned her back on him immediately she got into bed.

'You're late, pet,' he said as he began to touch her big hard breasts.

'Am I? Are y'sure? I thought it was next Wednesday.'

'No, it's this.' Jimmy had the dates she would be denied him fixed firmly in his head.

She immediately removed his hand and said tonelessly, 'I've only ever been late twice in me life before, and that was when it turned out I was expecting Georgie and Billy.'

As no man worth his salt could possibly permit his pregnant wife to risk her life working with explosives, added to which, his name would be permanently mud if the neighbours found out, Jimmy had no alternative but to insist manfully that Theresa leave her job at the end of the week. Within the space of a fortnight, his entire world had turned completely upside down, and so it was that very early on the last Monday in April, with the sun rising like a blurred jewel in the dusky sky and the birds singing sweetly from the rooftops, Jimmy Quigley slammed the door of number 20 Pearl Street, and made his way towards Gladstone Docks to start work again. It was ten and a half years since the crate had fallen on his legs.

To make matters worse, Theresa declared that, seeing as how she was pregnant, she wanted nothing to do with Jimmy in *that* way till after the baby was born. And, as if that wasn't enough to send a man mad with the injustice of it all, his daughter Kitty decided to leave home.

Kitty knelt, head bowed, in the back pew of the almost deserted church. There were just two other people, a man and a woman, waiting to go to confession. The curtain of the confessional was drawn back and a young girl emerged and began to say her penance. The woman rose, went into the small cubicle and drew the curtain across, just as Father Keogh emerged from the sacristy, quickly genuflected in front of the altar and came hurrying down the nave, glancing briefly at Kitty as he passed.

The door swung closed, and the church returned to its state of utter silence. The scent of incense hung in the air, along with melted wax and flowers.

'Should I or shouldn't I?' prayed Kitty, though it was useless and possibly sinful to ask such a question of God.

Should she go to bed with Dale Tooley, or should she continue to refuse? She'd known him barely a month, yet they'd seen each other every single time they were both free. He loved her. He'd told her so with mounting passion every time they met. And she loved him, there was not a shred of doubt about that in her mind. Not only that, these weren't normal times when women clung tightly to their virtue. There was a war on. The times were special and not lightly wasted on long courtships and engagements. In a few months, Dale would be sent to another part of the country, or even to another country altogether, and Lord knew when she'd ever see him again. He belonged to the 8th Army Air Corps Maintenance Division, and as soon as the airstrip and support buildings were finalised in Burtonwood he'd be off to do the same thing elsewhere.

Kitty clutched her hands together tightly and bent her head until her lips were resting on her thumbs.

'Hi, Kitty.'

'Hi, Dale.' Her mind wandered back to the night they met. The Andrews Sisters were singing 'I'll Be With You in Apple Blossom Time' when he'd taken her in his arms and her body began to tingle all over, as if she'd suddenly woken up from a long peaceful sleep. So, it was as simple as that, falling in love.

'Can I see you again?' he asked when the music finished. His bright blue eyes with their long thick lashes stared down into hers in the dusk of Pearl Street. He had short hair, like all the Americans, brown with the suggestion of a curl, and wide, sensual lips which curled upwards in a lazy grin.

'If you like,' she replied, which was a bit of an

understatement considering the way she felt. His arm was still around her waist, he was still holding her hand. People pushed against them, a football rolled into her leg, someone said, 'Kitty, have you . . .' Kitty didn't hear the rest.

'I do like. When?'

She tried to recall what day it was. The Americans had come to tea, so it must be Sunday. What shift was she on? Mornings, she remembered after a while. 'One night next week?'

'How about tomorrow?'

'Tomorrer's fine.'

She couldn't get him out of her mind all next day. It was hard to concentrate on her work, to carry out the tasks she was given with appropriate care and attention. Lucy was seeing Wayne that night and was in an equal tizzy of anticipation, though Kitty kept her own date to herself. She couldn't even bear to share his name with someone else, not yet.

He was coming by train and they met under the clock outside Owen Owen's. Kitty was there first and she felt her heart turn over when she saw his tall, lithe figure cross the road towards her.

'Hi,' he said. He lifted his arms, about to give her an impulsive hug, but changed his mind and dropped them as if worried she might think he was rushing things too quickly.

'Hello,' Kitty said shyly.

It was strange, but there was something extraordinarily special about just walking alongside someone you were in love with. Their arms brushed together from time to time, and, after a few minutes, he took hold of her hand. 'Where shall we go?'

'The pictures?'

'I'd prefer a drink, so we can talk.'

They went into the nearest pub. In fact, they didn't talk much, content to stare into each other's eyes and marvel over what had happened. He was from Boston, Kitty established that much. He was twenty-eight, had a college education, and was, like her, a Catholic.

She described her job in the hospital and told him about Jimmy and Theresa. 'One of her sons, Georgie, is making his First Holy Communion on Sunday.'

'Gee, I remember that day only too well. I was scared I'd choke on the host and spit it out.'

'So was I!'

The hours flashed by and they scarcely took their eyes off each other. Kitty drank in everything about him: his brown hands with their long broad fingers and the scar on the middle finger of his left hand, his wide, humorous mouth, the little mole beneath his left ear, the way he tapped his cigarette on the box before he lit it. After a while, his entire persona seemed so familiar, she experienced a sensation of *déjà vu,* as if she had been sitting opposite Dale Tooley in a Liverpool pub on numerous occasions before during her life.

'It's odd,' he said precisely at that moment, 'but I feel as if we've met before.'

They looked at each other in surprise when the barman shouted, 'Time, ladies and gentlemen, please.'

'This is a strange system you have,' Dale said, amused. 'At home, the bars don't close till the last customer has gone.'

'We have licensing laws over here.'

Outside the pub, he linked her arm as if they were an old married couple and said, 'I'll take you home.'

Kitty managed to convince him that he would miss his last train if he came all the way to Bootle. She wasn't even sure if he should walk her as far as Exchange Station. 'You'll never find your way back in the blackout.'

'Don't worry, honey. If I get lost, I'll ask someone the way or catch a cab. It's not particularly dark, anyway.'

A sliver of the new moon drifted in and out of the

black lacy clouds, giving just enough light to see by. They wandered towards the station, talking to each other in a desultory fashion, both knowing that this would be the first of many more nights together. In almost every doorway, couples could be dimly seen wrapped in a passionate, writhing embrace. Kitty's heart fluttered wildly at the mere thought of being kissed by Dale, and wondered if he would draw her into the occasional empty doorway, though the lack of privacy was a bit off-putting. Perhaps he felt the same, because they arrived shortly at the station, where a train was waiting on the line, the doors open, and he'd still done no more than hold her hand and link her arm.

'When can I see you again?' he asked politely.

'I'm free every night this week.' Lucy would have disapproved of her making herself so easily available, but Kitty didn't care.

He touched her lips gently with his finger, 'Tomorrow, then. Same time, same place?'

The woman came out of the confessional and the man went in. A small queue had formed on the pews outside, though she'd been too wrapped up in her own thoughts to notice them come in.

'If I go to bed with Dale, I really should confess it!' Her lips curved in a smile as she envisaged the Father's shocked response.

'A woman's virtue is her most precious possession and should only be yielded to the man she marries in the eyes of God.' The priest would never take account of the fact there was a war on. If the world was about to explode into smithereens tomorrow, a good Catholic girl should hold grimly onto her virtue to the bitter end. 'I'm thoroughly ashamed of you, Kitty Quigley. I would have thought you of all people would know better.' He'd probably give her a million Holy Rosaries as a penance.

That was another thing. Whichever priest was on duty, he'd recognise her voice. Two weeks ago, when she confessed to Father McGoughlin – without mentioning any names – that, no matter how hard she tried, she just couldn't get on with her dad's new wife, Father said sternly, 'Theresa's a good woman. Be patient, Kitty, and you'll soon learn to love the pure gold within,' and he'd told her to say ten Our Fathers and ten Hail Marys.

Last Sunday, she and Dale had gone over to New Brighton on the ferry. 'Jeez!' he gasped, when he saw the docks, crowded to capacity with just about every type of ship there was. 'Next time we come, I'll bring my camera. Dad'll be really interested to get a snapshot of that scene. He came to Liverpool as a kid when the family were on their way to America.'

Kitty had been surprised to find when they arrived in New Brighton that a few of the rides were operating on the fairground. They sampled each one, ate fish and chips in a cheap restaurant, then went to the Tower Ballroom and danced together blissfully for a few hours.

'I love you, Kitty Quigley.' His arms encircled her waist and hers were clasped around his neck.

'I love you, Dale,' she sighed and nestled her cheek against his.

'Then why,' he began impatiently. 'Oh, never mind, it doesn't matter.'

She knew what he was going to say. 'Then why won't you let me prove how much I love you in bed?' She also knew it mattered very much to both of them. Like all the couples she'd noticed on their first date, she and Dale had ended up in a shop doorway when they kissed goodnight. There was nowhere else to go. They'd found a doorway more private than the others, down a little cutting off North John Street, which became their own special place. The very second his lips touched hers, she felt an unbearable sweetness, a delicious giddiness that left her shaking. Then, their lips still together, he would undo her coat and slip his hands underneath her jumper and caress her breasts. With Dale's body pressed hard against hers, Kitty's heart would thump madly against her ribs and she would feel a strange, urgent ache between her legs, wanting him to go further, wanting him to touch her *there*, and wondering if she could bring herself to stop him if he tried.

But Dale never did try. Instead, he would implore her huskily, 'Kitty, honey, I can't stand it here. Let's take a room in a hotel.'

'No, Dale!'

'Why, honey, why? You love me, don't you?'

In the ballroom, his arms tightened round her even more. 'You're driving me crazy, Kitty. It's religion, isn't it? We Catholics are put in a moral straitjacket the day we're born. You make me feel as if I'm committing a sin by wanting you, but making love to the girl you adore isn't sinful, it's the most beautiful thing in the world.'

'Have you made love to girls before?' She felt a rush of pure jealousy at the idea of him with another woman.

He moved his head back, looked into her eyes and his mouth curled upwards in the lazy smile which always caused her tummy to do a somersault. 'Hell, honey, I'm twenty-eight years old and a normal guy with normal appetites.'

'Does that mean you have?'

'I guess so,' he said lightly. 'But . . .'

'Did you adore them?'

'No, I didn't as a matter of fact. And they didn't adore me, either. Look, Kitty . . .'

'So, it wasn't the most beautiful thing in the world, not then at any rate?'

He stopped dancing, roughly gripped her arm and led her to their table at the edge of the floor. He pushed her into a chair and sat down beside her. 'Kitty, you're making me feel like some sort of monster,' he said

312

angrily. 'I don't normally go around seducing young women. When it happened in the past, it happened naturally. I can't help loving you, I can't help wanting you more than any women I've ever wanted before, I can't . . .' He stared at her mutely, unable to continue, then buried his head in his hands. 'Aw, Jeez, Kitty,' he mumbled. 'I can't get you out of my mind every minute of every day.'

'I know, Dale, I feel the same,' she said softly as she removed his hands from his distraught face.

'I bet you've kissed all sorts of guys before,' he said wildly. 'I can't stand the thought of some other guy touching you.'

'Come on, let's go.'

Darkness had descended whilst they were in the ballroom, and a ferry could be seen sailing across the moonlit waters of the Mersey on its way back to the Pier Head. It would be a while before it returned, so they walked hand in hand down to the water's edge and watched the tide rippling onto the glistening sand.

'Let's find a bar,' Dale said. 'I need a drink.'

They were walking back when they nearly fell over a couple lying full length on the sands, then another, and another.

'It's like an obstacle race,' Kitty giggled.

'Darling, my darling, darling Kitty.' His arms came round her from behind and he forced her onto her knees, then turned her over so she was facing him when he almost fell on top of her. She tried to push him away, but he caught her hands and pressed his mouth against hers. Kitty went limp as the old, familiar sensation swept over her.

'I love you, I love you,' she gasped between kisses.

'Kitty!' he breathed hoarsely. He frantically began to remove her coat and she helped him undo the buttons down the front of her frock. When her breasts were bare, he bent to kiss them and Kitty almost screamed when his lips touched her nipples. She felt his hand slide underneath her skirt and her body throbbed with longing. She wanted . . . she wanted . . . She had no idea what it was she wanted. He was pulling at her pants, touching her between the legs, but there were too many clothes in the way. Kitty began to wriggle her skirt upwards.

'No!' said Dale. He moved away and sat on the sand. She saw the flicker of a match as he lit a cigarette. 'I'm sorry, but it's not going to be this way with us, Kitty.'

She lay there, loving him more than ever, and unsure if she was glad or sorry that he'd stopped. She began to adjust her clothes, and after she'd put her coat back on she brushed off the sand and sat beside him and saw the ferry was on its way back from Liverpool.

Kitty sighed. Her legs were hurting after so long on the wooden kneeler. She sat back, her mind made up, but it seemed disgraceful to come to such a decision in a church. If Dale hadn't stopped, her virginity would have already gone out of the window last Sunday. She wanted him every bit as much as he wanted her!

It was a lovely spring evening outside. Dale was on duty that night and she already missed him, but they were seeing each other tomorrow, Saturday. Next week, she would be on afternoons and there would scarcely be time to meet. He was going to do his best to change his duties so he had time off in the mornings.

As she walked along Marsh Lane, Kitty passed the chip shop where Theresa used to work. She came down to earth with a bump and remembered she hadn't yet been home. Dad had started work on Monday, so most days Kitty had hung about the hospital talking to the afternoon staff when they came on, then dawdled her way along Liverpool Road, and finally gone to church, because she didn't want to arrive at the house before he did. Theresa was impossible to get on with alone. 'I can't imagine growing to like her,' Kitty thought. 'No matter how hard I try, we'll never become friends. She never even talks to me. On the odd occasions she wants to ask a question, she asks it through me dad.'

'Will your Kitty be in for her dinner on Sunday, Jimmy?'

'Tell Kitty not to forget to leave her ration book on the mantelpiece before she goes to work.'

And all the time, Kitty was standing there, wondering if she had become invisible and was she supposed to answer Theresa directly, or reply via Dad? If it hadn't been for the distraction of Dale Tooley, she would have felt even more unhappy at home than she already was. She felt like an intrusive stranger, a trespasser in someone else's house. Theresa had, naturally, taken over the only other easy chair, and when everyone was in, Kitty was forced to sit at the table like a visitor while they listened to the wireless or she read a book. She felt in the way when she did her washing – and it was difficult getting washed herself with the lads around.

She had decided that Theresa didn't dislike *her* in particular, though she may have resented another woman's presence in what was now her home. Theresa just didn't like anyone, full stop. Even with her sons, she showed not the slightest affection, and although she never hit them, the poor lads were sent to their room, often without their tea, for the least little thing, as if she preferred them out of the way so she could get on with her endless washing, ironing and cleaning. Housework seemed to be the only thing Theresa enjoyed – apart from going to bed with Dad!

Now Theresa was expecting a baby, Dad was out at work all day, arriving home in a foul mood, and everything was even worse than it had been before.

'Hello, luv,' Jimmy said tiredly when she entered the house. 'Your dinner's in the oven.' He was in his chair listening to the wireless. Vera Lynn was singing, 'I'll be seeing you'.

'Hello, Dad. Where's Theresa?'

'She's gone round to Flint Street to see her mam.'

'Have the lads gone with her?'

'No, they're upstairs. Theresa sent them to bed before she went. The little buggers were getting on her nerves.'

'That's a shame. It's lovely out and there's still piles of kids playing in the street.' She felt sorry for the two lads, though got on with them no better than she did their mother. They were withdrawn, and suspicious when she occasionally bought them small presents on payday.

Jimmy looked at her severely. 'It's none of your business, girl.'

That was something else. She didn't get on nearly so well with Dad as she used to. He snapped her head off virtually every time she opened her mouth. 'I know it's none of my business, Dad. I merely said it was a shame.' She changed the subject. 'How did work go?'

'Hard, girl, hard.' Jimmy's legs had quite genuinely been giving him trouble. They ached like blazes all day long. 'Me knees are bloody killing me,' he complained.

Instead of offering to rub them or make a hot water bottle as she'd always done in the past, his daughter waltzed into the kitchen to wash her hair.

Kitty returned to the living room and began to comb her tangled curls in front of the mirror over the mantelpiece, humming 'Yours till the stars lose their glory' along with Vera Lynn. She'd contemplated having it cut short a few weeks ago, thinking it might look smarter and more sophisticated, but Dale had made her promise never, never to have it cut.

'It's beautiful hair,' he said, running his fingers through it. 'Your hair was the first thing I noticed the night we first met.'

Jimmy stared at her resentfully. What right had she to look and sound so bloody happy, when he felt as miserable as sin? She had another feller, a Yank, Dale something, though so far he hadn't graced them with a visit. At the rate she was going, she'd end up on the streets before long. He'd already decided, working back, that it was all Kitty's fault things had turned out the way they had. If she'd put up a better show when she'd gone to the Labour Exchange last September, she wouldn't have been sent to work at the hospital and they'd still be living the same comfortable life as they'd done for the previous ten years. Considering the way things had turned out, Jimmy wasn't sure if getting married again had been such a good idea.

'Is it all right if I make a cup of tea, Dad?'

'I expect so,' he said grudgingly, because he fancied one himself.

Since Theresa had taken over the housekeeping, there were no more endless pots of tea, and Kitty, conscious that the completely re-organised back kitchen was no longer hers, felt too uncomfortable to make a pot herself, even when she was dying of thirst, though she also contributed towards the housekeeping and part of the rations were hers.

A few minutes later, Jimmy was supping his tea. Kitty made a better cup than Theresa, who was inclined to make it a bit weak for his liking. Kitty ate her dinner, washed the few dishes, and sank into her old chair with the latest Vogue pattern book on her knee. It was time she had some summer clothes made. Dale liked her best in blue. She turned the pages, noting how plain and simple the styles were, and the skirts were much shorter, scarcely below the knee. This year, she would have enough money to buy new sandals – white, and perhaps a white cardigan, and a white handbag would be nice . . .

'What's that you're reading?' Jimmy asked.

'It's a pattern book, Dad. Brenda lent it me. I'm going to have a couple of new frocks made.'

'Are you now!' He searched his mind for something to say which would take her down a peg or two. She was getting on his nerves. It seemed thoroughly unfair that she should sit there picking frocks out, spending money like water, whilst he killed himself on the docks. He thought of something that would put her in her place. 'By the way, girl, Theresa and me were talking the other night and we decided it would only be right and proper if the lads moved into the back bedroom and you had the boxroom.'

Kitty stared at him in disbelief. 'But Dad, the boxroom's not big enough for an adult! And there's no room for me wardrobe and chest of drawers. Where would I keep me clothes?'

'Perhaps if you cut down on the clothes a bit, you wouldn't need so much space to keep them,' Jimmy replied nastily. 'Anyroad, you're hardly ever in, so I wouldn't have thought it mattered which room you had.' He felt a bit disconcerted when her hazel eyes filled with tears, having entirely forgotten how much he loved her. Still, a few tears wouldn't hurt. She needed reminding there were other things in the world besides Yanks and the pictures and having a good time. He'd lost control of Kitty since she'd started work. He felt a surge of the old power, knowing he was still able to affect her life. If she pleaded with him, he was only too willing to go back on the suggestion that she move into the boxroom. He hadn't meant it, anyroad. It was a lie that he'd discussed it with Theresa. She probably didn't give a toss where the lads slept.

But instead of pleading, Kitty didn't say a word. She slammed the pattern book shut, so hard that Jimmy jumped, and sat staring into the fire. After a while, she said, 'I'm just going along the street to see Sheila.'

Sheila was kneeling in the middle of the floor getting the

318

smaller kids ready for bed. Jess Fleming was there, a sleepy Penny curled on her knee.

'What's up with you?' Sheila demanded when Kitty walked in. 'You look as if someone's just hit you with a lemon.'

Kitty tearfully relayed the gist of the conversation she'd just had with her dad.

'The cheeky bugger,' Sheila gasped. 'The boxroom's scarcely big enough to breathe in. It's not fair, Kit, particularly when you give them so much money.' She turned to Jessica. 'Y'know, Jess, she hands over more than half her wages every week.'

'What are you going to do, Kitty?' asked Jessica.

Kitty shrugged. 'I haven't much choice, have I?' She threw herself into a chair. 'The thing is, I've slept in that room me entire life. When Theresa has the baby, perhaps they'll shove me in the washhouse. I feel as if I'm gradually being squeezed out.'

'Oh, Kit,' Sheila said sympathetically. 'Keep still, Mary!' She gave her youngest child a cat's lick with a flannel. 'Off you go to bed now! I'll be upstairs in a minute to tuck you in. Where's our Ryan?' She dragged the little boy from under the table by his heels. 'C'mon, you little bugger! Oh, I don't half wish our Cal was home more often to give me a hand with this lot!'

'Why don't you move out altogether, Kitty?' Jessica suggested.

'Where would I go?' asked Kitty, startled.

'With a regular income, you should be able to find yourself a little flat somewhere which would cost far less than half your wages.'

'If you do, Kit, don't go far, will you?' Sheila warned. 'I wouldn't half miss you if you weren't around.'

'Oh, I don't know,' murmured Kitty. 'It seems an awful big step to take.' The idea terrified her.

'You couldn't possibly be more miserable than you

are now, could you?' Sheila fought with Ryan to wash his face.

'I don't suppose I could,' Kitty conceded miserably.

'And whilst you're looking,' said Jessica, 'you're welcome to stay in my spare bedroom. Neither of us are in much, so we'd scarcely see anything of each other. You could come and go as you pleased.'

'I'll think about it,' promised Kitty, though she felt convinced she would never pluck up the courage to leave home for good.

She woke up and slowly opened her eyes. There was a sheet tangled around her legs and her body felt pleasantly languid. At first, she wondered where she was when she saw the ugly black wallpaper patterned with big pink cabbage roses. Her face grew hot when she remembered. This was the hotel room where she and Dale had just made love!

'Where shall we go?' he'd asked after a long loving kiss when he met her off the train at Exchange Station – they hadn't seen each other for two whole days. She'd come straight from work, because it was Saturday and he came off duty at midday.

When Kitty didn't answer straight away, Dale suggested helpfully, 'Your pubs aren't open yet, so shall we take in a movie? We can eat later on.'

'I've been thinking,' Kitty began hesitantly. She felt more than usually aware of his arm lying heavy on her shoulder. He seemed bigger than usual, stronger, and there was something alien about his American uniform. She suddenly felt as if she didn't know him at all.

'Been thinking what, honey?' he asked, grinning, when she went no further. He paused in the middle of Clayton Square, turned her face towards his and kissed her gently on the lips. In that instant, he became the Dale she knew so well, the man she was in love with.

'I've been thinking,' she said in a rush, 'that perhaps we should go to that hotel you're always on about.'

He paused again and looked deep into her eyes. 'Are you sure, Kitty? Are you sure?'

Kitty nodded her head vigorously. 'I'm positive.'

He found a place in a street behind the Adelphi, a shabby four-storeyed building, the sort commercial travellers used. Kitty quaked in case the manager asked for their wedding lines, and hid her hands so he wouldn't see she didn't wear a ring. The man, however, showed no interest once Dale had paid for the room in advance. He slid the key across the counter of the cramped reception area and said brusquely, 'Room seven, fourth floor.'

The wallpaper was hideous, none of the furniture matched, though the bedclothes were clean and the room smelt of polish. Kitty stood awkwardly in the middle of the room. Dale had turned into a stranger again and for the first time since they'd met, seemed stuck for words.

She sat on the edge of the bed and began to undo her coat, but her fingers had turned into thumbs and she couldn't manage.

'Let me do that,' said Dale. He knelt in front of her and helped her with the buttons. 'There!' he said, when the coat was removed. He placed his finger under her chin and drew her towards him and they kissed for a long time, only their lips touching. Then, as the heady sweetness swept through her body until she felt completely, and only too willingly, helpless against anything he might do to her, or want of her, Kitty slowly leaned backwards onto the bed. Only then did Dale take her in his arms. She could never remember afterwards them taking their clothes off, but they must have done, because suddenly Dale was naked on top of her, touching and kissing every inch of her own bare flesh. With each kiss, their passion increased until the

321

world outside ceased to exist altogether and they were aware only of themselves and their burgeoning delight.

'I'm a woman now!' she did recall thinking at the end when he thrust himself inside her. It hurt at first, and there was no particular sensation, except the exultation that she'd been possessed by a man, and the man was Dale Tooley, who she loved, and would always love for as long as she lived.

It was still daylight when Kitty woke, and as soon as she had established where she was and what had just happened, she saw Dale was standing profiled by the window, fully dressed. He was smoking, one hand in his pocket, and looked as if he was thousands of miles away from the shabby hotel in Liverpool.

'Perhaps he won't want me any more now,' Kitty thought fearfully. According to the nurses, as soon as a chap had got his way, he was off in search of fresher prey.

'Dale,' she whispered.

'Kitty!' He turned eagerly at the sound of her voice and came and sat beside her on the bed. The expression on his face was of total and absolute commitment as he bent and kissed her. She felt ashamed that she'd thought he might not want her any more. 'I thought you'd never wake up,' he complained.

'What were you thinking about just now?'

'Home – but now I'm thinking how beautiful you are.' He ran his hand along her thigh and Kitty shivered.

'Why are you dressed?'

'I'm longing for some food. I thought we could go out and have something to eat, then we'll . . .' He paused and grinned.

'Then we'll what?'

'Then we'll come back and do this all over again!'

Theresa was snoring like Vesuvius by his side, and no matter how hard Jimmy tried, he couldn't get to sleep. Apart from the snoring, he was worried about Kitty. It was well past midnight and she still wasn't in. For more than an hour, he'd been listening for the sound of her heels on the pavement outside, and at the same time kept glancing at the phosphorus fingers of the alarm clock to check how late it was.

At last! He heard footsteps and the front door opened. He slipped out of bed and went downstairs. She was already in the living room and in the process of turning the gas mantle up.

'Where the hell have you been?' he snarled.

She turned and smiled, oblivious to his anger. 'Oh, hello, Dad. I'm sorry I'm late, but I missed the last train. I managed to catch a tram and it seemed to take for ever in the blackout.'

There was something different about her. Her eyes were huge and luminous and her face glowed with an expression Jimmy had never seen before. She wasn't in the room with him, but elsewhere, a place where something wonderful had happened, which was still happening in the deep recesses of her mind. Jimmy could tell straight away what she'd been up to: he could almost smell what she'd been doing with her American. He was concerned, partly because she was his daughter and he didn't want her hurt. At the same time, he felt choked with jealousy at the sight of her radiant face. It wasn't fair. Nothing was fair.

The jealousy was predominant as he said in an ugly voice, 'This is my house, girl, and whilst you're under my roof, you're to be in by eleven o'clock. D'you hear?'

'Mmm,' Kitty murmured vaguely.

'And tomorrer,' he went on, determined to get through to her, 'we'll sort your things out and you can move into the boxroom.'

'There's no need to bother, Dad,' she said with a vivid smile. 'As from tomorrer, I won't be in your way any longer. I've just decided, I'm moving in with Jess Fleming.'

323

Chapter 15

The garage had begun to lose its thrall. Jessica couldn't be bothered advertising for other things to sell. Jack Doyle had put her off in any case, by suggesting she'd end up a rag-and-bone man like her father. The supply of bikes had virtually dried up and she hadn't touched a car in weeks, apart from putting in a gallon or two of petrol. When the private fuel allowance was abolished in a few weeks' time, there'd be even less of that to do. The business was almost back to the situation at the start, when she'd barely made enough to pay the rent.

Jessica sighed as she wheeled the few remaining bicycles outside. Penny ran behind trying to reach the saddle so she could push.

'Mind the spokes,' her mother warned.

Lately, it had seemed almost pathetic, selling second-hand bikes. How could she possibly have thought it such a great idea? Even if bikes were pouring in by the minute, it still seemed pathetic, and a rather second-rate way of making a living.

She dated her feelings of discontent back to the night she'd sung at the Dorchester. By making her feel cheap, Major Henningsen had caused her to wonder what she was doing with her life. When she'd lived in Calderstones, such a thought had never entered her head. She was happy buying clothes, filling the house with the latest gadgets, throwing dinner parties, cocktail parties, playing Bridge. Now she wanted something else and she wasn't sure what it was, apart from another child which she'd virtually given up on. Last week, she'd turned forty-six, though she hadn't told a soul.

'Perhaps I need to be in love!' she muttered. She felt envious of Kitty Quigley who'd moved into the spare bedroom a few weeks ago. Jessica had only made the suggestion because she felt in need of occasional company, mainly late at night after Jack had gone and Penny was fast asleep – and the extra money was useful. Kitty was obviously completely enamoured with her American, Dale Tooley. She'd brought him back for tea last Sunday, and Dale was clearly equally smitten. The pair kept exchanging glances, touching hands, and Jessica had felt excluded in the face of their total fascination with each other. She could tell they'd made love, and there seemed something remarkably innocent about it, so different from her relationship with Jack Doyle which seemed almost sordid in comparison.

A man drew in and bought two gallons of petrol. He patted the car's bonnet as he handed over the money. 'Have to take the old girl off the road soon,' he said mournfully.

'Shall we wake up Auntie Rita and demand a cup of tea, sweetheart?' Jessica suggested as he drove away.

'Auntie Rita got biccies?' Penny ran round to the side of the garage and began to thump on the door with her fists.

'Auntie Rita always has biccies, doesn't she?'

Jessica was about to knock on the door herself, when she heard a voice shout, 'Mrs Fleming!'

The Reilly children were on the opposite side of the road on their way to school. She waved to them, but to her surprise, Dominic ran across the road towards her waving an orange envelope in his hand. 'This came for you. Me mam signed for it. She asked me to bring it in case it was important. She said she hopes it's not bad news.'

Dominic made a startlingly ugly face at Penny, before

continuing on his way to school, just as Rita opened the door of her flat, looking more bleary-eyed than usual that morning.

'We're longing for a cuppa,' said Jessica, in the process of opening the telegram. She felt unconcerned. It was probably something to do with business. There was no reason why anyone should send her a telegram containing bad news, but as she read the unevenly printed words, she discovered that there was. 'Oh, no!' she murmured faintly.

'What's the matter, Jess?' Rita was suddenly wide awake and looked concerned.

'Would you mind looking after Penny?' Penny was already halfway upstairs, and Jessica desperately needed to be alone for a while.

'Of course I wouldn't, but Jess, what's happened?'

'Arthur's been killed in North Africa, a place called Trigh Capuzzo, but Rita, *I didn't even know he was there!*'

'I'm so selfish,' wept Jessica, as she sat in the office at the desk where Dennis Mott used to do his accounts. 'I ruined his life. *I killed him!*' Even as she wept, she knew she was being hypocritical. She hated people who pretended to be upset when someone they didn't particularly care for had died. But she *had* cared for Arthur, she had loved him in her own rather offhand way. Their marriage had been a mistake right from the start; she was too strong and he was too weak. Nevertheless, she felt devastated at the idea he was no longer there. Deep down at the back of her mind, she'd always had the thought that she and Penny could return to Arthur if everything else fell apart.

Rita came into the office, put a large glass of whisky on the desk and departed without a word.

Jessica picked up the glass and recklessly drained the contents in one go. 'Just when he was happy, just when he'd found the job he'd always wanted, I spoilt it all by leaving him in the lurch.' She recalled the night she told him she was expecting Penny, that she'd had an affair. He'd been more angry than she thought he was capable of, yet he'd still forgiven her, and he'd been devoted to Penny from the very minute she was born; a real father couldn't have loved his daughter more. 'And at Christmas, he even suggested I did it again.'

The more Jessica thought about Arthur, the guiltier she felt, and with the guilt came self-loathing and disgust at the maudlin way in which she was behaving. She regretted drinking the whisky so quickly, because, on top of everything else, her head had begun to swim.

'Oh, Arthur!' She laid her swimming head in her arms and began to sob brokenly, and was too wrapped up in misery to notice someone had come into the workshop.

'Are you okay?'

Jessica looked up. The last person in the world she felt like seeing at the moment was standing in the doorway of the office – Major Henningsen. He looked uncomfortable, as if he would have preferred to be several miles away.

'I'm fine.' Jessica sniffed and wiped her nose on her sleeve.

'You don't look it,' he said stiffly. 'Has something happened?'

'Yes it has, as a matter of fact. I've just learnt my husband has been killed.'

His thin lips curled. 'I thought you said you were separated?'

'We were, but that doesn't mean I didn't love him in my own peculiar way. We were incompatible, that's all.' Jessica regarded him bitterly. 'That's something a person like you wouldn't understand.'

'What do you mean, a person like me?' Perhaps it wasn't surprising that he should look slightly hurt.

'I meant someone who seems to have so little faith in human nature, who pre-judges everyone they meet and

327

assumes they're bad, and considers himself highly superior to the world in general.' By now, the effects of the whisky had completely taken hold. She was conscious that her voice was slurred and she didn't give a damn what she said.

Major Henningsen came into the office and eased his powerful frame into the chair on the other side of the desk. 'Am I really so bad?'

Jessica nodded. 'You're worse! I saw the way your lip curled when I told you Arthur was dead. You immediately thought me a hypocrite. You're incapable of appreciating that people can still go on loving each other after they've separated. Arthur was such a sweet man, so good.' She began to cry again. 'Oh, I *am* a hypocrite, I am. I was terribly cruel to him.'

'You can't stand weak people, can you? Particularly men.'

Jessica looked at him with red eyes. 'Is it so obvious?'

'It was obvious when I first met you. I'm not sure if I like strong women.'

'I think you can take it for granted that you don't. You clearly don't like me – not that I care, because I don't like you, either.'

'Well, at least we know where we stand!' He managed to crease his face into a smile. 'Tell me about Arthur. What did he do before the war?'

'You don't have to pretend to be interested.' She had a suspicion, though it went against everything she knew about him, that he was trying to be kind. 'In fact, I'd sooner you went away. I'd like to be on my own, if you don't mind. Oh, God!' She clapped her hands against her forehead as her head threatened to float away from her body altogether and a feeling of nausea engulfed her.

'I think it would be better if you weren't left on your own.' He nodded towards the glass. 'You've had too much to drink. The best thing for you to do is keep on talking. How long were you and Arthur married?'

Jessica thought hard. Her brain was so muzzy that Major Henningsen was beginning to look blurred. 'Twenty-three years,' she replied eventually.

'You waited long enough to have Penny.'

'So we did.'

'Was that your decision or Arthur's?'

'Neither. It was fate who decided I should have Penny.' Fate, Jack, Arthur. Fate, Jack . . . 'I think I want to be sick!'

Major Henningsen jumped to his feet. 'Where's the bathroom?'

She presumed he meant the lavatory. 'In the garden,' she gulped, 'but I'll never get there in time.'

Jessica threw up directly outside the workshop, then sank, groaning, onto the grass. 'What an idiot I was to drink it all at once!' She felt embarrassed at making such a show of herself in front of the man she so thoroughly detested.

His hand was on her shoulder like a ton weight. 'You should feel better now.'

'Should I? I feel utterly wretched,' Jess moaned.

'Utterly?'

'Please don't joke. I really do.'

'What you need is a strong cup of coffee.'

'Jess!' Rita appeared, closely followed by Penny. 'I just looked out the window – are you all right?'

Major Henningsen stood up and snarled, 'She needs coffee, black and strong.'

'I'll make some straight away.' Rita scurried off.

'Mummy,' Penny cried plaintively. 'Mummy, you fell over.' Frightened, she tried to crawl onto Jessica's knee.

'I'm fine, sweetheart. I'll get up in a minute.' Although Jessica tried, she felt too dizzy to move.

'Your mom's okay, honey.' Major Henningsen unexpectedly swung Penny up in his arms. 'She's just having a little sit down on the grass.'

Penny regarded him thoughtfully. She'd fortunately grown out of the habit of calling every man 'Dada'. She hid her head in the khaki shoulder. 'Don't like you,' she mumbled.

The major gave his rather cracked chuckle. 'You're in good company, honey. Your mom doesn't like me, either.'

Rita arrived with a bottle of aspirin and the coffee, which was as thick as treacle and tasted disgusting. After Jessica had drunk it, Major Henningsen helped her upstairs and she fell asleep in Rita's spare bedroom with a bucket handy in case she was sick again.

When she woke, it was six o'clock and, apart from a splitting headache, she felt much better. She refused Rita's offer of a meal, because the idea of food was objectionable at the moment. She walked home briskly, and Penny, excited by the unusually fast pace, waved her arms in delight.

Kitty was working afternoons and wouldn't arrive till late – if she arrived, that is. One night she hadn't come home at all and Jessica suspected she'd gone straight from work into town and spent the night with her sergeant. Still, she'd been told she could come and go as she pleased – and she was almost twenty-eight and could be presumed to know what she was doing.

Penny had already had her tea with Rita. She clung to her mother possessively, the events of that morning clearly still on her mind. 'Don't falled over again, Mummy.'

'Don't worry, love, I won't.' Jessica deliberately kept her up, waiting for Penny herself to announce that she felt tired and wanted to go to bed. When she did, Jessica sat beside the cot thinking about Arthur long after her daughter had gone to sleep.

At ten o'clock, she heard the King's Arms let out and the raucous sound of laughter as the customers hung round on the corner of the street, unwilling to return

330

home. A few minutes later, the back door opened and Jack Doyle let himself in. Jessica went downstairs, just as he shot the bolt in case Kitty came home.

'Hallo, Jess.'

Jessica nodded. 'Hello.' He was such a big, masculine man compared to Arthur, she thought dispassionately, though just as sensitive. He immediately guessed from the expression on her face that there was something wrong. Before he could ask what, she said, 'I got a telegram this morning. Arthur's been killed.'

He sank into a chair and groaned, 'Oh, Jaysus, no! He was a fine man, Arthur Fleming. I didn't know him all that long, but he became a good mate.'

She'd never told him his 'good mate' had realised Jack had made love to his wife, and couldn't be bothered to say so now. 'Under the circumstances, I'd prefer it if you didn't come round again, Jack. I'd like to call it a day.'

'But, Jess!' He looked poleaxed. His big face collapsed as he stared at her, utterly bewildered. 'But why now, Jess?'

Jessica was taken aback. She had assumed she meant as little to him as he did to her. 'I'm not sure why. It just seems all wrong.'

'It's a bit late in the day for it to seem wrong,' he argued desperately, 'particularly with Arthur gone. For the first time, it would have been all right.'

Jessica did her best to explain. 'I know I'm being unreasonable, but I feel very guilty and confused, I . . .' She stopped, wishing he would leave because she wasn't in the mood to try and sort out her muddled emotions just now. He would find it difficult, if impossible, to understand what it was to do with Arthur at this late stage. Though it wasn't just Arthur: there was the garage, the strange feeling of discontent she'd had lately, the urge to change the course of her life. 'But it's only eight months since I last changed it,' she thought. 'I can't go on moving here, there and everywhere every time I feel a bit unhappy. I've got to settle down some time, if only for Penny.'

Jack was frowning darkly at the fire. He bit his lip several times, as if there was something he wanted to say, but he couldn't quite pluck up the nerve to say it. 'Jess,' he almost gasped, then stopped and bit his lip again. 'Look, Jess, in a few months, once it seems proper like, we could get married!'

'Don't be silly, Jack.' Jessica gave a tired laugh. 'We'd make the most inappropriate married couple in the world.'

'But . . . but I thought that was what you'd always wanted!' His jaw dropped open in disbelief. Even tonight, he'd suspected her calling it off might be a come-on, a way of dragging a proposal out of him. He'd always thought he only had to ask and she'd agree to marry him like a shot.

'It's the last thing I've ever wanted.' She realised she was being as cruel to Jack as she'd been to Arthur. 'Of course, I'm immensely flattered,' she said quickly, 'but you and I would never get on together. Surely you realise that?'

'I love you,' he said simply. It came out more easily than expected.

Jessica smiled. 'I loved you too once, a long, long time ago. I was about twelve and you were courting Mollie. But I grew out of it, and so will you, Jack. We've just had something rather special for a while, but at the same time rather superficial. Now's the time to finish.'

He was too big a man to plead. 'If that's what you want,' he said stiffly.

'It is.'

'Tara then, Jess.' He left, unbowed and dignified, and returned to the house in Garnet Street where he'd lived ever since he'd married Mollie more than thirty years before. So, all that endless soul-searching had been a complete waste of time. Jess had never wanted

332

to marry him after all! He knew he would feel a terrible void, an aching sense of loss whenever he thought about the redheaded woman who had created such havoc in his life, not to mention his little girl, Penny. At the same time, there was a feeling of relief that once again his remaining years stretched ahead of him with calm predictability. There might be a few bumps on the way, but otherwise the pattern wouldn't change.

Major Henningsen telephoned Jessica the following afternoon. 'How's your head?'

'Back to normal. Look, I must apologise for . . .'

He cut in. 'Please don't apologise for anything. Considering the circumstances, it was entirely under-standable, but I suggest you stay clear of the liquor in future.'

'Apart from the occasional glass of wine, I don't usually drink,' Jessica explained, rather surprised at this show of magnanimity. 'I'm not used to whisky.'

There was a pause. 'Did you mean all those things you said about me?' he asked casually.

'What things were they?' Jessica's memory of the previous day's events was decidedly fuzzy.

'Something about me having little faith in human nature. I pre-judge people and consider myself super-ior.'

Jessica thought hard. 'Yes, I think I did.'

He made a humphing sound. 'You're no angel yourself.'

'The thing is, I know it and you don't,' she said crisply.

'Hmm. I wonder if you're right.'

'You could always ask your wife.' She felt curious to know if there was a woman on earth crazy enough to have taken him on. It was hard to imagine him with a family.

333

'I would need paranormal powers to do that. My wife died eighteen years ago.'

'I'm sorry,' she said quickly.

'It's a bit late for sympathy, but thanks,' he barked.

'Do you have any children?'

'One son, Peter, nineteen. He's in the army and has just been despatched to Australia, of all places.' For the very first time, there was a soft edge to his normally tough, terse voice. 'Anyway,' he continued brusquely, 'the reason I came to see you yesterday is we're having a concert, a big one this time, open to all ranks. It's being held in the main hangar of the base in Burtonwood on June seventh and we'd like you to sing. The star turn is a top comedian flying over especially from the States, so you'd only be part of the supporting bill.'

'I think I could stand that,' said Jessica.

Rita Mott crept in and out of the workshop all day and spoke to Jessica only in a whisper.

'For goodness' sake, Rita,' Jessica exploded eventually. 'Stop acting as if I'm an invalid or something. I've completely recovered. I'm fine.'

'You can't have got over losing Arthur so quickly, surely?'

'You're forgetting I'd already left Arthur. Even so, I'm very upset he's gone, but I can't cry for ever, can I?'

'You're ever so brave, Jess,' Rita whispered.

'I'm not. My father used to say I was as hard as nails – and I am. Do please stop whispering, Rita, I can hardly hear you.'

'Have you told Penny yet?' Rita asked in a normal voice.

'No, and I shan't. I shall probably tell her when she's older and more able to understand.'

Rita furrowed her brow. 'I wonder how I'd feel if Den was killed?'

334

'Try not to think about it,' Jessica advised. 'Where is Den now, by the way?'

'I'm not sure. Last time he wrote, he was still in that funny place in India. I haven't had a letter lately.' She looked at Jess, still frowning. 'Yesterday, when you were asleep, I wondered if I should give up on me parties for a while. Imagine if I got a telegram to say Den was dead! I'd feel terrible if I thought I'd been enjoying meself at the same time as he was killed.'

Nowadays, Rita's friends consisted of black Yanks from the storage depot in Marsh Lane, along with a couple of women who'd become regulars. According to Rita, the blacks were true gentlemen and far preferable to the whites.

'I shouldn't bother,' Jessica said carelessly, her mind by now on what she would wear for the concert in Burtonwood. Apart from which, Rita's hypocrisy seemed even worse than her own. 'You've had so many parties, Rita. What will a few more matter?'

Which, considering what was to happen later, was the worst possible advice Jessica could have given.

On Sunday, Jessica filled the van with the remainder of her petrol ration, and, leaving Penny with the Reillys, drove up to the Lake District to collect Arthur's things. She took her set of keys in case the museum hadn't appointed a new curator when Arthur left and the place was unoccupied. After ringing the bell on the side door several times, she noticed a small card attached to the main entrance which said, MUSEUM CLOSED INDEFINITELY, so let herself in.

It was rather eerie walking through the ground and first floors full of glass cases containing ancient relics which had survived civilisations several thousands of years old, as well as numerous broken, but priceless, statues which were missing several vital parts. Her footsteps sounded exceptionally loud on the mosaic-tiled floor. At one point, she froze, hearing matching footsteps from above and thinking there was someone coming down to meet her, but all was silent and she realised the sound was merely an echo.

The large flat was dusty, but as neat as a pin. Arthur had always been a tidy person and had put everything away before he left. Jessica quickly sorted through his papers, most of which were concerned with the museum's affairs. One of these days, she must write to the trustees and tell them Arthur was dead. They might be expecting him to take up the job of curator again once the war was over. She packed his clothes: the smart suits and silk shirts which he used to wear when he was a businessman in Calderstones, the old trousers and rough tweed jacket he'd gladly turned to when they'd moved to Bootle and he'd got a job, much to her disgust, as a lorry driver. He'd always loved driving.

'Poor Arthur,' Jess whispered. 'You would have been much better off with another woman.'

She sorted through the dishes and the utensils in the kitchen. Most she left behind. They might be useful to whoever took over the flat at some time in the future. If not, they could throw them away. She did the same with the ornaments which had been bought for a much bigger house. There was no place for them in Pearl Street. After hesitating over an elegant lamp with a peach-coloured ceramic base and matching pleated shade which had cost the earth in George Henry Lee's, Jessica decided to discard it. For one thing, she had no electricity, and for another, she felt strangely reluctant to weigh herself down with bulky possessions, though she'd take the radiogram, assuming she would be able to get it down the stairs. Perhaps she could swop it with Sheila for her battery wireless. She'd really missed a wireless since moving back to Bootle, and they were impossible to buy, either new or secondhand.

Penny's room was the last she entered. The drawers

were full of baby clothes. Jessica had never thrown a single item away. Perhaps even then, twenty months ago, there'd been the germ of the idea that she'd return to Jack Doyle and the clothes might be needed again. Some of the tiniest gowns and woolly matinee jackets were unworn because Penny had been such a big baby, over ten pounds, and the clothes were already too small.

Jessica sat down on the little chintz chair which she had chosen so carefully for the nursery and wept. Perhaps if she and Arthur had had babies of their own, things might have turned out very differently. She wouldn't have been nearly so selfish, for one thing. Penny was the only person she'd ever put before herself.

She packed the clothes carefully, along with the few toys that still remained, and began to carry the parcels and suitcases down to the van, managing to struggle, successfully, with the radiogram. Next week some time, she'd take some of the things to the WVS in Bootle. Before leaving the flat with the final load, she paused in front of the picture window in the lounge. The view was truly spectacular; the trees in full blossom, the bushes blazing, the hills a myriad shades of green. The trunks of the silver birches flashed and sparkled in the distance. There was, as usual, not a single soul to be seen.

But Jessica paused before this panoramic vista of nature in all its glory for merely a few seconds. It made her flesh creep, just as the inside of the empty museum made her flesh creep even more. She turned on her heel and ran down the stairs, along the tiled floors, hearing her footsteps echoing somewhere behind. She was trembling by the time she slammed the door and put the keys through the letterbox.

As she raced home through the peaceful countryside, urging the van to its maximum speed, she felt as if a final curtain had been drawn. Now Arthur had truly gone, and she and Penny were on their own for good.

*

'What's the world coming to?' gasped Fintan Kelly when he crawled out of bed one morning and found his call-up papers lying on the doormat of number 18. 'I'm forty-bloody-one!' Except for periods in Walton jail, he'd never spent a night away from his sister May before, and he felt frightened. He tried to pretend he was deaf when he went for his medical, but the MO caught him out by asking if he'd like a ciggie when his back was turned. When Fintan said, 'I wouldn't mind, doc,' and turned to take it, the MO didn't have a ciggie, after all. Instead, he gave an evil grin and barked, 'Passed, A-1.'

By the time Fintan was kitted out in his khaki army uniform, having reluctantly forsaken his spivvish suit with the wide kipper tie, he actually felt rather proud, though he bawled his head off when he had to say tara to May and his brother, Failey. Failey, forty-two, had become aware of his own vulnerability to call-up.

'Never mind, lad,' May sobbed. 'You're sure to win a medal, and if you don't, I'll try and get one for you on the black market.'

Most of the street came out to wave him off. 'What's the world coming to,' they echoed, 'when a man of forty-one's no longer safe?'

The situation in Russia was neither one thing nor the other. One minute the Jerries were on the offensive and seemed to be winning ground; next, the Russians were driving them back. The slaughter was horrendous; millions had already died.

At the same time the Japs, like Hitler, didn't seem to be able to put a foot wrong; Hong Kong, Malaya, Singapore, had all been conquered, and on the twentieth of May, they captured Burma. Flames soared sky high from the oilfields which had been set alight by the British on their one-thousand-mile retreat as the invaders seized the final gateway to China and the Pacific. British casualties were thirteen and a half thousand, three times that of the Japanese, though many troops managed to reach the safety of India. At the same time, the Japs were crawling like ants all over the Philippines. A couple of their submarines had attacked Sydney in Australia. Terrible tales had begun to circulate about the atrocities inflicted on their prisoners of war.

People yearned for a victory they could call their own. Instead, the Luftwaffe continued to bomb their towns and cities, and on the high seas British ships were being sunk with frightening regularity, several hundred every month. Of course, they'd sunk a few ships themselves, but the number seemed small in comparison to the horrendous toll achieved by the German navy with their U-boats.

In Africa, where they had once been winning, the German General Rommel continued to advance on Allied positions whilst the Eighth Army tried desperately to cling on.

Rationing was becoming even tighter at home. Staple foods like corned beef and white flour were banned, and the new National Loaf, a grey coarse slab of what purported to be bread, was unappetising to most people and virtually uneatable to a few, even though the Government claimed it was healthy and it was rumoured to be an aphrodisiac. An increase in purchase tax of sixty-six per cent had pushed up the price of a pint by twopence, and a pack of twenty ciggies had soared by a whole sixpence and was now two shillings and beyond the pockets of many.

A public opinion poll showed that people were dissatisfied with the way the war was being conducted, and in the House of Commons a vote of censure was moved against the Prime Minister. The members voted overwhelmingly to oppose the motion. There was no alternative to Churchill. He was all they had. They put their wholehearted faith in him, and in the indomitable spirit of the people of their country, to fight the war to the bitter end. Losing was not to be countenanced. Losing was for other countries, certainly not Great Britain.

Patients continued to arrive in their droves at the Royal Naval Hospital in Seaforth, where they were looked after tenderly, loved and given every care.

Outside working hours, most nurses' lives were a constant whirl of dates, dances, parties and films. They were driven partially by a desire to blank out the suffering they witnessed day after day, at least for a few hours.

In Liverpool, a major port, troops of a vast range of nationalities were constantly embarking or disembarking. There were French sailors, Canadian airmen, Australian soldiers, all in town for a few hours or a few days and anxious to show a girl a good time. As long as a young woman made it obvious when they first met in the queue for the pictures or in a dance hall, that she wasn't *that* kind of girl, the servicemen accepted the situation graciously, if reluctantly. What the men mainly wanted, were merely a few kind words, a hand to hold, a face to remember and lips to kiss, albeit briefly, before they set off into the terrifying unknown. As well as the transients, there were, of course, the Americans, who seemed to be everywhere.

The nurses swopped clothes, swopped boyfriends, swopped stories of the escapades they'd been up to the night before. Jenny Downing made a bet that she would go out with a different man every night one week, including Sunday – and she won. Inspired, Lucy tried the same thing and managed nine times in a row.

'Oh, this is a fine ould time to be young and alive,' Lucy crowed. Wayne, the young soldier she'd met at Jessica's, had been given his marching orders weeks ago. Since then, Lucy had been out with lots of other Americans and the latest was insisting they get engaged.

'It's only his way of getting me keks off,' she told Kitty blithely. 'He claims his dad's an oil millionaire and they've got this big mansion in Alabama. Do they have oil in Alabama?'

'I've no idea,' said Kitty. 'I'll ask Dale if you like.'

'Don't bother. I'm about to chuck him, anyroad. He's too bloody persistent. Every time we go out together, it ends up with me fighting for me honour. They seem to think us English girls are dead easy.' Lucy sniffed virtuously. 'As far as I'm concerned, any girl who sleeps with a Yank needs her bumps feeling.'

'I suppose so,' Kitty replied faintly. She must look too prim and proper to have slept with Dale, but if only Lucy knew! 'It'd be nice if you married a Yank,' she said, 'because we could visit each other once the war's over and we're both living in America.'

'Has Dale proposed?' Lucy's rather odd eyes widened in pleased surprise.

Kitty laughed. 'There's no need for him to propose. We just take it for granted we're going to spend the rest of our lives together.'

Dale had permanently reserved the hotel room with the black wallpaper. One weekend, when he had an extended pass, they'd actually lived there, as if the little dark room on the fourth floor was their home. They made love, wandered out for a meal or to the pictures, then returned to make love again. In spirit, Kitty was rarely away from the place where she and Dale reached such heights of pleasure and delight. But it wasn't just going to bed, it was merely being with the person you loved, who loved you, whose very presence could set your head spinning with a smile, a gesture of his hand, a turn of his head.

A few times, when she was on afternoons and Dale was unable to leave the base, Kitty had actually gone alone to the hotel, where she lay on the bed and thought how lucky she was that, out of all the millions and millions of men in the world, she had managed to find Dale. With her eyes closed, she visualised his face above hers, imagined his fingers roaming her body, creeping into the most secret of places. Within her mind, her hands caressed his hard, firm body. He entered her. It no longer hurt, the final act of love, but had become an exquisite, almost agonising joy, a tumultuous climax that left her panting and breathless.

'Dale, I love you,' she whispered, and wondered how on earth she could possibly last until the hour came when they would see each other again.

It was Kitty who heard the banging first, a frantic rat-a-tat-tat with the knocker on the front door. She glanced at the alarm clock. It was twenty past two. Groaning, because she had to be up at half past five for work, she staggered out of bed and went downstairs.

Because the light on the landing was left permanently on, she opened the door the merest crack. It was too dark to make out the identity of the person who had knocked. 'Hallo,' she called when nobody spoke. 'Who's there?'

'Who is it, Kitty?' Jessica was peering down from the top of the stairs.

'I don't know. They won't answer. Who's there?' Kitty called again. She listened hard and thought she could hear a sound. 'I'm sure someone's crying.'

'Is that you, Jess?' a voice quavered.

'Rita!' cried Jessica, astonished. 'What on earth are you doing here?'

A small figure fell against the door, pushing it open, onto the hallway floor. 'Can I come in, Jess? I've nowhere else to go.'

Kitty was shocked to the core when she saw the state of the woman once she'd been helped inside. 'Oh, my

God!' she gasped. Rita's face was covered in bruises and her eyes were so swollen she could scarcely see. Her lip was split, she'd lost several teeth and there were bloody gaps on her scalp where her hair had been pulled out in tufts.

Jessica was almost in tears. 'Oh, Rita, love, what happened?'

'Den arrived home in the middle of a party.' Rita's voice came out in a hiss and was scarcely audible. 'We were having ever such a good time. He told us he'd been in the fighting in Burma, but escaped across the border into India. He was in a terrible state, all gaunt and thin, and he could scarcely walk because his feet are still covered with sores. He lost his boots in Burma, you see. Poor Den!' Rita's bruised lips quivered and tears streamed down her swollen cheeks. 'The army sent him back on a month's leave to recuperate. He didn't let me know, because he wanted to surprise me. When he first came in, he just sat there, ever so polite, telling us all about it in this funny flat voice. Me friends were dead embarrassed. They listened and didn't say a word. Then, after a while, Den said, "Would you mind leaving? I'd like to have a word with me wife." As soon as they'd gone, he really laid into me. I thought I was a goner, Jess, I really did.'

Whilst Rita was speaking, Kitty was gently bathing her injuries with warm water and cotton wool, though she did it out of a sense of duty, not because she felt all that sorry for the woman. She'd never met Rita before, but from the odd things Jess had said, was aware of what went on in the flat over the garage. 'Are you sure there are no bones broken?' she asked in her best nurse's voice. 'You really should go to the hospital for a check up.'

But Rita insisted she was all right. 'I probably look worse than I feel.'

'Where's Den now?' demanded a distraught Jessica. 'How did you manage to get away?'

'Oh, Jess, you've no idea how mad he was! He said he was going to kill us both and he set fire to the garage. I got away when the fire engine arrived, and as I was running down the road, the petrol exploded. God! I hope poor Den's not dead.'

A few passers-by had stopped to stare at the still-smouldering wreckage of the building. Amidst the debris, Jessica could see the black twisted frames of her last remaining bikes. A shred of charred purple net fluttered from the telephone lines above.

'Oh, well,' she sighed. 'At least the problem of the garage is sorted out. I don't have to think about it any more.'

Rita had left very early that morning, having revealed she had a sister in Peterborough and would stay with her for the time being. 'We don't get on, but she won't mind putting me up for a while.'

Jessica had tried to persuade her to stay, at least for a few days, 'Until your face goes down a bit,' but Rita was adamant she didn't want Penny to see her the way she was. 'It'd only frighten her. I'd like Penny to think of her Auntie Rita as having always been pretty and glamorous, and please Jess, don't let her see the garage, either. Me and Penny used to have such good times there.'

So, wearing the black veiled hat which Jessica had reserved for funerals, Rita departed to catch the first train to Lime Street. She left her sister's address and asked Jessica to do her one final favour. 'Find out what happened to Den and let me know. I'd like to write to him if he's okay and tell him I deserved all I got.' Jessica promised she'd find out that very day.

With a final glance at the remains of the garage, Jessica made her way round to the police station to see if they knew what had gone on the night before. After convincing a haughty sergeant she was not just being nosy and it was very much her concern because she'd run a business on the premises until the day before, the man informed her that Dennis Mott had been found running amok down the road in search of his wife when the police arrived at the scene. 'We called in the military and they took him away. To be perfectly frank, madam, although I'm sorry about your business, I don't regret seeing the back of that place. It's not the first time we've been called to a rumpus there.'

He wanted to know if she knew the whereabouts of the missing wife. 'We'd like a few words with her,' he said in a threatening voice.

Jessica professed total ignorance of where Rita Mott might be. 'Yet I used to be so law-abiding!' she thought on the way home.

A jeep without a driver was parked outside the King's Arms when she turned into Pearl Street, and she hadn't been in the house more than a few minutes when there was a knock on the door. She opened it to find Major Henningsen outside. There was an odd look on his stern face that she couldn't quite define.

'I called you this morning,' he said in his usual curt tones, 'but the operator said the line was down. I wanted to make final arrangements for the concert on Saturday.'

'Come in,' Jessica said politely. She realised with amazement that he'd actually been worried she'd come to some harm – or, more likely, he was worried about his concert.

'Thanks.'

'I'm afraid there was an accident last night at the garage,' she said when he was sitting down. He looked entirely out of place in the little old-fashioned room.

'I know, I've been there. I was slightly concerned you'd been hurt, which is why I came round. I knew the street, but not your number, so I asked at the bar on the corner.' His eyes crinkled into a reluctant smile. 'I must say they're a friendly crowd of guys in there.'

He asked Jessica what had happened the night before, and after she'd told him, he said scathingly, 'It sounds as if the woman only got what she deserved.'

Jessica made a face. 'Strangely enough, that's what Rita said herself.'

He glared at her. 'You sound as if you don't agree.'

'I don't agree with violence, particularly when it's the strong against the weak. As to Rita getting what she deserved, I'm not sure. She merely took advantage of the situation she was put in. In a way, I always regarded Rita as an exaggerated version of myself. We even had the same red hair – though hers was dyed,' she added quickly. 'Not like mine.'

Major Henningsen regarded her curiously. 'And would you take advantage of a situation like she did?'

'I did once,' said Jessica calmly, 'and it completely altered my life.' It was very odd, perhaps it was because she disliked him so intensely and didn't give a damn what he thought, but she could say things to him that ordinarily she wouldn't have said to another soul, particularly a man. 'Have you ever done something, not that you're later ashamed of, but you would never dream of doing if the circumstances hadn't arisen?'

She got up and went into the back kitchen to fill the kettle with water. When she returned, he was slowly shaking his head. 'I don't think I have, no.' He smiled, a genuine smile this time, and she felt taken aback when his grim face was completely transformed. He actually looked rather boyish. 'Is that a good or a bad thing?'

'I suppose it depends on the circumstances,' Jessica shrugged. 'In my case, it couldn't have turned out better.'

'You mean you had Penny?'

She felt her face turn scarlet and the kettle nearly dropped from her hand. 'How did you . . . I mean, what made you say that?' she stammered.

346

It was his turn to shrug. 'You told me it was fate who decided you should have Penny. I put two and two together . . .'

Jessica put the kettle on the hob and turned it over the fire. 'Are you shocked?'

'Surprisingly, no.'

Before the conversation could go any further, the back door opened and Sheila Reilly came in with Penny in her arms. Her eyes glanced mischievously from Jessica to the visitor. 'I would have kept Penny longer if I'd known you had company, Jess, but she's longing for a nap and it's like bedlam in our house.'

Jessica introduced her to Major Henningsen.

'Call me Gus,' he said amiably, shaking hands.

Sheila promptly invited him to Melling on Saturday afternoon. 'Our Eileen, that's me sister, is having a party in the garden to raise funds for Russia.'

To Jessica's surprise, he graciously accepted, and even offered them a lift in his jeep. 'Ta, but I've got six kids and they'll never fit in,' Sheila said regretfully. 'Take Jess and Penny, though. A few people from the street are going, so I won't be short of company on the bus.'

After reminding Jessica they would have to leave the garden party no later than four o'clock in order to be on time for the concert that evening, he chucked Penny underneath the chin and left.

'He's a striking looking man, Jess,' remarked Sheila when Jessica returned to the living room after showing the major out.

'He reminds me of Mussolini,' Jessica said dismissively. 'How are you feeling today? You shouldn't be carrying Penny in your condition. She's a ton weight.'

As a result of Cal's short visit at Easter, Sheila had been delighted to find herself pregnant. 'I feel on top of the world,' she crowed. 'Not like last time when I had a miscarriage. Having babies must be catching, mustn't it? First Alice, then Theresa Quigley, now me! Oh, well,

I'd best get home and make the tea. My lot are dying of starvation, as usual.'

Penny decided she was no longer tired and insisted her mother read her a story. Jessica knew her favourite almost off by heart, and, as she read, it was other words she kept hearing in her head. 'Having babies must be catching, mustn't it?' 'If only it was,' she thought. She was a fortnight late with her period, but she was forty-six, well past the age when women usually bore children, an age when she could expect her periods to go haywire. It might be the change. She'd thought it was the menopause the last time, but it had turned out she was expecting Penny. 'I'll try not to think about it,' she decided. 'Then I won't be too disappointed if it turns out to be a false alarm.'

Jessica kissed her daughter's silky hair. 'Would you like a little brother or sister, sweetheart?' she whispered, but Penny wasn't interested. 'No, Mummy, want biccy,' she said.

'You've left something out,' said Jessica sternly.

'Want biccy, Mummy, please.'

Chapter 16

Saturday dawned dull and misty; feathery grey clouds flitted swiftly across the sky, occasionally revealing a brief, tantalising glimpse of the yellow sun behind.

In Melling, a mist still hung in the air at two o'clock, when the garden party was due to start. There were stalls at the front manned by several local women: one stall for handicrafts, the other laden with an inviting selection of home-made cakes and jam, jars of pickled cabbage and beetroot, and strawberries and rhubarb from Eileen's garden. A stone hot water bottle, two rarely seen and highly desirable lemons, and a set of notepaper and envelopes, comprised the raffle prizes.

By half past two, both front and back gardens were crowded and the stalls were almost bare. Trestle tables had been set up on the lawn at the back, and Eileen was busy in the back kitchen making tea.

'Where did all this stuff come from, luv?' Jack Doyle asked when he saw the heap of sandwiches and scones.

'The committee made it, Dad, the Melling Aid to Russia committee. I joined a few weeks ago. It seemed the least I could do, seeing as how that's where Nick is.'

To Jack's relief, she looked more her old self than she'd done for a long time. She wore a nice white blouse and a flowered skirt, and her blonde hair was tied back with a pink ribbon. Her cheeks, so pale and drawn recently, were flushed, and her big blue eyes were bright with excitement. She'd heard from Nick a few days before, and although the letter was three months old, at least it meant that in March he'd been alive and well, though he couldn't stand the cruel Russian weather.

'There's some nice hand-knitted gloves on the stall at the front, Dad,' she said. 'Why don't you buy yourself a pair for the winter?'

'I'll think about it, luv.'

Jack wandered off. He'd only come to keep an eye on the garden and make sure no-one walked on his vegetables. He thoroughly disapproved of such events as garden parties, fêtes and the like, because it didn't seem right to raise funds for the suffering masses in Russia whilst you had a good time on the side. If folks wanted to donate, then let them hand the cash straight over, not stuff themselves with scones and sarnies and cups of tea and make out they were being charitable. What would the starving people of Leningrad and Sebastopol think if they knew their plight was being used as an excuse for an afternoon out in an English country garden?

Two elderly straw-hatted ladies at a table nearby were discussing the recent Bomber Command raids on Cologne and Essen.

'Over a thousand planes!' one remarked. 'It seems terribly immoral. Cologne is such a beautiful city, or at least it was.'

'It was the slaughter of civilians that bothered me,' said the other. 'It means we've sunk to the barbaric level of the Germans. We're just as bad as they are.'

'Very true.' The first woman nodded her agreement. 'It said on the wireless the other day that they estimate at least twenty thousand people were killed.'

'How shameful!'

Jack couldn't stand it a second longer. 'Who the hell started the bloody war?' he demanded angrily.

The old ladies stared at him, blinking nervously. 'Why, the Germans,' one stuttered.

'And who were the first to bomb civilians?'

'The Germans,' they conceded together.

'In that case, d'you expect us to conduct the war like gentlemen? We've got to be not just as bad as the Germans, we've got to be worse, much worse, else the war'll go on for ever and bloody ever.' Jack could feel his temper rising. For months, people had been bemoaning the fact the Government wasn't doing enough. Now, just when they'd got their act together and were hitting back with a vengeance, they were being criticised for doing too much. 'How dare you sit there cramming your gob with me daughter's home-made scones and call this country barbaric and immoral?'

'I made some of these scones myself . . .' one of the old ladies began indignantly.

'Stuff your effing scones!' Jack said scornfully. 'We've got to do everything we can, bomb the whole of Germany to smithereens if necessary, in order to win this war. If we don't, there'll be Nazi stormtroopers marching all over the place, and you won't be free to criticise it then. Oh, no, you'll be taken out and bloody shot!'

'Oh, dear!' The elder of the ladies began to cry.

'Now see what you've done,' the other said accusingly to Jack.

'She'll be having something worth crying about if the Nazis get here!'

'Grandad!' Jack's grandchildren threw themselves at him. Sheila had arrived, along with a few of the folk from Pearl Street.

'What were you saying to those old women, Dad?' asked Sheila worriedly. The old ladies had decided to go home, both by now in tears.

'Just telling them a few home truths,' Jack replied smugly.

'I'll give our Eileen a hand.' Sheila disappeared, and the six children began to play havoc amongst the guests.

Jack sought out Paddy O'Hara and took his arm.

'Come on, Paddy, mate, and I'll take you round the garden. You can have some fresh strawberries straight off the bush.' Apart from his children, Jack had never been more proud of anything than his newly found garden.

'Is there nothing to drink, Jack, other than tea and lemonade?' Paddy asked plaintively.

'Nah!' Jack said disgustedly. 'There's an alehouse not far along the road, but there's no way I'm leaving here, not with me taters so close to the grass. Some idiot might tread on 'em.'

Paddy was left sitting contentedly beneath the apple tree with a cup of tea, a plate of sarnies and Rover, enjoying the unfamiliar scents of the summer country-side in full bloom.

Jack prowled the garden, glaring at everyone, wishing they would go home and leave his vegetables in peace, but they were all having far too good a time raising money for the starving Russians to leave. He was almost glad the day was such a dull one, as it would probably take a bit of the edge off their enjoyment, but, at that very moment, the sun perversely decided to put in an appearance and the entire garden was drenched in vivid golden light.

Somewhere, a woman laughed, and the sound was instantly recognisable. Jess Fleming! Jack turned swiftly. She had obviously just arrived and was standing outside the back door talking to Eileen, wearing a clinging green dress that showed off her red hair and her voluptuous figure to their best advantage. But what made Jack draw in a swift breath of ugly jealousy was the fact that she was with a burly American, an officer, who was carrying Jack's daughter, Penny, in his arms.

He would never have taken Jess for a liar! She had many bad qualities, but dishonesty wasn't one of them. When she'd told him she wanted to call it a day because of Arthur, he'd believed her, yet all the time she had a Yank stashed up her sleeve ready to take Jack's place.

Penny was looking at the chap coyly. He put her down and she ran off to join Sheila's girls, who were playing house underneath one of the tables, much to the annoyance of the people sitting there.

Jess disappeared inside the cottage and the Yank was immediately surrounded by a crowd of admirers, Aggie Donovan to the forefront. Jack had to concede he didn't have the same grinning, self-confident air that most Yanks had, as if he owned the place. In fact, he scarcely smiled at all. He was a tough-looking geezer, as broad as Jack, though not quite so tall, with stern, stubborn features and a forbidding gaze.

Jack went over to the edge of the admiring crowd and listened. 'And what do you think of England, Major?' someone asked.

'I think it's a very charming place, ma'am,' the American replied courteously.

'We were all terribly relieved when your country entered the war.'

'Is that so, ma'am.' He looked rather uncomfortable, and kept glancing at the back door as if hoping Jess would come and rescue him.

Jack wanted to ask if he knew one end of a gun from the other. The bloody Yanks hadn't been involved in a war for decades, yet Major General Dwight Eisenhower, who had never fired a shot in anger in his life, had just been appointed commander of the US forces in Europe. He was trying to think of a truly awkward question he could pose, when Aggie Donovan asked, 'What did you do before the war, luv?'

Jack was slightly taken aback when the Yank replied, 'I've been a regular soldier all my life, ma'am.'

'Aye, but you've never seen battle,' Jack put in sourly.

'Yes sir, I have.' Behind the rimless glasses, the man's cold blue eyes met Jack's. 'I volunteered for the last great war on the day I turned eighteen. I saw battle, as you put it, in the trenches of the Somme.'

'So did I,' Jack muttered. He realised this was a Yank he could find no fault with, so slunk back and leaned against the wall of the cottage, scowling. The major continued to field questions with a sort of polite embarrassment. All of a sudden he paused mid-sentence, his audience forgotten, as his eyes fixed on something way across the garden. Jack followed his gaze. Jess Fleming was crossing the grass with a tray of cups and saucers. One of her high heels twisted on the uneven ground and she almost stumbled. The major made a tiny move, as if he was about to go and help her, but Jess recovered her balance, laughed, and took the tray over to a table. The major relaxed and continued with whatever he'd been saying.

But this tiny, insignificant gesture told Jack the whole story. The American was in love with Jess!

Jessica was washing the last of the dishes when the huge figure of Jack Doyle appeared at the back door. 'Eileen's upstairs seeing to Nicky,' she said. It was the first time they'd come face to face since the day she'd got the telegram to say Arthur was dead.

'It was you I wanted to speak to, not our Eileen.'

The dishes washed, Jessica picked up a teatowel. 'This is sopping,' she murmured. 'I wish I'd known, I would have brought a couple.' She began to dry the dishes, saying brightly, 'Go ahead.'

Jack stuffed his hands in his pockets and frowned at his boots. 'I'm dead disappointed in you, Jess.'

'Why?' demanded Jessica, amazed. She paused, a wet plate in her hand. 'What have I done?'

'I don't like being fooled and lied to,' Jack said hotly. 'I think I've a right to have been told the truth.'

Jessica looked indignant. 'I haven't the faintest idea what you're talking about, Jack. I've never lied to you.'

'What about the American?'

She looked flabbergasted. 'What American?'

Jack felt unsure of himself. Her puzzlement seemed totally sincere. He jerked his head towards the garden. 'The one outside, the major,' he said.

'You mean Gus?'

'I don't know what his name is, but there's obviously something going on.'

Jessica's green eyes sparkled with amusement. 'You're too suspicious for your own good, Jack. There's absolutely nothing going on between me and Gus. I doubt if we could even be called friends.'

'But he brought you!' Jack floundered.

'That's right, and he would have brought your Sheila, too, if all the kids would have fitted in the jeep.'

'How did you get to know him?' Jack persisted.

Jessica was becoming annoyed. She recommended drying the dishes with an angry flourish of the tea towel and said coldly, 'It's really none of your business, Jack. You're behaving like a jealous schoolboy. If you must know, he came to the garage after there'd been trouble with some GIs in the flat upstairs. Following that, he asked me to sing at a concert. I'm singing at another one tonight.' She tipped her chin and glared at Jack, as if challenging him to try and stop her.

'I see.' Jack stepped outside. The American was at the bottom of the garden talking to Paddy O'Hara who'd lost his eyesight in the war to end all wars. They were no doubt chinwagging over their experiences in the trenches. The man looked up, then turned away, uninterested, when he saw it was only Jack who'd appeared.

Jack gave a bitter smile. 'You may think there's nothing between you, Jess,' he said, 'but I doubt if the major would agree. It's obvious the chap's mad about you.'

*

Jessica was quiet for most of the way to Burtonwood. She'd decided at the last minute to take Penny, instead of leaving her with the Reillys as originally planned. Penny sat on her knee, sucked her thumb and stared shyly at Gus Henningsen. She seemed to be acquiring a crush on him.

As they drove through the narrow streets of Rainhill, Jessica's mind was in a turmoil. It was Jack, not Gus, who was mad. Why else should he have come up with such an outrageous suggestion? Why, Gus had told her plainly on two occasions that she wasn't his type, and he'd done absolutely nothing to indicate the opposite. 'And *he's* not *my* type either,' she thought, 'so there's no reason why I should be bothered whether he's mad about me or not. I don't care for bossy, arrogant men like Gus Henningsen.'

She glanced across at him surreptitiously. He was relaxed at the wheel of the jeep, which he drove very fast and with great skill. She noticed his pale eyebrows were finely drawn and his lashes thick and short. His powerful frame, his strong-willed brow, the leather-gloved hands gripping the wheel, everything about him emanated strength and iron determination.

Quite out of the blue, a thrill of excitement coursed through Jessica's veins. Perhaps someone like Gus Henningsen was just the sort of man she needed. 'I've only ever known Arthur and Jack. I could wrap Arthur round my little finger, and I only wanted Jack for one purpose. He was strong, but much too conventional. There's something daring and unpredictable about Gus.'

The silence between them was comfortable and entirely without strain. They were almost there when Gus said, 'How are you going to make a few bucks now the garage has gone up in smoke?'

'I haven't given it much thought,' Jessica confessed. 'I've enough to live on, but I'd like to start another

356

business. I'd be bored silly stuck at home with nothing to do except housework.' From now on, the income from the properties would be hers. Responsibility for the debts incurred when the business went bankrupt had died along with Arthur. Jessica might have felt bound to honour them had the bank had more respect for her at the time they'd decided to call in their debts, but they seemed to think that, as a woman, she had no right to a say in financial affairs. It was the bank which had allowed Arthur to borrow more and more without any reference to Jessica, even though the haulage company was technically hers. Therefore, the bank could suffer the subsequent loss of the debts still outstanding. In other words, the bank could get stuffed.

Gus didn't comment, and as he'd been the one to break the silence, Jessica decided it was her turn to say something. 'I didn't know you were a regular soldier,' she remarked. 'Someone told me just before we left Eileen's.'

'Yeah! My twenty-five years were up in May. Naturally, in view of the hostilities, I stayed on.'

'What were you going to do with your retirement?'

'Retirement? Jeez, I'm only forty-three.'

'You know what I mean,' Jessica said testily. She was a bit put out, as she'd thought him older than forty-three.

'I intend starting up a business myself, something my boy, Peter, can come in on. After taking orders most of my life, I'd like to be my own boss for a change.'

Jessica felt confident that any business he started would be bound to succeed. 'I can imagine you on a range,' she mused, 'herding cattle like they do in the pictures.'

He gave his rather rusty chuckle. 'You've got me sized up all wrong, Jess. I was born in New York – my folks ran a bakery. New York is the greatest city in the world and I wouldn't want to live the rest of my life anywhere else. Peter's crazy for me to take on a car

357

dealership; Cadillacs are the favourite.' He chuckled again. 'I think he fancies being the chief demonstrator. He's always been mad for cars. He could drive at thirteen.'

A car dealership in New York! It was the sort of venture dear to Jessica's heart. She'd love to go to America when the war was over. It was a country ripe with opportunity. She glanced again at Gus as he turned the jeep into the base and wondered if he'd like a partner. If she sold the Bootle properties, she might raise enough for a stake in the business. Or – she felt another thrill of excitement – maybe he'd like a wife! It was all Jack Doyle's doing, but he'd made her realise there was, and always had been, some sort of chemistry between her and Gus.

Just to be awkward, Jessica had brought with her the red dress which had so irritated Gus Henningsen when she first wore it. She changed in a small room behind the officers' mess, along with the two young women who were professional tapdancers and first on the bill.

When it was Jessica's turn to go on, one of the tapdancers held Penny at the side of the temporary stage which had been set up at the end of a massive aircraft hangar. She knew she was at her best that night. She always was, with an enthusiastic audience who stamped their feet in appreciation and needed no bidding to join in the chorus of every song. When she'd finished and was about to take her final bow, Penny came running across the stage towards her, and Jessica swept her daughter up in her arms and waved a last farewell to the cheering boys in khaki.

She had hoped to ask Gus if he would take her home immediately her stint was finished, but he'd disappeared, and everyone else was far too taken up with the concert. The white-haired colonel who'd laid claim to her thigh at the Dorchester, and now seemed to have no memory of the incident, informed her a seat had been reserved in the front row so she could watch the remainder of the show.

Jessica had never heard of the comedian who entertained them for the entire second half, but apparently he was very big in the States. She thought him rather coarse and not the least bit funny, but the audience fell about the aisles laughing at his every word.

There was still no sign of Gus when they went back to the officers' mess after the show for the usual lavish refreshments. Penny was wide awake and in her element as she was petted and told what a cute little girl she was by virtually everyone there. As time wore on and the colonel gradually became more inebriated, he kept laying his hand on Jessica's bare shoulder and squeezing her arm, but this time there was no sign of Gus Henningsen to rescue her. Jessica rescued herself by changing back into the green dress she'd come in, which showed less flesh, in the hope the colonel wouldn't find her so seductive.

Penny was on a table being taught to tapdance when Jessica emerged. Soon afterwards, a young soldier appeared at her shoulder. 'Are you ready to leave yet, ma'am?'

'More than ready.' She noticed the colonel had spied her and was rapidly approaching. 'Are you taking me?'

'Yes, ma'am.'

Jessica hadn't realised how much she'd been looking forward to the drive home with Gus Henningsen. She liked talking to him – or not talking to him, as the case may be. There was a sense of ease between them, as if, deep down at heart, they understood each other. It meant Jack Doyle had been talking through the back of his neck. Gus wasn't even interested enough to take her home.

On the return journey, the soldier chatted volubly. He loved England, it was a great place, and he was looking forward to being transferred across to Suffolk in a few weeks' time. It was truly amazing that it took only a few hours' drive to travel the entire width of such an important country.

'Does that mean you're part of Army Air Corps Maintenance?' enquired Jessica.

'Sure does, ma'am. Gee, how on earth did you know that?' he asked in surprise.

'Someone I know is friendly with Sergeant Dale Tooley. She told me he was being sent to Suffolk at the end of the month.'

'I know Dale Tooley,' the soldier said. 'He's a great guy.'

'Kitty certainly seems to thinks so,' Jessica smiled.

The days passed and swiftly turned to weeks, and still Jessica heard nothing from Gus Henningsen. With the garage gone, he could no longer telephone. Jessica felt more than a little hurt. She tried to convince herself she didn't like him, but although she wasn't sure what her feelings were, she knew this was no longer true. For the first time in her life, she'd met a man who was her match. She would have liked the relationship to continue and see what developed.

'Not that we had a relationship,' she conceded to herself. 'We've only met a few times, and we were mainly unpleasant to each other.'

Instead of his memory fading, each day Jessica thought about him more. In the end, she decided to write to him. 'What harm can it do? Why should it always be the man who asks for dates?' She had no intention of giving up on Gus Henningsen so easily.

She suggested they meet in the Dorchester for dinner. It seemed to be the place where American top brass hung out. *I leave you to pick the day*, she wrote, *as obviously I don't know when you'll be free*. She finished off with, *Yours sincerely, Jessica Fleming*.

The day after she'd posted it, Jessica heard from Arthur's Commanding Officer, a Colonel Curtis, in North Africa. *Private Fleming was taking supplies of essential ammunition to a small group of men who had been cut off in the fighting, when his vehicle was hit by an enemy shell . . .*

Arthur had been *very brave*, and Jessica was offered the deepest sympathy for her sad loss.

Jessica wondered what Colonel Curtis's fate had been when General Rommel had taken the entire British garrison in Tobruk only the other day. Thirty-three thousand troops had been captured by an enemy force of barely half that number, another terrible defeat for Britain. 'Perhaps Mrs Curtis has had a telegram by now,' she thought bleakly.

She sorted through the things she'd brought back from the flat over the museum until she found a photograph of her and Arthur's wedding. She dusted it, put it on the sideboard, and sat staring at the photograph for quite a long time. Then she took it off and put it in a drawer, along with the letter from the Colonel Curtis. 'I can't stand hypocrites!' she said loudly.

It was Sunday, the last day they would have together before Dale was transferred. The weather was scorching and the sun beamed down like a fiery torch out of a clear, bright sky. Kitty wore a new blue and white check frock with short sleeves and big white buttons down the front, which Jessica said dubiously made her look like a nurse!

They met early and decided to spend the day in New Brighton. 'It's a great place. I really like it there,' Dale enthused.

The ferry was crammed to capacity with day trippers carrying bulging shopping bags, and children with their buckets and spades. Dale had brought his camera and took a snapshot of the docks for his dad, followed by several of Kitty standing against the ship's rail which was almost too hot to touch: one looking right, one left, and one looking straight at him with her tongue stuck out.

'If you'd like to tell me how that thing works, I'll take one of you together,' a man, who was watching the proceedings with great interest, offered.

So Dale explained how to use the viewfinder and when to press the shutter, and he and Kitty posed arm in arm against the rail.

'Give her a nice big kiss, and I'll take another.'

'I'll send you copies when I've had them developed,' Dale promised Kitty after the camera was returned.

'I'll keep the ones of us together in me handbag. Then I can take them out and look at them whenever I want, even at work.'

'Are you worried you're going to forget what I look like?' Dale teased.

'As if I would! Anyroad, I'll still be seeing you, won't I?' He was coming to Liverpool whenever he had an extended leave, even if it meant they would only have a single night in the hotel room with the black wallpaper which they now looked upon almost as a second home. When Kitty had her fortnight's holiday, she intended staying in a hotel in Ipswich, only a few miles from his new base. Today wasn't goodbye for ever, but even so, it was still unbearably sad.

'I don't know how I'm going to live without you!' She laid her head on his shoulder and he stroked her hair. For three months, Dale had dominated her life. They had fused together, become one person. Kitty felt as if losing him would be as painful as losing one of her limbs.

'I love you, Kitty Quigley.' He kissed her softly on the lips. 'You'll never forget that, will you? No matter what happens, remember I truly loved you. You're my girl. I've never loved anyone else the way I love you, and I never will.'

The ferry creaked and groaned against the solid piers of the New Brighton quay. Most people were already massed on deck waiting to disembark. 'Dale!' Kitty said nervously. 'You sound as if you've had a premonition you're going to be killed or something.'

Dale shook his head. 'Nothing like that, honey. I just wanted to make sure you knew how much I love you.'

'I already know that, don't I?' The massive gangplank was being lowered and Kitty seized his hand. 'Come on, let's go on the fairground first.'

The day was bittersweet. Kitty crossed the hours off in her head, the way dates were struck off a calendar: two o'clock, three o'clock, four. It was like the tolling of a fateful bell. Once it ceased, Dale would be gone.

After they'd exhausted every ride on the fairground, they strolled arm in arm on the crowded beach. Small children paddled naked in the shallow water, and further out, shimmering in the brilliant sunshine, the glassy river was full of swimmers.

Dale was carrying his jacket over his arm. Kitty modestly removed her stockings and let her feet sink into the burning sand. She paddled briefly, amazed the water could be so cold. Dale watched and laughed and warned her she might drown.

Later, they found a small patch of empty sand and he built a castle with his hands, topping it with a flag made from an old cigarette packet. 'There! I now crown you queen of this castle.'

'And I crown you king.' Their eyes met over the clumsily made castle and he leaned across and kissed her. She fell back against the sand and he took her in his arms and kissed her again. Neither cared that they were surrounded by people who were watching with great interest. As far as Kitty and Dale were concerned, no-one else existed at that moment in time. 'How many times have we kissed?' she whispered.

'Hundreds, thousands, millions. However many times, it's not been nearly enough.'

Kitty glanced at his watch: five o'clock. He was leaving first thing tomorrow and had to catch the last train back to Burtonwood.

'Hungry?' Dale enquired, smiling. The smile still had the power to cause flutters in her tummy. He stood up and held out an arm to pull her to her feet.

'What for?' Kitty licked her lips provocatively.

'For me, for food?'

'I'm hungry for both, particularly you.'

'We've just missed the ferry, so there's time for fish and chips, then we'll catch the boat and you can have me!' He'd developed a taste for fish and chips, and was relieved to be told they were sure to be available in Ipswich.

It was just gone six when they'd eaten and boarded the ferry back to Liverpool. The day was as hot as ever, and once again the boat was packed with perspiring people returning home with their tired children after their day trip to New Brighton. Kitty noticed several GIs with their girls. Everyone had caught too much sun, but despite their red faces and their obvious weariness, most looked enormously happy, as if grateful that, in the midst of the most terrible war the world had ever known, they'd managed to snatch a few hours away from the horror and pretend life was normal for a change.

As the ferry neared the Pier Head, the sound of music drifted across the water. 'I'll be with you in apple blossom time,' the Andrews Sisters crooned.

Dale and Kitty were leaning against the rail on the open top deck. He turned her towards him and slid his arms around her waist. 'Can I have this dance?' he murmured in her ear.

'There's no room to dance!' she protested. She felt close to tears and wished the music was something

364

different. It was the song they'd danced to the night they met, and, to Kitty, it seemed as if everything was being drawn into a tight circle.

'We'll waltz on the spot.' He began to twist her slowly around, their bodies glued together. A woman sitting nearby nudged her husband and they watched the young couple indulgently. 'They've got it bad,' the man remarked.

'Hi, I'm Dale Tooley.'

'I'm Kitty Quigley.'

'Promise you'll never stop loving me, Kitty Quigley.'

'I'll love you for ever,' vowed Kitty.

Jessica found herself staying up later and later. Without the garage, there was no need to rise with the lark, and she and Penny had time for a cuddle in bed before a leisurely breakfast. Now she had a wireless, Jessica usually waited for the midnight bulletin before she retired – Sheila Reilly had been thrilled to swop it for a proper radiogram. Also, the light nights were no encouragement to go to bed. With the clocks having gone forward two hours, the sky was still a pearly grey at midnight.

The curtains had barely been drawn when Jessica heard the door to the back entry open, followed by Kitty's footsteps in the yard. There was only one front door key, and she was reluctant to hang it behind the front door, otherwise the world and his wife would regard it as an open invitation to let themselves in.

'Hello, Kitty,' she called, 'you've missed all the excitement. Ellis Evans kicked Dai out tonight, and I mean that quite literally. Apparently, she found out he'd been having a bit on the side with Vera Dodds. She'd kicked him halfway down the street before someone rescued him. You've never heard such screaming and shouting.'

There was no response from Kitty and Jessica

365

remembered she'd been saying goodbye to Dale. The tap began to run. 'There's still some tea in the pot, dear. I think it should be warm.'

Still no answer. Worried, Jessica went over to the back kitchen doorway. Kitty was bent over the sink, splashing her face with cold water. 'Are you all right?'

Kitty turned. She looked like a clown: her nose was cherry red from the sun and there were equally bright patches on her cheeks, but the rest of her face was starkly white. Jessica was about to laugh, when she was shocked into silence. Kitty's eyes were two dark bitter holes that seemed to bore right through her. Instead of laughing, Jessica flinched.

'Come on, love,' she said compassionately. 'It's not the end. You'll be seeing him again shortly.'

Kitty shook her head, very slowly. 'No,' she muttered. 'No I won't.'

Jessica's heart sank. 'He hasn't chucked you, surely?' They'd been so much in love, the pair of them. Dale had fooled her every bit as much as he'd fooled Kitty.

'No, he hasn't chucked me. It's just that he told me . . .' Kitty paused and drew in a long shuddering, despairing breath. 'He told me *he's married*!'

They had made love with increasing desperation; fumbling, touching, kissing. Panting, they came together in a soaring passionate climax that left them both lost for words and breathless. Then they lay naked side by side, shoulders touching.

After a while, Dale sat up and lit a cigarette. 'Jeez, honey!' he said hoarsely.

Kitty began to run her fingers along his thigh. 'What will you be doing this time tomorrer?'

'Thinking about you!'

'Same here.' She laid her head on his thigh and kissed it. 'D'you think I'll like Boston? Is it much different from Liverpool?' They had never talked much about the

366

future, content to dwell on the delights of the present, but Kitty had always known there was an unspoken agreement that when the war was over they would get married and spend the rest of their lives together.

There was a long pause. Kitty lifted her head and looked at him, wondering why there was such a strange expression on his handsome face. 'Dale?'

His cigarette was down to the stub and he immediately lit another, which was also strange because Dale wasn't a chain smoker. Kitty released his thigh and sat beside him, tightly clutching her knees. She could read him like a book. Something was wrong. A knot of unease began to curl in her stomach.

'Kitty, honey,' he began hesitantly, 'there's something I should have told you.'

The words came tumbling out. He was married, he had two daughters back in Boston, he and Kitty had no future beyond the war.

Kitty listened, stone faced, as her life collapsed in dust around her ears. 'Why didn't you tell me before?' she asked dully when he'd finished.

'Because I didn't want to. You'd never have gone out with me if you knew I was married, would you?'

'No.'

'I love you, Kitty!'

He tried to embrace her but she shrugged him off. '*Don't touch me!*' she hissed.

'I wasn't just after a good time,' he said desperately. 'It was love at first sight. The very second I set eyes on you, I knew you were the girl for me.'

'But only for the next few months?' Why wasn't she more angry? Why didn't she tear him limb from limb, shout at him, scream, try to impress on him how much he'd hurt her, how deeply she felt betrayed? Because she hadn't got the strength, that's why. Her body felt dead inside and would always remain so. Without Dale, she could see no reason to go on living.

'Oh, God!' He flung the cigarette into an ashtray and said tragically, 'I've been fooling myself all along, living in a dream world. I kept telling myself that all that mattered was *now*. The future didn't exist. Kitty Quigley was my girl, full stop.'

'But it's me that's been fooled, not you,' Kitty muttered. She scarcely had the strength to speak. 'You lied to me . . .'

'I didn't lie, Kitty,' he protested quickly. 'I've been selfish and a coward, but I've never lied.'

'Then you've never told me the truth.'

'I would have if you'd asked.'

'It never crossed me mind to ask if you were married,' she whispered. 'Why are you bothering to tell me now, anyroad? I suppose you just want to be shot of me, so you can string another poor girl along as soon as you're in Ipswich.'

'As if I would!' Dale groaned. 'It was when you mentioned Boston, I couldn't go on letting you believe one day we'd be married. If we could, Kitty, you'd have been my wife months ago.'

My wife! The words tore at her heart. He already had a wife back in America. Kitty stared directly at him for the first time since he'd told her the terrible truth. She longed to hate him. She wished she could see something despicable about him, but he looked no different. He was still the same Dale and she loved him just as much. There was an almost irresistible urge to reach out and touch the little mole beneath his left ear. Instead, she asked coldly, 'What's your wife called?'

His lips twisted in a crooked smile. 'Kathleen.'

'Don't you love her?'

'Not the way I love you.' He sighed and reached for his cigarettes. 'We were brought up together, went to the same church, the same school. Her folks were best friends with mine. It had always been assumed we'd get married, and like a good Catholic girl and boy, we did.'

He shrugged. 'Kathy's a good wife, and I suppose, till now, I've always been a good husband. I've never been unfaithful before.'

Kitty gasped as the memories flooded back. 'The things you said! Even on the boat a few hours ago, you asked me to never stop loving you.'

Dale said slowly, 'You'll think me crazy, Kitty, but that's how I saw it at the time. If I close my eyes, I can still imagine us having kids and growing old together. It's only when I open them that reality sets in and I realise we're doomed. I could leave Kathy, but not my girls – and would you marry a divorced man in a registry office?'

'I don't know,' Kitty said hopelessly. She began to cry as the hopelessness engulfed her and she envisaged the years ahead without Dale.

'It's all so tragic,' Jessica thought angrily as she helped Kitty into the living room. 'Arthur, Rita, now Kitty.' When would it all end?

'It's hard to accept right at this moment, love,' she told the distraught girl, 'but you'll get over it. Remember when Eileen lost her little boy? She wrote and said she wanted to kill herself, but within a year, she was married and had Nicky.'

But Kitty wasn't listening. 'I trusted him!' she sobbed. 'I would have trusted him with me life. How could he do this to me? I still can't believe it's happened.'

'I suppose that's my cue to say all men are bastards, but they're not, truly they're not.' Neither Arthur nor Jack were capable of such selfishness; nor, she suspected, was Gus Henningsen.

Kitty veered wildly from one extreme to another. 'Dale's not a bastard. He loves me. He still wants us to meet whenever possible.'

'Would you do that, Kitty?' Jessica asked cautiously. She prayed the girl would answer no, else she would only be storing up more heartbreak for herself when Dale eventually left for good.

'I don't know,' wept Kitty. Her mind went back to the hotel room. She'd started to cry and Dale had taken her helpless body in his arms. Before she knew where she was, he was stroking her breasts, touching her. She wanted to resist, but seemed to have lost every shred of willpower. And it wasn't just that, she wanted him more than she'd ever done before. Their bodies became a tangled mass of heaving limbs, and she poured herself into him. Her nails scratched his back as he bent over her, groaning in sheer ecstasy towards a dizzy pinnacle never reached before. When Kitty came, she bit his shoulder and tasted blood.

Then, without a word, Kitty got off the bed and put on her clothes. She could feel Dale's eyes watching her every move. She paused at the door. 'Tara, Dale.'

He didn't reply, and before the door was closed, he too had begun to weep.

Chapter 17

It was well into the early hours before Kitty could be persuaded up to bed. She spent the remainder of the night tossing and turning, sitting up, then lying down, quite literally unable to grasp what had happened. Dale was married! He had lain with another woman, done the same things with her as he'd done with Kitty, murmured the same words, and one day he would lie with the other woman again.

It wasn't true. It couldn't be. She'd dreamt the whole thing, imagined it, because no way in this world could last night have actually happened.

The jangle of the alarm clock made her jump, although she was wide awake and expecting it. Kitty got out of bed immediately. Her legs were like jelly and she'd never felt so wretched, but despite everything, she was longing for a cup of tea.

She decided not to tell anyone at the hospital, but there must have been something about her face that gave her away. Everyone was very respectful and careful of what they said. Even Clara Watkins, when they were in the auxiliaries' rest room having their mid-morning break, said awkwardly, 'Bear up, Kitty. Everything'll turn out right in the end.'

'Will it?' Kitty replied politely.

When the shift ended, she went home, scarcely able to remember anything about the ten hours she'd just spent at work. Jessica had a pot of tea freshly made and greeted her with a warm hug. Jessica was being very kind, but Kitty was aware she shouldn't cause too much embarrassment in someone else's house.

After she'd drunk the tea, she said, 'If you don't mind, I'd like to lie down.' She wanted to get out of Jessica's sight so she could grieve in private.

She lay on the bed, and the same old thoughts came pouring through her head. 'How could he? How could he do this to me? *Dale!*' Her body was soggy with weariness, and after a while she fell into a fitful sleep. She was woken by the bedclothes being tugged. Unbeknown to Jessica, Penny had come upstairs and was trying to climb on the bed.

Kitty leaned over and lifted the child up. She loved Penny. She was such a dear little girl, it was hard not to.

'Sorry, Kitty.' Penny stroked her face.

'Sorry for what, luv?'

'Sorry Kitty sad.'

Kitty burst into tears. 'When you grow up, Penny, whatever you do, don't fall in love.'

Later that night, her dad came. Perhaps Jessica had told him that what his daughter needed was family.

'Oh, kiddo!' He took her in his arms and rocked her gently to and fro, every trace of resentment and envy entirely forgotten. His girl, his own flesh and blood, had been badly hurt, and he could feel the hurt twisting inside his own guts. Bloody Yanks. He'd like to throttle every single one of them. 'You know, luv, you can come back home this very night if you want.'

'No, Dad. I'm better off here. I only feel in the way with Theresa there.'

'Theresa!' There was a silence and Jimmy looked into the gentle, red-rimmed eyes of his daughter. 'I made a terrible mistake with Theresa.'

'I know, Dad.' Kitty nodded. 'I always knew, but you're stuck with her now and there's nothing you can do about it.'

'There's something lacking in the woman. I don't

372

know what it is. Perhaps she's got a screw loose or something. She doesn't mean to be cruel or unkind. She just hasn't got the nous to know any better.' Jimmy knew he'd been too quick to get married, too anxious to replace Kitty, who he felt had deserted him, with another woman. Theresa had made him feel young again, but only for a while. Now there was always an unpleasant atmosphere in the house and she barely spoke to him. He scarcely saw Georgie and Billy except at weekends. By the time he got home, they'd usually been sent to bed for some reason. 'I should have got to know her better,' he muttered. 'I was too fast off the mark.'

Dai Evans had come into work that day, bruised, but full of beans. Ellis may well have thrown him out, but he'd moved in with Vera Dodds. It made Jimmy aware he'd missed out, not with Vera whom he couldn't stand, but with some other woman, perhaps one more his age. He could have ended up having a dead good time instead of being stuck with Theresa. Still, as Kitty said, he'd made his bed and he had no alternative but to lie on it.

'How's work?' asked Kitty.

'Not bad,' Jimmy smiled. 'Fact, it's not bad at all. Working on the docks is different than it used to be. We're essential workers now, so we don't get pissed around any more. And the pay's good.' From odd remarks his workmates made, he discovered he'd become a figure of fun during the period he was pretending to be an invalid, but now he'd got his self-respect back.

'I'm ever so pleased, Dad.'

'So'm I, kiddo. Well, I'll be off now. Theresa's left me dinner in the oven. She seems to spend a lot of time round at her mam's lately. See you tomorrer, luv.'

'Dad!' Kitty clutched his sleeve.

'What is it, luv?'

'Those lads, Georgie and Billy. It's not right the way Theresa keeps them stuck in the bedroom. You need to put your foot down. They're your lads now, every bit as much as hers.'

Jimmy pursed his lips. 'You're right, kiddo. I'll see what I can do.'

It was a beautiful July evening, the very best of weather. Pearl Street was full of lads playing football against the railway wall and girls with their skipping ropes and whips and tops. Dominic and Niall Reilly were swinging on a rope strung from the lamppost outside the King's Arms.

Jimmy went indoors and called his stepsons to come downstairs. After a few minutes, they appeared on the landing.

'I said, come down.' Jimmy put his hands on his hips and looked at them sternly.

'But me mam sent us to bed early,' said Georgie.

'What for?'

The boy looked vague. 'I'm not sure. I think it was because our Billy asked for more bread and margarine.'

'If you come down, I'll do you some bread and marge – jam too, if there is any.'

'But what about me mam?' Billy said fearfully.

'Sod your mam and come down this very minute.'

The boys descended nervously. Theresa never laid a finger on them, but a look from her could make them tremble.

Jimmy cut four slices of bread and made them each a jam sarnie. 'Now, when you've finished that, you're to go out in the street and play.'

'Don't want to,' said Georgie.

'Why not?'

'No-one'll want to play with us. They think we're cissies 'cos we stay in all the time.'

'In that case, I'll come out and kick a ball round with

you. The other lads'll soon join in when they see me.'
He thought they'd be delighted, but both boys merely
shrugged, and Billy said listlessly, 'If you like.'

Their big white faces were still frightened whilst they
silently munched their bread and jam. Jimmy sat in his
chair and watched them. Obviously, they were scared
their mam would come in.

'Did your dad used to play with you?' Apart from the
day they'd met, Theresa had never once mentioned her
first husband.

To Jimmy's amazement, Georgie's face lit up. 'Yeah,
well, not play exactly. We used to go fishing every time
he was home.'

'Fishing!' exclaimed Jimmy. 'Did you now! Whereabouts?'

'In some river, I don't know where it was. We used to
get the bus.'

'T'weren't a river,' argued Billy. 'Our dad said it was
just a stream.'

'Did you catch much?' asked Jimmy, interested.

'Nah, just tiddlers. We'd bring them back in a jam jar.'

'Would you like me to take you fishing next Saturday
after I finish work?'

Billy burst out crying, much to Jimmy's horror.
'What's the matter, lad?' he asked, alarmed.

'I don't half miss me dad,' sobbed Billy.

Georgie was doing his best to blink back his own
tears. 'So do I,' he said, his bottom lip trembling. 'Our
dad was the gear.'

Poor little sods! It had never crossed Jimmy's mind the
lads were mourning their lost father. Bloody Theresa!
He cursed the woman for her lack of sensitivity. At the
same time, he cursed himself for thinking the lads were
merely being churlish, when in fact they were dead
miserable. Whilst they had been talking, they'd edged
closer and by now both were leaning against Jimmy's
knees. They were an ugly pair, but perhaps not quite as

ugly as he'd first thought. He had a feeling he could grow fond of them in time, and if the feeling was reciprocated, they could end up a proper family, excluding Theresa, of course. Or including her, if she ever turned out to be a human being.

He slapped them both on the shoulder. 'Well, lads, things are going to change round here. As from today, I'm in charge. You'll not be spending any more time in your room, you're to play in the street like the other kids. As for your mam, if she attempts to put her foot down, I'll . . .' Jimmy paused, unsure what he'd do.

'You'll bloody clock her,' suggested Georgie. 'Me dad always said he'd like to clock her, but he never did.'

By the end of the week, Kitty had managed to adopt an air of false brightness. She smiled a lot, though the smile never reached her eyes, and spoke very fast in a rather high-pitched voice. She didn't manage to fool her close acquaintances but, as she said to Lucy, 'I can't stand the thought of people feeling sorry for me. I can't go round with a long face for the rest of me life.' She giggled a touch hysterically. 'The patients'll never get better with a nurse who looks like the Angel of Death!'

Only in the solitude of her bedroom did she let herself go. Even then, she drew the eiderdown over her head so Jessica couldn't hear the sobs that racked her body night after night. It didn't help when she received a letter from Dale: he loved her, he missed her. Please could they meet again?

It took almost superhuman willpower for Kitty to throw the letter on the fire after she'd read it once. There was nothing she wanted more than to mend her broken heart by sinking into Dale's arms in their hotel room with the black wallpaper. But their romance was doomed. He himself had used the word: doomed. If she weakened and allowed herself to see him again, she'd have to go through all this again when the war was over and he returned to his wife and family.

A week later, another letter came with an Ipswich postmark. It was waiting on the sideboard when Kitty arrived home from work. The envelope felt thick, as if there was more than just a letter inside, and Kitty guessed what it contained. She flung it on the fire, unopened.

Jessica gasped, and the two women stood watching as flickering blue flames quickly seized the paper and it began to burn. The envelope went first, exposing the contents, the photographs which had been taken on the ferry to New Brighton. The one of Dale kissing her was on top – perhaps he'd put it there deliberately. Gradually, the flames took hold, the photos began to curl and burn, the two figures on the boat turned brown, then black, then completely disappeared. Soon, all that was left was a little square of grey ash. Jessica, noting the way Kitty was staring intently at the fire, seized the poker and dispersed the ash, so there was nothing left to remind her of the final day out in New Brighton with Dale Tooley.

Kitty had her curly brown hair cut very short. She'd lost her appetite and was losing weight and the short hair made her face look even thinner. Perversely, where once she'd been healthily pretty, the haunted expression in her large hazel eyes and the delicate contours of her suddenly hollow cheeks gave her an air of almost fragile beauty.

In the middle of July she turned twenty-eight, though pleaded with Jessica not to do anything special for tea. 'I'd sooner ignore it. I feel more like sixty than twenty-eight.'

'Whatever you say, love, though you're a bit young to forget about your birthdays.' Even so, Jessica gave Kitty a pretty cream georgette scarf and her dad bought her a tiny locket on a chain.

'It's real silver, kiddo. I got it from that pawnshop in Marsh Lane. The feller there said it's antique, whatever that means.'

Soon after her birthday, Kitty was on her way down to the office with papers for a patient who was about to be discharged, when a startled voice said, 'Kitty! I hardly recognised you with your hair like that.'

'Hello, Stan,' she said calmly. 'I didn't know you were back.'

Stan Taylor laughed. 'I've never been away. I was made permanent months ago.'

'I didn't realise. I've been rather taken up with other things lately.'

'So I've noticed. Whenever I've said hello, you looked as if you were a hundred miles away.'

'Sorry.'

'Seeing as you've recognised my existence,' he said eagerly, 'how about a trip to the pictures one night soon? It's ages since we had a chat.'

Kitty paused before replying. She had no wish to go out with another man again, but it would make a change to talk to someone who didn't know about the break-up with Dale. Jessica, Sheila, her dad, the other nurses — everyone talked to her in an artificial way, as if she were a child and they were terrified of saying something wrong. She knew they were being sympathetic, but it only seemed to emphasise how deeply she'd been hurt.

'As long as the picture's a musical or a comedy,' she said to Stan. 'I'm not in the mood for a romance.'

They went to a cinema in Waterloo to see Betty Grable in *Down Argentina Way*. Kitty supposed that normally she might have found it enjoyable, but she felt too numb to laugh and allow herself be carried away by the cheerful music.

When they came out of the cinema, Stan suggested they went for a drink in the public house across the road. 'The usual?' he enquired when they were inside.

'No, I'll have something stronger,' said Kitty. Her usual drink was half a pint of shandy. She remembered he normally drank rum. 'A rum and orange, please.'

'It's not like you to drink spirits,' Stan said when he returned with the drinks.

'I've changed since we last went out.'

'In what way?'

'I drink rum now, instead of shandy!' She began to sip the drink slowly and by the time she'd finished, she felt a little dizzy and the edges of her hurt became slightly blunted. She felt less sad.

'Would you like another?' asked Stan.

'I wouldn't mind.' Perhaps another drink would make her happy. 'Did you ever hear from Daphne?' she asked when Stan came back.

He made a face. 'Only that she got married.'

'What happened to the other girl, the one you fell in love with?'

'Nothing came of it.'

'I'm sorry, Stan.' She squeezed his arm. She'd always liked Stan, but now she felt almost affectionate. He'd also been let down by the person he loved, which meant they'd both been through the same tragic experience. It was a bit late in the day, but she wanted to convey the fact that she understood and sympathised.

'Never mind, there's still time. Another rum, Kitty?'

'Wouldn't say no,' Kitty replied thickly.

The barman called time just as she finished her third rum and orange. Kitty's legs felt unsteady when they left the pub and began to walk along Liverpool Road in the direction of Bootle. Stan put his arm around her waist to hold her steady.

'Thanks, Stan,' she hiccuped. 'You're the best friend in the world.' She stopped and looked at him with moist eyes. 'Am I your best friend in the world, Stan?'

'I want to be more than your friend, Kitty.' Stan's voice was strange, all tight and strangled. 'I've been in love with you for ages. You're the "other girl" I mentioned. I love you, Kitty.'

'Love!' Kitty laughed bitterly. 'There's no such thing as love. Love's just a joke. It doesn't exist.'

'But I love you,' Stan insisted.

'I don't love you,' cried Kitty. 'I'll never love anyone again as long as I live. Love turns to ashes on the fire.'

'Let's get you back to my place,' Stan muttered. 'You can't go home like this.'

'Jessica won't mind.'

'Who's Jessica?' Stan began to hurry her along.

'I'm not quite sure,' said Kitty seriously. 'But, whoever she is, she won't mind. Anyroad, what's wrong with me?'

'You're in urgent need of a cup of strong black coffee.'

'Haven't you got a landlady?' Kitty giggled. 'She might mind more than Jessica.'

'My landlady's on holiday.'

Kitty wasn't sure why it was necessary for Stan to take her upstairs when they reached his lodgings. 'Funny place for a back kitchen!' she remarked as he led her into an untidy bedroom with too much furniture.

'Lie down, Kitty. You'll feel better once you're lying down.'

She sank back onto the bed and the room swam around her. 'I don't like your wallpaper. I like black wallpaper with roses best.'

'Damn the wallpaper.' He bent over and pressed his lips against hers. 'I adore you, Kitty,' he said passionately, after a while. 'You've no idea how long I've dreamed of doing this.' He was fumbling with the buttons down the front of her frock.

380

Kitty just lay there and let him. She was still drunk, but the walk had sobered her up enough to realise what was happening. Stan, like all men, was merely taking advantage of an unexpected opportunity – Dale had done the same, except with him it had been a more long-term attempt to get her into bed. She knew Stan could be stopped. He wasn't a brute. All she had to do was fight or scream and he'd soon back away, but perhaps this was a way of escaping from the all-consuming misery she'd felt over the last few weeks. She reached up and put her arms around his neck, drew his face down to her breasts and let him kiss them.

'Kitty, Kitty,' he groaned.

She shoved her clothes down and he ran his hands up and down her body. He touched the places only one other man had touched before. There was a pause whilst he removed his clothes, staring at her naked body greedily the whole time.

They made love, but it was nothing like it had been with that other man. He didn't look like Dale or sound like Dale. He didn't feel like Dale. He was a stranger, a rather worthless stranger, but perhaps not so worthless as herself.

When they'd finished, Kitty felt dirty. She felt like a prostitute who'd sold herself, not for money, but for a few minutes of forgetfulness. Not only that, the transaction had been a waste of time. She'd forgotten nothing. Indeed, it only brought home to her how perfect her relationship had been with the man who had so cruelly betrayed her.

'That was wonderful, Kitty,' Stan said in a small voice. 'I'll make you that coffee now.'

'It doesn't matter,' said Kitty. 'I'd sooner go home.' She began to put her clothes back on.

'In that case, I'll take you.' He jumped eagerly off the bed.

'I'd rather go by meself, if you don't mind.'

'When will I see you again?'

'We'll probably see each other round the hospital,' Kitty said airily. She glanced at his crestfallen face. 'Tara, Stan.'

Convoy PQ-17, on its way to the Russian port of Murmansk with a cargo of tanks, aircraft and military vehicles, was being subjected to a vicious onslaught from German U-boats and planes. Day after day, Sheila Reilly listened to the wireless and heard a cultured voice announce that once again, 'Enemy planes have attacked British merchant shipping in the Barents Sea. Several British and Allied vessels were sunk.'

'There'll be none left to sink soon,' thought Sheila. She was in the yard sorting out the family leavings in various receptacles: bacon rind in a jar for Eileen's hens, potato peelings to make compost for her garden, bones for Rover, and silver milk-bottle tops which Aggie Donovan would collect, along with the waste paper and cardboard. There was scarcely any rubbish for the bin men nowadays.

'It's not knowing whether Cal's alive or dead that's the worst.' On the other hand, not knowing meant there was still hope. She hadn't yet had a chance to tell him about the baby.

It was going to be a boy. Brenda had suspended a needle and thread over Sheila's belly and the needle had swung clockwise, which meant a boy.

'I thought clockwise meant a girl?' said Brenda.

'Now you've got me all confused and I can't remember meself. I'm sure it's a boy.'

Sheila had begun to think up names. It had to be something Irish: Declan, Kevin – Patrick was a nice name and currently her favourite. But what if it was a girl? She'd always fancied Mavoureen, but Cal didn't like it, he thought it soppy. They'd argued over Mary when their youngest was born. Cal preferred Aileen,

382

but Sheila protested. 'I've been calling her Mary for months. I've always had a feeling I was carrying a girl.'

She pictured her babies inside her womb the minute she knew she was expecting. They weren't seeds or foetuses or whatever the doctors called them, but tiny, perfect human beings just an inch or so long. She could picture the new baby: it was about as big as her hand now and looked exactly like Calum. 'That's what I'll call him, Calum!'

But no, there was only room for one Calum in her life, and it was tempting fate to introduce another. It was like cancelling the first one out. Sheila felt frightened that such an idea had entered her head. Perhaps it was a message from God? It was his way of telling her that Cal was dead.

'Oh, dear God, please don't do that to me,' she prayed and she wiped her hands on her pinny and went back inside the house. But God had already done the same thing to so many other women. Why should he regard Sheila Reilly as special?

It was over a month since Jessica had written to Gus Henningsen. She'd almost given up on him when she received a postcard which said tersely, *Dorchester, Thursday, eight o'clock. G.*

When Thursday came, she made herself up with particular care, twisting her hair into a chignon at the nape of her neck. She'd already chosen what clothes to wear: a plain black costume with a frilly white blouse underneath.

'Are you sure you don't mind staying in with Penny?' she asked Kitty when she was ready to leave. 'Sheila will always have her if you'd prefer to go out.'

'Kitty read stories!' Penny put her arms around Kitty's legs and glared at her mother.

'I haven't much choice, have I?' said Kitty. 'I don't think Penny's willing to let me go even if I wanted to.'

As the evening was all her idea, Jessica left early to make sure she reached the Dorchester first. She sat in the bar and ordered a dry martini.

The barman slid the drink across and Jessica was about to pay, when a voice said, 'Let me buy that.' A short man with a very red face and wearing an expensive suit was reaching in his pocket. He'd clearly had too much to drink.

'No thank you,' said Jessica. 'I'm waiting for a friend.'

The man winked. 'That friend could be me.'

'Unless my friend has lost several stone in weight, shrunk six inches and had an operation on his face, I think that's unlikely.'

'Are you being clever, lady?' The red face turned pugnacious.

'No, I'm being realistic,' Jessica said coldly. 'Please go away.'

'Sir,' the barman interrupted courteously. 'I think the lady would prefer to be alone.'

'What's she doing hanging around bars if she wants to be alone?'

'Look, buster,' a gritty voice broke in, 'if you want to keep that nose in place, then take a hike. The lady's with me.'

'I'm becoming tired of rescuing you from drunken middle-aged men,' Gus complained when they were seated in the almost empty restaurant.

Jessica was conscious, in a way she'd never been with Jack Doyle, of the enormous power in his broad shoulders and bulging arms. He had removed his cap and his short-cropped hair glistened palely. If it hadn't been for his glasses, she could have visualised him in a horned helmet standing at the prow of a Viking ship.

'You weren't there to rescue me when your colonel started pawing me after the concert,' she pointed out.

'Sorry, but I was called out on an emergency. Some of our boys had got into a fight in a dancehall in

Manchester. The MPs had sorted them out, but it's my job to soothe ruffled local feelings. Anyway,' he went on with a grin, 'you seem perfectly capable of looking after yourself.'

'Really!' Jessica said tartly. 'What would you like to eat?'

He looked at her over the menu. 'Is this meal on you?'

'I invited you, didn't I?'

He smacked his lips with gusto. 'In that case, I'll have sole to start with, followed by roast beef.'

'You can have either sole or beef. There's a war on and you're not allowed two main courses.'

'In that case, I'll have the beef.' He laid the menu down and crossed his massive arms on the table. 'What's this all about, Jess?'

'I just wanted to see you, that's all. I haven't got any ulterior motive. You didn't get in touch with me . . .'

'Only because I've been away,' he explained. 'I was called to a conference in London, then did a quick tour of our British bases, flew back to the States for a week. We're very anxious our boys don't cause too much disruption in your country. We'd like them to be regarded as friends, not as the enemy.'

'One of your boys has caused disruption in my house.' Jessica told him about Kitty and Dale Tooley. 'The poor girl's heartbroken.'

Gus didn't look particularly concerned. 'I'm afraid there's not much I can do about that.'

'I didn't expect you to.'

The waiter arrived and Jessica gave him their order and requested a bottle of red wine. Gus looked amused. 'This is the first time a woman has asked me out on a date.'

'At our age, I think we've passed the point of who asks whom first.'

He said quickly, 'I intended getting in touch as soon as I got back, but found your letter waiting.'

'I'm relieved,' Jessica said bluntly. 'I thought you didn't want to see me again.'

He looked amused again, but also slightly puzzled. 'You're very honest. I can't help but wonder why?'

Jessica took a deep breath. Now the moment had come, she felt more than a little afraid. 'Because I can't be bothered pussyfooting around with all the preliminaries of courting,' she said, amazed her voice sounded so steady and self-assured. 'I think there's a possibility we might be good together on a permanent basis. I could turn out to be wrong. If so, we'll have lost nothing, will we?'

Gus no longer looked amused. He frowned at the table, looking grimmer than she'd ever seen him, as if Jessica's words had struck him dumb with anger – or perhaps it was terror! The waiter brought their meal and he made no effort to touch it.

'If you've already decided to run a mile,' she said lightly, 'stay and eat your dinner first. I'll have to pay for it now.'

He picked up his fork and began to shove the food around the plate. Still frowning, he muttered, 'I've decided not to run a mile. So, what happens now?'

Jessica swallowed. 'I think we should start by being open with each other. I'd like you to know everything about me, what sort of person I am, because I'm not terribly nice.'

'I've already managed to work that out for myself,' he said cuttingly.

She ignored him, and explained about the house in Calderstones where she used to live. 'It was what we call Mock Tudor, with five bedrooms and a double garage for the cars. Then Arthur lost the business which my father had built up, though it was just as much my fault for being so wrapped up with my own affairs that I didn't notice what was going on. That's when we moved to Pearl Street.'

'I thought you looked out of place there,' he commented drily.

'Oh, no,' cried Jessica. 'Pearl Street's very much where I belong. I was born there. My father was a rag-and-bone man. He used to wheel a handcart round the streets shouting for people to bring out their rubbish. Does that shock you?'

'It surprises me,' Gus conceded. 'What surprises me most is that you admit it.'

'When I lived in Calderstones, I didn't tell a soul. I used to pretend I was born elsewhere, but when I went back to Bootle, it didn't seem to matter.'

Gus had begun to eat, though he looked more interested in what Jessica had to say than he did the food. 'Is that when you had Penny?'

'Yes. Arthur and I never had children, and I always thought it was my fault.' Jessica sighed. 'I didn't mean to deceive him, it happened so suddenly I couldn't help myself, but then I found I was expecting Penny and I didn't care. Soon after she was born, Arthur got a job in a museum in the Lake District, but I couldn't stand it there. Like you, I'm a city person, so I left him and came home.'

'Poor Arthur,' Gus said in a hard voice. 'It sounds like you gave him a tough time.'

'I did. I thought he'd be happy messing round with his tiles and bits of statues, but he wasn't. He joined the army – you know what happened then.' Jessica breathed a sigh of relief. 'Now it's your turn.'

'To do what?'

'Tell me all about yourself! What skeletons do you have hidden in your cupboard? I'd like us to start off with a clean slate.'

He looked irritated. 'Lady, my cupboard is bare and my slate entirely clean. There's nothing to tell. I got married at twenty-three. My wife died two years later. I brought Peter up on my own. He'd just started college,

387

when we had Pearl Harbor. Against my wishes, he decided to join the army. That's it. That's the story of my life. Whereas yours might fill a book, I doubt if mine runs a page.' He finished his meal and threw the fork down with more force than was necessary.

Jessica's heart sank. She seemed to have misread the entire situation. 'Have I made a show of myself?'

'What does that mean?'

'Do you think me an idiot?'

'Yes.'

There was a long silence, during which Jessica wished the floor would open up and swallow her. She was conscious of the clink of dishes, the buzz of conversation in the restaurant, which had filled up considerably since they came in. The waiter came and removed their plates and asked what they'd like for afters. Gus wanted nothing to eat, but asked for a double whisky. 'Or bourbon, Jack Daniels, if you've got it.'

'Yes sir.' The waiter disappeared and the silence continued.

After a while, Gus said sarcastically, 'I thought you said there was no ulterior motive for this meeting?'

'I was lying.'

'Also, I'm not sure if my ears deceived me, but did you propose marriage?'

'Only in the very, very long-distant future, once we'd got to know each other properly,' Jessica stammered. 'Obviously, it was a stupid idea.'

He glared at her. 'Isn't proposing considered the man's job?'

'Normally, yes.'

'Wouldn't it have been . . .' he paused and sought for the right word, ' . . . let's say polite to wait for me to ask first?'

'Is there a possibility that would have happened?'

His drink arrived and he picked up the tumbler and swirled the contents around. For a few minutes, he brooded into the golden liquid, then he shook his head in wonder and said, 'This is one helluva night. Nothing like this has ever happened to me before.' Then he slammed the drink down on the table and whisky splashed out onto the cloth. Several diners nearby jumped and turned to see what was happening.

'Of course it would have happened!' he snarled. 'It's what I wanted the minute I first laid eyes on you, you damn crazy woman. I accept your proposal. There's no need to wait until the very long distant future. I'll marry you tomorrow if you like.'

Jessica felt her body flood with relief, and she bestowed upon him the most dazzling of her smiles. 'There's one other thing. I said I wanted to be honest with you. Now, I'm about to be brutally honest.'

'I wouldn't expect anything else of you, Jess.'

'The main reason I went back to Bootle was to start an affair with Penny's father. I make no bones about the fact I used him quite selfishly because I wanted another child. The thing is, I think I might be three months pregnant. Do you mind?'

Ellis Evans, stubbornly proud and deeply religious, was mortified that her husband had openly committed a carnal sin with another woman; so mortified that she stayed indoors, convinced the entire street were laughing up their sleeves and talking about nothing else. There was a certain amount of truth in this conviction: Ellis was too virulent a person to arouse much pity. Even so, she was one of theirs, and the neighbours were only too willing to offer tea and sympathy and settle down to a good gossip over Dai's philandering ways and Vera Dodds' morals – or lack of them – but Ellis refused to speak to anyone. She despatched her daughter, Myfanwy, on all the messages.

There was no sign of either Ellis or Myfanwy for several days, and after people had knocked on the door, banged on the windows, peered through the letterbox and climbed over the wall into the back yard, they realised that number 5 was empty.

'She's gone,' said the agent when he called on Jessica – she insisted he pretend to collect the rent, otherwise the neighbours would have noticed she didn't pay. 'There was nine and sixpence on the table and a letter to say she's gone back to Wales. Everywhere's been left spick and span, ready for someone else to move into. There's already five people after it, and there'll be dozens more once word gets round it's vacant, what with the modernisation you had done. It must be the only house in Bootle with an electric stove. Fact, you could move across there yourself.'

'I couldn't be bothered,' said Jessica. 'I've grown used to this place, and I won't be staying for ever.'

'Do you want to put the rent up? It's worth more than nine and six.'

'Make it eleven shillings.'

The applications poured in, nearly fifty in all, some offering double the rent for the first week if the landlord would only choose them. In the past, Jessica had always left such matters to the agent. He might sneak a look at the prospective tenants wherever they were currently living and make sure they were respectable enough for Pearl Street. This time, however, she told him she wanted to make the decision herself. Halfway through the pile of applications, she came to the neatly written letter she'd been looking for. She gave it to the agent next time he came round. 'I want this family to have it.'

He looked dismayed. 'Do you realise Jack Doyle's son and daughter-in-law live in Miller's Bridge? It's dead rough over there. You don't want those sort of people in one of your properties, Mrs Fleming.'

'Yes, I do,' said Jessica. 'And another thing, put the rent back down to what it was.'

Sheila had told her Jack had applied for number 5 on

390

behalf of Sean and Alice. 'Oh, it would be lovely having our Sean live opposite. I tried to persuade me dad to offer the landlord a few bob extra, but you know what he's like, straight as a die. He just came out with a tirade against landlords; capitalist filth, he called them.'

Jessica supposed it was the least she could do for the man who'd given her Penny and almost certainly a second child. She'd been sick that morning and felt queasy until midday, the first real sign of pregnancy. It was time to see a doctor.

Chapter 18

Calum Reilly came home in August. He didn't tell Sheila, but twenty-three ships out of the convoy of thirty-six had been sent to the bottom of the Barents Sea. Four hundred and thirty tanks had been lost, over two hundred aircraft, more than three thousand vehicles . . . He had no idea if anyone had bothered to count the number of wasted lives.

'It's a war of figures,' he said to Jack Doyle. It was Saturday and Jack had just arrived home from a day spent in his daughter's garden in Melling. A row of green tomatoes stood on the window ledge inside his living room to ripen in the sunshine. 'When I left school, nearly every lad in the class went into the Merchant Navy. Now, I'm the only one still alive. It'll be little short of a miracle if I'm here by the time this lot's over.'

'Miracles can happen, lad,' his father-in-law grunted.

'If the worst comes to the worst, you'll look after Sheila and the kids for me, won't you, Jack? There'll be another kid in January. Sheila's convinced it's going to be a boy.' Cal felt as if he were living on borrowed time; that one day, very soon, death was inevitable. Since coming home, he kept looking round for things to do in the house to make it easier for Sheila when he was gone. He'd put an extra shelf up in the cupboard under the stairs and given the yard a fresh coat of whitewash.

'You don't have to worry, lad,' Jack said gruffly.

'Sheila will never go short while I'm alive. There's years more work in me. Your kids'll be old enough for work theirselves by the time I'm ready to give up.'

'Thanks, Jack.' Cal laughed shortly. 'Let's hope you don't end up with your Eileen and Nicky on your hands, as well. Nick's got an even more dangerous job than me.' Whilst Cal risked his life in the seas around Russia, Nick Stephens flew the perilous skies. He'd only met Nick once, at his and Eileen's wedding. He'd liked him. In the normal course of events, they would have become great mates. But you could no longer look forward to events in the future, simple things like getting to know your sister-in-law's husband and going for a drink together after Mass on Sundays. Over the last few weeks, as his ship had sailed through the chill and unfriendly waters of the Barents Sea and the convoy around them rapidly diminished, the crew had begun to wonder if it was worth looking forward to their next meal.

Jack was staring into the fire. 'Nick's coming home,' he said slowly. 'Eileen only got the letter yesterday. He's been invalided out of the RAF.'

'What happened to him?' Cal prayed Nick hadn't been burnt. He'd heard of a chap who'd had his entire face destroyed when his plane crashed.

'The letter didn't say.'

'Jaysus!' whispered Cal. 'I'm not sure if that's good news or bad.'

'We'll just have to wait and see, won't we,' Jack sighed.

While Cal was home, one good thing happened to cheer him. Across the street in the front bedroom of number 5, little Alice Doyle gave birth to her first baby, a boy weighing five pounds, three ounces. To her delight, the baby, who she decided to call Edward after her long-deceased father, was the image of his dad, a tiny

393

jewel of a baby with a mop of jet black hair and already a hint of Sean's roguish charm.

'Isn't he the gear?' Alice said tearfully to her brothers and sisters who had collected proudly around the bed. 'Oh, if only Sean was here to see him! Still, I'm lucky, not like some women. At least I know he's safe and sound.' She kissed the baby's head. His hair felt like thick silk and he waved his fists around like a boxer. 'In fact, I'm the luckiest woman on earth. I never dreamt I'd end up married to Sean Doyle, who always had a stream of girls after him. And, if that weren't enough, we're living in a palace. I can't wait to go downstairs and make sure the electric stove's really there: sometimes I think I've just imagined it – an electric stove and a bathroom of our own! Even when I used to take in laundry from those dead posh houses along Merton Road, I never came across a woman with an electric stove.'

There was as yet no furniture in the parlour, and the stuff in the living room had seen many better days before it reached the Scullys' old place in Miller's Bridge and been moved on a handcart to Pearl Street, but Alice was used to poverty and couldn't possibly have been happier.

'Colette,' she said to her sister, 'go downstairs and make sure the stove's all right. I should be back on me feet by this time tomorrow, so I can keep an eye on it meself.'

Jimmy Quigley had been unable to pinpoint the location of the stream where Frank Beamish used to take his sons fishing. Neither lad could remember what number bus they caught, nor what direction they took once they were on it.

'There's a nice stream runs alongside the factory in Melling where our Eileen used to work,' Sheila Reilly told him. 'I've seen kids fishing there.'

'Me dad used to bring a bottle of lemonade and some

394

sarnies,' said Georgie when Jimmy confirmed his intention of taking them fishing on Saturday afternoon.

'We'll do things exactly the same as you did them with your dad, don't worry,' Jimmy assured him firmly. He couldn't remember when he last spent a day out in the country, and it seemed an entirely different world altogether when they got off the bus beside a little humpbacked bridge beneath which the crystal clear water gurgled merrily. The scenery was slightly spoilt by the giant munitions factory, so they strolled along the stream until they were surrounded by fields and the factory could only be seen in the distance. It was a lovely day, but then it had been a lovely summer so far, with scarcely any rain to speak of.

The boys took their shoes and socks off and had a fine time with the fishing nets – Jimmy had walked the length and breadth of Bootle until he'd found a shop which stocked them. After a while, he got bored. 'Is it all right if I read me paper?' he asked the lads. He was anxious not to do anything their dad wouldn't have done. He didn't want them to think, even though they would have been right, that he wasn't terribly interested in fishing.

'Yeah, our dad used to bring a book.'

Jimmy decided he would probably have liked Frank Beamish. 'Much better than I like his bloody wife,' he thought, grinning to himself, though there wasn't much to grin at. The situation with Theresa was more tragic than funny. She either didn't care or hadn't noticed he'd decided to put his foot down over the lads. In fact, nowadays they hardly ever spoke to each other, and the other day she'd cursorily suggested he might as well use Kitty's bedroom seeing as it was empty. When Jimmy tried to have it out with her and asked what was wrong, she looked at him in sluggish surprise. 'What do you mean, what's wrong? There's nowt wrong as far as I know.'

395

'I'll never get through to her,' Jimmy muttered aloud. 'Never!'

'I've caught a goldfish, Uncle Jimmy,' Billy yelled in triumph.

'Don't keep it if it's too big. It'll only die in a jar.' Jimmy felt pleased that a barrier had just been crossed. He'd suggested the lads call him 'uncle', and this was the first time one had done so.

'Our dad wouldn't let us keep the big 'uns.'

It was gone six by the time they arrived back in Pearl Street. Georgie and Billy had caught the sun, as well as several tiddlers, and looked happy and contented. 'Can we go fishing again next week, Uncle Jimmy?' Georgie asked eagerly.

'As long as it's not raining.'

'Our dad used to take us in the rain. We even went once in the snow.'

Jimmy gritted his teeth. 'All right,' he said, 'we'll still go, even if it's raining.'

It was another fine day several weeks later when Jimmy took his stepsons fishing. They didn't appear to mind if he disappeared into the alehouse by the bridge for a pint or two while they played with their nets in the water.

He was making his way back, pleasantly full of ale, when he noticed a young man in RAF uniform sitting on the bank on the other side of the little stream opposite the factory. The chap was in a daydream, shoulders hunched, his gaze fixed on something invisible to Jimmy. There was something odd about him that Jimmy couldn't quite make out at first. When he got closer, he saw the young man only had one arm. The left had gone and the sleeve was neatly pinned in half and dangled loosely.

Jimmy couldn't bring himself just to walk past without a word, yet the young man seemed entirely unaware of his presence. When he was directly opposite, Jimmy paused and said conversationally, 'Penny for 'em, mate!'

The chap nearly jumped out of his skin. He was a fine-looking young fellow with dark curly hair, rich brown eyes and a pleasant, open face. 'S-sorry,' he stammered. 'You startled me.'

'It's me that should be sorry,' Jimmy said abjectly. 'I should have crept past and left you to your thoughts.' He nodded at the missing arm. 'What happened?'

The young lad looked at his empty sleeve with an air of slight surprise, as if he wasn't quite used to the arm not being there. Jimmy guessed it wasn't long since the accident had happened. 'My plane crash-landed. The navigator was killed. I suppose I was lucky to get out alive.'

'I don't suppose you feel all that lucky?'

The chap smiled sardonically. 'Not yet.'

Jimmy sat down on the bank and took out a packet of Woodbines. There were only two left. 'Fancy a ciggie?' he offered. 'I'll throw them over.'

'No thanks, I don't smoke.'

'Don't blame you, mate. They're heavy on the pocket.'

'They're also bad for you,' the young man said severely. 'My wife used to smoke. She gave up not long before I went away. I often wondered if she took it up again.'

'Well, you'll soon find out. Are you on your way home now?' The question was scarcely out of his mouth when Jimmy realised it was a stupid thing to ask. If he was on his way home, then he wouldn't be sitting on the bank opposite, staring into space, and looking as if going home was the last thing on his mind.

The man's dark eyes clouded with misery and an expression of utter wretchedness came over his young face. Then, as if everything had been boiling up inside him, the words came tumbling out. 'To tell the truth,

397

I'm scared to go home. I asked to be dropped off here. This is where I met my wife. I was sitting in this very spot when she came out of the door over there and knelt by the water to splash her face. She looked like a mermaid. You've no idea what we went through before we could be married . . .' He stopped and looked at Jimmy appealingly. 'What will she think when she sees me like this?' He gestured at his missing arm. 'She'll have to cut my food in pieces for me, help me dress. I won't be able to pick my baby son up – Nicky was only hours old when I last saw him. I can't work in the garden or do things around the house.' He was on the verge of tears. 'Christ! I'll be less than useless.'

'I think you're exaggerating a bit,' Jimmy said gruffly. An emotional man, he was close to tears himself. 'You'll soon learn to do all sorts of things on your own. I reckon you'll soon be nifty with just one arm. As for your missus, if I were you, I'd be off like a shot. I bet she'd have a fit if she knew you were here. Is she expecting you?'

'I've no idea. I'm not even sure if she knows about . . . about this!' He shrugged his left shoulder hopelessly.

'Do you live far?'

'Just along the road.'

'Uncle Jimmy! Uncle Jimmy!' Georgie and Billy came running up and stared at Jimmy accusingly. 'You've been gone for ages. Did you forget about us?'

Jimmy stood up and put his arms around his boys. 'Just as if! I've been talking to this young feller for a while, that's all.'

The lads transferred their gaze across the stream. They stared at the figure in his blue-grey uniform with a certain amount of awe.

'Where's your arm?' demanded Billy.

'Shush, lad,' Jimmy cautioned.

The young man smiled. 'That's all right. My arm went up in smoke along with my Mosquito.'

'Are you a hero?'

'Of course not! I'm just a . . .'

'Yes, he is,' Jimmy broke in huskily. 'He's a hero, and he's about to go home to his missus.' He stared at the young man challengingly. 'That's right, isn't it, son?'

'I suppose so.' The man sighed as he eased himself awkwardly to his feet. He was about to walk away, when he stopped and said, embarrassed, 'I hope you didn't mind me coming out with all that guff? I'm not sure what came over me.'

'What guff?' Jimmy nodded sternly in the direction of the bridge. 'Go on, you're losing time.'

'Cheerio — and thanks!'

'*Is* he a hero?' Georgie asked when the young man had disappeared.

'He certainly is,' said Jimmy.

Kitty was having a wild old time. She was scarcely ever in. She would go dancing straight from the hospital and, sometimes, it was well gone midnight by the time she arrived home. Occasionally, she'd had too much to drink and her eyes shone with an unnatural brightness.

'It was the gear,' she'd breathe ecstatically when Jessica asked if she'd enjoyed herself. She'd started to use make-up, far too much, and her hollow cheeks were rouged, her lashes stiff with mascara. 'I danced every dance, but then I always do.'

'I'm not surprised.' She looked beautiful, but in Jessica's eyes her painted face was a picture of pathos as she put every waking minute into the effort of forgetting Dale Tooley.

Dale still wrote, but perhaps he was losing heart as his letters went unanswered, because they were growing fewer. Other letters came, though. Kitty heard from Harriet Mansell, who was working in a hospital in

America. *It's for black people only. I love it. I feel I'm doing something truly worthwhile. I was a useless auxiliary.* She hoped Kitty was happy. *You deserve to be, Kitty dear. You're the sweetest person I've ever known.*

Kitty cried openly over the letter. 'Happy! I couldn't possibly be less happy. And I'm not sweet, either, not any more. From now on, I'm going to be as hard as nails. Never again will I let a man do to me what Dale did.'

'They're not all like that, love,' Jessica tried to convince her.

'Aren't they?' Kitty cried scornfully. 'Huh! I won't wait to find out. As soon as one seems serious, I'll ditch him.'

She never gave anyone the opportunity to get serious. She had a good time at the dances, teasing her partners to distraction and letting them buy drinks all night if there was a bar, but she always left alone. After her experience with Stan Taylor, she decided to keep her body to herself from now on. Even the thought of being kissed was intolerable.

Glyn Thomas also wrote. Kitty had almost forgotten him. He was due in Liverpool shortly and would be staying with Jack Doyle. The very second he had parked his kitbag, he would be around to see her.

Jack must have told Glyn that she'd moved, because he turned up at Jessica's just as she was about to leave for a dance at the Rialto. He was in his sailor's outfit and his face wore the old irrepressible grin when Kitty opened the door. His arms were stretched out dramatically all ready to give her a monstrous hug, but his expression turned to one of dismay.

'You've changed, Kitty,' he said immediately. 'You never used to wear all that stuff on your face.'

'We all change,' she replied pertly and invited him in. Jessica was upstairs putting Penny to bed.

'How are you?' Glyn asked courteously when they were sitting down.

'Couldn't be better,' sang Kitty.

'You've changed a lot.'

'You've already said that.'

'It's not just your face, it's your manner.'

Kitty sensed he felt disillusioned. He'd carried a picture around in his mind of a fresh, innocent girl who no longer existed. What was it he'd said when they first met? Something about the face being the mirror to the soul and she was beautiful inside and out. She didn't care if he was disappointed. He was a man, and one of these days, like Dale, he would have let her down. She decided to refuse when he asked her out.

But she didn't have the opportunity to turn him down. After a few minutes of stiff conversation, Glyn decided it was time to leave, and made no mention of seeing her again.

'That's a laugh,' Kitty said to Jessica after Glyn had gone. 'He wanted us to get married a few months ago. Now he can't bear to lay eyes on me just because I'm wearing a bit of make-up. He said I've changed. If he loved me all that much, he would have wanted to know why.'

'He can't have been genuine,' Jessica said despairingly. Sometimes, sorting out Kitty's tragic love life could be a touch wearing.

'What man is?' snorted Kitty.

Rita Mott had taken lodgings in Peterborough and was working in a local factory. *I've been in touch with Den,* she wrote to Jessica. *He's in a military prison in Colchester, and he's willing to have me back. I do as much overtime as they'll let me. I never go out, and I put every penny aside so Den can start another garage once this bloody war's over. I miss the 'you know what' we used to talk about something rotten, but never again! From now on, it's just me and Den. Love to Penny. I really miss her—fact, I really miss you both. Your loving friend, Rita.*

'At least someone's sorted out satisfactorily,' thought Jessica in relief. That night, she wrote back to Rita and told her how pleased she was to hear she'd made it up with Den. *I've some news of my own. Remember Major Henningsen who called at the garage the day I heard Arthur had been killed? We're going to be married, I'm not sure when . . .*

Jessica laid down her pen. When?

Gus was pressing to get married straight away, bemused at her hesitation — understandably, since it was Jessica who'd proposed.

'But I said in the long-distant future,' she whispered to herself. 'I wanted to get to know him first. I don't love him!'

Although she wanted to be honest, she couldn't very well tell him that! She'd thought they'd make a fine partnership, that they'd be good for each other, but Gus had assumed from her words that night in the Dorchester that she loved him as much as he loved her.

'I never loved Arthur, not properly, not even when we were first married, and I was only a child when I loved Jack. It was no more than a schoolgirl crush. Perhaps I'm too selfish to love anyone except Penny — and this new one.'

She laid her hands protectively on her stomach. The doctor had confirmed she was definitely pregnant. After she'd sorted out her dates, he worked out the baby was due early next year: mid February.

Gus had offered to rent a house near the base: Warrington or Manchester. 'The sooner we get married, the better for the baby, though frankly, Jess, I must be out of my mind getting tangled up with a gal like you.'

'That's what makes us so suitable for each other,' said Jessica wisely. 'We don't have the same morals as other people.' This statement was in contrast to their so far decorous relationship. Gus had done no more than kiss her, which was also understandable in view of his desire that they be married soon.

He laughed. 'Don't we? That's news to me. I've been strictly moral all my life. You've bewitched me, Jess Fleming, right from the start. That's why I was so rude, I was trying to resist you. Now you're trying to tell me I'm some special sort of person just so you can get your talons even further into me. Now, about this wedding . . .'

'What about Peter?' asked Jessica.

'What about him?'

'What will he have to say about his dad getting married again?' Gus was obviously very proud of his boy and mentioned him a lot.

'Peter's an easy-going kid.' He shrugged his shoulders carelessly. 'He never knew his mother. He told me if I ever found him a new mom, she had to have long red hair and be called Jessica.'

'Seriously, Gus. He mightn't like me.'

'Pete likes everyone, but perhaps it wouldn't be a bad idea to keep your lurid past a secret between you and me. He might think I've taken up with a scarlet woman.' He grinned amiably. 'Now, for the second time, about this wedding . . .'

She wouldn't feel isolated, he assured her, as she'd done in the Lake District. Something was always going on at the base, and a few wives of senior officers were already there.

Jessica picked up the pen to continue with her letter to Rita, but paused, the pen poised over the paper. 'I'm not sure if I want to be in love after seeing what it's done to Kitty. And fancy being sick with worry all the time the way Sheila is over Calum! I never gave Arthur a second thought when he joined the army.'

She finished the letter to Rita and turned on the wireless. The ten o'clock bulletin reported good news from North Africa. After their triumphant capture of

403

Tobruk, the Germans had advanced as far as Alamein, but their advance had drawn to a sudden and surprising halt. According to the announcer, Rommel and his army still remained bogged down in this position several weeks later. A new Commander of the Eighth Army had just been appointed, Major-General Bernard Mont-gomery. In another part of the world, the Germans had arrived at the gates of Stalingrad, but the Russian people had declared, 'We shall never surrender.'

'Good for them!' whispered Jessica. She supposed she had better stay up till Kitty arrived home. The poor girl was still in a state and Jessica could do little to comfort her. She felt slightly ashamed of how much she was looking forward to Kitty's absence when she went on a week's holiday with her father at the end of the month.

Jimmy Quigley decided it had been a funny old year. He needed a break and managed to convince his daughter that she needed one even more than he did. The Government were urging people to spend their holidays at home and not use up precious space on the trains. Events had been arranged in local parks: band concerts, open-air plays and all kinds of entertainments. 'But even if we went somewhere different every day,' Jimmy said, 'it still means coming back to Bootle. I'd like to be somewhere different for a while. What about a bed and breakfast place in Southport? It's only a local train ride. What do you think, kiddo?'

'That sounds nice, Dad,' Kitty said dutifully. It couldn't have been more different from the holiday she'd planned with Dale in Ipswich and she didn't look forward to it a bit, though she supposed it would be better than moping round Jessica's. She could have gone to Brighton with two of the nurses, but that would have only ended up a continuation of the frenetic life she was already leading, which was beginning to wear her down.

'We'll take the lads,' Jimmy said firmly. 'There's no way I'd leave them with their mam, and *she*'ll not come, that's for sure. Anyroad, it's me bloody wife I need the break from!'

There was plenty of money in his pocket nowadays. One good thing about Theresa, she was careful with the housekeeping and required surprisingly little each week. Jimmy always had an argument ready if she asked for more, but she never did. As expected, she declared holidays a waste of time and money and said she would clean the house from top to bottom whilst they were away – much to Jimmy's relief, and, he suspected, the lads'.

He found a place which called itself a 'guest house' advertised under 'Holidays' in the Liverpool *Echo*, and wrote and booked. It turned out to be a rather cramped establishment above a cheap restaurant off Lord Street. Kitty's top-floor room was very small, with a single bed tucked underneath the sloping ceiling. The window caught the early morning sun and she could feel it warm on her face when she first woke up. Georgie, Billy and her dad were in a much larger room below.

Their landlady made liberal use of the new dried egg mixture which was being imported from America. Every morning for breakfast, there was dried egg scrambled on toast, dried egg fritters or dried egg fried flat with bacon or mushrooms.

After a few days, Kitty was glad she'd come. The weather continued to be glorious, and it was relaxing to start off the day with nothing whatsoever to do. Some mornings, she merely stayed in the lounge and read one of the books which were thoughtfully provided on a shelf in the corner, or else she wandered round the shops in Lord Street or strolled along the vast silver sands whilst Jimmy took the lads fishing or to the fairground.

They met up for lunch, invariably fish and chips, and the afternoons were usually spent much the same way as

405

the mornings. Evenings, they went to the pictures or played Monopoly in the lounge. The guest house was half full and there were a few other children for Georgie and Billy to play with. After the children had gone to bed, several guests stayed to listen to the wireless. To a chorus of cheers, on the first of September, it was announced that Major-General Montgomery was forcing Rommel to retreat in North Africa, though the news wasn't all good: Stalingrad was now under siege.

Kitty was beginning to get on well with the boys. They'd started to call her 'Auntie Kitty', but she told them just Kitty was enough. 'I'm your sister, aren't I? You don't call your sister auntie!'

'Our sister!' They stared at her, amazed. It was funny, Kitty thought, but they weren't nearly so plain as she'd first thought. The more she grew to like them, the better-looking they became. They got on like a house on fire with Dad. What was also funny, was the fact it was the lads who seemed to be making Dad happy, not Theresa. He seemed like a man reborn when he played football with them on the sands.

Her dad had changed unrecognisably from the man he'd been a year ago. 'Just like me!' Kitty thought. 'Except whereas he's changed for the better, I've changed for the worse. I'm not nearly so nice as I was.'

Sometimes, she wished life was still the same as it used to be, that she'd managed to convince Miss Ellis at the Labour Exchange that she needed to stay home with Jimmy. But if that had been the case, she would never have worked at the hospital. She would never have met Lucy and Harriet, or Martin McCabe and all the other sailors who had briefly flickered across her life.

On Thursday, a man of about Kitty's age appeared in the dining room for breakfast. He wore a smart black pin-striped suit and sat alone at his table, eating his food idly and smiling to himself. Several times, he spoke aloud. Georgie and Billy nudged each other and giggled, and Jimmy tapped the side of his forehead and whispered, 'He's obviously a penny short of a shilling.'

After the man had gone, the landlady came into the dining room. She was a florid woman with dyed black hair and crimson painted lips who always wore violently patterned overalls which, she said proudly, she made herself. 'Don't take any notice of Mr Grisham, he's harmless,' she told them. She went on to explain, in what Kitty thought was an unpleasantly ghoulish manner, that five years ago, Mr Grisham and his wife, who were from Birkenhead, had spent their honeymoon at her guest house. The following year, they'd come with their new baby, and the year after with their second-born. They continued to come, even after the war had started. 'He had a good job as a bank clerk. They wouldn't take him in the army because he had a weak chest, but that didn't stop him joining the ARP.' The landlady's eyes glittered. She was clearly enjoying her role at centre stage. 'One night during the May Blitz, the poor man was out doing his duty when his house took a direct hit and his wife and two kids were killed!'

She paused for effect and the guests dutifully supplied gasps of genuine horror. 'His mum looks after him now, but he comes back regularly.' She giggled. 'He thinks his wife and kids are with him. That's who he was talking to at the table.'

Kitty saw Mr Grisham walking on the sands later that morning and went up to him. 'Hallo, we're both at the same hotel.' He was a very ordinary man with thinning hair and light brown eyes, and looked rather incongruous on the beach in his formal clothes.

'Hallo.' He smiled at her, quite friendly, and they chatted about the weather for a while.

Kitty thought he seemed quite normal. 'I was just about to buy myself a cup of tea. Would you care to join me?'

407

'That's awfully nice of you, but I'm looking for my wife.' He glanced anxiously up and down the beach. 'I don't suppose you've seen her? She's not very tall with brown hair and I think she's wearing a blue dress this morning. She has two small children with her.'

'I'm sorry,' Kitty said sadly, 'but I haven't seen anyone like that.'

'Never mind, I'm sure to find her soon.' He tipped an invisible hat and continued with his walk.

Kitty stared after his retreating figure. She felt ashamed that she'd let herself get in such a state over Dale when there were people who'd suffered a million times more than she had. Compared to them, Dale was just a pinprick. It made her even more ashamed that she was using these other people's suffering to lessen her own. She walked back to the guest house and was pleased to find the lounge empty so she could sit and think. 'I've got to *do* something with me life. I can't go on the way I've done the last few weeks. What on earth must Jess think of me? I feel dead embarrassed over the way I've behaved.'

She'd hated every minute of the dances. 'I can't go back to that. I wonder if I could join the forces?'

The prospect of becoming a Wren or a WAAF was rather appealing. 'That's if they'd allow me to leave the hospital.' She was already working in an essential occupation. Nowadays, you couldn't just up and leave a job without permission from the Government.

'Hello there, kiddo.' Jimmy came into the room looking happily exhausted.

'Where's the boys?'

'I left them playing with some other kids outside.' He gave Kitty a pretend punch. 'Are you enjoying yourself, luv?'

'Much better than I expected,' Kitty conceded with a smile. 'I'm having a lazy ould time, but me head's been hard at work trying to sort me life out.'

'That bloody Yank!' swore Jimmy. 'I'd like to kill him.'

'It taught me a lesson, Dad.' She no longer thought, 'How could he do this to me?' but 'Why did I let it happen?'.

'Aye, but not a lesson y'needed to learn. I'd like to see you married, girl, with a family of your own.'

It was an effort for Kitty not to smile. He'd done his level best for ten years to make sure that didn't happen. 'I know you would, Dad,' she said gently, 'but I can't see meself getting married for a long while.' That's if she got married at all. Out of the blue, a sense of desperate loneliness swept over her, more keenly than it had ever done before. Staying with Jessica was only supposed to be temporary. If she carried on as she was, she would end up living alone, a spinster in an unskilled job with only the memory of an unhappy affair to keep her company in bed at night.

Kitty made up her mind there and then. The minute she got back to Bootle, she would do something drastic. Somehow, in some way, she'd set her life on an entirely different course.

The Dorchester Hotel was widely used by American servicemen and Jessica continued to meet Gus there for dinner once or twice a week. The staff in the Provost Marshal's office in Burtonwood had the hotel number and knew where to contact him if he was needed. He refused to stay for long in Pearl Street. 'You haven't got a phone, Jess. Say there's an emergency?'

'There's an emergency,' said Jessica the first time he complained.

'It's not funny. It could be something crucial.'

'You should have more confidence in your staff. You should delegate more.'

'Is that Jessica Fleming, businesswoman, speaking?' he said coldly.

Soon afterwards he left, looking annoyed. Jessica was slightly put out, feeling *she* should be put first, not the American Eighth Army Air Force, but eventually came to the conclusion that if he'd stayed, she would have thought less of him. Gus wasn't going to dance to her tune like Arthur or be coaxed around like Jack. Gus was his own man, which was what had drawn her to him in the first place. She would have to get used to not having her own way, at least not all the time!

She was humming happily to herself one night as she got ready to meet him. Kitty had offered to look after Penny. After her holiday, Kitty had gone through yet another metamorphosis. Whereas she'd once never been in, now she was never out. She didn't exactly look happy, but she appeared quite calm and never mentioned Dale Tooley.

'Are you putting on weight, Jess?' Kitty asked. 'That skirt looks awfully tight and it never used to.'

'It must be all the dinners with Gus,' Jessica said lightly. She showed surprisingly little for nearly five months pregnant, unlike with Penny when she'd grown as big as a house. Perhaps, now she was beginning to show, it wouldn't be a bad idea to marry Gus immediately and move elsewhere. She hadn't given it much thought before, she was too thrilled at the idea of being pregnant, but Pearl Street wasn't exactly a good place to be an unmarried mother. Even good friends like Sheila Reilly, so religious, would disapprove once they found out, and Aggie Donovan and those of her ilk could well give her a hard time. Jessica remembered the way some had turned on Eileen Stephens when a rumour flashed around that she was having an affair: the women had accosted her in the street, screaming their disapproval.

'I'll tell Gus tonight,' she thought as she went upstairs to change into a fuller, less revealing skirt. 'I'd like to get married secretly and not tell a soul.'

There was no sign of Gus when she reached the Dorchester. She asked the waiter if there was a table booked for Major Henningsen, but was told no. Jessica felt mystified. It was unlike Gus to be late and not to have reserved a table in advance. She ordered a dry martini and waited in the bar. After nearly half an hour, she had just decided to telephone the base, when the girl who worked evenings as a receptionist approached.

'Mrs Fleming? Major Henningsen's office has just called. They said they're sorry, but the major has been unavoidably detained.'

'Did they say why?'

'No, Mrs Fleming, just that he's been detained.'

'It wasn't Major Henningsen himself who spoke to you?'

'It was a young man. I would have recognised the major's voice.'

'Thank you.'

The girl returned to her desk and Jessica remained in the bar, sipping her martini and feeling annoyed. How dare he cancel a date right at the last minute? Was this what married life would be like with Gus Henningsen? Would he turn out to be the sort of man who always put his job first? At least he could have telephoned himself and asked to speak to her personally, not got some lackey to do it for him. Her anger grew, and after a while she went over to the receptionist and asked her to put a call through to Burtonwood.

'If you'd like to go into booth four, Mrs Fleming, I'll transfer the call as soon as I'm connected.'

Jessica's rage increased as she stood waiting in the booth. The nerve of the man! The second the telephone gave a brief ring, she picked up the receiver and demanded the Provost Marshal's office.

A young voice answered and Jessica asked to speak to Major Henningsen. 'I'm sorry, ma'am, but the major's not taking any calls at the moment,' she was told.

He was there! 'What do you mean, he's not taking calls? This is Mrs Fleming, a friend of the major's, and I want to speak to him immediately.'

'Sorry, but that would be more than my life is worth. The major's incommunicado. He doesn't want to see or speak to anyone.'

Jessica's rage swiftly melted. There was something wrong. 'Why?' she asked. 'What's happened?'

There was a pause before the young man said cautiously, 'I shouldn't really tell you this, ma'am, but he can only shoot me once, can't he? The major got the news a couple of hours ago. His son's been reported missing, believed killed, in Papua New Guinea.'

She had to get to him! She told the young man to inform the sentries on the gate that she was coming, otherwise she would be refused admission. 'Don't forget now, it's Mrs Fleming, Jessica Fleming. I'll be there as soon as I can.'

Jessica slammed the receiver down and ran out of the hotel into the road. 'I'll catch a taxi to Burtonwood!' she decided swiftly.

The nights were gradually drawing in, but it was broad daylight at half past eight. There was no sign of a taxi, so Jessica began to run down Brownlow Hill, wishing she'd worn different shoes because her heels kept catching in the spaces between the flags and twice she nearly fell. She felt angry again, but a different sort of anger this time. Why had Gus shut her out? Surely she was the first, perhaps the only, person he would want to see as soon as he heard about Peter? Her heart twisted when she thought about the big, outwardly unemotional man, grieving alone in his office. He wasn't the sort of man who would cry, not like Arthur. Gus was tough and kept everything inside.

Her heel caught again and this time she did fall, right onto her knees. She cried out in pain.

'Hey, missus!' A man came hurrying up and helped her to her feet. 'You're in a hurry, aren't you! Look what you've done to your stockings! They're all torn.'

'I have to find a taxi,' Jessica panted, the pain already forgotten. She had to get to Gus.

'Lime Street Station, luv. You'll find a whole row there.'

As the man had predicted, there were several taxis lined up outside the station. 'The American base at Burtonwood,' Jessica panted as she climbed into the one at the front.

'That's a long way, missus! If you don't mind, I'd like to see the money first.'

Money! She'd forgotten all about money. Fortunately, her purse contained one pound and several ten shilling notes. She shoved the open purse under the driver's nose. 'Will that be enough?'

'Plenty.' He set off and veered the taxi into the traffic. 'I've got to be careful. There's girls asked me to take them as far as Burtonwood before, and they offered something other than money for the fare once we got there.'

'I'm not likely to do that!' Jessica said coldly.

'No, but as I said, I've got to be careful.'

She didn't answer next time he spoke, and the journey to Burtonwood was made in total silence. It was almost dark by the time they arrived and Jessica was surprised to see a crowd of girls hanging around the gates. She paid the driver, but didn't tip him, and he said sourly, 'At your age, you'll look out of place amongst that lot.'

It took some time to convince the soldiers on the gate that she was expected. 'The Provost Marshal's office should have told you I was coming. If you haven't got my name, please ring them. It's Fleming, Jessica Fleming. I've come all the way from Liverpool.'

'Lady, there's girls over there who've probably come

all the way from Timbuctoo. I could spit as far as Liverpool.'

'It's all right, corporal,' another soldier called. 'Her name's in the book, Fleming. She's expected.'

Jessica knew the way to the Provost Marshal's office; Gus had pointed it out when he'd brought her to the concert. She started to run again, but the effort made her sick. She'd already run too much that night for a pregnant woman of forty-six.

The young soldier she presumed she'd spoken to on the phone was in the outer office. He blinked in amazement when the wild dishevelled figure of Jessica came storming in.

She closed the door and leaned against it, gasping for breath. 'Is he still here?'

'Yes, ma'am.' The soldier looked nervous. 'I should tell you, he took a bottle of Jack Daniels with him. It was full.'

'Right.' Jessica nodded. 'Is the door locked?'

'No. There was no need to lock it. The major knows only too well no-one'd be foolhardy enough to go in if he told them not to.'

'I'm not brave,' said Jessica, 'but I'm going in.'

The room appeared to be in total darkness, but perhaps Gus had got used to the lack of light, because when Jessica felt for the switch, a gravelly voice snarled, 'Leave it!'

'Gus, it's me, Jessica.'

'I know. What the hell are you doing here?'

'I wanted to be with you. Oh, Gus! Why didn't you tell me about Peter?' As her own eyes grew accustomed to the darkened room, she could see a dim figure behind the desk. There was something different about the wide, strong shoulders. They sagged hopelessly. Jessica could actually feel his pain. He didn't answer and his hoarse breath was laboured in the ensuing silence. 'Why, Gus?' she repeated.

'Do you really want to know, Jess?'

'Of course I do.' If only she hadn't run all that way! She wasn't sure if she could remain upright any longer. Her eyes searched for a chair. She saw one against the wall and almost staggered towards it.

'I've been crying,' he said dully. 'That's why I didn't tell you. I've lost my boy and it made me cry, but you don't like weak men, do you, Jess? You don't have much time for men who cry.'

'Gus! I love you, I don't care if you cry.' She'd said it! For the first time in her life, she'd told a man she loved him and meant it. She felt almost dizzy with the knowledge that she was in love, but perhaps it was something else that was making her feel dizzy. Sitting was no longer enough. She felt an urgent need to lie down and it was all she could do not to slide off the chair onto the floor. With an enormous effort, she managed to say, 'Peter's only missing. You never know, he might still be alive.'

'Missing, presumed dead, they told me.' Gus's voice was so thin she could scarcely hear him. 'My boy's gone.'

'Please don't lose all hope, darling . . .' Jessica paused as a tearing pain swept through her gut. Warm liquid oozed down her legs and she screamed, 'Gus, the baby! I think I'm losing the baby.'

Chapter 19

There'd been announcements in the paper for days, and children were told about it at school. The army were organising a major invasion exercise the following weekend to test co-operation between their forces, Civil Defence workers and the Home Guard, and also to judge how the civilian population of Merseyside would react to the arrival of the enemy.

People were instructed to stay indoors so the military would have the free run of the streets. The city and the surrounding area would become a war zone for two days.

As the weekend grew nearer, interest magnified. No-one had any intention of staying inside and missing out on all the excitement. Paddy O'Hara was only one of hundreds of veterans of previous wars to unearth his medals and set out early on Saturday morning to share the fruits of his experience with present day troops. He was shortly followed by Sheila Reilly, Brenda Mahon, and all their children who were going just to watch. It sounded better than a pageant or a May Day procession. Aggie Donovan borrowed a trestle table and set up a refreshment stall outside the King's Arms.

As the supposed invaders advanced on the city and the defenders took up their positions, instead of deserted streets, both sides found themselves surrounded by admiring groups of civilians who demanded they explain the workings of their machine and mortar guns.

When both sides met up and indulged in hand-to-hand fighting, the crowds fell about laughing, formed a circle and spurred the combatants on with cheers and shouts of encouragement.

The 'enemy' were asked what direction they were taking, and told how to avoid a waiting ambush by taking a short cut through a back entry. Dominic Reilly saw a long-awaited opportunity to become involved in the war and offered to act as a spy. When his services were rejected by one side, he offered them to the other, and sulked all day when he was turned down a second time.

Even those troops sprawled out of harm's way on the roof tops found they weren't immune from civilian attention to their welfare. Half a dozen soldiers concealed behind the chimneys of a row of terraced houses found themselves obliged to crawl along to a dusty loft window from which a hand emerged with a cup of tea and a voice shouted, 'Do any of you lads take sugar?'

When Eileen Stephens arrived to see her sister, she found Pearl Street almost deserted. Jessica Fleming was the only friend to be found in. She opened the door looking incredibly smart in her turquoise suit and matching pillbox hat with its fetching veil. Penny came running into the hall to see who'd arrived, wearing a red velvet frock with a lace collar, which Jessica explained Brenda Mahon had made out of a piece of old curtain, adding, 'I think she's going to grow up as mad on clothes as her mother. She insisted on a new frock for her birthday party the other week.'

'I'm sorry I didn't bring Nicky, Jess,' Eileen said apologetically. 'It was his birthday a few days after Penny's, but I didn't want to leave Nick by himself.'

'Is he no better, love?' Jessica asked worriedly as she showed Eileen in. Nick Stephens had returned from Russia minus his left arm, and was finding it difficult to adjust to civilian life with a handicap. He was depressed, refused to go out and objected to visitors, even his wife's closest relatives. To Eileen's further dismay, he took scarcely any notice of the son he'd only seen once before, on the night of his birth.

To Jessica's relief, Eileen's lovely blue eyes lit up. 'Oh, he's over the moon, is Nick. He's managed to land a desk job in the RAF. Unfortunately, it's in London, but he'll come home weekends whenever he can. He only heard the other day and you wouldn't believe the difference it's made. He said he no longer feels useless and "surplus to requirements", as he put it. The other night, we actually . . .' She paused, and her cheeks turned pink. '. . . Well, we did something we hadn't done since he came back.'

'I'm ever so pleased, Eil, I really am.'

'Y'know, Jess,' Eileen said thoughtfully, 'a year ago, when Nick had to leave the maternity home within an hour of me having the baby, I had the strongest feeling I'd never see him again. I was beginning to wonder if I'd been proved right. It wasn't the Nick I used to know who's been living at the cottage over the last few months. It was a stranger who couldn't bear to touch me. I still loved him, but I desperately wanted the old Nick back.' She smiled gleefully. 'And now I've got him! He insisted I leave Nicky with him when I came out today. He said, "It's about time I got to know my son." Of course, he feels dead awful now because he didn't do it sooner.'

'So, it's turned out perfect!' Jessica couldn't possibly have felt more pleased for her friend, though at her words, a shadow fell over Eileen's face. Of course, it would never be perfect without Tony – and Nick had lost an arm.

Eileen sighed, then seemed to pull herself together. 'Why are you and Penny all dolled up, anyroad? You look as if you're off to a wedding.'

'I am,' Jessica said quietly.

'Anyone I know?'

'Someone you know very well. Me! I'm marrying Gus Henningsen in the Register Office at one o'clock. Kitty's the only one I've told. I kept it a secret from the street as I didn't want any fuss.'

'Jess!' Eileen jumped to her feet and gave Jessica a hug. 'I'm dead pleased. Congratulations! Where are you going on your honeymoon?'

'Nowhere! We're going to the Dorchester for lunch, then Gus will go back to Burtonwood and Penny and me are coming home. He'll be along later if he can get away.'

Eileen burst into tears. 'I'm sorry, Jess, but ever since this bloody war began, I cry at the drop of a hat. I hope you and Gus and Penny will be very happy.'

'Don't cry, love,' Jessica said emotionally, 'or you'll have me at it. I'll spoil my make up and I've just used the last of the mascara.'

She'd cried a lot over the last two weeks, more than she'd done in her entire life. She'd lost her baby and her grief was made worse by the awareness it had been her last chance to have a second child.

'It's all my fault,' groaned Gus. By then, the whole awful business was over. An army doctor had been called, and Jessica cleaned up and moved to an emergency bed in the First Aid Centre.

'No, it's my own fault,' Jessica said weakly. 'I should have had more sense than to run the way I did.'

Gus was sitting on a chair beside the bed. He looked at her despairingly. 'But you wouldn't have if I'd had the good sense to call you myself with the news about Peter.'

'Neither of us acted rationally. People do all sorts of silly things in terrible situations.'

'I'll never be able to forgive myself. Two kids gone in

419

one night, first Peter, then yours. Lord Almighty, Jess! I'm not sure if we can come through this.'

Jessica reached for his hand. 'As soon as I'm back on my feet, we'll get married and come through it together.'

His face twisted into a grimace which Jessica realised was Gus being tender. 'Are you sure, darling?'

'I'm positive.' It was only then that Jessica remembered about Penny. 'Kitty's got to be up for work early in the morning.'

'I sent my sergeant to collect Penny. I told him to say you were ill, that you'd just fainted. He should be back soon.' Then Gus said bleakly, 'Do you realise, Jess, that Penny's now all we've got left between us?'

But Gus turned out to be wrong. Several days later, Private Peter Henningsen, aged nineteen, was found, badly injured and more dead than alive, in the thick foliage of a Papuan jungle. Within hours, he had been flown to the safety of a hospital in Australia, where his young healthy body was responding well to treatment.

When Jessica heard, she took the news strangely. Normally down to earth and impatient with superstition, she felt as if her child had been lost in order to save Gus's. She even imagined God, whom she wasn't sure she believed in, asking her to make a choice, 'Will you give up your unborn child for Peter?' and spent many hours wondering what her reply would have been. The sensible part of her mind told her she was being silly and merely looking for justification of her bitter loss in order to feel better. If she could find a reason for the tragedy, it would be easier to bear.

Kitty was delighted to hear Jessica was getting married, and promised to keep the news strictly to herself.

'Gus is looking round for a property to rent close to the base,' Jessica told her. 'I'd prefer to stay in Pearl

Street, but it wouldn't be fair on him. He's on edge the whole time if he's not in easy contact with his office, and I doubt if I could have a telephone installed in wartime. That means I'll be moving soon, Kitty.'

'I'll miss you and Penny, Jess,' Kitty said serenely. Her holiday had certainly done her good. Lately, she'd been looking increasingly pleased with herself.

'The thing is, dear, you could have this house if you want it. I know the landlord very well and I'm sure he could be persuaded to transfer the rentbook to your name.'

Jessica thought that Kitty would jump at the idea. She'd only be a few doors away from her dad, with whom good relations had been completely restored, and she was becoming fond of Theresa's boys. Not only that, her lifelong friends lived in the street. But to Jessica's surprise, Kitty shook her head.

'I wouldn't feel right, taking a whole house to meself. There's whole families need it far more than I do.' Kitty looked at Jessica with shining eyes. 'Anyroad, I'll be off meself soon. I've joined the Merchant Navy as a nurse. I intended telling you once I got me first posting. It should come through any day now.' It had seemed like a miracle at the time. Kitty had gone back to work after her week in Southport, determined to do something different with her life, and there, on the noticeboard, she had found the ideal solution. The Merchant Navy were advertising for volunteers to serve on hospital and troopships. It meant there was no need to get permission to change her job. She'd applied immediately, gone for interview and been accepted. All she was waiting for was an advice to say what ship she would serve on. 'I won't be coming back to Bootle any more, except to visit me friends and family,' she said. 'I've no idea what I'm going to do when the war's over, but I've no intention of settling down for a long time.'

It all seemed a bit extreme to Jessica, but she wished

the girl good luck. 'I'm glad you've got over Dale Tooley,' she added.

'I haven't,' Kitty said simply. 'The time we were together was so perfect, that I doubt if I'll ever get over Dale. You'll probably think me stupid, Jess, but in me head there's two Dales: the one I went out with for three months, and another one who told me he was married. I could easily forget the second in time, but I'll never forget the first.'

Jessica, who was in the throes of trying to decide if her lost baby's life had been sacrificed for Peter Henningsen's, said drily, 'I don't think that's stupid, Kitty, not at all.'

'There's something else I won't forget, Jess,' Kitty said warmly, 'and that's how kind you've been. I'm not sure how I would have coped without you.'

'I did my best, but I don't think I truly understood how upset you were. It's only now I realise what you went through. The idea of Gus doing to me what Dale did to you, is so beyond the bounds of possibility that it's never crossed my mind.'

'That's the way I thought,' said Kitty.

'I'm sorry, Eileen, but I shall have to leave for the Register Office soon.'

Eileen immediately jumped to her feet, but Jessica insisted there was just time for a glass of sherry. 'I wouldn't mind one myself. Now the time's come, I'm feeling a bit nervous.'

'That's understandable,' Eileen assured her. 'Is a car coming for you?'

'No, I'm walking. We're supposed to keep vehicles off the road today.' Jessica giggled. 'I hope we don't get taken prisoner on the way.'

'It's sheer bedlam out there. If it was a genuine invasion, the Germans'd turn tail and run. They'd think they'd landed in a giant lunatic asylum. I'll walk part of

422

the way with you, if you don't mind, and see if I can find our Sheila.'

They left shortly afterwards. Eileen wandered off in search of her sister, and Jessica Fleming, hand in hand with Penny, made her way through the happy and excited crowds towards the place where she was due to marry Major Gus Henningsen.

Kitty's posting came through the following Monday. She was ordered to join the troopship *Nero* which would sail from Portsmouth on the first of October, five days later. A travel docket was enclosed for the train.

She had already worked out her notice at the hospital, but went in for a final time to say goodbye to the good friends she'd made over the last twelve months.

'It's been the best year of my life,' she said to Nurse Bellamy.

'We've enjoyed having you,' the nurse said crisply. 'Perhaps when the war's over and things are back to normal, you might consider a career as a professional nurse. You could probably skip the first year's training in view of your past experience.'

'I'll think about it,' Kitty said seriously. The idea was already on her list of options when the time came to make a decision on her future.

Lucy cried profusely when they said goodbye. 'It won't seem the same without you, Kitty. Clara is still as thick as thieves with Valerie. I hope whoever takes your place won't side with them, else it'll be me against all three.'

'I thought you were getting married to what's-his-name at Christmas?' Kitty had lost track of the names of Lucy's never-ending boyfriends and fiancés.

'Harry! Oh, he turned out to be a drip, so I chucked him,' Lucy said witheringly, 'but I met this dead good-looking Yank at a dance last night.'

They promised to write. Kitty said goodbye to the

nurses who vowed they'd keep close track of the *Nero* in the papers, then sought out Clara Watkins. Although she'd said nothing to Lucy, there was bad news in store for Clara. One of the nurses had confided that her husband George had been seen in a pub in town with Valerie Simmonds, and they appeared to be *very* good friends indeed!

Clara was in the kitchen preparing the dinner trolley. Kitty didn't waste words. 'I'd like you to keep an eye on Lucy for me,' she said bluntly. 'She's young enough to be your daughter, Clara, and it's not fair the way you and Valerie gang up on her.'

'Lucy can be a little bitch,' Clara sneered, though she had the grace to look slightly ashamed.

'She's never been a bitch to me. She's a good kid and she has a hard time at home. I've never asked anything of you before, Clara, but do me one first and final favour, be nice to her. Anyroad, it's best to be on good terms with your mates at work. You never know when you'll need one as a friend.'

'I'm really sorry you're leaving, Kitty,' Clara said grudgingly. 'I've always liked you, though I may not have shown it. For your sake, I'll try to get along with Lucy from now on.'

Kitty was saying her last goodbye to the Wren at the reception desk, when a pretty, well-dressed woman came into the building through the main entrance. She looked vaguely familiar and Kitty was trying to remember where they'd met before, when the woman said, 'How are you?'

'Fine,' Kitty said courteously. 'I'm afraid . . .'

The woman laughed a trifle patronisingly. 'You don't remember me, do you? I'm Miss Ellis from the Labour Exchange. I've come to see Staff Nurse Bellamy. It's Kitty, isn't it?'

Kitty remembered the rude way in which Miss Ellis

had spoken to her, as if she was worthless and ignorant. 'No,' she said coldly. 'It's not Kitty, it's Nurse Quigley. Goodbye, Miss Ellis.' With a toss of her head, Kitty swept out of the door, though on the way home, she regretted her rudeness. All in all, she had much to thank Miss Ellis for. She'd learnt a lot over the past year. One thing, she would never allow anyone to speak to her in such a demeaning way again.

Jimmy Quigley was panic-stricken when Kitty told him the news. 'You're leaving! But it sounds dead danger-ous, kiddo. You could be killed. I need you, girl, I need you here with me.'

'You've got a wife now, Dad,' Kitty said gently, 'and a family of your own. You don't need me any more.'

'Theresa's no good. It's you I want, Kitty, me own flesh and blood.' How on earth would he live without his Kitty on hand?

'Once Theresa's had the baby, she might come round. And don't forget, Dad,' Kitty reminded him, 'that the new baby's your own flesh and blood.'

'Jaysus, kiddo, you've really knocked the wind out of me sails. The lads'll be heartbroken when I tell them. They're dead fond of their big sister.'

'I'm not disappearing off the planet for good, Dad. I'll be back to see you, don't worry.'

Jimmy came round to Jessica's every night as soon as he finished work, as if he wanted to spend as much time as possible with his daughter before she went away.

'What's all that lot for?' he asked the night before she was leaving, pointing to a small pile of clothes which were folded on the table.

'I've been sorting all me stuff out,' explained Kitty. 'I thought I'd take them round to the WVS. I've got a handbag, some old shoes and a couple of books as well.'

'But what about when you come back, luv? You'll need those things then.' He panicked again. Kitty seemed determined to leave no trace of herself behind. There would soon be nothing left to remind him of his girl. 'I'll store this lot in me loft for you.'

'If you like, Dad.' Kitty understood and let him take the few things, though she knew she would never need them again.

Next morning, about twenty neighbours accompanied Kitty to Marsh Lane Station to wave farewell when she caught the train. Jimmy had taken the morning off to accompany her as far as Lime Street Station.

'I'm sick to death of goodbyes,' sobbed Sheila when the train had disappeared. 'Folks are forever leaving, and not all of them come back.'

'Remember when we started school – it was our very first day,' Brenda Mahon reminisced, 'and everyone was making fun of that little kid from Dryden Street who had a terrible squint? Kitty was the only one who wouldn't join in. She went out of her way to play with him at break time, although she was only five and it must have taken an awful lot of courage.'

'She was always a lovely girl, Kitty Quigley,' Aggie Donovan said tearfully, 'though I must say I was surprised when she took up with that there Yank.'

Gus had found a furnished bungalow which was ready to move into in a small village only a short distance from Burtonwood. He took Jessica to visit it before signing the lease. It had been built for a young couple only four years before, but when the man was called up, his wife had gone to live with her parents in Chester. The furniture was new, and although not Jessica's choice, she decided she could live with it until the war was over and they all went to live in New York.

As soon as she was back in Pearl Street, she started to pack her belongings. 'I seem to do this regularly once a year: first Calderstones, then Bootle, the Lake District. I travelled a long way, but I always ended up back where I started. Now I'm leaving Bootle for the third time in my life, but this time I know I'll never be coming back.'

She felt a mixture of joy and infinite sadness. Bootle was her home and would always remain so in her heart, but things moved on, life was unpredictable. Three years ago, she was living in Calderstones, childless and married to Arthur. Now, Arthur was dead, she had Penny – and an American husband.

She found herself thinking about Arthur a lot. Although she knew it was a case of shutting the stable door after the horse had bolted, she wished desperately she'd been nicer to him. Jessica vowed that she would never do anything to Gus or Penny that she would regret later. 'I think I've already changed a little for the better. Years ago, I would never have had such patience with Kitty. I would have told her to pull herself together, to stop moaning and get on with it.'

On her final night in the street where she was born, after Penny had gone to bed, Jessica slipped into the Reillys' to say a private farewell to Sheila and give her Penny's baby clothes, sadly no longer needed for the child she'd been expecting herself.

'I know I'll see you briefly in the morning, but I just wanted to wish you all the best for the future, Sheil. I pray that everything turns out well with the new baby and one day soon Calum will be home for good.'

'It said on the wireless we've turned the corner.' Sheila hated goodbyes. She was doing her level best not to cry.

'That's right. We've been told to wait up for the midnight bulletin.' Jessica stood awkwardly in the middle of the room. 'Will your dad be along soon? I'd like to say goodbye and he won't be around tomorrow.'

'He's gone to a lecture with Kate Thomas. Me and our Eileen keep hoping something'll come of it between them, but I don't think so, somehow.'

Jessica didn't think so, either. 'Give him my love, then. Well, cheerio, Sheila.'

'Tara, Jess.'

The two women embraced stiffly and promised to visit each other soon. Jessica went home and switched the wireless on low. The faint strains of a choir singing 'Greensleeves' came from the set. This time, it wasn't merely a false hope, it definitely appeared as if things were going their way for a change. Algeria had capitulated, the Australians were doing well in New Guinea and the Americans had landed on the Solomon Islands. Although Stalingrad was still under siege, the Russians were gradually getting the upper hand. Nature having taken her relentless and predictable course, snow already lay thick on the Caucasus and the invaders were faced with another paralysing Russian winter. In North Africa, forty thousand enemy prisoners had been taken when Major-General Montgomery and his troops attacked El Alamein, and the RAF continued with their heavy raids on German cities.

Jessica listened to the music as she emptied the drawers of the sideboard. She hadn't been there long enough to fill them with the usual rubbish which accumulated over the years. The suitcases and boxes were waiting in the parlour ready to be loaded in the van. She'd almost forgotten about the van, and discovered there was enough petrol to get her as far as Burtonwood. The bungalow had a garage, and, you never knew, the van could be worth something once the war was over.

In the right-hand sideboard drawer she found the letter from Arthur's Commanding Officer, together with the photo of her wedding. She was about to throw them both on the fire, when she decided to keep them instead. 'I know I'm starting a new life with Gus, but it doesn't mean I should cancel out everything that's happened before. Arthur specially asked that Penny should never forget him. She might want to know what he looked like when she's older.'

She hoped Gus would manage to get there that night. Once the men were all safely back and the base had settled down for the night, he usually came so they could spend a few hours together. He was determined to give her another child to replace the one she'd lost. 'It's still not too late, Jess. Lots of women have children well into their forties.'

But not in their late forties. Jessica had a strong feeling in her bones that it was all a waste of time, though trying was better than it had ever been with Jack Doyle. Still, she had Penny – and she also had Peter, the son she'd never met.

Jessica was so lost in her thoughts that Big Ben had begun to chime before she realised it was midnight and the news was about to begin. She quickly turned the wireless up. Bruce Belfrage was the announcer. His normally calm voice was jubilant. 'The enemy is in full retreat in North Africa.'

The great German General Rommel had been beaten! The tide had turned. Throughout the land, cheers went up, particularly when the news was relayed by loudspeaker to workers on the late shift.

For some, the news had come too late to raise a cheer. They were glad, of course, but had already lost their loved ones. Others, more cautious, wondered how many more years would it be before they reached their final goal: victory!

In Pearl Street, there was a knock on the door of number 10 and Jessica Henningsen hurried down the hall to let her husband in. 'Have you heard the good news?' she asked excitedly.

Gus nodded. 'There's a few guys celebrating on the corner and they told me.' He kissed her and she nestled in his arms. 'What was it Churchill said – "Into the storm and through the storm". Well, we're halfway there, Jess. It won't be long before we're through the storm completely.'

Chapter 1
1939–1940

'Rose!' Mrs Corbett bellowed. 'Where are you?'

'Up here, madam.' Rose appeared, breathless, at the top of the stairs. 'Making the beds.'

'I'd have thought you'd be finished by now.'

'I've only just started, madam.'

'Huh!' Mrs Corbett said contemptuously. She always seemed to expect her maid to have begun the next job, or even the one after that, leaving Rose with the constant feeling that she was way behind. 'Well, get a move on, girl. I want you in uniform by eleven o'clock. The vicar and his wife are coming for coffee.'

'Yes, madam.' It was exceptionally warm for June and there were beads of perspiration on Rose's brow when she returned to the colonel's room and began to plump up pillows, straighten sheets and tuck them firmly under the mattress. Colonel Max was Mrs Corbett's son, a professional soldier, presently home on leave. He was a much nicer person than his mother, very kind. She was always sorry when he had to return to his regiment.

Mrs Corbett, on the other hand, was never kind. She apparently thought the more Rose was harried, the harder she would work. But Rose already laboured as hard as she could. That morning, she'd been up at six, as she was every morning, to light the Aga. On the dot of seven, Mrs Corbett had been taken up a cup of tea, two

1

slices of bread and butter, and *The Times*. The colonel had been given his tea on the dot of eight, by which time his mother was having a bath, the coal scuttle had been filled, the washing had been hung on the line, the numerous clocks had been wound, and Mrs Denning, the cook who lived in the village, had arrived to make breakfast.

While the Corbetts ate, Rose sat down to her own breakfast, although, more often than not, the bell would ring and she would scurry into the dining room to be met with complaints that the eggs were overdone, the kippers not cooked enough, or there wasn't enough toast, none of which was Rose's fault, but Mrs Corbett behaved as if it was.

Breakfast over, she'd start on the housework; shake mats and brush carpets, dust and polish the furniture, which had to be done every day, apart from Sunday, Rose's day off, but only after ten o'clock, when the Aga had been lit and, if it was winter, fires made in the breakfast and drawing rooms, the morning tea had been served and the beds made.

Today, the housework would be interrupted because the Reverend and Mrs Conway were coming for coffee and she would have to change out of her green overall into her maid's outfit; a black frock with long sleeves, a tiny, white, lace-trimmed apron and white cap. Thus attired, Rose would answer the door and show the visitors into the drawing room where coffee and biscuits were waiting on a silver tray and Mrs Corbett would rise to greet them, her big, over-powdered face twisted in a charming smile.

Rose wasn't required to show the visitors out. She would change back into the overall and get on with other things; cleaning the silver, for instance, or ironing,

2

the job she disliked most. Mrs Corbett examined the finished work with a hawk's eye, looking for creases in her fine, silk underwear and expensive *crêpe de chine* blouses. Even the bedding had to be as smooth as freshly fallen snow. Rose would be bitterly scolded if one of the pure Irish linen pillow slips hadn't been ironed on both sides, something she was apt to overlook.

'You'll make some man a fine wife one day,' Mrs Denning had said more than once.

'I can't imagine getting married,' Rose usually replied. She did so again today. Both women were in the kitchen, where the windows had been flung wide open in the hope a breath of fresh air might penetrate the sweltering heat. A red-faced Mrs Denning was preparing lunch and Rose was sorting out yesterday's washing, putting it into different piles ready to be ironed. Mrs Corbett was still entertaining the Conways in the drawing room.

She picked up the iron off the Aga and spat on it. The spit sizzled to nothing straight away and she reckoned it was just about right. She put another iron in its place.

'You'll get married,' Mrs Denning assured her. 'You'll not be left on the shelf, not with those big blue eyes. How old are you now, Rose?'

'Fifteen,' Rose sighed. She'd been working for Mrs Corbett and keeping The Limes spick and span for over two years, ever since her thirteenth birthday. Holmwood House, the orphanage where she'd been raised, wasn't prepared to keep the children a day longer than necessary and Mrs Corbett had been to examine her and assess her fitness for the job, which for some reason involved looking inside her ears and down her throat.

'I want someone strong and healthy,' she'd said in her loud, sergeant-major voice. She was a widow in her

3

sixties, a large, majestic woman with enormous breasts that hung over the belt of her outsize brown frock. She wore a fox fur and a tiny fur hat with a spotted veil that cast little black shadows on her dour, autocratic face.

'Apart from the usual childhood illnesses, I've never known Rose be sick,' Mr Hillyard, the Governor of Holmwood House, had smoothly assured her.

'But she doesn't look particularly strong. In fact, I'd describe her as delicate.'

'We have another girl that might do. Would you care to see her?'

'Why not.'

Rose was sent to wait outside Mr Hillyard's office and Ann Parker was fetched for Mrs Corbett to examine, but rejected on the spot. 'She's too coarse; at least the other one has a bit of refinement about her.' Every word was audible in the corridor outside. 'What's her name again?'

'Rose Sullivan.'

'She'll just have to do. When can I have her?'

'She'll be thirteen in a fortnight. You can have her then.'

Two weeks later, at the beginning of May, a car had arrived to take Rose away from Holmwood House, a place where she had never been happy and where the word 'love' had never once been mentioned or felt. The driver got out to open the door and take the parcel containing all her worldly possessions. He was a handsome man, old enough to be her father, with broad shoulders and dark wavy hair. His skin was burnt nutmeg brown from the sun. She learnt later that his name was Tom Flowers and he was, rather appropriately, the gardener who doubled as a chauffeur when Mrs Corbett needed to be driven anywhere.

He hardly spoke on the way to The Limes, merely

4

muttering that if she was good and behaved herself, she'd get on fine with her new employer. 'She's a hard taskmaster, but her bark's worse than her bite.'

Rose was soon to discover the truth of the first part of this remark, but never the second.

The Limes was a square, grey brick building with eight bedrooms set in five acres of well-tended grounds. Inside was comfortably furnished, though on her first day she didn't see the rooms she would soon come to know well, as Tom Flowers took her round to a side entrance, through a long, narrow room with a deep brown sink, a dolly tub, and a mangle. A sturdy clothes rack was suspended from the ceiling.

He opened another door and they entered a vast kitchen with a red tiled floor and white walls, from which hung an assortment of copper-bottomed pans, from the very small to the very large. Waves of heat were coming from a giant stove. The shelves of an enormous dresser were filled with pretty blue and white china and there was a bowl of brightly coloured flowers on the pine table that could easily have seated a dozen.

'Mrs Corbett's out for the day,' Tom Flowers informed her, 'and Mrs Denning, the cook, won't be back for a while. I'll show you your room. Once you've unpacked, perhaps you'd like to go for a walk around the village. Ailsham's a nice place, you'll like it. Just turn right when you leave the gates and you'll come to the shops about a mile away.'

'Ta,' Rose whispered.

'Come on then, girl,' he said brusquely. 'You're on the second floor.'

He marched out of the kitchen, up a wide staircase, then a narrower one, Rose having to run to keep up.

The door to her room was already open, her things on the bed. Tom Flowers said something that she presumed was 'goodbye', closed the door, and Rose was left alone.

She sat on the bed. It was quite a pleasant room with a sloping ceiling. The distempered walls, the curtains on the small window, and the cotton coverlet on the bed were white. There was a rag rug on the otherwise bare wooden floor, a little chest of drawers, and a single wardrobe. Later, when she opened the wardrobe to hang her too short winter coat, she found a black frock that was much too long and a green overall that would have fitted someone twice her size.

But Rose felt too miserable to unpack then. Unhappiness rose like a ball in her throat. Tom Flowers' footsteps could be heard, getting further and further away, and with each step, the unhappiness grew until she could hardly breathe. She lay on the bed and began to cry into the soft, white pillow. She wanted her mother. That could never be because her mother was dead, but she wanted her all the same. All she could remember was a blurred face, a soft voice, soft music, arms reaching for her as she toddled across the room, being cuddled by someone who could only have been her mother. Then one day the soft voice stopped and the music was no more. She had never been cuddled again. The voices since had been harsh, even when she was told that her mother had died. The birth certificate she'd been given with her things stated 'Father Unknown'. She had no one. Now she didn't even have the orphanage, where at least she'd felt safe. She was completely alone in the world.

All Orion/Phoenix titles are available at your local bookshop or from the following address:

Mail Order Department
Littlehampton Book Services
FREEPOST BR535
Worthing, West Sussex, BN13 3BR
telephone 01903 828503, *facsimile* 01903 828802
e-mail MailOrders@lbsltd.co.uk
(Please ensure that you include full postal address details)

Payment can be made either by credit/debit card (Visa, Mastercard, Access and Switch accepted) or by sending a £ Sterling cheque or postal order made payable to *Littlehampton Book Services*.
DO NOT SEND CASH OR CURRENCY.

Please add the following to cover postage and packing

UK and BFPO:
£1.50 for the first book, and 50p for each additional book to a maximum of £3.50

Overseas and Eire:
£2.50 for the first book plus £1.00 for the second book and 50p for each additional book ordered

---

BLOCK CAPITALS PLEASE

name of cardholder ....   *delivery address*
                                    (if different from cardholder)
address of cardholder ....

....

....

       postcode ....   *postcode* ....

☐   I enclose my remittance for   £ ....

☐   please debit my Mastercard/Visa/Access/Switch (delete as appropriate)

card number ☐☐☐☐☐☐☐☐☐☐☐☐☐☐☐☐☐☐

expiry date ☐☐☐☐   Switch issue no. ☐☐

signature ....

prices and availability are subject to change without notice